Praise for bestselling author Michele Hauf

"Hauf delivers excitement, danger and romance in a way only she can!"
—*New York Times* bestselling author Sherrilyn Kenyon on *Her Vampire Husband*

"With action-packed excitement from start to finish, Hauf offers an original storyline full of quirky, fun characters and wonderful descriptions. And the sexual tension between CJ and Vika sparkles. Readers won't want to put this one down."
—*RT Book Reviews* on *This Wicked Magic*, Top Pick!

"This quirky story has a fair amount of humor and a lot of heart as well."
—*Harlequin Junkie* on *The Vampire Hunter*

"Nothing at all tame about this book. Lots of messy, dangerous sex, complete with teeth, the way vampire sex should be."
—*Brazen Reads* on *Beautiful Danger*

"I love the world building this author creates in her books."
—*Romancing the Dark Side*

"*Kiss Me Deadly* is an addictive read, one that won't be put down until the final page is completed."
—*Examiner.com*

Michele Hauf has been writing romance, action-adventure and fantasy stories for more than twenty years. France, musketeers, vampires and faeries usually populate her stories. And if Michele followed the adage "write what you know," all her stories would have snow in them. Fortunately, she steps beyond her comfort zone and writes about countries and creatures she has never seen. Find her on Facebook, Twitter and at michelehauf.com.

Books by Michele Hauf

Harlequin Nocturne

Saint-Pierre Series

The Dark's Mistress
Ghost Wolf
Moonlight and Diamonds
The Vampire's Fall

In the Company of Vampires Series

Beautiful Danger
The Vampire Hunter
Beyond the Moon

HQN Books

Her Vampire Husband
Seducing the Vampire
A Vampire for Christmas
"Monsters Don't Do Christmas"

Visit the Author Profile page
at Harlequin.com for more titles.

Michele Hauf

MOONLIGHT AND DIAMONDS

AND

THE VAMPIRE'S FALL

HARLEQUIN® NOCTURNE™

Recycling programs
for this product may
not exist in your area.

ISBN-13: 978-0-373-60151-6

Moonlight and Diamonds and The Vampire's Fall

Copyright © 2015 by Harlequin Books S.A.

The publisher acknowledges the copyright holder
of the individual works as follows:

Moonlight and Diamonds
Copyright © 2015 by Michele Hauf

The Vampire's Fall
Copyright © 2015 by Michele Hauf

This edition published by arrangement with Harlequin Books S.A.

For questions and comments about the quality of this book,
please contact us at CustomerService@Harlequin.com.

® and TM are trademarks of the publisher. Trademarks indicated with ® are registered in the United States Patent and Trademark Office, the Canadian Intellectual Property Office and in other countries.

Printed in U.S.A.

www.Harlequin.com

CONTENTS

MOONLIGHT AND DIAMONDS

Chapter 1

"Achoo!"

Stryke Saint-Pierre chuckled at the power sneeze that had blown out of Summer Santiago's two-year-old mouth. Her dad, Vail, instead of wiping his daughter's nose and cooing reassurance, lifted his head and fiercely scanned up and down the Parisian street. They stood before the Hawkes Associates building, along with Rhys Hawkes, Vail's stepfather. The trio were enjoying the cloudy day and discussing Rhys's need for help.

"See any?" Rhys, a tall, salty-haired half vampire, half werewolf, asked his son.

Vail, full-blooded vampire, nodded across the street.

Stryke followed the vampire's nod and spied a lanky man wearing a blue hoodie, tattered jeans and combat boots who strode down the sidewalk. The stranger glanced toward them. Red eyes glowed.

"Demon," Vail confirmed. "He's cool, though. Doesn't appear as though he means any trouble. Does he, sweetie?" He kissed his daughter's curly blond hair.

"Demons are not my favorite breed," Rhys muttered. "But he looks harmless. She still allergic?" he asked Vail.

Vail, with coal-black hair and silver rings on his fingers that glinted even with the lacking sunlight, nodded. He explained to Stryke. "Ever since Summer had a little run-in with Himself last year she's been allergic to sulfur. Good demon alarm, though."

"How does a baby have a run-in with Himself?" Stryke had been in Paris all of two days and was staying in an apartment owned by his grandfather—the rest of his family was, as well—and what he'd learned since arriving was that paranormal breeds of all varieties were in abundance here as compared to Minnesota, which he called home.

"Himself kidnapped her," Vail provided. "Long story. She's good. Wasn't hurt. But you know. Allergic now. I have to head out. Lyric is probably already at the tailor's waiting for me. I have to try on the tuxedo again. I hope the tailor got the studs right this time."

Stryke smirked. Vail wore black velvet jeans and a crisp black shirt with black lace around the wrists. And there was enough silver and diamonds on his wrists, ears and rings to flash signals to the moon. The vamp defined glamour rock, but with a bite.

"I sent a suit to your apartment, Stryke," Vail said. "Your mother reported to my wife that her sons hadn't properly packed. Ha! Anyway, not sure if they'll fit you with a tux for the wedding. But in case not, I thought you could borrow one of mine. I sent one to your brother

Trouble's apartment too, but that guy is a block. Not sure my stuff will fit him."

Indeed, Stryke hadn't packed anything fancy for the family wedding. When he'd learned it was black-tie, he'd shaken his head and tried not to moan too loudly. Suits were not his style. But it was generous of the vamp to send him a loaner. Stryke's shoulders were broader than the vampire's and his biceps were definitely bigger, but he figured he could make it work. Unless it was velvet. It was probably too late to specify a more subtle fabric choice, so he'd keep that worry to himself.

"Thanks, man." Stryke met Vail's fist bump and then tweaked Summer's button nose. "See you at the wedding, Summer."

The shy toddler tucked her face against her dad's neck yet, with a giggle, peeked back at Stryke.

"Hug?" Stryke held out his arms.

Surprisingly, she stretched out her arms and he took her into a bear hug. A hug from a kid defied explanation. Stryke wanted a pack of his own. Soon. The urge to raise a couple of sons, and heck, why not a few daughters too, was strong. Hugs seemed a very necessary purpose to life.

"She likes you." Vail retrieved his daughter.

Summer said, "Puppy?"

"Ha! She's already got a nose for the wolves," Vail said.

Stryke playfully barked at her, and Summer giggled.

"See you at the wedding!"

The vampire strode off toward the red Maserati convertible parked down the street. Stryke and Rhys waved to Summer in the front car seat as the twosome rolled by.

"That's the third Maserati in so many years," Rhys commented on the sleek vehicle that sported a noticeable dent on the passenger door. "That boy needs to take a driver's course."

"Wow." Stryke shoved his hands in his front jeans pockets. He couldn't imagine having the kind of disposable income to afford a six-figure car—three times over. While set for life, thanks to investments, he lived a middle-class existence in a small town. He gladly claimed the title of redneck. Happiness to him was living simply.

Though he wouldn't mind hooking up with a pretty Parisian werewolf while here. The available females back home were slim-pickings, and his werewolf had never had the pleasure of dating another of his breed. It was what he most desired. That, and starting a family that he could call a pack.

Finding a woman had actually become necessity since Stryke's father had given him the task of starting a new pack. Malakai Saint-Pierre was ready to retire and travel the world with his wife, Rissa. The Saint-Pierre pack consisted of only family. They needed a strong new pack in the area. A diverse pack made up of many families. It was how the werewolves in Minnesota would finally grow their numbers.

The Saint-Pierre pack's scion was currently Trouble, Stryke's eldest brother. Trouble hadn't the calm control to step into his father's position as principal and lead others. Malakai had said as much to Stryke. His oldest brother was a loose cannon, who picked fights at the drop of a shifty glance and reveled in partying all night. Slightly ADD? Always possible with Trouble.

Stryke was eager to head a pack and had the confidence to do so. But to grow a pack a man needed a good woman at his side.

"So you said you were going to stay on a bit after your family heads home?"

"A few days, for sure." Stryke returned his attention to Rhys, who owned Hawkes Associates, a sort of bank/savings/storage conglomerate that catered to all paranormal species. "My parents and brothers and sister are here for five days. But Grandpa Creed said we could stay in the apartments as long as we like, so I'm going to fit in some touring when the wedding is over."

"When you're not wandering and checking out the sights I'd love it if you'd consider helping me out. I'm shorthanded and have a lot of work in the office. My assistant is out of town on his honeymoon. I've a pickup with the Order of the Stake. It would be simple. You'd meet Tor and he'll hand over the artifacts."

"Is the Order of the Stake what I think it is?"

"Yes, they are an ancient order of mortal knights who hunt vampires. But they're cool. Vail informs for them on occasion. Torsten Rindle does their spin. He also handles exchanges with Hawkes Associates. Sometimes the knights in the Order come upon treasure or, let's just say…their victims' belongings have to be cataloged. They've recently acquired a demon artifact that I bought for my own collection. It wouldn't take long. But I don't have the time to run over there myself with all this wedding stuff."

"I can do that. Doesn't sound too difficult. Tomorrow?"

"Yes. I'll text you the information and provide Tor with your name. Thanks, Stryke. I appreciate it. Oh, and now that I think of it… Here." Rhys tugged out two tickets from his jacket pocket. "You have any interest in gallery showings?"

Stryke shrugged. "I do hope to catch some of the museums and culture while I'm in town. Always willing to put new ideas in my brain and learn what I can about art and history."

"I think this is a seventeenth-century jewelry collection on display. I got the tickets weeks ago, but won't be able to make it tonight. As grandparents of the groom, my wife and I have to attend a rehearsal dinner tonight. Tedious."

Stryke accepted the tickets. He wasn't much for jewels, but he'd made the decision to take in as much of the city as he could while here. This was the first time he'd been overseas. He wasn't sure he could survive being cooped up in an airplane for nine hours to ever make the return visit, so while on land he would do the town up right.

"Maybe one of my brothers will go along with me. Do I have to dress up?"

"You'll probably want to wear the suit Vail sent to your place. Thanks, Stryke. I'll call you in the morning with details on the job."

Rhys clapped a hand across Stryke's shoulder then wandered back inside the six-story black granite building where he did business.

Stryke tucked the tickets in his back pocket and shook his head as a bright pink Vespa scooted by. A gorgeous woman wearing a skirt commandeered the scooter. She even wore high heels. The women here were so different from back in the States. They liked to look good, no matter what the activity.

He didn't understand a single word of the language, so he had gotten more sneers and snide side glances than he'd experienced in a lifetime. He was taking it in stride. He wasn't the sort to anger easily. That was his brother Trouble's forte. Maybe by the time he boarded the plane for the return trip home he'd actually know a bit of the language and have found that fantasy werewolf he dreamed about meeting?

Then again, he'd be thankful to not starve—because

he couldn't ask for what he wanted in French—not get arrested, and not make a fool of himself if a pretty woman *did* glance his way.

And if he was lucky he might happen upon some danger. Because before he started the dream family and pack, he needed to satisfy a soul-deep craving for adventure. His brothers always seemed to find danger and excitement in spades.

Stryke had survived a near-death experience last winter. Time to live his life and make the most of it.

Private gallery, 10:00 p.m.

Two hundred people wandered about the airy gallery off the Rue de Rivoli. Excellent turnout. The champagne flowed, and the silver-dusted vanilla macarons catered from Pierre Hermes were nibbled even by those women who would never deem to smudge their lipstick. It wasn't the calories, *chéri*; it was the humility of being seen chewing in public.

Blyss Sauveterre had owned the gallery for two years and it wasn't so much a labor of love as her means to keep tabs on society. By featuring a new exhibit every month she ensured the flow of the rich and famous in and out of the gallery doors never ceased. The diamonds on display this evening were once Marie Antoinette's prized possessions. Gifts from her lover, Count Axel von Fersen.

Blyss wasn't sure she believed the provenance. Axel Fersen had been a rake, a solider, an opportunist. Had he really garnered enough wages to afford such elaborate diamonds for the queen? History painted him more a lover than a businessman, which she was inclined to agree with. Whether or not he'd had an affair with the doomed queen? She certainly hoped that part was true.

The fantasy of it all intrigued her, and no one this evening had questioned the story behind the beautiful gemstones glinting within their rococo silver-and-gold settings.

The exhibit tonight was a preshow to the grand event Blyss and her assistant planned to feature perhaps next month—the unveiling of *Le Diabolique* to the public.

Le Diabolique was a fifty-carat black diamond that glinted red from within. History told that it had been given by a seventeenth-century Belgian duke to the French Queen Anne. It had been stolen less than a week after she'd taken it in hand. The diamond had been recovered and stolen throughout history many times over, and rumor told that anyone who possessed it faced great torment, wickedness and terrible evil. If not the ultimate misfortune of death.

Blyss believed the rumors. The diamond would prove her greatest torment should she not pull off the heist properly this evening. Part one had already been accomplished. Now the handoff.

"Blyss!"

Her assistant, Lorcan Price, was bedecked in a pink bespoke suit and bright purple bow tie. He adjusted his thick black-rimmed glasses and crossed the room, weaving between patrons and wielding champagne flutes in each hand. He gained her side and pressed a cool champagne glass into her hand.

The man seemed to possess a sixth sense about how to please her. Bon mots uttered at the precise moment she was beginning to doubt herself, a compliment about her designer shoes, even a conspiratorially catty wink from across the room during such events as tonight.

Blyss tilted back a few sips of bubbly, eyeing the crowd over the crystal rim as she did so. Most men had a woman draped on their arm this evening and looked oh-so-bored. If they were wise, they'd pay attention to those things that attracted their partners' eyes, such as all things sparkly. Blyss's usual type, an older man who wore an expensive suit, tended his nails and hair, and who reeked money, were spread throughout the gallery. Some had even come alone. Such fortune.

But tonight she required someone different.

"The show is going well," Lorcan said in his quiet yet enthusiastic voice. "The duchess Konstantinov has suggested to me she may loan the gallery her grandmother's sapphire collection. She's from old Russian money. Wouldn't be surprised if they've a Fabergé egg stashed away, as well. Isn't that spectacular?"

"Exquisite," Blyss agreed. Yet the intrigue of whether or not the duchess did own a Fabergé egg didn't pique her curiosity. Her heart wasn't in the moment. Too much to think about. The plan must go off or she faced a horrible future.

"Is all well with the, erm…big surprise?" he whispered conspiratorially.

"Oui, bien sur." At least, not if anyone cared to study *Le Diabolique* too closely. "Soon, Lorcan. But I don't know about announcing it tonight."

"I will leave it to you, then. You do have the only key to the storage room."

Always trying to gain that access, Blyss thought. Maybe someday she would trust him to tend the acquisitions. But not yet.

"Keep working the room, Lorcan. And do be sure to introduce yourself to Madame Horchard. She's filthy." As in rich. A shorthand the two of them shared. Because if there was one thing that had drawn Blyss to Lorcan, it was his desire to climb the social ladder by means of attaching himself to money. "I must make another round through the gallery."

They bussed each other's cheeks. Lorcan knew well that Blyss abhorred getting her lipstick or her hair mussed.

Clutching the goblet, she strode slowly through the crowd, nodding in acknowledgment to those she knew. Normally she noted the flash of bling on ears, at necks, and wrists and fingers. So *she* had managed ten carats from her lover? Lucky girl. But tonight her mind was a scatter. Nerves made her tense.

Her heartbeats thundered. She inhaled and then exhaled deeply, vying for calm. She hated this feeling of desperation that had settled into her being the past few days. She'd thought to have perfected her life and that smooth sailing was all her future held.

Until her father, Colin Sauveterre, had shown up at her door a month ago, slobbering drunk and crying. His gambling debts had caught up to him. He'd needed her help. But by helping him, she had placed herself on a precipice that loomed over a dangerous fall.

Would she ever again feel safe and sure? As if her life was exactly as she had designed it? All she desired was to drop her shoulders and relax, knowing all was well. And that she fit in.

Exhaling heavily, she drew in a breath of courage. She could do this. She *had* to do this.

She managed a fake smile to a dignitary whose name she could not recall, and drifted away from the velvet-and-glass displays that featured dazzling diamonds and colored stones in gorgeous settings from the seventeenth and eighteenth centuries.

Rubbing a hand along her lace dress, Blyss cursed the fact her palm was moist. Nerves were not her thing. She could work a room peopled with hundreds and never let them see her sweat. But tonight was different. And she hadn't found the right man yet.

But she remained hopeful.

Trading her empty flute of champagne for a fresh one from a waiter's silver tray, she glided through the room and out into the large gallery that housed marble sculptures and where many had gone to chatter louder and more gregariously than the smaller room allowed.

The men were of all varieties. Old, young, middle-aged. Handsome, ugly, oddly alluring. Black ties and designer labels, mostly. Some lesser suits, of which she did not recognize the designer. The women were all dressed to dazzle and reveal.

The couture made her wish she had a credit card that wasn't maxed out. Alexander McQueen? Oh, yes, please.

Blyss revealed as much as the other women. The black lace dress was cut low in the back to expose almost everything, and the front featured a deep V that clung to her breasts yet revealed their inner curves. A thigh-high slit on the floor-length skirt showed off her red-soled Louboutins. Diamonds at her neck and ears were prizes earned on the quest for the rich and bored who hunted for a sparkling trophy to hang on his arm. But never commitment. No, she chose her men for their expiration dates—and the wanderlust in their eyes. And if they suggested something longer than a fling or a few weekends in Madrid? She quickly extricated herself.

It wasn't easy maintaining the lifestyle she enjoyed, but every kiss, every extravagant meal, every late night hookup in a lavish hotel room was worth it. Blyss adored luxury.

Most of all, she adored being adored.

Hmm, now there stood a possibility. The man chatting with the waiter over by the Rodin. She hadn't seen him at any of the gallery's previous functions. He was tall, nicely tanned—perhaps from yachting?—and wore his hair in a close shave against his head. Bright white teeth flashed beneath his blade nose. An easy stance advertised a certain laissez-faire. He didn't care what others thought about him.

Blyss could not relate to lacking concern. As well, something about him didn't quite fit him among the elite crowd. Was it the fabric that stretched at his broad shoulders? The suit had been poorly tailored. Or his seeming awestruck gaze as he took in the festivities? He was...big. Almost awkward. Like a boulder tossed into a flower garden.

Well, he wouldn't be here without an invite. And Blyss tendered her invites carefully. He was worth checking out—if not, using.

Stryke wandered through the marble-walled gallery, taking in the sculptures by artists he'd only read about in books. Yeah, so he was probably the only one of his brothers who claimed to read. Much unlike his brothers, who hadn't the patience or interest in fine arts, he enjoyed learning new things and bulking up his cultural-knowledge quotient.

He took in the elite crowd who sipped champagne and nibbled caviar-coated crackers. He assessed every step, every gesture, every cut of fabric and deviously delivered bon mot. Diamonds glinted at ears, necks and cuff links. He was pretty sure the clothing cost a small fortune, and didn't even want to guess at how long he'd have to work to afford the diamond choker around that old lady's neck.

He wasn't currently working for a paycheck. After a short stint as a volunteer fireman—the fire station had been closed due to budget problems—he was looking for something to fulfill his need for action and danger.

It didn't need to provide a paycheck; he was set for life. But as well, if it involved helping his own breed then he would be even more attracted to taking on the job.

These people were not his breed. They were human. Not his crowd. On the other hand, he was accustomed to existing among humans because that was simply life as he knew it. Wasn't as if a private werewolf haven existed on an island in the Pacific.

He wouldn't be interested if it did exist. He liked humans. They were just like him, but without the propensity to grow fur and flick out the claws when the mood struck. Poor humans.

Tonight's biggest surprise? His brother Blade had come along with him. The last of the Saint-Pierre brothers he would have guessed had an interest in art. Reclusive almost to the extreme, Blade had nodded and muttered something about "getting away from the crazy chicks and their wedding talk."

And yet, Blade had left fifteen minutes ago with his arms wrapped around sexy blonde twins wearing matching red miniskirts. So Blade's idea of art was a little different than most.

Stryke had flown to Paris with his family. His parents, Malakai and Rissa Saint-Pierre, and their children, Trouble, Blade, Kelyn and Daisy Blu. Stryke's aunt Kambriel was marrying Johnny Santiago in a few days. The Santiagos were the Hawkes side of the family, and they were vampires.

Fine by him. As with humans, he had nothing against vamps. His grandfather Creed Saint-Pierre was a vamp, and Blade was actually half faery—as well as vampire. It was all good so long as there were werewolves in the mix at the wedding.

Stryke had heard Europe's werewolf population was

booming and the females were in abundance, much the opposite of his native hometown. He hoped that was true. It would increase his chances of meeting a female werewolf, falling in love and getting married.

If only reality proved as simple as the fantasy.

Stryke likely wouldn't hook up so easily as Blade had tonight. He was no slouch when it came to dating, but he did tend toward a specific type. Pretty, yet slightly tomboyish, able to embrace fun and a lover of all things outdoors, including snuggling by a midnight bonfire and long walks through the woods.

Was that asking too much? He didn't think so.

And yet he wasn't feeling attraction to any of the women. All of them were dressed to the nines with hair that must have taken hours in a salon and makeup that had probably been professionally applied. The diamonds flashing on fingers, necks and ears could light the New Year's Eve ball dropped in Times Square. He guessed none of them would even look at a man whose bank account didn't scream high seven figures.

Didn't matter. Now that Blade had taken off, he could focus on the art. He'd browsed through the jewelry display. Diamonds were just sparkly chunks of carbon, right? He couldn't figure their appeal. Here in this large open area many sculptures held court. Carved from white marble, he was awestruck how the stone looked as if it was real, warm flesh. As if he should touch one of them the statue would startle. Cool.

He glanced around. Would an alarm go off if he did touch one? He crossed his arms to fend off the compulsion but the suit coat tugged at his shoulders. Vail was definitely less broad in the shoulders than he was.

A waiter offered more champagne and he refused. "Thanks, man—er, *non, merci.*" Yeah, he'd picked up a

few French words. He would be working the language
like a native in no time.

Stryke heard all languages babbling about tonight.
Earlier he'd listened to a couple of women chatter in
English about their hemlines. Why were the conversa-
tions he could understand the boring ones?

A crew of well-suited men passed him, each with a
gorgeous looker draped on his arm. Stryke tilted back
his shoulders. He didn't need a woman to look important. He preferred his females a bit tussled and wilder,
anyway. The princess of his pack would need endur-
ance, patience and, hell, she must be fun, too. And like
beer.

"But maybe I should reconsider lace," he muttered
as his eyes landed upon a sheath of black lace caressing the most gorgeous figure he had ever seen. He felt
sure he couldn't even dream up something so luscious.

Black lace caressed long legs and hugged a tight ass
and narrow waist. Red-manicured fingernails glided
over a hip before gesturing as she spoke to another
woman. The gesture directed Stryke's eyes to the deep-
cut neckline that exposed the cusps of perfect, round
breasts. And up the slender neck where a single diamond glinted, yet didn't distract from the soft, pale skin.

Petal-pink lips caught his interest. Kissing those lips
would be better than tasting the home-brewed beers he
enjoyed and brewed in his basement. Kissing those lips,
and running his fingers through that soft dark hair that
was pulled up in back yet fluffed on top to frame black-
lined eyes could ruin a man for other women.

After a man kissed those lips, there would be no
going back. And to stroke his fingers down her neck
and arrive at the curves of her breasts? Mercy.

Think rednecks and beer.

Stryke smirked and caught himself laughing quietly. He didn't do stuff like moon over a gorgeous woman. That chick was so out of his league he'd never get closer than the nosebleed seats. He bet she would never wear flannel or even consider a hike through the pine forest out back of his home.

And yet, she was something to look at. Much more intriguing than the sculpture of a naked man immediately to his left.

So he let his gaze linger as he strolled closer, hoping to catch a whiff of her scent. It would be expensive, for sure. His werewolf senses picked up too much from the room. Perfume, aftershave, champagne, salted crackers, sweet treats, body odor. The sensory assault was overwhelming, but he knew how to turn it down and had done so within minutes after arriving.

Now he sought to home in on her scent. A piece of her to tuck into his memory and take along with him tonight. Something upon which to dream.

As he neared, she dismissed the person she was talking to and brushed close to him, not noticing him, but Stryke felt her heat pierce his borrowed suit and dress shirt. Her body heat was visceral. And her scent was sweet but not like sugar, more like a garden full of flowers with bees buzzing among the petals. Subtle yet intensely heady.

His wrist jerked as she passed, and Stryke swung to see what had happened. "Oh, shit. Uh…" He followed as she walked, unknowing, until she did realize and turned to bump chests with him.

"Sorry," he said. "My cuff link is hooked on your dress. You passed so close." He twisted his wrist, but could feel the resistance. "Uh, *parlez vous Anglais*?"

"Interesting way of picking up a girl," she said in a

cultured voice that belonged in a jewelry box aside all that was precious. And on the box? A sign labeled Don't Touch. "*Oui*, I can manage English when I must. Can you get it unhooked?"

"Give me a minute. Your dress is all lace and so delicate. I don't want to tear it."

"Please do not, *monsieur*. It's one of my favorites."

He'd snagged her right over the ass, and he worked the back of his hand against her derriere, feeling guilty for the stolen touch, yet at the same time, loving the freebie. The diamond cuff link Vail had loaned him was worth a pretty penny, he felt sure. One of the clasps holding a stone had dug its clutches into the thin black lace.

He straightened, standing beside her with his hand behind her and fingers curled so he didn't blatantly cup her ass. Causing a scene was the last thing he wanted to do, so he'd act casual. Mercy. She smelled good. It was all he could do not to tilt his head against hers to sniff her hair.

"My name's Stryke Saint-Pierre, by the way."

"Blyss Sauveterre," she offered. And oh, yes, she was. "What sort of *pre nom* is Stryke?"

"The one my parents gave me. Uh, I'm from the US."

"That is obvious from your accent," she said with not even a smile.

Nope. He wasn't going to win her over this way. Damn. Way to spoil things. Worst pickup ever. Now to extricate himself without humiliating her more than himself.

"Uh, could we move over near that column where there's more light?"

He nodded toward a marble column at the edge of the gathering. Not a lot of people milling on that side

of the gallery. They'd be granted some privacy to perform this delicate operation.

"If it'll deliver me of your groping hand, then *oui*."

She started toward the column and he followed, but
it was easiest to let his fingers gently curl about her
behind. Yeah, it wasn't cool, but what about this situation was cool?

Once at the column he pulled her around to the other
side, where they found privacy and better light.

"Excuse me for what I'm going to do," he said.

Her lips pursed. Her bright green eyes were the most
valuable jewels in the room tonight. And those pink lips.
They looked moist and so wanting of a kiss. No chance
of kissing them after this embarrassing debacle. Not as
if he'd a chance with this delicious bit in the first place.

Stryke bent behind her to work at the tangle. She
slid a hand down her hip, uncomfortable, he guessed.
And impatient. God, she smelled amazing. All flowers
covered in sugar and fluttering over him until he was
buried in sweetness.

"So this is how American men meet women?" she
asked over her shoulder. "Snag them like a *poisson*?"

Poisson? What was that? Poison? Hell, he didn't
know. "Not generally. I like to take a less aggressive
tact when I'm interested in a woman." Though certainly
he was on the hunt. Wrong breed, though. This one he'd
have to toss back. Ah! *Poisson* meant fish. "I suspect
I'm not your type anyway."

"What, or rather, who do you guess is my type, Monsieur Stryke?"

When she said his name like that Stryke wished they
were the only two in the gallery, and that he had the
courage to kiss her and steal away more of her elegant
French words.

"Your type…" He stood and kept their close proximity by running his hand over her hip, and said, "…is rich."

She quirked a perfectly arched brow. The eyeliner circling her beautiful bright eyes had been drawn out at the corners in a catty tease. As he had with the marble statues, Stryke reminded himself not to touch. This wasn't the venue or crowd that appreciated his kind of sensual curiosity. He'd have to save the smoothing of his fingers over her skin for the bedroom. Which was never going to happen.

"So you do not qualify?" she asked. "Rich?"

"I do well enough."

In truth, he could probably beat most of the people here tonight in a show of financial statements, but he didn't like to brag. He was most comfortable living below his means. And if a woman judged a man by his checkbook? He wasn't interested.

She tapped his free wrist where the diamond cuff link glinted. "I suspect you do."

He wasn't about to correct her assumption. Why create another mark against him?

"I've been in Paris two days," he offered. "I have to say you've made the trip worthwhile."

"How is that?"

Leaning closer, just managing the skim of his coat front against her back, he spoke near her ear when a curl of her hair tickled his cheek.

"You've pulled me out of my world and into a fantasy. Not often that happens to a guy. Would it be cross to ask if you've a boyfriend?"

"It would."

He nodded. Yeah, he wasn't going to score interest from this glamour girl.

She tilted her gaze at him and he couldn't determine if she was disgusted or maybe intrigued. "Have you managed to detach yourself?"

He displayed the cuff link he'd freed from her dress minutes earlier. But since she'd been engaged in talking, he'd not informed her of her freedom too quickly. And the stolen moments of standing in her air? Priceless.

She clasped the cuff link. And then he remembered it wasn't his. He shouldn't just hand it over like that.

"Blyss," he repeated, not addressing her, more feeling the taste of her on his tongue.

She dipped her lashes before looking directly at him and dragging the diamond cuff link across her kiss-me-now lips. *"Oui?"*

Oh, man, those lips said things he wanted to be true. He breathed her name again. It was so appropriate. Every pore on his body inhaled her perfume and imagined her sugar-flower taste as her silken skin glided against his body.

Before he could claim the cuff link, she strode off. Long legs moved her swiftly, high heels clicking the marble floor. The hand behind her back toggled the diamond cuff link, allowing it to catch the light teasingly. She didn't reenter the crowd, but instead veered toward the curved marble wall where he had earlier seen the waiters coming and going.

Before walking through an open doorway, she cast a look over her shoulder at him. The cuff link was in her mouth, glinting between those luscious lips.

Stryke's jaw dropped open. He didn't need an interpreter to guess what she was saying.

Come claim it. If you dare.

Chapter 2

Stryke Saint-Pierre was one gorgeous man. And polite. While he could have copped a feel when they'd been tangled out on the museum floor, he had remained the consummate gentleman. Too bad for her. Blyss wanted to feel his deft fingers smooth over her derriere. She wanted to lose herself in the rugged smell of him, the roughness of him.

And she wanted to feel that now.

She strode down the dimly lit hallway toward the back office. It was her office, but she shared it with Lorcan, her assistant, and used it principally for paperwork, business calls and the occasional make-out session with a sexy man. It was what she did. She saw an attractive man. She wanted him. She won him. The winning part gave her immense satisfaction. And sometimes a sparkler for her finger or ear. She was choosy, most certainly, and discreet. And never greedy.

Tonight the win was born of necessity.

"You live in Paris?" she called back.

"Staying for a week or so, then heading back home to Minnesota."

Perfect. He'd be gone and out of her hair as soon as she had accomplished her task.

Minnesota? Blyss vaguely imagined a tundra with blowing winds and snow and—not of interest to her.

As she unlocked and opened the door and strode into the office, she surreptitiously glanced over a shoulder to catch the strut of the man's long, confident strides. Following at a distance. Smart man. Well, she did have something of his that he wanted back. The cuff link was too small to sell for any worthwhile amount, so she would give it back.

But first, to enact part two of tonight's plan.

Stryke closed the door behind him.

"Lock it," Blyss cooed. She stood across the room and turned, back against the wall, one leg bent and a black patent leather shoe heeling the wall.

The man's long fingers flicked the steel door lock. Something about those sexy, strong fingers. She needed to feel them on her body. And she would. And the man's name was Stryke. So bold and macho. Everything about him screamed alpha—yet to think that term gave her a shudder.

She eyed the small drawer at the corner of her desk. Inside was the key to securing her future. She must concentrate on the task at hand. Not on his virile attraction or her increasing need to surrender to that virility.

"Where are you staying?" she asked, because it was important.

"On that little island behind the big church."

The man was quaintly rustic. But that smile of his

was dangerous. It said to her, "I like to have fun, and if you're lucky, you can go along for the ride." Blyss couldn't remember when last she'd had fun with abandon. Had she ever?

"Île Saint-Louis?" she guessed, keeping her growing desire for his touch under control by pressing her palms against the wall behind her.

"That's the one. My grandfather owns one of the buildings and my entire family is staying there. We're in town for my aunt's wedding. The apartment I'm staying in is right above a candy shop. In the mornings I wake up to the smell of chocolate."

"Oh, I know that one. About center of the island."

"Yeah, exact center, I'd guess. It's a neat little neighborhood. I haven't done much exploring since arriving, but I hope to walk the city tomorrow. So…"

His eyes followed the lines of her body, up the slit that exposed her leg, which was darkened by a sheer black stocking. A red bow teased at the top of the stocking. All carefully planned, of course. Blyss thrived on male attention. It fed a part of her soul. If not her bank account.

He strode toward her and she smiled and placed the cuff link between her lips. He wanted her. She wanted him. Too bad this was to be a business engagement.

"Quickly," she said around the cuff link. "I can't be away from the event for too long."

"Is that so?" He stepped before her and plucked the cuff link from her mouth. They matched in height, but that was only because of her heels. She tapped his long blade of a nose, gliding her finger down it and to his lips, which were firm and, over the upper, topped with stubble. His tongue lashed her finger and she pushed it into his mouth for him to suck. "You want me?"

He pressed closer so she could feel the fabric of his suit brush against the lacy dress, yet he didn't push his body against hers. Teasing? Or not so daring as she had hoped?

"You are like those diamonds displayed out in the gallery," he said. "Pretty to look at, yet a man could never dream to possess them."

"Good boy. So you know you'll not be walking out of here tonight with me on your arm."

"I get your game. A quickie with a stranger?"

"*Quickie* is a vulgar term. I prefer *an amorous liaison.*"

"I like the sound of your French words, glamour girl. Then I guess I'd better get to it. Quickly," he whispered against her ear.

The brush of his mouth along her jaw made her sigh and tilt her head back, wanting him to paint his warm breath along her skin and to, for one moment, feed her the warmth she sought.

Stryke's hands glided up her thighs. One stopped at the ribbon that topped her stocking. The tickle of his finger shimmered a delicious hum through her mons and core.

"Mustn't tug," she admonished. Placing her hand over his, she again claimed the cuff link.

"Let me guess. You don't like to be mussed."

She slid her hands down to his fly and unzipped him.

"No mussing, it is," he groaned tightly.

He was hard and ready. Just the way she wanted him. But before they began, she lifted his wrist and stuck the cuff link through the buttonhole. "I'll let you keep this trinket."

And gliding her hands inside his coat, she slid them up his back between the crisp dress shirt and the silk coat lining. So many pockets lining the interior. Excellent. And then back around to unbutton his trousers and push them down.

"Take me," she insisted, defiantly holding his wondrous gaze. She did love it when they seemed shocked, the treat of a stolen liaison so unexpected to them. "Fast and hard."

His swallow was audible. But he didn't balk. Pushing up her dress, he lifted her against the wall at the same time. She wrapped her legs about his hips. His erection fit like a hot steel rod against her mons.

"You're soft and you smell great, and you're so hot," he babbled as he found his way inside her.

Blyss gasped as his thickness entered her in a smooth glide. She hadn't required lubrication because she'd been turned on since he'd gotten caught on her dress. Mmm, he felt like hot, hard steel. Every in-and-out motion teased at her apex, and she thought she might even climax, even though simple thrusting generally didn't do it for her.

She glided her fingers through his hair, seeking to grip hanks but it was so short, like uncut velvet. And then she did something she never did with her hookups. She didn't even think about it. Her head simply tilted and her mouth sought his. He tasted like champagne. His moan echoed inside her, stirring up her own moan. His powerful biceps flexed under her hands. His hips slammed her against the wall.

Gripping him at the back of his neck, she kissed him deeply, wanting to get lost in him, to find… *No. Mustn't be a fool.*

Stryke gasped harshly, yet quickly muffled the noise by pressing his mouth against her neck, his teeth pressing gently into her skin. "Shoot, I didn't use a condom…"

"I am on the pill," she whispered. "No worries."

"Whew." And as his body shook against hers, she reveled in his quick yet furious orgasm that shuddered his body against hers. Until she remembered…

The desk drawer beside her slid open with ease. She palmed the item she'd placed inside earlier and then slid her hand inside his suit coat. He was lost in the orgasm, oblivious to her actions.

"That was so—mmm, good." His eyes sought something in hers, so desperately, Blyss felt as if she'd done something wrong. "You're…" He sniffed, pushing his nose against her neck again and lingering at the base of her ear where her hair must tickle his face. "God, you smell good. But there's something…"

She dropped her legs and tugged down her skirt. "What is it?"

"I don't know. I just…" He pressed a hand over her breast, and it was only then that Blyss noticed how her heartbeats thundered. She'd love to do it again with this one—to actually take her time and find her own orgasm—but…

She would see him again. He just didn't know that yet.

"You're beautiful," he said. "But you don't belong here."

The hand at her chest suddenly felt like a two-ton weight. Blyss gaped. She shook her head. "Why do you say that?"

"I don't know why I feel that, but I do," he said. "Something about you. Are you…lost?"

A knock at the door sounded.

Stryke quickly zipped and Blyss tugged down her

dress and adjusted the red ribbon at the top of her silk stocking. "Lorcan?" she called.

"You busy?" a British voice called from outside the door. They'd done this drill before. He knew never to simply open the door and walk right in.

"He's my assistant." And such perfect timing!

She pushed by Stryke and strode toward the door, hands smoothing over her hair. "I have to get back. They'll be looking for me. You should leave now. Please."

She unlocked the door and opened it, revealing Lorcan waiting outside. He knew better than to show a cheeky grin or even a raised brow. The man was ever discreet. She returned the same courtesy to him. Turning, Blyss gulped down the longing that had been planted there by Stryke's sensual prowess. She'd wanted to linger.

Really? Linger against his heat, his overwhelming essence of man, sex and muscle? Sounded delicious. But indulgence in what her heart desired was something she never allowed.

Stryke passed her and slowed, as if he wanted to say something to her, but with Lorcan standing in the doorway, his eyes respectfully gliding along the door frame, Stryke simply nodded and walked out.

"Don't go back into the gallery!" she called after him. "Please."

He nodded as his strides took him down the hallway and away from her.

And she turned and strode back to the desk, palm pressed over her heart and biting her lip to prevent the tears.

Tears? What had he meant when he'd insinuated she was lost? Perhaps he hadn't been such a wise choice, after all. It was too late to alter her plan. She'd already completed the main step.

She would have to see Stryke again. And she looked forward to it. She dreaded it, as well.

"Everything all right, duck?" Lorcan asked.

She nodded. "I'm sorry. You know sometimes I just…"

"No need for an explanation. I'm headed out myself with a pretty young thing. Wanted to let you know I'm leaving. Unless you need me to stay and lock up?"

"No. Thank you, Lorcan. I've the security guard and the waitstaff will be around, as well. Go have some fun. I'll see you in a few days."

"Yes. We'll cement our plans for the showing then, eh?"

She nodded.

If all went well, that showing would never occur. And the only one aware it had failed would be her. She had a plan for keeping Lorcan in the dark about it.

He left the office door open, and Blyss bent and peered past her assistant to see if she could still see Stryke's back, but he was gone.

"The Île Saint-Louis," she whispered. "Now to step three in the plan. This will be the most difficult."

And if her heart got in the way again she truly would be lost, as he'd guessed.

Talk about the cold shoulder.

Stryke actually shivered as he strode down the darkened hallway, passed by the gallery and aimed straight for the exit.

Outside, he shrugged off the uncomfortable suit coat and tossed it over a shoulder. He should have hailed a cab, but he could see the river Seine from here. One thing he'd learned since arriving in Paris: if a man could locate the river, he'd never get lost. There was the left bank and the right bank, and the river. And he knew the island where he was staying was to his left.

It would be about a twenty-minute walk. He could use the fresh air. It was July and even nearing midnight the air was sultry. But not as sultry as the sexy handful he'd just held up against the wall.

"Blyss," he murmured.

And yet.

"What happened back there?"

Earlier this evening he'd donned a borrowed suit, met Blade on the street before the chocolate shop and entered the gallery with hopes to view some interesting artwork. A couple of rednecks mingling with the snooty set. It was supposed to be a kick. Stryke hadn't expected to pick up the hottest chick in the place.

And to have sex with her.

Blade and his miniskirted twins had nothing on what he'd scored.

But the craziest thing of all? There had been something about her. And it wasn't her beauty or her bold tease or the quick but satisfying liaison. He toggled the cuff link she'd returned to him. Her scent had been… Well hell, he didn't know how to categorize the uniqueness of her. Beyond the sweet flowery perfume, he had scented something deeper. Intriguing. Familiar?

"Crazy," he muttered as he strolled along the river. Lights on the buildings cast a spectacular show across the Seine's darkened waters. He marveled that tourists were out in full force. The City of Light truly never slept.

"I was caught in the moment. And what a moment."

Would he ever see her again? If he returned to the

gallery would she give him the time of day? Acknowledge they'd shared that moment?

Probably not. A woman like Blyss probably picked out a man to please her then tossed him aside without a glance over her sexy, bare shoulder.

Yet she hadn't gotten off. He'd come so quickly. Hadn't been able to stop himself. He felt bad about that. Normally he tended to a woman's pleasure before allowing his own. But the moment had jumped on him and he'd been swept away. He should have dropped to his knees and...

The assistant had banged on the door, ruining the whole thing.

Stryke paused at an intersection and glanced back the direction from which he'd come. A brightly lit Ferris wheel spun through the Paris sky to his left.

Why had he walked away? He should have waited around for the guy to leave and then got her phone number.

Was his hasty retreat because he'd felt as if she'd rejected him by pulling away from him so quickly? Probably. The woman defined classy. So out of Stryke's universe. Probably ate caviar and champagne for breakfast, then skirted around Paris in a Lamborghini painted pale pink, the color of her lips.

Rubbing his brow, Stryke shook his head and walked across the street on the green light. Smirking, he shook his head again. "It was a hookup," he muttered. "Let it go."

But with the lingering scent of flowers imbued on his skin, letting go was easier thought than done.

Chapter 3

Torsten Rindle was an interesting fellow. Stryke met him in a parking lot on the left bank down the street from a vast city park. The man drove an olive-green van, and he'd opened up the back doors to reveal some boxes sitting in the stripped-to-the-framework interior.

Tor was tall, slender and dressed in a tweed vest and pleated trousers. A polka-dot tie tightened about a crisp white dress shirt, of which, the sleeves were rolled to his elbows. A cicada was tattooed on the underside of one of his forearms, but otherwise, he appeared a dapper Englishman.

Stryke liked his accent. So *Downton Abbey*. Not that he'd ever watched the show. Okay, maybe once on a date a girl had suggested they cuddle on the couch and watch TV. The things a guy did for a little snuggling.

"So Hawkes Associates is strapped for help?" Tor asked as he carefully peeled back the packing tape from the top of a cardboard box.

"Actually, Rhys Hawkes is busy with a family wedding. Which is why I'm in town. The bride is my aunt."

"Ah yes, Johnny Santiago and his girl are tying the knot. Good couple. Vampires."

"Yes, indeed." And this guy worked for a secret order that hunted vampires. "You, uh…ever try to stake them?"

"Me?" Tor grinned, exposing a boyish charm. "I don't do the stake. I'm spin. Someone has to make sure the mortals didn't see a vampire bite a person's neck, but instead, just happened upon a couple actors rehearsing for a show at the Moulin Rouge. You know? The Order of the Stake only pursues those vampires who are a danger to humans. Like me. I'm human." He turned and offered his hand to shake. "Sorry, didn't do this properly. Torsten Rindle. Human."

Stryke shook the man's firm grasp. "Stryke Saint-Pierre. Werewolf."

"I like werewolves," Tor offered, folding back the flap on the box. "But you guys can be a challenge when pissed off."

Stryke tilted his head in acknowledgment. "Nothing wrong with being a challenge."

"So." Tor gestured Stryke approach the back of the van to peer into the box. "This is what I've got."

"Rhys said your knights sometimes pick this stuff up from a slain vampire's lair?"

"This artifact came from a vamp who was trafficking in magical accoutrements. Most of the stuff—herbs, nostrums and small ritual objects—we toss. But there were some decidedly demonic artifacts mixed in with the more innocuous stuff. Didn't want to keep our hands on this, nor did we want it sitting around for any Tom, Dick or Edward to get his hands on."

"May I?"

Tor nodded. "You'll be taking it with you anyway."

Stryke peered into the box and spied what looked like a staff of sorts. About two feet long, it was sleek, resembled steel and the top portion jutted up into prongs, which looked as though they should be clasping some wizardly sort of crystal.

His fingers neared the staff and then he flinched. "Is this what I think it is?" he asked.

"Demonic scepter." Tor reached in and pulled out the item as if a child's toy and waved it before Stryke. "Demons can do very bad things with it."

Stryke took a step back and put up his hands. "That's silver, man."

Tor studied the length of the scepter, then nodded. "Yep, probably is. A good conductor of magic. I suspect a stone or some such fits in the prongs. Most likely the stone is required to activate the thing. Be thankful it's missing. Here you go."

"Dude, I am not touching that thing. Silver is—"

"Ah, right. Sorry. But the silver has to actually enter your bloodstream to do you werewolves harm, right?"

"In theory. But I had a bad experience with a silver-tipped arrow last winter." He clutched his left biceps. "Almost died. I'm not taking any chances."

"Yikes." Tor carefully set the scepter back in the box. "Take it in the box, then."

"So it's cool sitting in this plain old brown box?"

"Should be." Tor tugged out the box and handed it to Stryke. "But I'd get it back to Hawkes Associates and secure it with wards as quickly as possible. Just to be safe."

Stryke thought he felt a wave of heat emanate from within the box and glow in his biceps. He winced. His brow began to sweat. His mouth dried. Flashes of last winter when the silver had fought to take his life disoriented him. But a healthy dose of wolfsbane had defeated the poison.

"Stryke? You okay?"

"Huh? Uh, yes." Best to get the hell out of here fast. "Thanks, man. Do I need to pay you?"

"We've an account with Hawkes. It's all been taken care of. Nice to meet you, Saint-Pierre. Stay wary."

"Really?" Stryke asked, but Tor had already slipped around the side of the van and he heard the driver's door slam shut.

"Wary," he muttered as the van pulled away.

Again he felt the heat emanate from within the box. "You don't have to tell me that. Me and silver do not have a good history."

If he was going to run into more silver working for Rhys, he'd have to start carrying some wolfsbane with him.

Blyss touched up her eyeliner in the mirror, drawing it out in a cat's-eye tease. Her brows were tweezed and shaded to perfection. A hint of blush. And bright red lips. Her usual daytime look. She liked to look sexy, and yes, she knew she was pretty. Men told her as much all the time. But sometimes it was hard to justify the beauty when she knew a beast lurked within.

She shook her head at the mirror's reflection. *Do not fall into those dark thoughts.* She'd moved beyond such thinking and was managing her beast. Had been for years.

Only, now her life had started to unravel in incredible ways. Her supplier, Edamite Thrash, had always been kind and just with her, but even he could not put up with her missed payments. She was behind a year, and she needed to refill her supply soon. Only a few pills remained in the glass jar she kept on her vanity.

She must not allow the beast reign.

There was no questioning Edamite's generosity by letting her go a year without paying. She'd had no choice but to divert her funds. Her father, well… She hoped he had learned a lesson and would never gamble again. But Blyss knew better.

Her bank account was in the red, and her social life was faltering. While usually she relied upon extravagant gifts from her lovers to seed her finances, she had not received a gift in months.

And she'd been given a week to procure an item for Edamite. An item so valuable he would forgive her debt and cover her for the next year's supply. An item that she had obtained and then placed in another person's care to divert suspicion. An item she must claim today so she could clear up matters with Ed.

She exhaled heavily, watching her shoulders slump in the mirror. Quickly, she corrected, pushing her shoulders back and lifting her chin.

Never let them see you suffer.

She'd worked too hard to establish her position among the humans. Blyss Sauveterre, Parisian socialite and gallery owner. She'd even been photographed with celebrities and had once made the gossip page after a weekend fling with a Russian duke.

She adjusted the combs, brushes and makeup on the vanity table before her so they lay straight and evenly spaced. She liked neatness. She was so close to avoiding a complete life catastrophe and smoothing over that annoying bump in her road. Control was her only means to relax.

Yet now Stryke Saint-Pierre had strolled into her life.

Her reflection frowned. She had been attracted the moment she'd laid eyes on him walking the gallery floor. And the attraction had been like nothing she had ever felt for a man before. She'd wanted to feel his hands roaming her skin, his mouth tasting hers. And she'd gotten that.

She wanted it again.

No. He is just the diversion.

Right. *Stick to the plan.* She had to see him again today. In order to retrieve what she'd planted on him, she needed access to his personal things. She must get close to him without raising suspicion.

Seduction would be necessary. And while seduction should prove a simple task—a job, nothing more—Blyss knew once she again stood in Stryke's arms, all bets would be off. She'd fall into his beautiful brown eyes and sexy smile and wish only for his masterful kiss. A kiss that had left her breathless in the gallery office.

A kiss she wanted to taste again.

Shaking her head furiously, she battled with the devil and angel hovering above each shoulder. She would never be an angel. She tried not to be so devilish. But this afternoon she must tempt and seduce. And win back her standing with her supplier.

Because if she did not, she must then face her beast. And that was something she could not bear.

Outfitted in hazmat gloves and a face mask, Rhys Hawkes had been waiting for the delivery in his office. Stryke had chuckled, but then asked when he would be issued his own safety equipment.

"Sorry," Rhys said as he took the silver scepter from the cardboard box. "I knew it was silver, but the thought to warn you didn't occur at the time. I'll have the company car outfitted with some precautionary equipment."

"Precautionary," Stryke repeated as he followed Rhys into an open vault that stretched back about twenty feet and featured an aisle four feet wide. He strolled his gaze up and down the security boxes, each fronted by a digital entry pad. "What all is in these boxes?"

"Gold, silver, coins from ages past. Magical items. Demonic accoutrements. Personal possessions that hold such great power the owner fears keeping them too near. Everything you can imagine. This is the preliminary holding cell for items the owners intend to retrieve instead of having them stored long-term. As well, I keep items I've purchased in here—like this scepter—until a spot can be coded for them below. I've a marvelous warehouse underground this building. I'll show it to you sometime."

"Kind of Warehouse 13, eh?"

"Hmm?" Rhys punched in a code and pulled open a drawer. He hadn't gotten the reference to the sci-fi show Stryke caught on replay every so often that featured a massive storage shed for items and devices of supernatural origin.

"So that wasn't a very dangerous job," Stryke commented. "You know I am capable if you've a particularly harrowing task."

"Oh, indeed." Rhys closed the drawer and tugged off his gloves. "You looking for some danger, Saint-Pierre?"

"Always."

"Your father told me you're the wise one of his children. Sort of the calm center amid a storm of fur and trouble."

"*Trouble* being the key word in that statement. My brother definitely lives up to his name."

"Malakai also tells me he's encouraged you to start a pack?"

"Yes, Dad wants to retire. And we could use a more varied pack where I live. A mixture of families."

"Always wise to integrate the pack with new blood. So you are married?"

"No, but I'm looking."

"Heh. I'd introduce you to my granddaughters at the wedding—Trystan's girls—but no. I don't want you taking any from my family across the ocean."

"Thanks. I do have my eye out while I'm in town."

Rhys patted him on the back and led him back out to the office. "You enjoy the show last night?"

"It was interesting." If not curious. And a boost to his ego. Until Blyss had shoved him out the door, and then his ego had fallen onto the concrete. "Met a gorgeous woman."

"Ah? Werewolf?"

"No. Doubt I'll find such luck so quickly."

"You two have a date, then?"

"I think we've done the date, the first kiss, the— Let's say it was sweet while it lasted."

"Parisian women can be baffling. Such pretty baubles to admire, but try to nudge beneath the sparkle and learn them?" Rhys shook his head. "I am thankful for a long and loving relationship with my wife. Dating nowadays would stymie me. People don't even talk anymore. They text. What is that about?"

Stryke offered him a shrug. He wasn't much for texting. A long talk and hand-holding were more his style.

"But if you're looking for a hookup in town," Rhys continued, "talk to Johnny. He knows a lot of—"

"Vampires aren't really my style. But thanks, Rhys. I'm going to head out. Unless you've more work for me?"

"Not at the moment, but I'm sure I will in a day or two. Thanks for helping out, Stryke. See you at the wedding this weekend."

On the way home Stryke stopped for a crepe from a food stand across the cobbled street from Notre Dame. He'd been eyeing this stand every day since arrival. Worth the dive into unhealthy. Sickeningly sweet chocolate oozed out around thick slices of banana between the folded crepe.

Bananas were always healthy, right?

He consumed the crepe and wandered in through the lobby of the apartment building. Knocking on the door to the apartment his brother Blade was staying in, he waited, but no answer. Must still be out with the twins.

His parents were likely helping with the wedding stuff. And Kelyn had been serious about seeing the sights. The youngest Saint-Pierre brother had left the building this morning with a map in one hand and his iPod set to a city tour.

Shaking his head in admiration over Blade's roguish prowess, Stryke headed up to his place. He surfed the television but couldn't understand French or the Indian-language stations, though the talk shows that emulated the confrontational style so popular in the US were a hoot.

After fifteen minutes all the hair-pulling and shoving annoyed him. Time to head out and explore the city. Maybe he could pick up Kelyn's scent and join him. He scanned out the window and eyed the row of shops across the river. He'd start there because he was pretty sure one of them was a bookshop.

A knock at the door must be a family member. Expecting a brother or even his mom or dad, Stryke answered the summons and chuffed out his breath at the sight of who it really was.

The sexy siren stood with one arm raised, her hand grasping high on the door frame, while her sinuous body slinked and seduced in red velvet. The dress hugged her from breasts to curvy hips. A party this early in the day? Stryke decided that every day—all day—was a party for this glamour girl.

"Blyss?"

She winked and strode across the threshold, handing him a filmy black scarf. He fumbled with it, not sure whether to scrunch it up and toss it aside or press it to his nose to inhale her scent. He compromised and brushed it over his face as he tossed it aside to land on the kitchen table littered with toast crumbs from a hasty breakfast.

Following the click of her high heels into the living room, which was bare of furnishings, save for a baroque couch and chair set that looked as if it hailed from the eighteenth century, Stryke waited for her to announce her reason for the visit.

Did he need a reason? Hell no.

The woman he'd thought to never see again stood not six feet away from him, looking like a sex goddess wrapped in red. Her dark hair was pinned up again, with a few wispy tendrils drawing his eye directly to her elegant neck. Right there. That was where he really wanted to kiss her.

She turned and crooked her finger at him and he almost lost it right there. But he was cool. Mostly. He got an instant hard-on, though. No fancy suit today, just a T-shirt and loose blue jeans that had gotten remarkably tighter.

"How'd you find where I'm staying?" he asked as he padded up to her and didn't dare touch her. Yet. She smelled like flowers. And again he got lost in a meadow of blossoms.

"You told me you live above the candy shop. Only one on the island."

"I didn't think I'd see you again after that hasty send-off last night."

"*Excuse moi.* I sometimes slip out of hostess mode, and then when I realize my guests are untended, I refocus with a vengeance. It's a thing with me."

"You often slip out of hostess mode at such gatherings?" Meaning, did she screw strange men in the office much?

Blyss tilted her head and fluttered her lashes.

Did he care what she did with other men? She was here now. She smelled like flowers. Looked like sin. And it was obvious she hadn't come for a chat.

Stryke pulled her to him in a swift move that married their bodies at hips and chest. He felt her nipples harden beneath the velvet and his hand glided to one breast to squeeze. There was something about a woman intent upon getting exactly what she wanted. And he sensed this flawless piece of female was here on a seek-and-have-sex mission.

He dipped his head to her breasts. The dress was cut low, and he dashed his tongue under the velvet. She gasped and leaned into him, asking for more with her body.

"I hope you're not busy," she whispered. "I don't normally stop by without first calling, but I didn't have your mobile number."

Mobile was what the French called the cell phone. He lashed his tongue over her firm breast. "Was only planning on sightseeing. Mmm, Blyss, you are incredible."

Her hand slid up under his T-shirt, fingernails gently clawing his abs. "And you are *très fantastique*, Stryke."

He slid the thin red strap off her shoulder and pulled down the dress to expose her breast. Kissing and suckling her erect nipple, he moaned at the pleasure of the surprise. And his inner wolf stirred, sensing the connection to—hmm…to what?

Something about her called to his feral instincts in ways that no woman ever had. It puzzled him, but then again, he couldn't question it too much. Maybe later.

Her leg hooked about his and she gripped him at the back of his neck, pulling him hard against her breast. When he nipped her skin she gasped. She liked that. A little rough? He'd always thought himself a gentle lover, but he could amp up the intensity if that was what she wanted.

Squeezing her other breast while he sucked in her nipple, he gripped her ass and lifted her so she wrapped her legs about his. The bedroom door was five steps away. Moving blindly, he managed to miss the door completely and crush her up against the wall. He knew she liked this position.

"Sorry, was aiming for the door."

"Your bedroom is through there? Yes, let's try it on a bed this time, *mon amour*."

My love? Oh yeah. She was here for more than a social call.

This time he made it through the doorway and they tumbled onto the king-size bed made with simple white linens and a scatter of fluffy pillows. He didn't let her go, though. Instead he pulled down the other dress strap and the dress fell to her waist. Burying his face against her breasts, he breathed in what was surely expensive perfume. He'd fallen into a rose garden.

She tugged at his shirt and he slipped it over his head. Cooing, Blyss ran her hands over his chest, setting his nerve endings ultrareceptive to all things good.

"So ripped," she murmured. "American men are so much more than the French man."

When he was about to foolishly say it was the wolf in him, she pressed a finger to his lips. "Let's not talk. Let's taste." She lashed her tongue under his jaw. "And touch." Her fingers slid over his crotch and curled about his erection. "And devour."

"Devouring sounds good to me."

Stryke made quick work of his fly, unzipping and shrugging out of his jeans. Boxer briefs hugged his erection, but they didn't stay up for long. Blyss shoved them down his hips and grasped his aching hard-on. The contact felt like fire singeing him in the sweetest way. He hissed.

She coiled her fingers about him and squeezed. Oh, yeah, that was twenty kinds of all right.

Stryke was about to kiss her mouth, but the red lipstick stayed him. She was so pretty, so perfect. She deserved mussing, but he'd do it in another way. Planting the kiss on her neck, he nuzzled there and gently bit down along her shoulder. Her hands busied themselves with his cock and he would come too fast if she kept it up.

He grabbed her wrists and pinned them up by her shoulders. This time, he intended to orchestrate their liaison. No coming for him until she did first. He owed her one. She cooed, her tongue dashing out to lick those teasing red lips. He'd caught her. Now what would he do with her?

Indeed, what to do with this gorgeous bit of glamour that surprised him at every turn and whom he wanted to figure out. And yet, he did not. The surprises were what made her so exciting.

Rocking his hips against hers, he teased at her hot, sticky wetness with his cock. She moaned and murmured, "Yes," but he was inclined to tease a bit longer.

The dress hugged around her waist. Her thigh-high stockings glided like silk against his legs. She still wore the shoes, and thinking about those spiked heels hardened his cock even more. He wanted to feel her softness and her dangerous sharpness all over his skin.

So when she struggled against his hold on her wrists, he relaxed his grip and allowed her to push at him. He rolled to his back, pulling her on top of him in a smooth movement. Straddling him, she pulled off the dress and tossed it to the floor.

Afternoon sunlight beamed across the bed and her body glowed as if she were a sun goddess. Stryke glided his hands up her stomach. When he cupped her breasts, she tilted her head back, offering her succulent fullness to him. She wiggled, her moistness heating his cock. And with a shift of her hips she managed to take him inside her.

"I don't have any—" Stryke never had unprotected sex. Werewolves could get mortal women pregnant.

She tutted him. "You didn't last night either, no?"

Right. She'd said she was on the pill.

"Lover, you are steel between my legs. Mmm…"

He closed his eyes and fell into the exquisite rhythm of her rocking above him, feeding off him, milking him, pairing with him. Bonding—no.

When two werewolves had sex together in werewolf form they bonded for life. It was a serious deal. And while he hoped to someday bond with a werewolf and make a family together, this woman was merely human and he just wanted to have fun with the glamour goddess.

Blyss cupped his hands, still wrapped about her breasts, and squeezed. Murmuring an approving sound, she quickened her pace, up and down, bringing him to climax with expert skill. Stryke's hips bucked up against her, and when she pressed her hands to his chest and watched him ride out the pleasure, he thought surely she was looking inside him for some secret.

The secret was that he was stymied by her interest in him. But then again, maybe he should stop thinking like a Northwoods hick and accept the Parisian ideal. Whatever that was.

Slipping his fingers between her legs, he found her swollen apex and stroked her until she gripped at his shoulders and tossed back her head. The scent of flowers and salty sweetness and…something so familiar filled his senses as she cried out in pleasure.

Stryke inhaled deeply, testing the scent she gave off and wondering… It was too familiar not to recognize. Was she really? There was no mistaking her feral scent. He knew it from long runs in the woods with his brothers while they were in wolf form and from the rush of adrenaline the wolves got when chasing prey.

As Blyss's body softened above him, Stryke gripped her by the shoulders. "You're a werewolf?"

Chapter 4

Blyss pushed out of Stryke's demanding grasp and shuffled off the bed. She clasped her hands across her breasts, the urge to protect herself heightened by his out-of-the-blue question. And his strangely accusatory tone. Inhaling, she fought to not mentally return to that moment in high school—the moment life had turned against her.

How could he have known?

In all the years she had been taking a pill to suppress her werewolf, never had anyone guessed her truth. Sure, she tended to live and socialize only with humans. Not too often a human was going to make the jump to ask "Could you be a werewolf?" But on occasion she sensed a vampire or other in the crowd—vamps could be so obvious at times. None had ever guessed at her beastly origins.

Yet Stryke knew. In the moment when she had cried

out as an orgasm had swept through her, and then he too had come—

Was it possible another werewolf could scent her during an aroused state?

Apparently it was. But not simple arousal, rather climax. It was the first time she had come when with him.

"Blyss? Are you…?"

A frightening truth assaulted Blyss like a blow to the gut. The only way Stryke could possibly guess such a thing about her was if he was also a wolf.

She had just slept with a werewolf.

Oh, mercy, what terrible thing had she done?

"It's okay." He moved to the edge of the bed, his hands up to placate. His eyes softened, as did his voice. "I didn't realize you were my breed. I'm werewolf," he offered, obviously sensing her distress. "I didn't realize what you were last night in your office. Usually I can scent another of my kind. Maybe your perfume overwhelmed my senses."

"I can't talk about this right now."

The innate instinct to flee when cornered moved Blyss's limbs. She excused herself to go to the bathroom and rushed across the hardwood floor. With the door closed behind her, and the cool bathroom tiles beneath her bare feet, she turned on the faucet and splashed her face with tepid water. Her reflection could not overlook that twitch at the corner of her heart that manifested in a frown. Her hair was tousled, her lipstick worn away. Her eye shadow still looked perfect, but…

Nothing was perfect. He knew.

And while she should have laughed off his guess and made a grand and confident exit as stunning as her entrance, she couldn't simply leave. She had come here for a reason. Her very life depended on securing the black diamond she had planted in Stryke's suit pocket.

Merde. Stryke Saint-Pierre was a werewolf.

Her heartbeats dropped to her stomach. Blyss pressed her palms to the cool vanity sink, bowing her head. He hadn't scented her because the pills she took to suppress her werewolf made her virtually human.

"How did he know?" she begged her reflection.

It had to have been the sex. When she had climaxed and her body had released…something had clued him to her heritage. Pheromones or something like that. No man had noticed before because she'd never had sex with a werewolf.

What luck—the one man she had picked out from the crowd to help her should be the very man she needed to stay away from. Wanted to stay away from. But now could not.

Not until she found what she'd come for.

She straightened and nodded firmly at the mirror. She would go out there, dress, and she had to check the closet for the suit he'd worn last night. How to do that without raising suspicion? And how to avoid the werewolf questions?

She wanted to run away from it all. As she had so many years ago when her fellow classmates had stared at her with horror.

"You can do this. You *have* to do this." She winced. Could Stryke possibly help her? No. She had a plan. She would stick to it. "He must never know what kind of trouble I'm in."

With a few adjustments to her hair and a pat of a towel to dry her face, Blyss wandered back into the bedroom. Her lover stood by the window, naked, with an erection. The sun beamed across his face and shadowed his body, silhouetting that proud jut of manhood before the glass. Gorgeous. Something she would miss. She already missed him. The whole man. His kisses. His firm yet loving touch. His sexy smile…

Hell, what was she thinking? *Get your head on course.*

Blyss sat on the end of the bed. She picked up the red velvet dress from the floor. Where was her purse? Must have left it in the kitchen when she'd entered. "Your water is nice and hot here."

"Is that a good thing? I mean, isn't it all over the city?" He strode over to her and stroked his fingers over her hair. A shiver trickled down her neck and tightened her nipples. He smelled like fire and strength and sex. It was annoyingly distracting.

"Usually takes mine five minutes to warm nicely in the winter," she provided in an attempt to stick to the plan. "I may live off the Champs-Élysées, but the plumbing doesn't care that it is the ritzy section of town."

"Is that the street with all the fancy shops on it? The one that leads up to Napoleon's statue?"

Blyss smiled and stood to face him. She trailed a finger down his chest that was dusted with brown hair. His muscles gleamed in the sunlight.

"It's not a statue. It's a monument. The Arc de Triomphe was erected by Napoleon to commemorate his military victories." She kissed his jaw. Avoided touching his hard-on. Not an easy task. "Wish I had a toothbrush."

"I might have seen an extra in the drawer. Give me a few minutes to brush my teeth. Then I'll set one out for you. Okay?"

"Perfect."

He kissed her on the mouth and she pushed away from him. "I just said—"

"Are we going to discuss the werewolf thing?"

Heartbeats rammed against her rib cage. "I don't want to. I... No. Please let it go, Stryke."

He sighed and nodded. But for a few seconds he studied her. Trying to look inside her? Figure how he had missed that she was a werewolf?

If only she had known the same about him.

Finally, Stryke strolled toward the bathroom.

Tearing her gaze from his sexy backside, Blyss sighed. The life she led was a difficult achievement. And she did strive for it. But it was to be her undoing.

When the bathroom door closed, she slipped the dress over her head as she made a beeline for the closet door. Inside, the walk-in closet was vast and empty. Only the first rack held a few items. Two pairs of men's shoes sat on the floor beside a large empty suitcase.

She touched the hung items. A few T-shirts. Some jeans and a pair of dressier slacks. One white dress shirt. Nothing designer. And one black tie that wasn't silk but rather something like polyester.

Blyss shuddered. The man's wardrobe was hideous. Not a natural fiber in the lot, and yet the suit last night had been Zegna, if she was not mistaken. And she rarely misjudged couture. Though it had been poorly tailored to fit him, it had been expensive. She was sure of it.

Where was the suit?

"Hey."

Blyss startled. She hadn't heard Stryke's return and now he stood in the doorway, filling the space with an easy confidence, shoulders set back and head tilted. He'd put on a pair of jeans that hung low, revealing the hard cuts of muscle that veered toward his groin like some kind of traffic alert that screamed "Go this way!"

"What are you doing?" He held a boxed toothbrush in his hand.

"Uh, just…looking." She spread her palm down the front of one of the T-shirts. Shit. What to say? "I'm a bit of a snoop." Weren't all women? "A girl can learn a lot about a man by standing in his closet."

Oh, bad save, Blyss. Very bad save.

"Is that so? Tell me what you've learned about me?"

"That you're a terrible traveler. Didn't you say you were in town for a wedding? Where's the suit you wore last night?"

"It was a loaner. I dropped it off at Vail's earlier today. I've been doing a lot of running around for my family, picking up things they need for the wedding."

"Vail?"

"A vampire. He's the father of the groom. I borrowed the suit for the night. I've been informed by the female faction of all this wedding madness that I'll have a rental for the wedding. Although…I imagine Vail will probably wear the suit for the wedding."

"Vail," she muttered. "I don't think I've heard of him."

"You probably haven't. Vamps tend to stay off the radar."

"Yes, I suppose."

He discussed vampires with her so casually. As if it was something she was familiar with and engaged in discussion every day. The paranormal breeds were something she avoided with a passion. And talking about them made her uncomfortable.

"But since you don't want to discuss the werewolf thing, I'll assume vampires are off the table, too?"

She nodded and dropped her hand from the front of the dress shirt.

"So, do you want to go to a wedding?" Stryke offered as he waggled the toothbrush before her.

Blyss accepted the packaged offering and tapped it against her lower lip. A wedding with vampires? Oh, mercy no. But if the suit was going to be there? Had she any other choice?

The last thing she wanted to do was associate with werewolves and vampires.

"Weddings are always fun," she managed to say brightly. "When is it?"

"Saturday. It's an evening wedding. I'll pick you up around six?"

She nodded. "It's a date."

Step three of the plan had failed miserably. On to step four. Emergency procedures.

"I'll need your address."

Blyss strolled out into the bedroom, stepped into her heels and spied his mobile phone on the nightstand beside the bed.

"I'll enter it for you."

She typed in her address on the contacts app, but she didn't enter her number. She never gave any man her number.

When Stryke took the phone he leaned in to kiss her, but she performed a twist and managed to avoid the contact as his lips brushed her cheek. She clicked toward the bedroom door, abandoning the toothbrush with a toss toward the bed.

"I'm so sorry to rush off, but I have to get back to the gallery!"

She didn't listen for his reply, but suspected he was probably kicking himself for inviting her to the wedding after that cold brush-off. Of course, now the man would have another day to think and wonder over her. Not a good thing.

Grabbing her scarf and purse as she breezed through the kitchen, she hastened through the front door and skipped toward the elevator.

A vampire wedding would prove a challenge. But if she did not find the suit, she would not be able to pay off Edamite Thrash. And life as she knew it would never again be the same.

"It freaked me out," Stryke said to his brother Kelyn as they strolled down a narrow cobbled street somewhere in the 5th arrondissement. Trouble walked ahead of them. "I had no idea she was werewolf."

"Something must be wrong with her," Kelyn offered in his usual quiet tone.

Of the four Saint-Pierre boys, Kelyn had no wolf in him and was 100 percent faery, thanks to their mother's genes. Physically he looked like no one in the family—save their mother—and was tall, lithe and pale. He usually covered the faint white markings that traced his arms, chest and back of his neck. Faery markings even he wasn't sure about. His violet eyes had a tendency to make women swoon. And Stryke had heard more than a few whispers about Kelyn's prowess between the sheets that made the ladies collapse in delighted exhaustion.

His *sidhe* brother seemed to navigate Paris as if he knew the city, yet used the ley-line excuse when Stryke asked about it. Faeries were inexplicably connected to the ley lines that crissed and crossed across the planet.

Trouble, who strode in front of them, his shoulders swaying with each sure stride, eyed a pair of women in stilettos and brandishing patent leather purses as they sat sipping café au lait before a chic café. The dark-haired Trouble winked and nodded to them. The women ignored his blatant flirtations with a chill Stryke was all too recently familiar with. Blyss's quick escape earlier had made him want to check if icicles had formed on the doorknob.

There was something up with her. Beyond the weird aversion to discussing the fact they were both wolves. That was why he'd asked her to the wedding. He needed to know more. And—to have one huge question answered.

"The city girls are snobs," Trouble said as he slowed and parted Stryke and Kelyn to walk between them. "I can't get a rise out of any of them. I'm ready to go home."

"I like Paris," Kelyn commented. "It feels familiar. And Stryke found himself a werewolf without even trying."

"Dude, really? How'd you score that?" Trouble wrapped an arm about Stryke's neck and gave him a noogie. "Thought you were at some fancy-schmancy gallery last night with Blade? Did you hear about Blade?"

"What?" Kelyn asked.

"Scored twins," Stryke confirmed.

"That man is a master," Trouble said in awe. "But a werewolf, eh? 'Bout time my little bro hooked up with his own kind. Dad will be happy to hear you are serious about starting a pack. Where'd you find her? Vail hook you up?"

"I met her at the gallery. I think she's the owner, but we didn't talk about much. Mostly I pushed her up against the wall and had a quickie." Because brothers shared everything. And he had to tell someone about the insane but amazing encounter.

"Nice." Trouble wasn't the most discerning when it came to women. He liked them fast, sexy and amiable. And they couldn't be too fancy or prissy. Trouble was a man's man, and he liked a woman who did all the kinds of things he liked to do.

Same with Stryke. If she couldn't handle a fishing rod or ride behind him on the four-wheeler while careening through a muddy field, well then, that was it.

Blyss was none of the above. But hell, she was his Paris fling. And what happened in Paris stayed in Paris. Right?

"She stopped by my place earlier for more sex," Stryke explained, "and it was the first time I realized she was wolf. When she came, I scented her. How the hell could I have not known before then?"

"Weird." Trouble pounded his fists together, a sort of tic. "What did she say about it?"

"She didn't want to talk about it. I had sex with a werewolf. You know how rare that is? Back in Minnesota the packs guard their females so well, if you can manage a date it's like breaking into Fort Knox. I don't have a clue why she didn't want to talk about it when she learned I was wolf. But I'm seeing her again. Taking her with me to the wedding."

"I'll sniff her out," Trouble offered. "See what's up."

"Keep your nose away from my woman," Stryke said with a less-than-gentle nudge to his brother's ribs. "I'll figure it out. She's…complicated."

"Ah, hell, complicated women are not for me." Trouble wandered ahead again at sight of a gaggle of tourist girls who couldn't be a day over the age of sixteen.

"This way," Kelyn called, and they veered to the

right to distract their brother's wandering attention. "Let's get something to eat at that gyro place we ate at last night."

"I'm going to head across the river," Stryke said. "I want to walk through the Tuileries and check it out."

"The what?" Trouble asked.

"It used to be the royal gardens a few centuries ago."

"Dude, I don't care about flowers."

"I know. That's why I'll head there by myself." And he didn't need the harassment of his brothers should he manage to find Blyss's place while pretending to be interested in some stupid flowers. "I'll see you two later."

The brothers exchanged fist bumps, and Stryke headed across a bridge laden with padlocks and toward the garden. He'd eaten a sandwich after Blyss left and wasn't hungry yet, so he didn't miss the food break. Trouble could eat all the time. And Kelyn, well… That kid rarely ate. So he was odd. Stryke worried about him at times. This world was not the place for Kelyn, but he wasn't sure Faery would welcome him either.

The Tuileries was a disappointment. Where were the flowers? It was mostly espaliered trees and trimmed shrubs and some marble statues. The French had strange ideas about gardens, that was for sure.

Crossing a wildly busy roundabout intersection, Stryke then wandered down the Champs-Élysées, taking in the elegant storefronts and dodging tourists who wielded armloads of shopping bags. He pulled out his phone and clicked on Blyss's address. The GPS located her immediately. About two blocks from where he stood.

Spying a stand selling flowers, he detoured.

"Can't show up uninvited *and* empty-handed."

He purchased some flowers then wandered deeper

down the narrow streets that hugged three- and four-story buildings that he guessed must be centuries old. He knew Paris had been drastically redesigned sometime in the nineteenth century by Haussmann, and Napoleon had also torn down many structures, but the ancient history remained. Everything was elaborate, the building fronts featuring carved stone edifices and mascarons and even gilding on some of the stone and ironwork. Locked gates and digital entry systems clued him he had entered a ritzy neighborhood.

Stryke suddenly felt very underdressed in his Boundary Waters T-shirt and jeans with the worn hems dusting his scuffed Doc Martens. Maybe this was a bad idea? Showing up at a socialite's pied-à-terre looking like a tourist? He wasn't even sure what pied-à-terre meant, but it sounded cool.

He paused on a street corner paved in cobblestones. A red Vespa scooted by, and an elderly woman with gray hair bound behind her head and a pair of leather chaps nodded at him. The image made Stryke smile and he decided to go for it.

But as he stepped off the curb he heard the click of high heels.

"Are you stalking me, Monsieur Saint-Pierre?"

He turned to find Blyss looking like some kind of magazine model in a tailored pink dress and matching high heels. One hand clutched a slim purse and in the other dangled a dainty bag sporting the store name Pierre Hermé. She'd changed since seeing him only a few hours earlier.

"Uh, I was in the neighborhood and I thought I'd see if I could find your place." He held out the red roses, bound with twine. "These made me think of your lips."

She strolled slowly across the street, her eyes never

leaving his, and the sexy tilt of her head pretty much went straight for his loins. She traced a delicate fingernail along a rose petal. Stryke could smell her perfume and the sweetness inside the bag she carried. Must be pastries. Yet he couldn't scent her wolf now.

"So you've found me." She walked across the street, away from him.

That was it? She hadn't taken the roses. "Uh, maybe you want to invite me up?"

She paused before a steel door, her fingers perched upon the digital entry pad. Did she have to think about it? Yep, he should have tried more for suave instead of tourist with his look today.

She punched in the code, pushed the door open and strode inside. She didn't close the door, so Stryke took that as an invite to follow. The woman had a way with leading him places. And he liked what happened once he arrived.

Closing the door behind him, he saw she walked through a small open courtyard lined with militantly trimmed green shrubs and simple flowers. It was amazing how Paris had all these hidden gems of greenery tucked in private courtyards. Reminded him of being home in the country.

Well, not really, but he'd use his imagination. It was necessity when surrounded by tarmac, buildings, and nothing but humans for miles and miles.

Blyss veered right and disappeared into the cool shadows.

He hastened his steps to keep up with her. Normally, Stryke could follow another werewolf by scent alone. Why was it that he had only sensed her innate wolf when they were having sex? It was as if the adrenaline had to be rushing through her system to stir whatever pheromones his wolf could react to.

And he understood the subject of their breed was off-limits. It shouldn't bother him, but he couldn't help being curious. How often did Blyss happen upon another werewolf? Was it so common to her that she'd grown bored of the discussion? Couldn't be.

He'd lucked out. And as little as he knew about her, he did like her. Could something come of this? He daren't hope, but at the same time, his inner wolf howled with joy.

Blyss opened her front door. Stryke looked so innocently hungry staring at her with that adoring expression and underlined by the gorgeous bouquet of roses. The wedding wasn't until tomorrow but she believed his excuse that he had been walking in the area.

She never invited men into her home. It wasn't wise. Once invited in, it was often difficult to make them leave after she tired of them. And they sometimes returned. It was a sticky business to have to deal with.

And this particular man was more than man. He was werewolf. The last creature in this world with whom she wished to be intimate.

Alas, she had ignored any intuition that would have kept her safe from that emotional danger. And even as she vacillated with grabbing the roses and slamming the door in his face, the compulsion to pull him in by that awful T-shirt and let him have his way with her was even stronger.

She couldn't resist his wild allure. It was an accidental allure, she felt sure. The man wasn't a master seducer. Though he was an amazing lover. And he wasn't suave or polished, as she preferred her men. He was a rough and awkward man from the United States, of all places, who had happened to fall into her scheme, and now he was milking it for all he could. Because he knew something about her that others did not.

Would he use that information to blackmail her such as Edamite Thrash had?

He thrust the roses forward. Sweet blackmail, if there was such a thing. And that smile. She wanted him to teach her all the things that smile promised.

Blyss took the bouquet by the ribbon-wrapped stems, and then she grabbed her suitor by the shirtfront and pulled him inside. Turning, she walked down the long hallway, roses dangling at one side, man clutched at her other side.

If she was going down the wrong path, she might as well do it big. At least, until the wedding was over and she held the key to her future safe in hand.

Chapter 5

Stryke followed Blyss down a long white hallway and into a kitchen that gleamed white and silver. It looked like something out of a minimalist designer's dream. White marble countertops, not an appliance on the counter, no signs it was a kitchen if not for the sink and sleek, glass-fronted fridge that sported wine bottles down one side.

Placing the roses on the counter, Blyss veered left into a living area that featured a white furniture set beneath a ceiling that was entirely glass. It was like standing in a conservatory without the plants. Everything was white. He didn't dare sit down because he'd been walking through Paris. His shoes must be dirty.

How could a person relax in a place so white?

The gorgeous contrast of pink silk and blackest hair and eyebrows turned and tilted a brilliant red smile at him. "I didn't think I'd see you until Saturday. But now that you're here…"

She pushed her hand up under his T-shirt, her glossy nails gliding over his abs. At the erotic touch Stryke sucked in a breath. The intention in her eyes was apparent. This woman went from cool to boiling faster than a rocket ship.

He abandoned his need to ask about her werewolf and instead slid a hand about her hip and pulled her to him. Her fingernails dug in at his chest, and one of them tweaked his nipple. Yep, that gave him a hard-on.

"You are so hard to resist," he growled.

"Then why must you? I certainly have no intention of denying myself what I want."

"I'm guessing you are a woman who likes to be spoiled."

"Very much so."

"Then why me?" He caught her hand against his chest, the shirt between his hand and hers. Leaning closer to her face, he tried to scent her innate wolf but could not. "Am I just a fling?"

"Of course you are." She kissed his mouth without making a connection—more like breath against breath—just enough of a tease to keep him close to her. "I never get attached to a man. It's a rule. Can you deal with that, Stryke?"

It sounded fifty ways wrong. But he needed only one reason to stay. And that reason had grown hard as steel, standing at attention, ready for some action.

"Works for me," he said and lifted her up against him.

As her thin pink skirt slid up high, she wrapped her legs about his hips and Stryke set her on the back of the white sofa. He bent to kiss along her neck, smelling only the sweet flowers that blossomed on her skin. The heat of her combined with the sweetness melded into an intoxicating perfume that he inhaled deeply. Still no wolf. He'd ask her about it later.

He slid down the zipper at the back of her dress, his fingertips strolling slowly over her skin, the straightness of her spine, until he felt the sexy divots that topped her derriere. There he rocked his thumbs against the concave curves.

"I gotta taste you." He pulled her from the couch, turning her, so her gorgeous ass faced him. Bending to lick the Venus dimples above her hips, he curled his hands around in front of her mons. One glided up toward her breasts; the other sought the moist warmth between her legs.

"Blyss," he muttered against her sweet skin. It wasn't so much her name as an experience, and he intended to take it to the maximum. "So good."

She turned and put up a foot on one of his shoulders, forcing him to kneel. So that was the way of it?

"S'il vous plaît," she asked sweetly.

He didn't know what that meant but that wasn't going to stop him from taking and giving what he desired. Stryke kissed her mons and glided his hand up her thigh until her wetness enticed him to dash his tongue down her hot seam. Mmm…he was hungry now.

He lashed at her sensitive apex and her body shuddered in response. Fingers clasping his hair, she balanced there on the back of the couch, one leg sliding over his shoulder, the other, toes barely touching the floor.

Reaching up, he was rewarded with her hand clasping his. She squeezed tightly every time his tongue hit the spot. She moaned appreciatively.

The best feeling a guy could have? Kissing a woman between her legs as she came, her thighs squeezing his face and her hands tugging him in desperate release. That he could make her ride a high like this gave him immense satisfaction. He felt pride and also needed to feel her heat wrapping about his cock.

Before he could stand, Blyss sank to the floor and straddled him, taking his erection inside her. She was so wet and still spasming from the orgasm. The tug and tease on his cock lured him to a speedy orgasm.

Werewolf or not, this woman was something else.

Blyss woke to the sun beaming across her face. Half of the apartment was capped by windowed, cathedral-style ceilings. She thrived on the sunshine, and this bedroom with the slanted ceiling and the windows that faced the eastern sky fed her very soul.

She yawned and then realized there was a tremendous body heat lying next to her. He mastered the bed, as if staking a claim.

She silently swore, clutching the bedsheets up over her breasts. And yet, she could only blame herself for this mistake called Stryke Saint-Pierre. When she'd spied him on the street yesterday afternoon, she should have stepped around the side of a building and pressed her back to the wall as if a thief fearing capture, and waited for him to leave. But something about him had inexplicably compelled her. Drew her to him as if starved for the lust and sensual cravings he seemed to fulfill every time he touched her.

She turned onto her side, and the movement startled him awake. He reached over and pulled her against his chest, sliding his hand up her stomach to cup her breast. He whispered sleepily, "Come here, glamour girl."

Mercy. If this was a mistake then why did lying next to Stryke feel so right?

* * *

Stryke dressed as the shower clattered in the next room. Blyss had woken, slipped out from under his arm and padded toward the bathroom. "See you tonight," she had called. "You can let yourself out."

A cold send-off.

He considered pulling his clothes off and lying back on the bed in wait. They could make love again. He could lose himself in her. Fall into her strange world of glamour, perfection and sensory disguise. Because he forgot everything when wrapped in Blyss's arms.

But he knew she wanted him gone by the time the shower stopped. Call it instinct. She was a hard one to figure. She was hot and wild in bed, but out of it she was like porcelain. Smooth and cool to the touch. And not at all wolflike.

He glanced about the bedroom, seeking something, anything, that would clue him to her breed. Not sure what he was looking for exactly. Wasn't as if wolves kept totems around signifying their packs, or—

He wondered what the name of her pack was. Obviously, she didn't live within the pack, as most tended to gather in large compounds. Of course, many had a central gathering place while the members had their own homes and lived away from the pack.

That was how he planned to form his pack. A central compound for gatherings while the individual families lived in their own homes. It was a good way to build a strong yet diverse community.

Tilting his glance upward, he squinted at the bright sunlight beaming through the overhead windows. He hadn't taken the time to look up last night to sight in the moon. He bet lying here beneath the full moon was awesome.

That was, if the full moon didn't tug at his need to shift to werewolf. The last thing he'd do in this city was shift and risk being seen in werewolf shape. He wondered where Blyss went to shift.

So many things he wanted to ask her, and yet there was no way to bring up questions without causing her affront. He was damn sure she'd slap him or storm out again should he even whisper the word *werewolf*.

His shoes were out in the living room somewhere. Stryke wandered down the hallway. He was afraid to touch anything for fear of leaving a stain. Near the couch he shoved his feet into the Doc Martens, and as he was walking down the hall to the front door, his phone rang.

He closed the front door behind him and answered.

"Stryke, where are you? I thought you were going to help with errands today?"

His mother, Rissa. Indeed, he had offered to ferry her about Paris as they collected whatever was needed for tonight's ceremony. His mother was at the Santiago mansion today. They lived in the 7th, which if he knew the city—and he did not—might be across the river from where he currently was. It was near the Eiffel Tower; he did know that much.

"I think it'll take half an hour to find the place," he said to his mother. "Then you've got me for most of the day."

"Most?"

"Are you going to release me from servitude to get ready for the wedding?"

His mother laughed. "Of course. Could you pick up some *pains au chocolat* on your way here?"

"I have no idea what that is, but I'll try my best to sniff some out."

"Chocolate pastries, son. Point your nose toward chocolate. You know how much I love my sweets."

"Will do. See you in a bit, Mom."

The phone rang again before he even stuffed it back in a pocket. This time it was a brother asking for directions home from someplace beyond the ring road that circled the city proper.

"Don't you have GPS, Trouble?"

"I did, until I lost my phone. Dude, it's like country out here. But the countrywomen sure are fun. Kelyn and I met a bunch of faeries last night. They are hot. Where are you, anyway?"

"I'm finding much better luck in the city," Stryke offered as he exited the courtyard and strode over the cobblestones. "Listen, I have no idea where you are. I'm headed to the Santiagos' right now to drive a carload of wedding-crazed women all over."

"Ah hell, sounds like you got the shit job today."

"It'll make looking forward to this evening and my date with Blyss all the sweeter."

"She's the wolf who's weird about it, right?"

"Right. I think I see a place selling those chocolate things Mom wanted. I gotta go. Why don't you have Kelyn fly up above the trees and locate your position?"

"Good call. See you later, bro."

Blyss sat before the vanity in a lace pink La Perla bra-and-panty set. Pink marabou fluffed on the toes of her kitten-heeled slippers. Carefully, she drew eyeliner beneath her lower lid. Her hair was still up in a towel, but she liked to do her eyes before drying it. Rest of the makeup was done after her hair. It was a two-hour morning ritual.

And it was nearly noon.

She could have lingered in bed with Stryke well into the afternoon. His skin against hers had been insanely exquisite. His hands gliding across her limbs, caressing a breast, even tracing her lips, was a feeling she didn't ever want to forget. His mouth at hers. His moans harmonizing with hers. His hard, hot cock buried within her.

Blyss sighed, and her reflection blinked, messing up the eyeliner.

"What the hell am I doing?" she muttered as she swiped a tissue over the mess. "I don't turn into a swooning schoolgirl when a man knows how to make love to me. I remain calm and distant, and thank him for whatever sparkling gift he wishes to give me."

Stryke had gifted her gorgeous red roses. Nothing that could be resold, such as diamonds or platinum, or even a new car. She'd collected hundreds of thousands of dollars in gifts over the years. All of which were now gone. Ransomed to pay for her addiction.

"It's not an addiction," she whispered. "It is necessity."

Because she couldn't live as a werewolf. It was unthinkable.

And she did still own one gift—the gallery. Would she have to sell it to pay for her habit?

It wasn't a habit; it was her lifestyle.

The mobile phone sitting on a silver tray played the opening organ notes from Schnorr's Toccata and Fugue in D Minor. The caller ID was blocked. Blyss knew exactly who it was from the ringtone. She drummed her fingers on the vanity.

The phone rang insistently.

She finally picked it up. *"Oui?"*

"Mademoiselle Sauveterre."

Even knowing who it was, her heart dropped to her gut. And it pulsed so erratically she clutched at her stomach, feeling as though she would be sick.

"You have *Le Diabolique*?" the deeply calm yet sinister voice asked.

It was Edamite Thrash. A demon. Her supplier.

"It is in transit. I'm to collect it tonight."

The diamond had been their deal. If she obtained the *Diabolique* diamond, he would forget that she owed him five hundred thousand euros and also front her for another year's supply. Those pills were what suppressed her werewolf.

"I don't understand, Mademoiselle Sauveterre. I know the diamond has been taken from the gallery."

How he knew about that secret operation, a crime she intended to keep out of the media by replacing the original stone with a fake, was beyond her. She hadn't been in to check on the fake today. There was no reason to. And if Lorcan should see it he wouldn't be able to tell it was a fake.

"I had to divert suspicion from me in order to get it out of the gallery," she said. Any chance of Lorcan finding the diamond on her had to be reduced. The handoff to Stryke had been the only plan she could live with. She hadn't expected the suit loan, though. "I will have it in hand tonight and can bring it to you tomorrow."

"I'll send a car for you in the morning." The phone clicked off.

Blyss dropped the phone on the marble vanity. Her makeup supplies scattered, spilling across her lap, and she caught her face in her palms. Tears slid down her wrists.

There were six pills left in the jar she kept on the vanity. And she must take one today.

She sat up abruptly. "No."

Racing down the hallway and into the kitchen, she clicked on the iPad and selected the calendar app. Counting out the days, she tapped her finger on the end date. And there, at the bottom of the day square, was a tiny circle.

"Full moon," she gasped. "Oh, mercy, this can't happen."

Chapter 6

After he'd parked in front of Blyss's building, Stryke adjusted his tie in the rearview mirror. He was oddly ambivalent about this evening. He had an unnerving suspicion about Blyss, and it hadn't anything to do with the fact she wouldn't admit to being werewolf to him. It had everything to do with what he'd found in the pocket of Vail's suit. He didn't know Vail well, and the guy did like his sparkly gemstones, but really?

He struggled with giving Blyss the benefit of the doubt or straight-out questioning her before they got to the wedding. And then he decided to play it by ear. If his suspicions were correct, she would reveal herself. And he wouldn't like that.

He didn't want her to be anything but the glamour girl he loved to make love to. And hell, he knew this was a fantasy. There wasn't a woman in the world like her. It was foolish to entertain the idea that she could be a part of his future, the werewolf wife he wanted and needed to start his own pack.

Even if she never wanted to see him again, he would always have memories of her.

Plucking the white flower from the cup holder, he held it by the tiny plastic vial that held a few drops of water to preserve its freshness. Daisy Blu, his sister, had told him this was freesia. The bride, Kambriel, had them stuck all over in the wedding bouquets. It smelled like the best kind of perfume. Yet it was a simple flower, so opposite Blyss.

He slid out of the steel-gray Audi Rhys Hawkes had loaned him and strode across the cobblestoned street. He'd been borrowing a lot from his aunt's new in-laws, but Rhys had insisted, and besides, he'd use it if Hawkes had any more jobs for him while in town. It was a lot nicer than the twenty-year-old Ford he drove back home.

Blyss buzzed him in at the entry and Stryke strode through the courtyard and to her door, where she met him with a kiss to both his cheeks. The French called the double-cheek kiss *bises*. He'd learned that from the groom's mom, Lyric, this afternoon. But he wouldn't let Blyss get by with that noncommittal greeting. Before she could pull away, he pulled her to him and kissed her long and deep. He felt her soften in his arms, and then her fingers clutched at his biceps and she pulled him over the threshold.

She wanted him. And he wanted her.

His hand roamed up her leg, noting a slit in the long skirt that allowed him free rein across her skin. His fingers danced over the lacy tops of her thigh-high stockings. He hadn't intended to push her against the wall and have sex with her—the wedding began in less than an hour—but...

"No," she gasped as she pulled away from the kiss, but then kissed his eyelids and the tip of his nose. "You'll muss me."

"I like you mussed, glamour girl."

"Control yourself. *S'il vous plaît.*"

Stryke pressed his forehead to her shoulder. Yeah, she was right. Though he had the sinking feeling this would be his last opportunity at ever having sex with Blyss again. Tonight truths would be revealed. He just hoped they weren't more startling than discovering he'd had sex with a werewolf unawares.

He displayed the tiny flower for her and she tilted her head in wonder. "What is it?"

"Freesia. Smell it."

She sniffed, her eyelids closing to reveal dramatic dark and sexy eye shadow. Her red lips parted and a tendril of dark curl fell across her forehead. Diamonds hung at her ears and a single diamond glinted at her neck.

Stryke wanted to devour her. But she was right. He mustn't muss this jewel before the big soiree.

"Smells like candy," she offered. *"Très jolie."*

"It's from the bride's wedding flowers." He pulled the tiny flower out from the vial and flicked off the water droplets. "May I?"

She nodded.

He tucked the flower into her thick black curls, then sniffed it. "No match for you."

"You are a sweet man, Stryke Saint-Pierre. I…" She suddenly looked aside.

Yeah, she was riding the same vibe as he. They both knew this night was going to end with a big kiss-off.

"Are you ready?"

She picked up a sheer black shawl from the floor,

and smoothed a hand over her violet skirt that fell to the floor in a filmy swoosh. She looked garden-party ready, save for that sexy slit up to the thigh.

"Let's do this," she said, locking the door behind her, then heading out to the street. "You've a car. Delightful."

Stryke was sure she'd expected a cab and was thankful for the loaner. The wedding was in an old rented mansion in the 8th arrondissement. He had already entered the directions into the GPS, though he'd been to the place a few times already so he could look around while Blyss pointed out the landmarks along the way.

The Champs-Élysées was a big long stretch of elite shops and tourist traps. The street was double-wide and filled with cars, tourist buses, sports cars and the occasional bike weaving in and out of traffic as if it owned the road.

Blyss pointed to her favorite haunt: Louis Vuitton. "I love their purses." She clutched hers, a little pink number that had some weird finger holes along one side in the shape of skulls. "This one is Alexander McQueen."

"Uh-huh," Stryke said. Best thing to do when a woman dropped into shopping mode was just nod his head and agree. "So if all the shops along this road are spendy then why do I see a McDonald's over there?"

"They are not all so expensive. There are the DVD rental stores, as well. So gauche."

He could only smirk at her obvious disdain for those lesser shops. Taking the roundabout by the Arc de Triomphe, he marveled that the setting sun beamed under the arch. Paris was a beautiful city, but it would take him a lifetime to see everything and to begin to feel comfortable in this land of the tourists and foreign babble.

When they were but a few blocks away from the

wedding site, he took her hand and squeezed it. "I just have to warn you…"

He stopped the car at a stop sign, and she turned a wondering gaze on him.

"My whole family is here for this event. So there's going to be lots of questions and stares, and you can expect downright ogling from my brothers."

"How many brothers do you have?"

"Three. Be cautious of Trouble. He's a flirt. So is Kelyn. And, hell, Blade has this sort of silent seduction thing going on that seems to render women into puddles of mush. He was at the gallery with me, but left fifteen minutes later. With twins."

"I know those twins." She chuckled. "I'm sure I'll be fine. Social events are my thing. I can mingle with the best of them."

"Right, but I'm sure you haven't had to dodge questions like 'How long have you been dating?' and 'When are you getting married?' Expect that stuff from my family. And my dad, well, he expects me to start a pack and if he sees me with a werewolf—I want to warn you in advance."

"I see. No problem, Stryke. I can do this. Are we dating or just friends?"

"I, uh…" He'd love to answer that they were dating, but he wasn't stupid. This felt more like an extended hookup than anything.

"We are lovers," she decided. "That should give them something to whisper about behind our backs. Yet your father won't have reason to believe we are committed to one another."

Her wink twirled Stryke's world out of orbit. He almost gushed out that he loved her, but he knew that would be a stupid reaction to a beautiful woman calling him her lover. He wasn't some idiot who fell head over heels before the first gorgeous woman who gave him the time of day.

"Lovers." He kissed her hand. "I like that. And, uh… they'll also want to know that you're wolf. My father again."

"Ah." She stared straight ahead. Stryke noted the delicate muscle in her jaw pulse once. "Well, you know the answer to that, don't you?"

"I do, but— Why do I sense it's not something you want to talk about?"

"Because it isn't. And can we leave it at that?"

"The place is going to be swarming with werewolves. And vampires. And witches. And probably a few faeries."

"I can deal."

But why she had to "deal" bothered him. What was wrong with hanging with her own kind? Had to be better than some boring gallery showing among vapid humans. Now was not the time to get into an intense conversation. He'd save it for later.

If later didn't blow up in his face.

Stryke drove onward and spied the building. "There's parking around back. Do you want me to let you off at the front?"

"No, I'd like to walk in on your arm."

If she kept saying things like that he may turn into that gushing idiot before the night was over.

Social events were Blyss's air. She lived for the champagne and small talk. Mingling was her language. Air-kisses and light bon mots were her toys.

But as she stood in the reception hall draped with crimson chiffon and twists of black roses amid dozens of people, she realized this event would try her. It was a wedding between two vampires. She doubted there was even a human in the crowd.

Humans were the species she most related to. She strived to be human.

A mix of paranormals buzzed about the dance floor and chattered over the bubbly. But she couldn't determine who was what. Her heightened werewolf senses were suppressed. As she preferred. Yet she felt the lone man on the raft right now. Unsure if she would sink or swim.

And the trouble with paranormals was that most lived for hundreds of years and yet aged slowly. A person could never tell if they were talking to someone their own age, or in fact, a five-hundred-year-old vampire who may have a witchy wife who had passed the millennial mark. It was enough to make Blyss nervous.

"You cool?" Stryke asked.

He hadn't let go of her hand since they'd walked in, and while normally she would untether herself from her date and float among the masses, at the moment Blyss preferred the leash.

She nodded. "I need some champagne. Could you grab me some from that oncoming tray?"

Stryke scored two goblets, pressing one into her shaky grasp with a sweet kiss to the base of her ear. "Don't worry. There may be vamps and witches running amok, but there are lots of wolves here tonight, as well. You're in good company, glamour girl."

That was the least comforting reassurance.

"They are dancing already?" she asked. "Did we miss the ceremony?"

"No. According to what I've gleaned from the female faction, tonight is all backward. Johnny's band is playing for the dance right now. Later, when the clock strikes midnight, they'll get hitched."

"Interesting. Johnny is the groom?"

"Yep." Stryke pointed over the dance floor toward the stage. A decidedly goth band sang a catchy tune that had all the guests dancing amid a flicker of strobe lights.

Hooking her arm in Stryke's, she followed as he pushed through the crowd. The male eyes tilted toward her as they passed. Blyss couldn't manage to lift her chin and beam as usual. This night couldn't end quickly enough.

"Hey, man!"

Blyss turned to find Stryke hugging a burly man with wide shoulders and dark hair, and his eyes immediately went to her. A quick assessment found he wore a leather kilt and combat boots beneath the crisp white dress shirt and black suit coat. Even more interesting.

"This your girl?"

"This is Blyss Sauveterre. Blyss, my oldest brother, Trouble."

Trouble took her hand and kissed the back of it, but Blyss noticed he sniffed at her skin for a few seconds before tugging her into his embrace and hugging her. He was strong, and he smelled great, but she wasn't accustomed to such gregarious greetings.

Stepping back on wobbly heels, she managed a smile at the unrefined behemoth. "You're quite the friendly one."

"And you smell great. Flowers and sex. Gotta love that."

"Chill, Trouble," Stryke warned. He slipped his hand into Blyss's and she was grateful for the grounding connection. "He's the rowdy one in the family, in case his name didn't clue you in."

"She's a looker, bro. Good catch," Trouble said while tilting a wink at his brother.

"I think I saw faery triplets back that way."

Trouble bounced on his toes to see over the crowd. "Where?"

Stryke pointed again. "We're going to say hello to Kelyn. See you around, Trouble."

Blyss hugged up close as he led her away from Trouble's smirking summation of her. "I think I prefer the cool calm brother."

"That would be me," he confirmed. "Don't let Trouble scare you. His bark is worse than his bite. He's all show. Except when he picks a fight. Then you'd better run. Hey, Kelyn."

A man Blyss would never have guessed was related to the well-muscled Stryke and Trouble turned and greeted them with a nod. He was tall, blond and slender, and his violet eyes smiled before his mouth met the emotion. A faery?

"Kelyn, this is Blyss. Kelyn's the youngest Saint-Pierre brother," Stryke offered. "Not sure where Blade is tonight."

"Ah, Blyss," Kelyn said. "The woman from the gallery." He eyed Stryke, and Blyss sensed they were communicating silently. Had he told his brothers about his wild discovery that she was werewolf? Likely.

"How are you finding Paris?" Blyss asked, if only to break the brothers' communication.

"It's to my liking. But I don't sense Faery here."

Good, she hadn't had to ask after his breed. Interesting mix in the family, to be sure. "I'm sure you know Faery does not survive over the well-populated areas.

But there is FaeryTown. Rather a dodgy area, though, if I must say."

She'd only been told what it was like by her brother, Kir. Blyss had as little interest in faeries as she did werewolves.

"I've heard about FaeryTown and may check it out," Kelyn offered. "Interesting wedding, eh? Dancing and eating first, and saving the ceremony for the end?"

"Thought it was a vamp thing," Stryke said and his hand glided up Blyss's back. "Speaking of eating… Want to find something to munch on?"

"Sure."

The food table was covered in red linen and sparkled with silver candelabras laden with more of the black roses. Stryke popped various hors d'oeuvres into his mouth, while Blyss managed a crunchy bit of toast with caviar. She wasn't hungry. In fact, her stomach was churning. When would Stryke introduce her to Vail? Only then could she leave this crowd of misfits behind.

"Rhys!" Stryke chewed the last of a cherry tart, then introduced Blyss to a handsome Frenchman with salt-and-pepper hair and a generous smile. "Rhys Hawkes is the groom's grandfather," Stryke explained, "and he's been giving me some work to do while I'm in town."

"Hawkes Associates," Rhys said as he shook Blyss's hand. Of all the people she had met tonight, he felt the most grounded and sincere. Truth in his eyes. But what was his truth? Werewolf? Vampire? "And you are?"

"I'm sorry," Stryke said. "This is Blyss Sauveterre."

"Is that so?" Rhys's smile was warmly reassuring. "Isn't your family with the Valoir pack?"

Blyss tightened her jaw, but quickly softened it. "Yes, of course."

"Excellent. That pack is well regarded in my book.

Listen, I hate to be quick, but I'm getting the wink from my wife across the room. Viviane adores this song. Johnny wrote it for her. Time to dance."

"So you do have a pack," Stryke commented as they again wove through the crowd of black ties and silk-and-satin gowns. "Valoir, eh? You've been hush-hush about, er, things, so I didn't want to press."

"I'm no longer with the pack," she commented and set her empty goblet on a passing tray. "I'm going to look for the ladies' room, if you don't mind?"

"Sure. But you look perfect."

"Just a little touch-up. You know we girls can't make it through any event without primping," she said and walked away as quickly as she could.

If she had been forced to converse further about her pack, Blyss would have had to confess more than just her absence from Valoir. She wasn't prepared to do that. And she wouldn't need to, if she could find the vampire Vail, who had loaned Stryke the suit. Pray, the vampire was wearing that very suit this evening.

Weaving through the crowd, using her clutch purse as a shield she held in front of her chest, she almost walked right into a tall, broad red-haired man who turned and caught his hands against her shoulders. "Sorry, lady. Wow."

He stepped back to look her over, running a hand over his tousle of hair. "You here all alone, pretty lady?"

"I'm with Stryke Saint-Pierre," she said, with the intention of swiftly bypassing him and avoiding conversation, but he caught her about the waist and spun her around.

"So you're the glamour girl Stryke caught? My father mentioned he was looking to hook up with a wolf.

You are so pretty." He blatantly sniffed the air between them. "Would have never guessed you for wolf, though."

She managed a smile and shrugged out of his grasp.

"Sorry." He offered his hand to shake. "Trystan Hawkes. Father of two eligible werewolf daughters and trying to protect the hell out of them tonight with all the single young wolves stalking the crowd."

"A doting father. Always refreshing. I was heading that way. If you'll excuse me."

She made a dash and almost cleared the ballroom with the hallway in sight when a gaggle of giggling bridesmaids scurried up behind her. Red skirts swishing, they rushed on their stilettos toward the same door she had spied.

"Sorry!" a woman with braided pink hair called back. "Emergency pee break!"

Blyss paused and pressed a shoulder against a cool marble column. A tuft of red chiffon dusted her head. The black roses had no scent. She didn't need the facilities, and the privacy she had been seeking would not be found in the ladies' room.

Sighing heavily, she turned to face a man who gave new meaning to *sexy*. He was tall, dark and dressed in black velvet, and silver rings glinted on his fingers as well as diamonds in both his ears. His eyes were black and his smile was slightly crooked. He'd flipped his hair back in a rock-star swoop and his smile made her want to fall to her knees and sigh in adoration.

Had to be vampire. He wore the dark, fanged vibe so well.

"Vaillant," he said, offering his hand to shake.

Blyss shook and told him her name. "I'm here with Stryke Saint-Pierre," she provided weakly. "Wait. Vaillant? Are you Vail? The father of the groom?"

"Ch-yeah. So you've heard about me? Makes sense. Why is such a gorgeous catch as you hanging out all by yourself? Isn't Stryke taking care of you?"

"I needed to catch a breath of air away from the crowd," she offered. Assuming a modicum of cool, Blyss set back her shoulders and traced a finger down the front of Vail's suit. "This is nice." Yet the lapels were velvet.

Not the suit she needed.

"Thanks. Black's my color."

"The suit you loaned Stryke the other evening was classy, as well."

"Yep. Zegna all the way."

"I had thought you'd wear it tonight."

"No, I gotta bring out the romantic stuff for the big event." He tilted a shoulder forward and Blyss then noticed the silver studs spiking up as if a warrior's armor. "My wife loves it when I work the rock-star vibe."

Blyss pulled her hand away from the velvet. Wife. Of course. She didn't want to start any rumors. Or fights, if indeed Stryke's father had an eye to her as a potential wife for his son. She was glad she hadn't been introduced to her lover's father yet. But it didn't matter anymore. Her mission had hit a brick wall. No suit. No diamond.

"I think the ceremony is starting soon," Vail said, checking his wristwatch. "I have to go and make the announcement for everyone to file in to the next ballroom. Nice meeting you, Blyss."

She mumbled a *bonsoir* and turned to search for Stryke, but her eyes unfocused and she again felt as if she balanced upon a raft amid treacherous waves. Edamite Thrash was sending a courier in the morning to pick up *Le Diabolique*. What would she do now?

Was there a way she could possibly get into Vail's closet tonight? Had she any other option? Where could he live? And did vampires sleep through the mornings, as she'd heard rumors, so she could sneak in without detection?

What was she thinking? She was no cat burglar. The snag from her own gallery had been possible because she had received the diamond and had processed it herself. She'd been vague with Lorcan about plans to exhibit it, which was why he hadn't questioned its absence yet.

Come to think of it, she hadn't heard from Lorcan since the Marie Antoinette showing. Generally they checked in with one another every day.

A warm hand slid around her waist. Blyss stiffened, until she realized who it was. Stryke kissed her at the base of her ear. Briefly she relaxed, sinking into his presence, until she remembered that now was no time to relax.

"Flirting with Vail?" he asked.

"Hmm? No. It's not called flirting if you don't get their number." She tossed out the tired old line because right now her brain wasn't functioning properly. "He wasn't wearing the suit."

"Nope. Let's go find a seat, shall we?"

Stryke nodded to Kelyn, who sat across the red-carpeted aisle from him. He caught his little brother's wink. Trouble kept giving him the head nod, as well. Yeah, he was sitting with the most gorgeous woman in the entire room. Hands down, he had won the Paris woman search among his brothers.

But when he'd seen Blyss talking to Vail, and running her fingers along his suit pocket, his heart had fallen. She had to have known it was a different suit, right?

While the officiate read through the vows, and Kambriel and Johnny stood facing one another, Stryke couldn't help but be distracted by the woman sitting next to him. He could smell the freesia and beyond that the traces of her floral perfume. But he couldn't sense her innate werewolf. Hell, he could pick out every werewolf in the room by scent alone. It wasn't an odor they put off, but something internal, a knowing they shared among their breed. He could even scent a few vamps because some carried an iron-tainted tinge of blood about them.

He tried to pay attention to the ceremony. The bride wore black latex, and the groom, clad in black velvet, wore a caterpillar of silver rings along one ear and his boots were studded and wrapped with silver chains. Johnny Santiago sang goth rock with a local band who had entertained friends and family tonight. Kambriel had lived in Minnesota all her life until running away to Paris to "find herself" a few years ago. It looked as though she'd found happiness.

Could he ever be so lucky?

Stryke threaded his fingers through Blyss's. What a woman to spend the rest of his life with. Yet it was an irrational thought. He knew nothing about her. Sure, they had some amazing chemistry between them. But what kind of distortion made her werewolf so imperceptible to him?

And would he really have to ask her the big question? The one that had troubled him since the night he'd returned home after the gallery showing and had shoved his hand into the inner pocket of the suit coat. He'd found something odd, interesting and couldn't believe it had belonged to Vail.

He had to do it. He would do it. Now, while it was relatively quiet and they sat toward the back. The bride and groom had recited their vows, and the officiate was babbling on about loving one another until death parted them. Long wait, if they could avoid the stake.

"So were you disappointed Vail wasn't wearing the suit?" he whispered close to Blyss's ear.

"Uh…" Startled, she flashed her bright greens at him.

Right. He'd caught her out.

"Were you looking for this?" He reached into his pocket and pulled out the incredible black diamond that seemed to glow red from within and which was the size of a small plum.

Up front, the officiate pronounced the couple happily married and called for, instead of applause, a blessed moment of silence.

Blyss gasped and reached for the stone. "How did you—?"

Amid the silence a surprisingly loud sneeze echoed out.

Johnny, the groom, glanced over the crowd, his eyes landing on his little sister, Summer. "Ah hell," the vampire muttered.

Chapter 7

"Demons!" someone shouted. The entire audience jumped to their feet. Shouts to protect the women were answered by demonic growls.

Blyss grasped for Stryke's hand, but he snatched the diamond away. "I need that!"

"No time for this argument." Stryke's eyes scanned the crowd and focused on the back door, where the bride had walked in and down the red-carpeted aisle. His jaw tensed.

Blyss grabbed him by the suit lapels. "Just hand it to me."

"We'll discuss this later. You have things to tell me." He gripped her by the shoulders. "Yes?"

"I'll tell you everything if you'll give me the diamond."

"I'm going to hang on to it until after your confession. Now stay behind me. There's a lot of them. Hell, what are demons doing here?"

Screams and shouts erupted. Demonic growls curdled over the gaiety. The brother Blyss knew as Trouble charged for the dark-skinned red-eyed demon in the lead of what looked like a cavalcade of demons. All around her Blyss saw people spring into action, and it wasn't just the men. Witches attempted to repel the demonic approach with chants and gestures, and the witch with the dark purple hair even threw fire—of which, a demon caught in his mouth and gobbled up as if candy.

The bride was swept off the dais in a swish of black latex by her groom, but neither left the fray as demons poured down the aisle, slapping at vampires and werewolves to clear their way. The bride slid up her skirt to reveal a dagger strapped to her thigh. The groom smirked and pulled out knives from the holsters beneath his velvet suit coat.

Stryke punched a slender demon with long, disjointed arms and wicked talons. The demon growled, infusing the air with a foul miasma.

Stryke reached back to shove Blyss away. "Stay close."

She appreciated his need to protect her, but all she wanted was to grab the diamond and get out of there. She hadn't seen him put *Le Diabolique* back in his pocket. Right now he lifted and swung a demon over the buffet table, bringing it down on the chocolate fountain in a spectacular crash.

A demon leaped from the aisle and landed before Blyss. The creature inhaled through long slit nostrils— all the demons wore their true forms—the gills on his cheeks fluttering. "You are the one."

Blyss choked down a scream. Grasping at her throat, she stumbled and went down, landing on her butt and up against a marble column. Stryke was nowhere to be seen. The wedding guests engaged in a wild tangle with an assortment of demons. She smelled blood and sulfur. And she tasted her own fear.

The demon looming over her opened his mouth to reveal chunky, dull teeth. A scream rattled at the back of her throat.

"D-did Edamite send you?" she asked.

"Thrash?" The demon chuckled. "Heh. If that's how you want to play it? Sure, Thrash sent me."

He hadn't. This demon was working for someone else. She knew it from his dismissive attitude.

"Hand over *Le Diabolique*," the demon demanded, thrusting its blocky hand out for something.

"I don't know what you want!" She tried to scramble away, but a meaty hand slapped onto her ankle.

Overhead flew a tatter-winged demon, screeching wildly. Somewhere, an infant sneezed repeatedly.

Blyss heard someone shout congrats for defeating a demon. A death cry preceded the spill of sticky black blood that spattered her cheek. Struggling against the hand that gripped her ankle, she looked up to spy one of the Saint-Pierre brothers, the dark one with the long hair she'd seen at the gallery. He held a long, curved blade that dripped with black blood.

The demon managed to drag her body across the marble floor. Blyss grasped for chair legs, but they were metal foldables and clattered off balance with every one she grasped.

"Got him!"

Her ankle was suddenly free. Stryke stood over her, repeatedly punching the demon in the face, and finally picked him up and shoved him toward the brother with the blade, who caught the creature on his steel. The demon shattered into black bits that scattered and settled like dust.

And suddenly Blyss stood in Stryke's arms. "You okay? Blyss?"

She nodded, tilted her head against his chest. Demon blood stained his shirt and he smelled of sulfur. Yet when he bracketed her face and kissed her, she returned the seeking touch. Safe. She'd initially sought safety in his embrace that night in the gallery office, but had brushed it off as stupid. But right now, she fell into the feeling.

"I'm so sorry," she muttered. Guilt struck as if a demon's tongue spearing directly into her heart. "This was all my fault."

"What are you talking about? It was a random wedding-crasher incident. Bunch of demons heard about two vampires getting married. That's it. We're all safe."

"No, Stryke, the demon after me wanted it. The diamond. Do you still have it? Where is it?"

He patted his coat pocket, then shoved his fingers in, but they came out with nothing in hand. "Must have dropped it."

"What? No!"

"Listen, Blyss, I don't know what's up with that funky black diamond, or why you slipped it into my coat pocket the night at the gallery, but if there's something deeper going on here, you'd better tell me."

"I…I can't." She tried to stand by herself but it felt as if her knees would give out. "It's too personal. I have to find that diamond." She began searching the floor, strewn with chairs and bridesmaids' bouquets and ripped lace and demon blood. "Please help me find it!"

"Hey, Stryke, you and your date okay?" Vail asked.

"Yeah, we're good. How's everyone?"

"Head count shows only demon casualties. But a few got away. We're sending out a hunting party to track them. You in?"

Stryke nodded. "I'll put Blyss in a cab and then join you."

"Excellent. I've troops to gather." Vail wiped black blood from his face and winced. "That stuff tastes nasty."

Blyss shook her head when Stryke offered his hand. "I can't leave until I've found it."

"It's not here! I must have dropped it, and someone, likely a demon, grabbed it."

"But you don't understand."

Stryke knelt before her. With a stern twist of his finger, he tilted her chin up to look at him. "Enlighten me."

She sighed, weighing the consequences of a confession. She looked around. Everyone was in tatters. A few women were sobbing, but most were celebrating the win, including the bride, who wiped a black smudge from her groom's cheek before kissing him. What a way to start a marriage.

Had this been her fault? Who could know that the diamond would be here? Even she had thought it would be found in Vail's closet.

This didn't make sense.

"I think they came looking specifically for *Le Diabolique*," she said quietly.

"What?"

"I don't know how they knew the diamond was going to be here. But the one that was after me asked for it by name."

Stryke hissed. "What the hell is it?"

"It's just a diamond. I don't know what it means to the demons." Edamite had told her about it. And she had chosen to look the other way and let him have it, no matter the consequences. Because at the time what mattered was securing her future. "I...I have to leave."

He gripped her upper arm tightly. "But you stole it from the gallery. You must know what it means to the demons. Were they the ones you were to hand it off to?"

"No. I don't believe the ones here tonight were working for Ed—"

Blyss pulled away from Stryke and ran for the exit doors. She couldn't do this now. Not this confession. Much as the whole family deserved it. The best thing she could do for them was to get the hell away and never show her face to any of them again.

Stryke followed on her heels, gripping her by the arm again. She could sense his anger and smell his wolf. Whenever her emotions were stirred she could sense her breed. It was disturbing, yet she couldn't deal with that at the moment.

Stryke hailed a cab, which pulled over immediately. He opened the back door, but held her firmly when she tried to enter. "You brought this upon my family?"

"I'm sorry. I didn't know this would happen."

"You admit it?"

She nodded.

"It's over between the two of us."

He shoved her inside the back of the cab, more gently than she'd expected. When she pulled in her feet, he leaned in, looking to say something more. He couldn't meet her eyes. His jaw was so tense. But then he shook his head and closed the door.

Stryke's brothers joined him at the curb, and she saw them talking to him, but Stryke's gaze remained on hers as the cab rolled away.

If they intended on tracking the demons perhaps they would find the diamond.

She'd lost this one. She'd lost…

…everything.

"I can't believe that bitch," Trouble said as the cab drove away. "You're going to let her get away, Stryke? She was the one who brought those assholes on us!"

"Give it a rest, Trouble," Kelyn said. The tall, cool faery bumped his fist gently against Trouble's shoulder. "Stryke never has been lucky at love. The day he finds a good woman…"

Stryke closed his eyes and inside he felt the wince. So he'd had a tough couple of years with women. Blyss had been different. Perfect. A glamour girl so out of his league he'd have to climb a staircase just to touch her feet. And he had known they had an expiration date. He'd even suspected that date was tonight.

Well hell, wasn't as if he'd actually given the relationship any hope. The last woman he could imagine standing at his side while he led a pack was Blyss Sauveterre.

"She screwed you," Trouble said as he wandered down the sidewalk. "This way, guys. The demon scent goes north."

Stryke clenched his fists and turned to follow the half dozen men who intended to track down the demons.

For as perfect as Blyss was, she had cleverly hidden a nasty dark side. How could she have done that to him? To his entire family?

Though really, she hadn't been the one to bring the diamond into the wedding. He had. Blyss had only thought she might find it in the coat pocket where she'd left it. But he had found it that night and had waited for her to ask about it yesterday. When he'd caught her in his closet he'd known what she was looking for, but still, she hadn't said a thing.

If she had been using him, would she really have had sex with him that much? They'd done it more than a few times. And this morning he'd woken in her bed. No means for her to search for the diamond then. It was as if she'd actually wanted to have sex with him for no reason other than that she'd been attracted to him.

He wanted to believe that.

Right now, Stryke didn't know what to believe.

What was important about the diamond? It was black. Yet he'd almost thought to see a glint of red in the center when he'd held it up to the bathroom light. Was it demonic?

Then why was Blyss after it? Had she stolen it from the gallery? Her own gallery? So many questions, and… he shouldn't be asking them. He'd put her in a cab and sent her off. End of story. He did not need her kind of trouble.

Her soft, sexy, seductive kind of trouble.

"You all right, man?" Blade brushed his shoulder as they strode into a dark alley. His older brother didn't talk much, but when he did, he meant it.

"Not sure. I think there's more to this, and part of me thinks Blyss could be in trouble."

"You should follow your instincts."

Wise words from the one brother who had experienced more than his share of pain in his short lifetime. "First let's go kick some demon ass."

"Try to keep up, brother." Blade strode onward, a curved blade clenched in his fist.

As far as a demon slaughter, the results of tracking the demon scent led the crew of wolves and vampires to an empty warehouse. The sulfur trail ended abruptly, and someone conjectured a witch's hex might have facilitated that under-the-radar sneak.

Vail, the vampire leading them, talked to Trouble and Stryke.

"It was probably a wedding crash," Vail decided.

Trouble eyed Stryke hard. Like, why didn't he speak up about his nasty girlfriend? It wouldn't matter if Stryke did reveal Blyss's involvement; they'd come to a dead end.

"Sorry for the disastrous wedding, guys," Vail offered.

"Are you kidding?" Trouble pounded a fist through the air. "Dancing, food and ass-kicking? That was awesome!"

"I'll keep my ears open," Stryke said to Vail as they headed back. "And my nose to the air. I'll let you know if anything turns up."

"Cool. I think it was a spectacular end to a great party myself. And Summer is safe, so it's all good."

Stryke refused Kelyn's offer of a ride home. They were on the right bank close to the huge forest that edged the city. He was pretty sure if he walked east he'd wind up on the Champs-Élysées. That fancy street where she liked to shop.

He didn't want to see her again.

And he did.

He needed answers. And he would get them.

Blyss rang him in immediately. Stryke wandered through the courtyard. The scents of yew and flowers seemed too fresh and out of place after the night he'd had. He wondered now how Johnny and Kambriel were handling the destruction of their wedding ceremony. Though he distinctly recalled seeing Johnny hugging Kambriel and kissing her amid the melee, while both had brandished blades dripping with black demon blood. And Vail had agreed it had been a hit.

Vampires. Go figure.

The door to Blyss's apartment was open. Stryke walked in, closing it behind him. He wandered down the long hallway to the kitchen. It was well after midnight, but moonlight beamed through the skylight in the adjacent living room, casting a pale glow across Blyss's shoulders. Standing beside the marble counter, with her head bowed, she didn't face him. She sniffled.

"I didn't think I would see you again," she whispered.

"You and me both, sweetie."

"Désolé," she said softly and turned to him. "It means I am sorry."

Stryke rubbed his scalp, winced, then splayed out his hand before him. "I know it's late, but I think you owe me some answers."

She nodded. Shivered.

He couldn't stand there and look at her, fallen and so small. He crossed the floor and wrapped his arms about her, and she stood and pressed her breasts against his chest.

"You mean something to me, Blyss," he confessed. "And if something bad is going on in your life right now I want to help. And that means you need to come clean about it all. You've got to trust me."

Her fingers clung to his shirt, tugging, tears spilling hotly through the fabric. "Oh, Stryke, it's become so terrible and big. I can't do this alone anymore."

He bowed his head and kissed her temple. "You don't have to. I'm here."

"Were you able to track the demons and…?"

He knew she wanted to ask about the diamond. All he wanted to know was what it meant to her. "Dead end. We gave up. No sign of the diamond."

Blyss's body went weak against his. She pulled him down with her as she collapsed. He lifted her in his arms and carried her into the bedroom. There, he sat on the bed and held her, sobbing gently, until they both fell asleep.

Chapter 8

Stryke woke on Blyss's bed. They'd fallen asleep in each other's arms still dressed. His shoes were on. And everything he touched, lay on or could see was white. Oops. He carefully extricated his hand from under her shoulder but managed to wake her.

"Sorry," he said.

She blinked lush lashes and yawned. "Morning?"

"Yeah, I fell asleep with you. Sorry, I should have kicked my shoes off. Just a little smudge on your bed-sheets."

"Doesn't matter. Oh. I must look a terrible mess. I'm still in my gown." She sat up and caught her fingers in her tangled hair. "Oh, *mon Dieu*."

"You look gorgeous, as always."

"Please don't lie to me, Stryke. You don't owe me any kindnesses."

He touched her cheek below a faint smudge of black

makeup. "Your eye stuff is a little smeared, but it works for me."

She touched her cheek and looked aside. "I'm so sorry. I promised I would tell you everything last night. I want to. I need to, but…" Her sigh rifled down his spine.

"Why don't I run out for some *pains au chocolat* and orange juice? That'll give you some time to freshen up, and then we can have a chat."

"Thank you. Take the key lying on my vanity with you. You can let yourself back in. That'll give me a chance to take a shower."

He kissed her at the temple, but she flinched. Probably because she suspected she looked a mess. There was nothing about Blyss that could offend him physically. But he was leery about what she would tell him, so he'd not overthink this.

Leaving her in the bedroom, he collected his suit coat and the key. Demon blood stained his white dress shirt, so he buttoned up the coat and strolled outside, through the courtyard and…

What was that scent? Smelled familiar—

Stryke felt an excruciating pain fire at the back of his neck. He immediately knew he'd been clubbed by something more than a fist—and then he blacked out.

Stryke came to and realized he was stumbling down a long steel-walled hallway toward a glass door. Not voluntarily, either. He struggled, but determined the men on either side of him were both taller, bulkier and stronger. The instinctive urge to shift to werewolf tingled at his bones, but he wasn't sure where he was and didn't want to risk wolfing out if there were humans near.

But if these guys were stronger than him he guessed

they were not human. When he inhaled, the distinctive scent of sulfur coiled in his nostrils.

What was up with the demons lately? Since arriving in Paris, they had been pointed out to him by Vail and Rhys. They'd crashed the wedding last night. Blyss was somehow inextricably involved with demons.

And now he was being escorted by a pair of demons to the devil knew where.

A glass door opened automatically as they approached, and the demons shoved him through the doorway to stumble forward across a gleaming black marble floor. It was some kind of office. Two walls were all glass, probably many stories up. Rain sheeted the windows. At the opposite side of the room loomed a black desk with a silver lamp upon it and a sleek silver computer. Behind it sat a man with his back turned to them.

"What the hell?" Stryke asked.

The man behind the desk spun around swiftly and snarled. "You brought me *this*?"

Stryke tried not to take offense from the remark, but really? The man's coal hair was slicked back to expose small hematite horns at his temples. And on the knuckles he flexed were also small, gleaming growths that looked like hematite thorns and which Stryke sensed could serve a stinging punch.

"Uh, boss, you said to take him when he leaves the building."

"I did not say *him*," the demon said icily. Below the thorny growths on his fists were dark markings that looked like tattoos, but Stryke suspected they were much more evil in nature. Generally tats on a paranormal were magically enhanced. Bad mojo. "I told you to grab her when she leaves the building. Her!"

"Uh…"

Stryke cast a smirk over his shoulder at the idiot henchman who struggled for an answer to his idiocy.

"Who are you?" Stryke and the man behind the desk asked each other simultaneously.

"I..." The man stood, tugged at his neat black tie and said, "...am Edamite Thrash. Businessman. Collector. Purveyor of Essentials. And you..." The demon's left nostril nudged up. "...smell like a werewolf."

"Stryke Saint-Pierre," he offered, now unwilling to take offense from a demon's snide assessment of him. "Why the nab? Were you going after Blyss? Are you the one she was supposed to get the diamond for?"

Edamite's expression softened from tight disapproval to a surprising smile. "Ah. So you are colluding with her?"

"Colluding? I barely know her. Well—" No need to explain how well he knew her. And no matter how conflicted about the socialite he was at the moment, that was no reason to throw her under the bus to save his ass. "What's going on?"

"Where is *Le Diabolique*?"

"Is that the name of the black stone? I don't know. It was lost last night. A gang of your thugs came after it. Crashed a private wedding."

"My thugs? I do not have thugs, Monsieur Saint-Pierre. They are minions. Tell me exactly who you believe was after the diamond."

"If you don't know your own people, I certainly can't help you there."

"Make him remember, Inego," Edamite said curtly.

Stryke took a punch to the middle of his back, directly on his spine. The pain was beyond belief and he couldn't stand for the sudden loss of muscle control.

He dropped to his knees as another thick demon fist swung up into his jaw. Blood trickled down his throat.

He caught the next punch with his palm. The demon sneered at him and narrowed its red gaze—and Stryke forgot about the other henchman, whose claws tore the side of his neck.

He dropped to his palms and spat blood onto the marble floor. These two did not fight fair.

"I don't know anything," he managed to say, wincing at the stinging pain seeping from the cuts. His blood dripped onto the black floor. Assholes.

Swinging back his arm, he called up his claws and delivered triple slices across the face of one of the demons. The henchman stumbled backward, hand gripping the black spurts of blood.

"Cease!" Edamite called as the other demon growled and swung toward Stryke.

Stryke didn't take orders from a demon, so he gripped the henchman's wrist and snapped it back so quickly the bone broke and splintered out from the flesh. Shoving him off to lick his wounds by the other, Stryke turned toward Edamite.

"You next?" he challenged.

"Blyss," Edamite insisted. "How are the two of you involved?"

Retracting his claws, Stryke growled deeply as he stood at full height and stretched back his shoulders imposingly. "I met her a few days ago. The diamond was a surprise."

"So you're telling me Mademoiselle Sauveterre doesn't have the stone?"

Stryke shook his head. Though he knew little about this situation, the feeling that he needed to protect Blyss was strong. Had to be why she had been so frantic about obtaining the diamond. And he could only be thankful they had nabbed him by mistake.

"Are you threatening her?" He punched a fist into his palm. Thrash may look imposing but he wasn't half as built as he was, and Stryke was always willing to jump into the fray.

Laughing, Edamite gestured subtly with a forefinger.

Stryke was suddenly lifted by both minions and pummeled in the face, chest and gut. The punches came so rapidly, he couldn't return with defensive punches. It was all he could do to keep his wits about him.

"Hold him!" Edamite charged.

The horned demon leaned over Stryke and blew a gust of black smoke into his face. Sulfur entered his senses and clutched his brain, causing him to black out.

He came to outside. Sitting against a brick wall. In an alley, he guessed, for both directions to either side led down a narrow path and out to streets where cars passed by. The tarmac was wet and his pants leg and dress shirt were also wet.

Unsure what had gone down, Stryke suddenly had the thought that he'd left Blyss waiting for orange juice and pastries. How long had he been gone? Where had they taken him? He didn't know the city. And he'd blacked out twice, so he had no clue to his whereabouts.

And he hurt. Everywhere. "Damned demons."

He pushed up to a stand and spat blood to the side. Rubbing his neck, he felt the scabs from the talon cuts. Yeah, this was going to take a good day to heal and feel up to par. But at least he'd gotten in some good punches himself.

Edamite Thrash. Businessman and collector? Purveyor of Essentials? What the heck did that nonsensical bullshit mean?

Didn't matter. "If he's threatening Blyss, he'll have to go through me to even breathe her air."

Stryke winced as he wandered down the alley. Right. The demon *had* gone through him and look who was bleeding now.

He should have wolfed out while in the marble office. Could have taken out those demons, no problem. But he still didn't have all the pieces to a strange and aggravating puzzle.

Blyss could provide some of those pieces.

Turning onto a main street, he caught his reflection in a storefront window. His face was mottled with bruises and his lips swollen. No black eyes, though. Score! Not. And blood drops dotted the front of his white shirt, some red, but more than most black.

"I need a shower."

He tried to button up the suit coat but only one button remained. Wandering down the street, he tucked his head. Thankful his cell phone was still in a pocket, Stryke brought up the GPS app and within a few minutes pinpointed his location. A couple miles walk to Blyss's place. He'd stop at a McDonald's on the way and eat breakfast, then pick up the pastries and orange juice for her. It was already past noon.

He always kept his word. Even if it was a little late.

Chapter 9

Three hours after he'd left, Stryke arrived at Blyss's front door. She'd had more than enough time to shower, put on some makeup, get up her courage to reveal the big secret—and then lose that courage when she'd decided after hour two that he wasn't planning to return. That he'd given up on her. That he never wanted to see her again.

Smart choices.

So when her handsome werewolf lover stood in the doorway holding a bakery bag, a carton of orange juice and smiled through a pair of bruised lips, tears spilled down Blyss's cheek. She hugged him, crushing the bag against his chest, and held on longer and tighter than she probably should have. But it didn't matter. He was here. He hadn't given up on her. And she needed someone on her side right now.

"I didn't think you'd come back." She sniffed away tears.

"Took a long detour."

"I can see that." She stepped back and studied his bruised face and then noted the bloodstains on his shirt. There were more than from last night. "What kind of a detour?"

He handed her the bag and orange juice. "It's an interesting story. I think it'll mesh with what you have to tell me. Or I suspect so. What's with the tears? You didn't miss me that much, did you, glamour girl?"

She nodded and sniffed away yet another tear.

He gestured beyond her. "Let's go sit down and talk."

Blyss hurried down the hallway and put the juice in the fridge, leaving the pastry bag on the counter. She wasn't hungry. And if Stryke was, he could help himself. Taking him by the hand, she led him into the living room, capped by the skylights, which beamed in gorgeous bright daylight. It was too bright for her, and she had probably smeared her makeup when crying, but she resisted the urge to go check it.

It was now or never. She'd never gain his trust if she didn't lay it all out in the open.

"Were you really crying because you thought I wouldn't return?" He brushed his finger under her eye to wipe away a tear.

She nodded. "Men don't usually come back to me. Not unless they want something."

"I do want something. The truth. Because these bruises? Got them from some demon thugs."

"I don't understand." She gently touched his cheek where the bruise was already green and fading. Werewolves healed quickly. "Why are demons after you?"

"They're not after me." He sat on the sofa and patted the seat beside him. "They wanted you. But when idiots are sent to do a job…"

Blyss sat on her knees beside him, tucking her skirt along her legs. Stryke reached for the simple diamond suspended from a platinum chain about her neck and tapped it. It was the only valuable piece of jewelry she still owned. Her father had given it to her after a winning streak so many years ago.

"It's all about the black diamond, isn't it?" he asked. "And Edamite Thrash."

At the mention of that name, Blyss gasped. She bowed her head, catching her breath. It felt as if her heart had leaped into her throat and swallowing it back down was awkward. "Is that who gave you those bruises?"

"I was knocked out in your courtyard as I left earlier. I woke up in a fancy office building and was escorted into the demon's lair. Thrash's idiot henchmen had been charged to bring you to him. And the diamond."

She nodded and drew in a breath of courage. "I was supposed to bring him *Le Diabolique*—that's what the diamond is called—and my debts, both past and future, would be wiped clean. And since our gallery was exhibiting it, it was easy enough to steal. But getting it out of the building without causing suspicion was something else. Lorcan—you met my assistant—he doesn't know, and I didn't want him involved."

"You needed to hand it off to an unsuspecting party for a clean getaway."

She nodded.

"So our little tryst in the gallery office was a ploy to sneak the diamond into my pocket?"

"It started that way."

It was never going to sound good, no matter how she put it. But truly? Something about Stryke Saint-Pierre begged her to let him know her truths. All of them, even the dark, ugly ones.

"You were a dupe I picked out from the crowd. And yet, I keep returning to you for a reason."

"Because you were looking to reclaim the diamond."

"That's one reason."

He crossed his arms over his chest and huffed. "Seems like the only reason to me."

"I could have broken into your apartment and searched your closet. I didn't need to spend more time with you. I certainly didn't need to have sex with you again. And again. I—I wanted to."

He chuckled softly, shaking his head. "Do not tell me you actually feel something for me. I won't buy it."

"I do."

"Please. Miss Precise and Always In Control? Your whole life is planned down to the last detail like your perfect hair and impeccable makeup. I'm one of those details."

"I know it won't hold weight against my confession of using you, but, Stryke, there is something about you. I admire you. And I, well… Let's say when I take a lover it's for one purpose."

"Which is?"

"Because I want something. Material items. Valuable jewels and gifts. I like to be spoiled. I've established a particular lifestyle that enjoys fine things. Sex is a means to getting what I want. But with you…" She dared to meet his brown eyes. "I don't want anything."

He met her gaze with a challenging glare that cut through her heart as if with a silver blade. "Except a large black diamond that glints red and which all the demons in Paris are hungry to get their hands on. Blyss,

this is wild. I want to believe you, but this is really…"
He sighed. "…fucked."

"I used you to get the diamond out of the gallery. I'm
not proud of that, but it was a necessary evil. But believe me, every time we've been together, I was using
you for my heart."

He scoffed.

"I like you, Stryke," she rushed out. "Every chance
I've been with you was a selfish grasp at something
good."

He rubbed his palms over his face. "I like you, too.
Despite getting a feeling, that first night, that something weird was up after finding a big black diamond
in my pocket."

That he had kept that knowledge a secret when he'd
found her snooping in the closet made him as devious
as her. Almost. All right, not at all. He was trying to
figure things out and had every right to do so.

"I told myself it was probably something Vail left
in his pocket," he continued. "But when I found you in
the closet looking for the suit, I knew it had been you.
That's why I invited you to the wedding and put out the
idea that Vail might be wearing the suit. And when I
saw you with Vail…"

"I'm sorry. I was desperate. I need that stone."

Stryke sighed and shook his head. "I don't know
what it is, but there's something about you that keeps
me coming back."

"I feel the same way."

"Then be honest with me, Blyss, and tell me what I
really want to know. Avoiding talk about werewolves
bothers me."

"Stryke, I…can't. Not right now."

"Uh-huh. You're asking a lot of me. But if I can

shove that elephant in the room aside—which is going to be tough—right now, you need to tell me how you got involved with Edamite Thrash. And what, exactly, this diamond means to him and all the rest of the demons. When I told him demons crashed the wedding, and that I suspected it was over the diamond, he got real nervous. I don't think the demons who showed at the wedding were his thugs."

"You think demons that *don't* work for Ed are the ones who crashed your aunt's wedding?"

Blyss turned on the couch and tapped her lip with her finger as she thought about it. She'd only ever seen one or two henchmen, as Stryke named them, when she had to go to Edamite's office for business. And none had ever come to her home.

They'd taken Stryke from the courtyard? Why hadn't Ed waited for her to bring the diamond to him as they had agreed?

"Ed told me it holds a demon within," she murmured.

"The diamond?"

"Yes. Some evil, powerful demon. I assumed he was going to release it. But that didn't concern me. I just wanted to hand it over to him and…"

Stryke's phone rang but he ignored it. "So if there's some demon trapped inside the diamond, that might be reason for other demons to want it, as well. And maybe they wanted to get to it before Thrash could?"

"It's possible. It's a guess. I don't know much about demons and what they do. Ed is like this kingpin sort of demon. He's got a firm grasp on most of the demon activity in Paris. He also collects all sorts of paranormal ephemera. Dangerous stuff. He buys and sells it like a drug dealer."

And she knew all too well how desperate a person could get for the drugs Edamite sold.

Again Stryke's phone rang, and he checked the screen, but then directed his attention back at her. "How did you get involved with Thrash?"

A fourth and fifth ring sounded. "Would you please get that?"

Reluctantly, he answered. "Hello? It's Rhys Hawkes," he said to her.

She could hear the other side of the conversation because the volume was turned up high.

"Hi, Rhys. Wild wedding last night, eh?"

"Indeed."

"I hope Johnny and Kam are okay?"

"They're fine. Everyone is fine. Just a few scratches and a lost deposit on the building. I understand the woman you invited to the wedding may have had something to do with the demon attack?"

Stryke met her gaze. "I don't know, man." He ran a palm over his short-cropped hair. "Whatever was up last night, she's an innocent. I know it."

Blyss clasped his hand and he squeezed, then winked at her.

"As I've said, there was no harm done," Rhys's voice echoed out. "Normally, I would let it go. Keep a vigilant eye for demons in the future because you know, things happen. But not after what happened early this morning."

"What's that?" Stryke stood, wandering to the window that looked out over the vast sea of Haussmann rooftops.

"Hawkes Associates was robbed," Rhys offered. Blyss had to tilt her head to hear it all. "I found the safe in my office open. The safe I use to store items until they can be placed in a permanent position in the warehouse."

"What was taken?"

"Only one thing. Which is odd, considering the valuable jewels and coins I store for my clients. The silver scepter was stolen."

"Wait. Didn't I just accept a scepter from Tor for you?"

"The exact one. The one missing some stone or jewel in the top."

Stryke turned to Blyss, raising an eyebrow. She shook her head, silently conveying her confusion. She was hearing only about half the conversation now.

"It's a demon scepter," Rhys offered. "So it makes me wonder if that's what the demons were after last night at the wedding. But then I tell myself, no, they must believe I wouldn't walk around with a scepter in hand. So are the two incidents related? I don't know."

"I'm talking to Blyss right now. Can I call you in a bit, Rhys?"

"Sure. I wanted to let you know what was stolen, see if you had any thoughts. It could be entirely random. I'll have to mark it as a loss."

"Right."

"Though, if you had the time, it might not be a bad idea to try to track the scent trail. I can pick it up, but since you handled the scepter most…"

"That's a good idea. I can come over right away. I'll see you soon, Rhys. Thanks for letting me know about this."

"Sure thing."

"A scepter?" Blyss asked after Stryke had hung up. "I don't understand."

"It was a fancy silver thing. Like something a king

holds when he sits on his throne. But it was missing the main piece. You know the top of the scepter is usually clasping a big jewel or probably—"

"Le Diabolique?"

Stryke nodded. "Did Edamite mention anything about a scepter?"

"No, but again, it wasn't important to me to ask questions."

His discerning look said so much, but Blyss wasn't ready to tell him all. "Rhys wants me to come over and try to track it."

"I'll come along."

Stryke lifted a hand, as if to stop her. He gazed into her eyes for so long, she felt his touch, and it was more gentle than she'd expected. Finally, he nodded. "Yeah. You know more than I do. I think it would be a good idea for you to come along. Two noses will serve better than one."

Stryke picked up the trail from the massive safe where Rhys had temporarily stored the scepter. With Blyss at his side, they tracked outside, around the building and down a street for half a mile before he paused and had to focus on the scent of sulfur in order to determine if the trail turned left or right.

"What do you think?" he asked Blyss as he clasped her hand. Focus was required not to get lost in her gorgeous scent. "Left or right?"

"Don't ask me."

He turned to look into her eyes, seeing the glamorous socialite and not the werewolf he expected. She was decked out in a classy black dress and perfect makeup. The shoes were killer, but she'd said she could run faster than he could when he'd questioned whether she could keep up.

"Don't you have the scent?" he asked. "I saw you lean over the storage box in the safe. It's a distinct odor."

She shook her head and brushed a curl of hair from her long lashes. "I'm just following you."

"But I thought you were helping? Blyss, didn't you pick up the scent in the office?"

She shook her head again.

Hadn't she tried to focus on the scent? Or was she so distracted by the crazy goings-on lately that she couldn't find that focus? So much about her baffled him. And there was yet much to learn. They hadn't finished their conversation. She still held secrets. And he guessed those unspoken words were about her werewolf.

But right now, he wanted to stay on the scent. He had an opportunity to prove himself to Rhys Hawkes, and he wouldn't let that go. Because he liked working for the man, and even if he did plan to leave Paris soon, he always did a job 100 percent. He had been the one to bring in the scepter; he felt responsible for its loss.

"Left," he decided, picking up the scent.

Blyss's heels clicked quickly behind him.

"We're nearing the Pigalle," she commented.

"Pig alley?"

"It's the red-light district. At night it attracts tourists and prostitutes. The streets are lined with sex shops and assorted dives."

"Sounds like my brother Trouble's kind of place." He clasped her hand and they crossed a double-wide street, pausing on the middle intersection to wait for the light. The air was scented with motor oil, some kind of summery flower that blossomed on the nearby trees, and human musk and salt. The faintest tendril of sulfur wavered in and out of his senses. "This way."

"Oh my goddess."

"What?" he asked. The scent lured him toward the black metal doors of a nightclub.

"This is Club l'Enfer. Are you sure you've been on the scent? This place is always occupied by demons. You could have picked up anything."

"Let's go inside and find out." He pushed the door open to expose a black maw and the distant sound of drumbeats. "Ladies first."

Blyss remained on the sidewalk. This was not her scene. She avoided contact with paranormals, and this club was all about the paranormals. Had she never gone to the wedding last night, would she have protected Stryke and his family from this problem? Probably.

"Too scary for you?" he asked with a challenge to his voice.

"This club is generally filled with demons and vampires. I'm not sure werewolves go in there. At least, not often. Maybe I should wait outside?"

He pulled her to him and held her against his body. It was the first time today that he'd taken a moment to hold her. And it felt wonderful. As if only they two existed in the world. And all the bad stuff that had crashed around her shoulders did not exist. He was still wearing last night's shirt spattered with blood and his face was bruised. Yet when he kissed her, she sighed. It was a sweet, quick kiss, but it stole something from her.

And she wasn't sure she wanted that something back.

"I'll hold your hand. It's day. I'm sure it's not rowdy until later, eh?"

She nodded. He clasped her hand. "I won't let anything hurt you."

She wasn't afraid of getting hurt. She'd already been

hurt. What Blyss was afraid of was facing the truth that lurked within the darkness.

They strolled inside. Immediately a broad-shouldered bouncer stepped before them. Red eyes glowed as he looked over Stryke, sniffing and then nodding as if he approved. "But what is she?" The bouncer thumbed a thick digit at her.

"Werewolf," Stryke said. "Promise."

Casting a wary summation over her, the demon finally stepped aside and muttered, "Not much going on right now."

They wandered into the din, which was no brighter than the insides of a coffin, Blyss decided. The walls, floor and ceilings were black. The dance floor flashed like red flames set on a low burner. A few people swayed to some recorded heavy-metal music. A few of the dozens of tables held lonely souls before them. Caught in a daze as they stared into their drinks.

It could be any bar that catered to humans. Her kind. But Blyss didn't do bars. Period. She hated the feeling of utter desolation that enveloped when wandering among the drunk and weary-eyed patrons.

A shiver traced her system. She clutched Stryke's hand.

"You still have the scent?" she asked as he scanned across the balcony and over the empty stage.

"No, I've lost it. But whoever stole from the safe at Hawkes Associates came here. I can feel it. I wonder if we can get through that door over there. Might lead backstage."

He walked around the dance floor and she dutifully followed. Every so often her shoes stuck to the sticky floor, and she winced. This was abhorrent, and it smelled awful. Not so much like demons but like smoke and sex and all the nasty body odors of creatures she'd rather not consider.

If she never recouped her losses, would she someday find herself in such a low and desolate place?

Before Stryke got to the back door, the bouncer once again stood before them. "What are you looking for, buddy?"

"Uh, was tracking a friend. I have his scent." He tapped his nose. "I'm worried about him. Didn't come home last night."

"There's no one back there. I think it's time for you and your pet to leave."

Blyss bristled at the term. The demon did not believe she was wolf and probably assumed she was Stryke's human pet. Ugh. Well, that was as it should be if her world was moving along the trajectory she had planned for it. Not the pet part. Normally she wouldn't be caught dead hanging around a werewolf.

But oh, she couldn't step away from Stryke. Not now. He'd gotten under her carefully applied veneer. And she liked the feeling of him so close to her. Everything about the feeling was wrong. Unless she could make it right. And the only way to do that was to come completely clean to him.

"Let's go." She grabbed Stryke's hand. "I need to tell you everything."

He turned a surprised look on her.

"The scepter can wait," she whispered. "Will you help me?"

"Help you?" His surprise turned to worry, and then he nodded and quickly escorted her outside.

"Let's take the Métro," she suggested because there was a station right across the street. While she avoided the Métro more than she avoided paranormals, she just wanted to be home, where she felt safe, and with Stryke.

Chapter 10

They entered the apartment in a tangle of kisses and groping hands and stumbling feet. Blyss wanted to be a part of Stryke, to feel him all over her. She couldn't deny the combustible attraction she felt when near him. Werewolf or not, she needed to know every part of this man.

"Thought we were going to talk?" he mumbled between kisses to her neck, the rise of her breasts, her collarbone. He slipped off her dress sleeve, his fingers tracing shiver-tickles down her arm.

"I need to know you first," she said on a gasp. "A man. A wolf. I want to feel your strength, Stryke."

"I don't know how this will change things," he said as they stumbled into the bedroom and landed on the bed. "But you won't hear me protesting. Blyss, you're so hot and wanting. My greedy glamour girl. I like that."

"Then give me everything you can," she whispered as she unzipped and shrugged down her dress. He pulled it off her and tossed it to the floor. The silk would wrinkle; she didn't care. "Get undressed. Quickly!"

He still wore the bloodstained shirt, which was quickly relegated to the floor, followed by his dress trousers, shoes and boxers. That was one rental suit that would not receive a return on the deposit.

She gripped his erection and pulled him onto the bed. She wanted him inside her. She wrapped her body against his and he glided between her legs, entering her, thrusting briskly at first and then slower until they barely moved yet the world swirled around them.

His tongue teased at her nipple. A finger slicked her clit. They maintained the slow rhythm, but it was too much to contain. Release overwhelmed them both and Stryke's body stiffened above hers, his muscles tensing and then relaxing as she shivered into a delicious orgasm. She thought he growled—it was some kind of wolfish sound. And then he collapsed to her side, yet rolled over to kiss her on the shoulder.

"The only time I really know you are werewolf is when we have sex." he said. "You get all hot and bothered and your true nature is revealed."

"It's the only time I can recognize your wolf, as well."

Blyss stared up through the overhead windows. The sky was bright. She felt terrific. Depleted and exhausted, yet also somehow…different. Complete? That a man could complete her was not a belief she subscribed to. Yet she felt somehow *right* lying beside Stryke. Even knowing he could sense her true nature.

And he smelled homey and warm, like sex and salt and everything she wanted to immerse herself in. The glide of their moistened skin against skin allowed her to gauge his strength. And the skim of the stubble on his jaw as he kissed down from her shoulder sent new shivers through her body that felt like joy.

For as little as she knew this man, she felt as if she could trust him. That, of all the people walking this world, this one would accept her.

The time had come to reveal all. Pray, he could accept her awful truth.

"All right." She blew out a breath and brushed aside a curl of hair from her lashes. "This is my story. You may hate me after I've told you, so I am thankful that we've had one last moment together. It means a lot to me, this being comfortable with you. I've never felt like this with any other man. It's so special."

He rolled to his side and propped up on an elbow, catching the side of his face against a palm. "I'm sure there's nothing you can say that will scare me out of your bed. Even demons haven't scared me away from you."

She stroked his neck where the talon cuts had healed yet faint dark lines remained. He nuzzled his face against her hand. It would be so easy to curl up against him and make slow love right now. But she couldn't conceal anything from him anymore.

"You wanted to know how I got involved with Edamite Thrash. I sought him out after learning he might have the fix I needed for my life. It was about six years ago, right after I'd left Valoir."

"You purposely left your pack? Banished?"

"No, I wasn't banished. My brother stood up for me, asking for a lesser punishment. I was expelled with the condition that I could return if I wished. And then, only if I accepted my wolf. I was honored they chose not to banish me."

Banishment was forever and left the werewolf permanently scarred as a sign to others that he or she had been extricated from the pack, usually for a crime against their own or for committing a deed so foul none in the pack could condone it.

Blyss hadn't harmed anyone. Yet her deed could be considered foul by some. Who was she kidding? All in the pack had voted to expel her. Including her mother.

She inhaled a breath of bravery.

"Stryke, my deep, dark secret is that I hate being werewolf. It's nasty, messy and horrible. Ever since the shift came upon me at puberty I've felt wrong. As if I was born into the wrong body. Shifting is not easy for me, and coming back from a shift into this human body is terrible. I feel ugly and— Oh, you're making a face."

His wince smoothed away and he shook his head. "I'm… I don't know what to say."

Who could know how to react? Blyss was aware she was one among millions who felt as she did. She'd never in her lifetime met or heard about other werewolves who denied their very heritage.

"This life I have now?" she said. "The diamonds and glamour and socializing? It is the life I've created that suits me best. No shifting. No fur or claws, or nasty running through the woods on all fours. No feeding on small animals or living among—well, wolves."

She shuddered. Memories of living in the pack were ugly. She had only ever been close to her father and brother, Kir. She rarely saw Kir nowadays. And her father had abandoned his family for another woman when Blyss was younger. Pack Valoir had banished Colin Sauveterre for his propensity to engage in illicit love affairs with demons and vampires. Now she saw her father a few times a year, and not on her terms, but because he showed up at her door groveling. Sometimes she wished he could get his act together so she didn't feel as if she had to keep an eye on him.

Stryke sat up and brushed his hands over his face. "Blyss, what you're saying... It's like... I don't know. It's like denying your heritage. How can you not be what you were born to be? My mind goes to people who are gay and try to deny it, or even—hell, a person of color who denies their race. It's wrong. I couldn't imagine being anything but wolf."

"Then you should understand that I am not denying what I am but am trying to be what I know I should be."

"That doesn't make sense." He stood and paced beside the bed, the glow from a streetlight worshipping his naked form. His skin gleamed. The tight muscles strapping his thighs and buttocks a lure to her sensual lusts. "You were born a werewolf, yes?"

"Of course. Our breed can only be born."

"Was one of your parents something else? A faery?"

"No, both my parents are wolves. As is my brother, Kirnan."

"You've a brother? What does your family think of you trying to be something you're not?"

"Stryke, I am trying to be the thing I feel I was born to be. And my family..."

Blyss sighed and sat up against the pillow. She couldn't look at him, couldn't face his accusing stare. Yet she felt his concern in her heart. He feared for her even while not completely comprehending her situation.

"My mother thinks I'm insane. My father tolerates me only because he was banished from the pack a decade ago after he'd had an affair with a demon. And there's the money. I've bailed him out more times than a child should have to. Mom and Kir remain in the pack.

Dad lives on his own with his demon girlfriend. And I am where I need to be."

"But you weren't banished from the pack?"

"I can return if I accept my werewolf."

"Will that ever happen? How?" He sat on the bed, leaning in to seek her truths. "How can you not be werewolf?"

"Right before leaving the pack, I heard there was a means to suppress my werewolf. Pills."

"Pills?" He shook his head and exhaled. Again he stood and paced. "You take pills to not be wolf? That sounds impossible."

"I take a pill to prevent my werewolf from demanding release every full moon. I get them from Ed."

"The demon?" Stryke blew out a breath. Hands to his hips, his back to her, he bowed his head, eyes closed. "So that's why you owe him money? Why you needed to get the diamond?"

"A year's supply of pills costs five hundred thousand euros. I take them daily. I do need to shift only one full moon every year. Sort of a means to let out everything I've suppressed. It's awful."

She sensed his utter horror at her confession. His back muscles were tense, as was his neck. He couldn't look directly at her. She had lost him. But there was no turning back now. She had to put it all out there.

"I've but a few pills remaining. And the full moon is closing in. I owe Ed for this year's supply still because I needed to divert the money elsewhere."

"Elsewhere?" he muttered. Sitting on the bed, his back to her, he caught his palms on his knees. "Continue."

"My father has a gambling problem. He was in debt. A nasty bunch of vampires were after him, a tribe who is known to hunt wolves. I paid off his debt thinking I could easily get the money to replace it. I…have a tendency to collect expensive gifts from my lovers. It's how I've survived."

Stryke's body bent forward, his head shaking as he exhaled.

"Not lately, though," she continued. Her heart pounded. Her soul ached for exposing her terrible truths. And she couldn't stop, although she knew every word was only driving a wedge deeper between the two of them.

"When Ed heard that our gallery was exhibiting *Le Diabolique*, he called me in and offered the deal. I had no idea the diamond was anything more than a stone. A demon trapped within? The legend of it is that whoever has held it through history has suffered a terrible fate. It's been in the hands of royalty, thieves, murderers and more royalty. But it's never been in demon hands."

"So you were going to hand over this nasty diamond to a demon, who had plans to do God knows what with it?"

"And in turn Ed would forgive my debt and cover me for the next year's pills. I need those pills, Stryke. Without them…"

"You're just a werewolf." He turned to pin her with an accusing gaze. It felt like silver cutting into her veins and sizzling directly to her heart. "A werewolf like me. Now I understand why I couldn't scent you in the gallery. And why you were so upset when I pinned you for werewolf. You must have been disgusted to know you'd just had sex with a werewolf."

He grabbed his pants and shuffled them up, swinging an arm through his bloodied shirt as rapidly.

"I can't listen to this," he said. "All I've ever wanted

my whole life is to fall in love with a beautiful were-wolf and make a family. I'm looking for a wife, Blyss. I'm to start a pack so my father can retire. And what happens when I begin to think I may have found that woman? She is the one wolf in the world who doesn't want to be a wolf."

He charged out of the bedroom, shoes in hand.

Blyss didn't call for him to stay. He had every right to be angry. To be disgusted by her. She knew the feeling. She'd been disgusted by wolves all her life.

Until she'd met Stryke Saint-Pierre.

Chapter 11

Stryke kicked off his shoes inside his apartment's kitchen. He tore off his shirt and tossed it across the back of a chair. He strode into the living room, smacking a fist in palm. The intense need to punch something tightened his muscles. He usually matched Trouble while sparring. He could use a punching bag right now.

Blyss didn't want to be a wolf.

What. The. Hell?

He couldn't conceive of such a notion. How could a person not want to be something they had been born to?

Blowing out a breath, he paced before the windows that overlooked the Seine. The view was gorgeous. He should be out touring the city, taking in the summer air, holding hands with a sexy werewolf…

Okay. Stop.

He was a rational man. He was able to look at things from more than his perspective. All his life he'd been a pseudo counselor to his brothers and their troubles, especially regarding women. He could do this.

If he considered what Blyss had revealed to him, he could understand that there were people in this world who wanted to change their circumstances. That no matter how others looked at them, and assumed them to be happy, they might never be happy with their life. So, sure, he could grant that Blyss wasn't happy. Hadn't been happy. And she'd taken measures to find a certain happiness that better suited her.

He shrugged his fingers over his scalp. "But not a wolf?"

Here he'd thought he'd happened upon a good thing. A gorgeous woman, who was also a werewolf, who seemed to like him and definitely seemed to enjoy having sex with him. He'd thought they'd hit it off. Had even allowed himself to take a step toward thinking she could be *the one*.

Yet the truth was, she had been using him. Mostly. He could believe her when she'd explained that initially she'd been looking for a dupe to carry the diamond out of the gallery, and then she'd warmed to him as a lover.

He wanted to believe that. He wanted to believe in something.

But it was too late. Tomorrow his family boarded a plane for the States. So long, Paris, romance and Blyss. Sure, he'd intended to stay a few days longer, but he would eventually leave.

Could he leave her?

"I need a shower." He'd been wearing the same clothes for two days. And he needed a good night's sleep. With hope, the morning would bring a new perspective.

* * *

The morning brought Stryke upright in bed with a name on his lips. "Blyss."

And all the angst he'd been feeling returned. Jumping out of bed and pulling on his jeans and a shirt, he wandered into the kitchen but wasn't hungry, so he swung back into the living room.

A knock on the door jerked him around from his fervent pacing. He marched to the door and pulled it open, cautioning himself from growling. Kelyn and Trouble barged in.

"We're heading to the airport this afternoon," Trouble said. "You packed and ready?"

"No."

"What?" Kelyn asked.

"I…" And he made a knee-jerk decision. "I'm going to stay on for a while longer."

"What the hell for?" Trouble asked. "I mean, the city is cool. It's got sexy chicks walking around, if you can sift through the crazy tourists and find a real Parisian femme, but seriously? I'm so ready to head back home."

"Rhys Hawkes has more work for me." Stryke summoned a simple excuse. "It's interesting work. And I like the city, so yeah, as long as I've a place to stay, I think I'll hang out for a while."

And there was one other, bigger reason.

"What about that chick you brought to the wedding?" Kelyn guessed correctly. "Is it true what I heard that it might have been her fault the demons attacked?"

"That's probably not true." He didn't want his brothers going after Blyss because of something she may or may not have been involved in. Because if Trouble smelled trouble then he'd stick around for the dangerous fun. "It's a complicated deal."

And Stryke didn't want to discuss it with his brothers. They would form an opinion of Blyss, and he'd rather they not think of her negatively. She was a complicated woman. And he decided right then and there that he wasn't going to walk away from her just like that. He couldn't. If there were demons looking for the diamond, Blyss could be in danger.

"Demons or not, she was one hot chick," Trouble said. "Isn't that the kicker? The dangerous ones are always the most exciting."

"Yeah? Then your ultimate match will probably knock you into tomorrow," Stryke offered.

"Hey, I'd like that." Trouble rubbed his jaw and bounced a couple of times on his feet. Boxer's moves. Their eldest brother was a frenetic bundle of energy. "So you want to head out to that street where they sell those chicken sandwiches with all the fries?"

"The Greek restaurant," Kelyn provided.

Dozens of restaurants tucked within the 5th arrondissement served up shredded chicken gyros on soft pita bread, slathered with tzatziki sauce, and piled with veggies and mountains of crispy fries. Heaven.

"Sounds like a plan," Stryke offered. "Is Blade around?"

"Yeah, we'll grab him on the way out the building. We'll get Dad, too. He's been complaining that Mom made him take her to all the froufrou restaurants that serve a carrot stick and a blop of mush."

Stryke grabbed his shirt and shoved his feet into his shoes. He needed a hearty meal and some time hanging with the guys. He could worry about the crazy werewolf glamour girl later.

Blyss pulled a bottle from the wine cooler, turned around—and dropped the bottle on the marble floor.

The glass shattered. Cool liquid splashed her ankles, and shards of glass cut across her bare feet.

Edamite Thrash stood in the kitchen. His pale gray eyes narrowed on her, his mouth equally as narrow. The horns at his temples caught the sunlight with a glint. She hadn't heard him enter, but she knew he was powerful. He must have the ability to transport himself wherever he wished. She wasn't up on demon abilities. Didn't want to be up on them either.

"Cabernet 1945?" he asked. "Pity."

With a sweep of his hand, the black glass pieces re-formed into the bottle, and the wine puddles refilled it. The undamaged bottle found its place onto the kitchen counter.

Blyss was no longer in the mood for a glass of wine. She'd been anxious and had sought something to calm her nerves. Yes, at eleven in the morning.

"What are you doing here?" she had the audacity to ask.

"Talked to your lover yesterday. He's a werewolf," Ed said with unexpected surprise. "What's up with that? I thought you were anti-werewolf?"

"It's complicated" was all she could answer. Because it was. And she didn't want to chat with Ed. "I'll get the diamond. I promise."

"My confidence in you actually accomplishing that task has waned." Another gesture of his fingers glided her across the floor to stop abruptly before him.

Blyss stepped back but her thighs met the countertop, keeping her an arm's reach from the demon. "I'll find it. I need to."

"Right. Because you're almost out of pills. Full moon on the horizon. Without those pills you'll be getting your wolf on. That is, if you live that long."

Blyss held her breath. The threat was nothing new.

"Are you aware a demonic scepter has also been stolen?" he queried. He pressed his fingertips together before his chest. The deadly thorns on his knuckles glinted menacingly. They looked as if carved from obsidian, and Blyss knew one slice from them could render most dead from the poison contained within.

"No. A scepter? What does that have to do with the diamond?"

"Everything. The diamond fits into the head of the scepter. Once *Le Diabolique* is placed in its rightful position, the scepter is capable of releasing the demon contained within. Xyloda is what it is called."

Her jaw dropped open. "But I thought that's what *you* wanted to do with it?"

He did want to release the demon. Or so she had assumed. He hadn't actually told her what his plans for *Le Diabolique* were.

"You think to know so much?" he asked in a measured tone.

Did she? Or did she only assume she knew his plans for the diamond? What else could he possibly have wanted it for?

Ed tilted his head to study her, his eyes glowing red. She noted a surprising change in his expression. The icy hardness melted at the corner of his tight mouth. And the red glow receded.

"A ritual is required," Ed continued. "The blood of twelve demons is required to release Xyloda from *Le Diabolique*. Twelve rare demons."

"Well, if they're rare—"

"Silence."

She did not tolerate a man speaking so rudely to her, but she knew better than to stand up to Edamite Thrash.

"All that means is you've yet time to obtain that which I've tasked you to get for me. And I have no choice but to let you seek it because you have a connection to the one man who may be able to sniff it out."

"Stryke? But—"

Ed flicked his fingers toward her. Blyss's feet left the ground, and her chin tilted up as if he was lifting her. "Bring me *Le Diabolique* before the moon is full. If you do not, I will kill your father. And then I will kill your mother and your brother. Then I will take off the Saint-Pierre werewolf's head while you watch. But I won't kill you, because to watch you shift to the one thing that appalls you most will give me great pleasure."

Blyss dropped to her feet and Ed disappeared from the kitchen. She caught herself from falling to her knees by grasping the counter behind her and leaning across it. Teardrops splashed the marble surface. Her heartbeats clambered against her rib cage.

How was she going to find *Le Diabolique*?

She needed Stryke's help. And he had walked away from her, disgusted by the choice she had made with her life.

Chapter 12

Blyss watched from a distance as the Saint-Pierre family piled into a stretch limo and rolled away from the island. En route to the airport, no doubt. Stryke had mentioned they were here for only the week.

Too late. She'd missed him! Now what to do?

She should have never agreed to get the diamond for Thrash. Yet Ed had always treated her well in the years she had been buying the pills from him. Today had been the first time she had felt genuine fear being near him. What evil would he unleash on the world when he finally got the diamond and scepter? What was the demon Xyloda? She shivered to consider the menace of which it could be capable.

A walk had felt necessary to rid herself of the anxiety, and she'd needed to get out of her home and away from the spot where Ed had stood and threatened her.

The Île Saint-Louis had been a long stroll in her

heeled Louis Vuitton suede boots. Good thing they were comfortable. And now her only hope had left. He'd washed his hands of her. Yet she had been compelled here, to where he had stayed. Because she hadn't known where else to go. And she thought that maybe, if she offered to pay Stryke, he would stay and help.

Of course, she hadn't any money. The only thing of value she hadn't hocked yet was the diamond she wore around her neck. It wasn't worth more than five thousand. A pittance to what she owed Thrash. Could it have been enough to interest Stryke in tracking demons for the one woman he must hate more than demons?

Didn't matter anymore. She was alone with no one to turn to.

A hand glided up Blyss's back, and she spun about, prepared to slap whoever touched her— "Stryke?"

"Sorry to scare you. I saw you standing here and couldn't figure out why."

Lowering her hand, she offered a shrug. "I was… I thought you had gone. I saw your family drive away."

"Headed home to Minnesota. They've had enough tourism for a while. I, on the other hand, am looking forward to a trip to the Eiffel Tower today. Might even take the stairs to the top. I hear that line is shorter."

"Infinitely shorter. I imagine a man like you could run up the stairs and not feel winded when you reach the top."

He shrugged. "I need to let off some steam. The workout will do me good."

He probably needed that workout because of her. Blyss looked aside, not wanting to look into his bright brown eyes because she knew she'd see the hurt there. Hurt caused by her.

"So, you're staying?" Her voice cracked slightly. "Just to do the tourist thing?"

"Yep. There are a lot of sights I'd like to see."

She nodded and looked aside. Dare she ask him for help? No, she couldn't. He owed her nothing. And she had already taken too much from him.

"I'm sorry I left the way I did last night," he offered.

"No. You had every right. I'm not the most upstanding person."

"Don't say that, Blyss. You were doing what felt right to you."

"Thank you. You are quite the man."

"Yeah, well, I was too hasty. Judging you. I shouldn't do that. I don't want to do that. You have every right to feel the way you do about your...werewolf thing."

"It's what I'm comfortable with."

He touched her chin, forcing her to look at him. "I think I could be comfortable with you."

"You're lying to yourself. You want a werewolf, Stryke. You want the picket fence and the pack. I can't give you that happily-ever-after." And her heart cringed because it was a truth she despised.

"All I want from you right now is trust," he said.

"I do trust you."

"And maybe companionship?" His eyes gleamed with sunlight. "I do have another reason for staying. You. We've started something. It's a weird something, to be honest with you. But it's a something that I don't want to end so abruptly. If that makes any sense."

"You really mean that?"

He kissed her. Hand gliding along her neck and up the back of her head, he held her there as the kiss mastered her, filled her. Spoke to her all the things he probably couldn't put into words. It said: *let's try this*. At least, that was what she hoped it said.

"I'm going to keep my options open," he said as he pulled away. "But you know, I'm not rich. I suspect I'm not exactly tops on your wish list either."

"I think it's high time I focus on something beyond the material."

"Really? Because if you owe some asshole demon half a million dollars, I'd think right now would be an excellent time to focus on laying your hands on some cash."

Blyss smiled. "You'd think. But I don't want that from you." Then she sighed, because she did want something from him. And it wasn't an easy friendship or a sexy kiss. "Time for total honesty and the reason I'm here. I need to track *Le Diabolique*. You know why?"

"I suspect Thrash has threatened you."

"He's now threatened to kill my entire family if I don't bring him the diamond by the full moon. He told me there's a ritual required to call the demon out from the stone and it requires the blood of twelve demons. It'll take a while for whoever has the stone to collect all those demons because they are rare. I hate telling you this, because once again, I need something from you."

"Just ask, Blyss. I stayed in Paris because I want to help you."

"You—you did?"

He nodded.

She swallowed down the lump in her throat. His generosity was immense and so selfless. And she deserved none of it. He was truly one in a million. She couldn't afford his kindness.

"Blyss, talk to me. Tell me what you need."

"I, uh…" She exhaled. For all he knew about her,

he was still standing before her. And that meant a lot. "I need your expertise in tracking. I need your help locating the diamond. I need so much from you and I've done nothing to deserve it."

"You need help. That's all that matters."

"It shouldn't be. I should have, at the very least, done something to deserve your help."

He leaned in and kissed her again before whispering, "You've touched my heart. That's reason enough."

She didn't want to cry. She didn't deserve his kindness or his sweet words. He was being too nice. And she didn't know why. But right now, she didn't have time to question that kindness.

"How will we find the diamond?" she asked softly.

"We need to go back to Club l'Enfer. I think Johnny, the groom, knows the place. I'll give him a call and see if he's got a suggestion how to get into the back rooms. Come on."

He grabbed her hand while he pulled out his phone with the other. Walking her up to his apartment, Stryke talked to Johnny while they did so. By the time he opened his front door, he closed the phone and gestured to walk inside.

"Johnny said the place is owned by Himself. It's a demon and vamp hot spot."

The devil Himself owned the place? Blyss shivered.

Stryke embraced her from behind, nuzzling his face aside her neck. "You're not coming along with me this time. L'Enfer is no place for a woman like you."

"You mean a silly girl who walks around in diamonds and high heels?"

"I mean, a woman who will most likely be construed as only human. You don't give off the werewolf vibes,

Blyss. The bouncer thought you were my human pet before. It's best you stay behind."

"But I don't want you to go there alone. It's dangerous. Can Johnny go with you?"

"He's on his honeymoon. He suggested I check with Vail. It would be better to go in with numbers than alone. Why don't I walk you home? Then after dark I'll go check out the club. It'll be wiser to go there when the place is full. Best chance to find whoever might have taken the diamond."

"I'd like to stay here until you go. If you don't mind? I won't bother you. I'll just curl up on the couch with a book or something."

Stryke chuffed. "No books in the place. Much to my annoyance. Though there is a travel guide on the coffee table. Let's do this. We'll head out for a nice meal, an afternoon of chatting, getting to know one another beyond what we've done in bed."

"Sounds lovely, and I don't deserve—"

Stryke kissed her quickly, then said, "Stop telling me what you don't deserve. You deserve whatever I'm willing to give you. And what I want to give you is another kiss."

And that kiss was the best kiss Blyss had ever received. Because it was a promise. The man wore integrity like a brightly gleaming badge. And with his kiss he gave her hope and the desire to make his dreams come true.

Happily-ever-after? Blyss didn't believe in the fantasy. But maybe it was worth a try?

Blyss handed Stryke her mobile after they'd been seated in The Lounge Club in the Hotel Regina. She loved this cozy restaurant and had eaten here a few times.

"Put your number in there," she said. "And…you can copy mine, if you like."

He took out his phone and did so, with a wink to her. "Why do I sense I've just crashed some golden gate that would normally be bolted and barred with digital codes that not even a seasoned thief could crack?"

She took her phone back and tucked it in her purse. "I never give my number to a man. You have cracked my code, Stryke. And I'm not saying that because I need help from you."

"I can tell when you're being genuine. You look me directly in the eye and it's as though I can see clear into the next life in those gorgeous greens of yours."

"That's quite a distance. What's going on in the next life? And where are you?"

"I'm right here, sitting next to you," he said and moved around the curved bench so their shoulders hugged. "Is it cool if I sit so close?" He stretched his gaze about the room. "Kind of a fancy place. I don't want you worrying about whispers."

"Let them whisper," she said and tilted her head to kiss his cheek. "Mmm, you always smell good. But you don't wear cologne."

"It's all me, glamour girl. Plain, showered and just your average wolf."

She tilted her head with a smile. "You're not an average anything. Most especially not a, er…"

"You don't like the topic of wolves much, do you?"

"I strive to walk a life parallel to all things wolf. I respect the breed. I just don't relate to it. As for you, I imagine your perfect life would involve living in some country cabin surrounded by miles of forest. Having a werewolf wife who is barefoot and pregnant, busy creating the pack you so desire."

"You hit it on the head. But she doesn't have to be barefoot if she doesn't want to be."

"So Louboutins would be all right?"

"I don't even know what that means."

"Louboutins are a brand of shoe. I own many pairs."

"Ah. Those sexy pumps you're always wearing? Not sure how they'd go over out in the country. Kind of *Green Acres*. But I could get into that fantasy."

"Green Acres?"

"Yeah, it's a TV show from decades ago that featured a New York millionaire and his wife who packed up and moved to the country. He embraced the farmer's lifestyle while she wandered about in her pretty clothes and shoes and dreamed of moving back to the big city."

"So they eventually divorced?"

Stryke smirked and sipped from the water goblet. "Nope. They were in love. Love conquers all challenges."

"Getting the heel of my Louboutin stuck in the mud is not a challenge I ever want to face."

"I know that about you. Don't worry, glamour girl. I won't toss you over my shoulder and haul you out to the country. Unless you ask me to." His wink softened the tension in her neck and melted the bars about her heart.

If he kept saying the right words she might follow him anywhere.

The waiter arrived and Blyss could but sigh. Having Stryke toss her over his shoulder and take her anywhere he pleased sounded like a delicious adventure. And if she had to, she'd even trip across the forest floor in her Louboutins if she knew he waited for her with his arms held open.

"Uh, Blyss?"

She waded out of her thoughts and back to reality. The waiter frowned at Stryke.

"You'll have to handle this one for me," he muttered conspiratorially. "This guy isn't much for my English."

"Of course." In French, she ordered him filet mignon and a nicoise salad for herself. A bottle of Krug sounded lovely, but she declined. She hadn't the finances to cover the cost, and she didn't want to put Stryke out.

Wow, this roughing it was really quite a change from the usual tossing aside all caution and ordering anything she might care for, along with the wine. But as well, it felt strangely freeing. Blyss the socialite would frown upon the man sitting next to her in jeans and a T-shirt.

Who was she now that the very sight of Stryke's easy confidence and devil-may-care smile tapped into all her desires and made her lean in toward him for any contact she could manage?

"So what am I eating tonight?" he asked.

"It'll be a surprise."

"If it's frog legs…"

"Don't worry." She kissed him on the cheek. "I may not know how to cook, but I do know how to take care of my man."

"So no cooking? Ever?"

She shook her head. "I was never taught. I have standing meal orders from the area restaurants. Cooking is not something that interests me." She smiled again. "Yet another mark against me on your list, I suppose?"

"I don't have a list."

"Really? Your *Green Acres* fantasy doesn't appeal to me," she offered. "And you really do need a wolf. Someone who can race through the woods with you."

He did. And yet. "You say that with a certain reverence. Memories from childhood of doing just that? Racing through the woods?"

She shook her head. "I doubt it. I've forgotten a lot of my childhood. I don't think of it. It's not important to me."

"Or maybe the mask you wear won't allow you to think about all those things you left behind?"

She clasped both palms about the wine goblet, but didn't drink. "I do wear a mask. It's the woman I let the world see."

"The woman running away from the wolf?"

Her fingers curled more tightly about the goblet. Stryke wasn't about to retract that question. She was hiding from things she didn't understand. "When you came into your wolf, didn't anyone show you the ropes? Guide you along?"

"I don't want to talk about this."

He touched her wrist. "It's important to me. I want to learn about you, Blyss."

"Why? We don't have a future together. Haven't you figured that out yet?" Why had she said that? Her cruelties would push him away. And yet, cruelties were a part of the mask that protected her from heartbreak.

"I know our future isn't bright," he offered. "But I like you. And I'm here right now, for good or for ill, trying to help you out. Will you at least talk to me?"

She nodded. Because moments ago she had been grasping for the fantasy at Stryke's side. Could she risk the heartbreak? It could be worth it, if only to have these few wondrous days with the most amazing man she had ever known.

"I used to go to a public school," she said softly. Fine. The final bits of her truth must be revealed. Her mask cracked and fell away.

"Ah." Stryke nodded knowingly.

"It was during my sophomore year. That awkward time for teenagers."

It was difficult enough to go through puberty and gain the need to shift and heightened senses, and hell, the desire to howl at odd moments. But to do it in a public school, surrounded by humans who sought any little oddity to tease? Why hadn't her mother warned her? Or even allowed her to complete her schooling at home?

"Did you ever see that movie *Carrie*?" Blyss asked. "It was sort of like that. Only my first shift came on me during an outdoor track event. I began to shift and raced into the nearby woods. The wolf came upon me so fast, my clothes tearing and falling away. And, as you know, you shift right back from *were* form and are left there naked and stunned by what just happened. I was found by a group of mean girls. They hadn't seen the shift, but finding me naked without an explanation? I can't even talk about it."

He clasped her hand, and she melted against his shoulder, sniffling back tears. To show such emotion in a public restaurant was unthinkable, but she couldn't stop the tears that needed release. And, thankfully, she felt safe with Stryke holding her hand.

"I know it's stupid," she started.

"It's not stupid. Your pack should have prepared you for the first shift. Your…mother?"

"She's always been self-possessed. And my brother was much older than me. He'd been out of school for years. He's an Enforcer."

"What's that?"

"Sort of a werewolf cop. We police our own here in Europe. Kirnan is one of the highest-ranked wolves in pack Valoir under the principal and the scion."

"You're proud of him."

"I am. I wish we could be closer. But I struggled with my wolf so much after that first shift. I wanted out of it all as soon as I could make it happen."

"When did you leave your pack?"

"When I was seventeen. A vampire in school be-friended me. We weren't like besties, but he was kind and told me about some girls who went clubbing at the elite clubs and were able to…" She sighed.

There was a limit to removing the mask. She didn't want to tell Stryke all the things she had done in order to survive on her own. All that mattered to her now was what happened to her moving from this day forward. Desperation had gotten her to this point. She didn't want it to continue.

"Are you happy?" he asked.

She tilted a look up at him. His deep brown eyes gentled her anxiety. And yet… "I'm not sure what hap-piness feels like."

The confession gripped at her heart. No one should ever have to confess such a thing. And yet it was her truth. Her deepest, darkest truth.

"Being with you makes me happier than I've been in a long time," she whispered. "But I've already gone and spoiled my chances of us ever having a trusting relationship."

"And I am a wolf. Not your favorite kind of guy."

She smiled through tears. "I've never actually given a wolf a chance. You seem pretty cool to me. Not half as hairy as I'd expect."

"Wait until you see me wolfed out. Which probably won't happen. Because the glamour girl keeps away from all that mess. The full moon is in a few days.

Don't you need your pills? What will happen if you don't get them?"

"I'll shift. I do it once a year, as I've explained. I hate it. It's so messy."

"If messy is the worst complaint you've got about the shift then maybe you just need to learn to let your hair down and…"

Stryke's phone rang. He didn't want to take the call—it would be rude, he gestured—but Blyss encouraged him to dismiss himself to the lobby. It could be important. Promising he'd be right back, he headed out of the restaurant.

"Vail? Sorry, I'm out with Blyss at some fancy restaurant. What's up?"

"I found a witch who might have some information on the demonic ritual that's required to release *Le Diabolique*. I figured if you knew what you were dealing with you might be able to stop it before it happens."

"Works for me."

Vail gave him the witch's address and said she expected him tonight. She said he'd know the house when he arrived; it was the only octagon-shaped house in the city.

When he returned, he discovered the food had arrived at their table. Maybe. Was that tiny medallion of dark stuff on his plate the food? And there were three peas artfully arranged around it in a dash of red stuff.

"Filet mignon," Blyss offered. Her salad looked much more filling, but Stryke nodded politely and sat.

He wasn't sure if he should cut the thing or swallow it whole, but to be polite, he made nice by cutting it in six small pieces. The peas barely topped off the meat in his stomach.

By the time the bill arrived and he handed the waiter his credit card, he was praying she wouldn't hear his stomach growl.

Blyss leaned over and kissed him. "Not full?"

"Well, uh…"

"Please. That wouldn't have filled a baby, let alone a strapping man like you."

"I'm good." For about five minutes, he figured. "That was Vail on the phone. Want to visit a witch?"

"I wouldn't place it on my top-ten list of fun things to do, but sure. Why not?"

Chapter 13

The witch's house was indeed an octagon. Eight white walls, capped by a turret-like roof and red slate tiles. The yard was larger than most in the neighborhood and was filled to the edges with lush green plants, trees and shrubs so abundant they looked as if they belonged in a tropical climate.

Stryke pushed open the creaky iron gate and someone popped up from behind a shrub. A tall, broad-shouldered man with dark hair and a keen stare. He wore a leather apron filled with gardening tools wrapped round his hips, and chain-mail gloves clasped a particularly nasty strand of thorned vine.

"Who are you?" the man insisted, eyeing both Stryke and Blyss with a pit-bull sneer.

"We're here to see Libertie St. Charles."

"It's rather late for a social call."

"I called earlier," Stryke offered.

"Ah yes. You the werewolf with the demon problem?"

Stryke nodded. He didn't sense the man was anything but mortal, but he could feel strength resonate from his body. He decided then and there that he'd be an equal match to him should the need to go head-to-head arise.

He was thinking like Trouble. Always assessing the possible competition. *Just be cool,* he coached inwardly.

"Go ahead, then." The gardener stepped forward happily. "I'm Reichardt, Libby's boyfriend. She's inside making cookies. Be sure you do not leave without sampling a cookie."

"Thank you," Blyss said as they wandered down a mossy stone path to the front door.

Twilight painted a beam of setting sunlight across the path. Stryke wasn't a fanciful sort, but he thought he saw a twinkle skitter amid the tall blades of emerald grass. Nah. Couldn't be. Maybe?

The red front door magically opened inward when they'd breached the top step. Stryke and Blyss exchanged glances.

From within the house, a woman called out, "Come in! I'm in the kitchen."

Blyss clasped his hand and they wandered beneath a massive crystal chandelier in the center of the living room. He bent to kiss her and whispered, "It's going to be okay."

"Thank you," she whispered, but he sensed a catch to her voice.

She was nervous. And he was, too. Not about talking to a witch, but rather, *could* he actually help Blyss? Was he promising her something he couldn't deliver?

He wasn't sure how to track *Le Diabolique* now that the trail had gone cold. He hoped the witch had an idea.

Through swinging white doors, they entered a cheery, vast kitchen that smelled of melted chocolate and brown sugar. A woman wearing a curve-hugging purple dress and a white-and-pink polka-dot apron stood up from closing the stove and turned with a wide smile on her face, which was framed by red hair.

"You must be Stryke Saint-Pierre," she said, offering her hand to shake. "Mmm, firm grip. Definitely werewolf."

"And this is Blyss Sauveterre," he introduced his anxious partner.

The women shook hands. "Your hair is gorgeous," Blyss offered. "So vibrant."

"Thanks. It's natural. As is everything else," she said with a slide of hand over her ample hip. "I'm not getting a read on you, though, sweetie. Werewolf?"

Blyss nodded.

Libby leaned closer to Blyss as if to peer into a child's eyes. "You sure, sweetie?"

"I, uh, take pills to suppress my wolf."

"Ah." Libby righted. "That explains it. No judgments here."

Yet she did slide her eyes down Blyss's figure in an assessment that Stryke felt was more judging than she would admit.

"So, you two are wondering about the *Diabolique* diamond and the spell to remove the demon from within? Who would want to release that nasty demon? I mean, seriously? You know the demon's name? Xyloda. Sounds like some kind of prescription drug that'll screw you up big-time. Ha!"

"We would like to keep the demon inside the stone,"

Stryke said. "But most important, we need to find the stolen diamond and…" Then he'd hand it over to Blyss and let her do as she wished with it.

But would that make him responsible for unleashing untold evil if Blyss handed the stone to Edamite Thrash and he then released the demon within? Stryke could not live with that.

Now was no time to state his doubts. First, they had to actually find the missing diamond.

"Come with me," Libby directed, taking off the apron and hanging it on a hook near the door. "I've found the spell already."

She led them into another clean, bright white room. It was some sort of study or lab, and the table stretching in the middle was glossy and high-tech. It was lit by halogen lights from beneath the glass surface of the table. As well, the cupboards hugging the room were glass and lit with bright white light.

"The spell room," Libby offered. "My sister Vika designed it. She's into ultraclean high-tech stuff. I prefer a little less order to my things, but I haven't gotten around to making it less sterile, if you will. Been spending most of my time with Reichardt. He used to be a soul bringer, but now he's completely mortal and learning all about the world. He loves to garden."

"Isn't a soul bringer an angel?" Stryke asked.

"Yep. Used to be, anyway, until he took his earthbound soul. I gave it to him. Held his halo above his head and—bam! Mortal. So. You two a couple?"

"Yes," Blyss offered, while at the same time Stryke wasn't sure how to answer.

He glanced at Blyss. She smiled up at him. He took her hand and kissed it. "Yes," he said. "We are."

At least until she got what she wanted.

Which he was oddly okay with. He wanted her to be safe and to have the life she desired. And if that meant not being a werewolf? He'd hand over the diamond and kiss her goodbye. Remember his adventure in Paris forever. And lament a lover lost. On to the next story.

Right?

He met Libby's green gaze and sensed she understood what he was thinking. Could she read his doubt?

"So the weird thing is…" Libby pulled a white linen cloth away from a large, ancient book that sat on the center of the white table. "…we happened to have a demonic grimoire in the library. Not sure how or why. My sisters and I only practice light magic. Demonic magic is very dark. Malefic, even. We leave that stuff for Vika's man, Certainly Jones. He's a dark witch, but the world needs dark magic to balance the light, you know?"

Stryke had no clue about magic and how it worked or what the various forms were. He did know Desiderial Merovech, who lived back home, an ancient witch who was the keeper of the Book of All Spells, an actual grimoire that contained all magic spells ever written or cast. It was constantly, and magically, updating itself. Creepy, but kind of cool. And she had saved his life when he'd been nicked by a hunter's silver-tipped arrow. As well, she had helped Blade recover from a torture so heinous his brother had been forever scarred by it.

So magic was cool, in his opinion.

"This is it." Libby pushed the book forward. Stryke and Blyss stood on the opposite side of the table. Both leaned forward to look over the old paper with dark writing scribbled across the page. "Don't get too close," she warned. "The magic will sense your innocence."

"I don't think I have to worry about that," Stryke joked.

"There are degrees of innocence," the witch stated seriously. "You are innocent of all malefic magic. At least, I hope you are."

"Right." Stryke stepped back a pace along with Blyss. "What does it say?"

"Is it written in Latin?" Blyss asked.

"Yes. It details the spell, and how when all the blood sacrifices have been made, then they must be added to the stone to release the demon."

"Blood sacrifices?" Blyss said on a gasping tone.

"Twelve demons must be sacrificed simultaneously," Libby explained. "They are each a different breed of demon and some quite rare. It may take a while to gather them all. Which could buy you two some time."

"Does this spell list the twelve demons?" Stryke asked.

"It does. Why don't I copy it out in English so you can understand it? It won't take but ten minutes. While waiting, the two of you go help yourself to some cookies."

Reichardt waited with the plate of cookies in hand. Stryke politely took one, but after the first bite, he nabbed two more. The former soul bringer nodded in agreement as the threesome enjoyed the most delicious cookies Stryke had ever tasted.

The conversation was stilted, but he did manage to seem enthusiastic over the clump of silvery-green herbs Reichardt showed them and asked them to smell. Very pungent and not like any kind of cooking spice he'd ever encountered.

"For death spells," Reichardt said with a wink. "I harvest it for Certainly Jones, Libby's brother-in-law."

"The dark witch," Blyss confirmed at Stryke's lifted brow.

"Right. Witches are an interesting bunch," Stryke said.

"Indeed."

Libby spilled into the room on an air of hyperenthusiasm and before handing Stryke the list apologized for the hearts dotting the *I*s. "Reichardt thinks it's funny I do that. I just like to spread the love," she said. "The world is desperately short on love, isn't it? Well, save for Reichardt and me. He's my sweetie."

"And she's changed my air."

"Aww, I adore you, lover." The witch kissed her cookie-eating former soul-bringer gardener of a boyfriend.

Hugging both of them, and sending them off with a spoken spell for their best future, Libby and Reichardt watched them leave down the path before closing the red door.

"Now what?" Stryke asked as he handed Blyss the spell.

"I don't know. I thought you might take the lead."

He wrapped her into his embrace. "I can do that. I need some time to think about it. I have no idea where to start hunting for demons. Want me to take you home?"

"Sounds good."

"How about we head to my place and muddle over what we've got?"

She nodded and turned against his body, allowing him to lead her. She was lost and fragile, and he didn't want to hurt her or break her.

But was it even possible to protect her from the ultimate harm? If they couldn't find the diamond, she'd never get more pills. And without that Blyss would have to face the one thing she had kept out of her life so well.

Blyss had not balked when Stryke had suggested they pick up chicken gyros on the way. Food was a necessity after that pitiful afternoon snack he'd had at the fancy hotel. He suspected fast food was the last thing she would ever eat, but as she settled before the white marble counter in her kitchen and forked in her first taste, he noticed her shoulders relax and she even smiled as she sipped wine.

"Not bad," she said. "This came from that sorry little restaurant? I'm impressed, even. I've never walked in the 5th where all the tourists go."

"That is not a surprise." He swallowed a few bites, eating the sandwich as it was meant, with both hands instead of a fork. This was heaven. He should have ordered a couple for himself. "You like neat and orderly. I think it's time…" Stryke dipped his finger in her wineglass then snapped it toward her chest, dispersing red droplets across her skin and blouse. "…you get messy."

"Stryke, don't. This is silk—I wish you wouldn't."

"Wishes don't always come true, glamour girl."

He bent to lave the wine off her skin with a lash of his tongue. Blyss's protest ceased with a pleasurable moan. He'd never thought to pair wine with chicken gyros, choosing water to go with his, but this vintage was delicious. Or probably it was because he now followed a droplet down between her cleavage and caught it as it curved along the side of her breast.

Blyss stroked his hair. She slid a leg along his thigh and cooed. She was in the mood. And so was he. But first, he had a point to make.

He picked up the goblet, and before she realized what he would do, he poured the remaining wine down the front of her chest, soaking into her silk shirt and down her belly. She jumped, but he caught her by the wrists, drawing her close and pressing his tongue against her slick skin.

"But my blouse—"

"Fuck the silk," he growled. "I'm going to mess you up, glamour girl."

Stryke pulled her blouse off and Blyss let it fall to the floor where the wine had puddled. The shirt was a loss. And the man remained determined as he lapped his tongue up her stomach to her breasts, where he circled around one nipple and then the other. She almost wished there had been more wine. She would have poured it over her skin.

But what he did next made her shriek and struggle to get away from him. He reached for her plate, slapping his fingers on the food. White cucumber sauce coated his fingers. He then smeared the cool goop over her stomach.

Blyss backed up against the fridge, moaning at the ickiness of it—until his tongue lashed over her hip and up along her side where the sauce had been painted.

She couldn't prevent a satisfied moan. Even as she gripped his head, wishing his hair was longer for a good hold, and tried to pull him away, with her other hand, she pulled his shoulder closer, wanting him there, everywhere on her skin. Tasting, licking, teasing.

"I like the red sauce, too," he murmured.

When he reached for the plate again, she grabbed a handful of the finely shaved chicken and fries and tossed it at him.

Stryke gave her an incredulous gape. "Really?"

"You want to get messy?" she challenged.

Her clothes were ruined. And she didn't see a way out of this mess unless she fought. So fight she would. She grabbed another handful of lettuce and sauce, and lobbed it against his neck and shoulder. She dashed away from him before he could grab her.

Pulling off his shirt, Stryke licked his fingers. "Now you're in trouble."

"*Oui?* A little food never scared me."

She was bare-breasted and smelled like Greek food, and something had dripped down behind her skirt, but she kept an eye on Stryke's hands. She grabbed the wine bottle, which had about a goblet remaining in it and, holding the base, flung the neck outward, catching Stryke across his chest with the wine.

"Mmm," Blyss cooed. "I could take care of that for you."

"Then come here." He gestured with his fingers. A teasing grin enticed her around the counter to drag her fingers through the sauce and wine on his chest. He grabbed her by the wrist and spun her around.

She didn't hear him open the fridge until it was too late.

"Oh no." She struggled, but slipped on something.

He hugged her against his chest with one arm, while he drew something out of the fridge with the other hand. The cream was cold as it hit her skin, tightening her nipples to hard buds. His tongue followed closely, warming them and sucking at the cream. He hummed and dropped the cream carton on the floor, pulling her to him and sliding his hands down to grab her derriere.

"This needs to come off." He tugged at her skirt and found the zipper at the side.

While he slid down her skirt, Blyss managed to wrangle the can of whipped cream she'd bought to top some petit fours she'd ordered last week. A bend of the nozzle delivered a froth of white whipping down the side of his face, and when he realized what she was doing, he pulled back. She blasted his chest with it and drew lower.

"You're going to need to strip too, *mon amour*," she said. "I know where I want to taste this."

He didn't argue. He zippered down, his pants dropped and he kicked them aside. Splaying his hands to display ripped abs, defined hips and an upright erection, he said, "Bring it."

"Ooo la la!"

Blyss squirted whipped cream down his stomach and drew a line along the length of his hard shaft. Dropping to her knees, she lashed her tongue down his stomach. Tasted amazing and she didn't even think about calories. This was crazy. But it was kind of fun not caring what anyone else would think of her.

Pulling him toward her by his cock, she licked the head of him, tasting the whipped cream and sucking until his moans deepened and his sticky fingers threaded into her hair.

"Blyss, that's… You are one hungry woman."

It didn't take long to bring him to a shuddering climax. Stryke cried out in pleasure, his hips bucking. The sound of his pleasure was a wicked delight in and of itself.

Blyss sat back against the open fridge, her hand landing in a puddle of cream and her head tilting against the stainless steel.

Her lover was covered with smeared whipped cream, wine and cucumber sauce. As was she. And he looked amazing, his muscles tight and flexing as his body shook with the tremendous force of climax. A beautiful man.

That had messed her up. And she had enjoyed the messing. She couldn't remember a time when she'd forgotten to be perfect, to not worry about her hair, and certainly not about getting food on her clothes. Or face. Or... Oh, that couldn't be good to get between her legs.

Standing, she slid her fingers up her lover's abs, greasing the wine and whipped cream in a finger-painted design. "Shower," she said and pulled him down the hallway.

They lingered under the hot shower. Stryke soaped up Blyss from head to toes. He even sucked her toes into his mouth and tickled between them with his tongue. She hadn't expected such an erotic thrill from that touch. And he licked between her fingers, kissing them from tip to hand. Another delicious sensation that skittered throughout her system. She came three times in the shower. She never wanted to leave.

Why did the man have to be a werewolf? He was the perfect lover, even the perfect partner—except for that one small detail.

A huge detail.

The water shut off and Stryke wandered out onto the tiled floor to claim a fluffy white towel from the warming rack. But instead of handing it to her, he teased her with a matador's flick of cape. "Come here, glamour girl."

Normally the moniker would annoy her, but coming from him, in his teasing tone, Blyss loved the way he claimed her. She stepped into his arms and he wrapped her up in the warm towel and hugged her.

"Sorry to have messed you up," he said.

"I'm not sorry at all. I needed that."

"I'll clean up the kitchen for you."

She'd forgotten about that mess. Now would have been a terrific time for the maid to stop by. But she'd had to fire her three weeks ago when her savings had dried up.

"We'll do it together," she said. "It'll make faster work."

The doorbell rang, and Stryke's head went up. He sniffed the air instinctually. Something she had never seen previous lovers do. The move was so alpha, so commanding. It excited her all over again. "You expecting someone?"

"No." She grabbed the silk robe from the hook on the bathroom wall and wrapped it around her body. Hair still wet and dripping, she squeezed it over the towel she'd dropped. "I'll see who it is. You…"

His clothes were a mess. She intended to put them in the wash before sending him away today.

The doorbell buzzed again. "Just stay here," she said and headed to answer the door.

She hadn't a peephole to look through, and at times like this Blyss really missed the werewolf's heightened ability to scent others. Clenching a hand in a nervous fist, she opened the door. "Oh. Hey. I haven't seen you for a while."

"Blyss. Sorry to stop by like this, but I've been thinking about you. Just catch you in the shower?"

"Yes—"

"Who the hell is this?" Stryke strode up behind her, his hips wrapped with a towel and his chest puffing up as he eyed the tall man in the doorway.

"Who the hell am I?" her visitor asked. "Who is this, Blyss? And why…?" He sniffed and tilted his head curiously. "Is he a wolf?"

Chapter 14

"Kir, this is Stryke Saint-Pierre." Blyss could feel Stryke's posture stiffen in defense behind her. "Stryke, this is Kirnan Sauveterre. My brother."

"*Brother.* Nice to meet you." Stryke offered his hand and Kir shook it. "Uh, sorry." He wore nothing but the white terry-cloth towel around his waist. "We were just, uh…"

"I don't want to know." Kir stepped inside, his long casual strides moving him down the hallway. "Didn't mean to interrupt, but— What the hell?"

The kitchen looked as though the fridge had exploded.

"You don't want to know," Blyss singsonged as she gestured her brother to head toward the living room. "Give us five minutes to put some clothes on. If you're hungry…" She glanced over the mess on the floor.

"I'm not," Kir said. "You two do what you gotta do. I can entertain myself."

The wolf chuckled as Stryke and Blyss headed into her bedroom. His clothes were wet and covered in food, but that was the only option for now. He snapped his jeans out over the shower and scraped away the cucumber sauce. A sniff took in only faint scents. "Not too bad," he decided.

"I may have a men's T-shirt that will fit you," Blyss called from the depths of her closet. "Ah, here!" A blue shirt flew out from the closet and landed on Stryke's head as he returned to the bedroom.

He didn't want to know who this had once belonged to. He sniffed it. Smelled like fabric softener and not another man. Whew. He pulled it on and the cotton fabric stretched over his biceps and pecs. Tight, but he'd survive.

Blyss appeared in a soft red jersey dress that hugged her curves and looked like something he'd like to snuggle up against and never let go.

"You're gorgeous, as usual," he said. "And your brother is going to wonder if I peed my pants." He looked over his soaked jeans. "I remember you mentioning you had a brother, but I didn't think you and your pack…?"

"He stops by a few times a year. We still love one another, but he had a hard time accepting my choice to leave the pack. And, well, I'm glad when he visits. He reminds me of things and makes me question myself. But you do that, too."

"I make you question yourself?"

She nodded, but didn't elaborate. Stryke decided if she questioned her decision to not be wolf then he was damned glad to stir that up in her.

"He'll stay and chat for a bit."

"Do you want me to leave?"

"No." She tucked a few pins in her hair, making it look as if she'd styled it up just so. "I wish you'd stay. Please?"

"Good, 'cause I really don't want to go outside looking like this. And I'm going to need another shower after he leaves. I smell like a chicken gyro."

"And wine," she said, then kissed him. "Kir may have some info on the demons in the area. He once mentioned to me that the Enforcers run into them at times."

"Then I'm all for a chat." He followed her to the kitchen, where they veered around the food puddles, and into the living room, where Kir stood looking up through the skylights.

Blyss's brother was tall, had light, curly brown hair and wore a leather vest over a long-sleeved shirt. A gun holster was strapped across his chest, but there was no weapon in it. Not that Stryke could see. The wolf stood with hips squared and hands akimbo. Imposing. And rightfully so, because surely the brother would be suspicious of any half-dressed man he found in his sister's house. And smelling like cucumber sauce didn't help either.

"Food fight, eh?" Kir asked. His grin was easy and not at all accusatory, even when he slid his gaze down Stryke's attire.

"A little fun," Stryke offered. "You ever eat at the Greek places in the 5th arrondissement?"

"Love those chicken gyros. I thought that's what I smelled. Good choice. Stryke, was it?"

"Yes. I'm from Minnesota. My family is—or rather was—in town for a wedding. I'm sticking around awhile longer. Rhys Hawkes has some work for me."

"I'm aware of Hawkes Associates. The pack keeps

some valuables with them. Hawkes is half werewolf, half vampire?"

"Yeah, but it's weird because when he's vamp his werewolf brain is in control, and when wolf, his vamp brain wants him to drink blood. That would be a hell of a condition to keep in check."

"No doubt." Kir glanced to Blyss. "So how are you, sis?"

"*Très bien.* As usual. What about you? How is *ma mere*?"

"Do you really want to know?"

Stryke sat on the couch while the siblings remained standing. He wanted to learn more about Blyss but he didn't want to intrude on anything private. 'Course, he was stuck here until his pants dried out.

"She's still harsh and judgmental," Kir offered with a chuckle. "Good ole *ma mere.* I wanted to stop by and see if you needed anything. But it looks like all is well. Okay, I'll just ask." Kir turned to Stryke, but addressed his sister. "You've hooked up with a wolf. Does that mean…?"

"Non," Blyss said quickly.

Stryke looked aside. Yeah, he was the mistake. Much as he liked to believe they were growing closer, he knew it was all an illusion. Wishful thinking on his part.

"I didn't know she was wolf," Stryke offered, "until…well."

"My senses are as a human's," Blyss offered to her brother. "I've explained this to you before. Stryke is, well, he's a good man. But I didn't know he was werewolf when we first met."

The brother was understandably confused, but to his credit he didn't push the issue. Probably he'd been dealing with his sister's refusal of their breed for a long time.

"So Blyss tells me you're with some kind of enforcing team?" Stryke tossed out in hopes of warming the chill that iced the air. "What's that about?"

Kir sat on the chair opposite Stryke. Blyss lingered by the wall, arms crossed, yet her gaze lingered on her brother.

Kir said, "The European wolves police their own. Various enforcements teams are spread throughout the countries. My pack, Valoir, is responsible for policing Paris. We keep an eye on those packs that may be gaming, victimizing vamps. Lately there's been a weird uptick in demonic activity in the city. We don't police demons, but we like to keep an eye on everything."

Stryke stabbed a look at Blyss. She shrugged and nodded. An approval to ask what he really wanted to ask.

"Did you hear about Hawkes Associates getting robbed a few days ago? We think it was demons because all that was taken was a demon scepter."

"No, but I did hear something about a demon attack at a vampire wedding?"

"That was the wedding we were at." Stryke again exchanged looks with Blyss but she flickered her gaze aside. Apparently whatever she was involved in she'd not revealed to her brother. "They were after a demonic diamond."

"Like Kir said," Blyss broke in, "he doesn't police demons, just werewolves."

"It's all right." Kir leaned forward, interested. "I had no idea it was a demonic artifact that was the lure to the wedding incident. A diamond? Do you know anything about that, Blyss?"

She sighed and her shoulders dropped. Stryke sensed she didn't want to discuss this with her brother, but if the guy could help, wouldn't she welcome his knowledge on the local demons? Time was ticking away. The full moon was fast approaching.

"It is called *Le Diabolique*," she offered. "It is a rare black diamond that contains an all-powerful demon. Edamite wanted me to obtain it for him."

"Thrash?" Kir turned to face his sister. "He's the one, isn't he? The demon's a good guy, but—is he your supplier?"

Blyss nodded and bowed her head. Apparently her brother had not known that information. And it was difficult for Blyss to reveal that part of herself to him.

"Come here," Stryke said gently, and she sat down beside him. He wrapped an arm about her shoulder and nuzzled her against his chest. She relaxed against him. Felt good to know he could be the soft place she needed to land.

To Kir, he said, "Thrash has threatened her because she owes him money. She was trying to hand over the diamond to him and everything went wonky. And now we know the diamond fits into the stolen scepter. The demons who have both pieces can release the demon within once they collect twelve rare demons and make a blood sacrifice."

Kir whistled and shook his head. "Blyss, why didn't you come to me?"

"Because this isn't your problem. I know what you think of me. I try not to bother you or *ma mere*. I made a choice when I walked away from Valoir. I'm a big girl. I can take care of myself."

"I don't want you to have to take care of yourself," Kir said tightly. He shoved his hands over his scalp and shook his head. "You helping her, Stryke?"

"I am. Or I'm trying to. I'd like to track down the demons and return the diamond so Blyss can get Thrash off her back. And there's always the bonus of preventing demons from releasing some insane evil on the world. What did the witch call it?"

"Xyloda," Blyss provided.

"If you have any information about the local demons," Stryke said to Kir, "I'd appreciate your help, man."

"There is a group that has been particularly rampant lately. I don't know locations or even names, or if there's a specific leader. Like I said, the Enforcement team keeps tabs, but it's not high on our priority list. But I can certainly look into this further."

"I can tell you everything I've learned so far," Stryke offered. "I tracked the scent the night of the wedding to Club l'Enfer."

"Yeesh." Kir stood and began to pace. "That's Himself's territory. I can't imagine The Old Lad would have an interest in something like unleashing a demon. Sounds like competition to me. You want to head over to the club and have a look right now?"

"Great idea." Stryke stood. The tight shirt stretched across his chest. "I think I need to stop and get some clean clothes along the way. I'm staying over on the island behind Notre Dame. Blyss, do you mind if I go with your brother? I promised I'd help you clean up."

"I've got it. But, Kir, I don't want you getting involved. You've enough to do with the Enforcers."

"Blyss, you're in trouble. This involves me. Don't ever think otherwise."

She nodded.

Stryke bent to kiss her. "You going to be all right alone?"

"Of course."

"You've got my cell number. I'll call and check in with you on the hour."

"Why?" Her eyes frantically searched his. "Do you think I'm in danger?"

"Thrash has been here once."

Kir lifted his head at that statement.

"He's kidnapped me and threatened you, Blyss. Yeah, I think I need to keep a close eye on you now. Let me do this. Let me protect you."

She kissed him and whispered so Kir couldn't hear. "Thank you."

Kir and Stryke stopped quickly at his apartment on the Île Saint-Louis, where he changed into fresh jeans, a T-shirt and leather jacket. Blyss's brother didn't ask for clarification on the food debacle. He wasn't stupid. And Stryke appreciated the man's discretion, even though he was bursting with questions.

Such questions being: What were the packs like in Europe? Were they big, small, located in the cities or country? Was pack structure the same as in the US with the principal leading the pack followed by his scion as second-in-command? Did they have as big a tiff with the vampires as the wolves back in the States? Granted, the werewolves and vampires were supposed to be peaceable, but that was more PR than actually put into practice.

And were the pack females as prized here in Europe as in the United States? So much so that only a rare few male wolves actually married their own breed because of the shortage of females.

And while he'd picked up that Kir was none too pleased with his sister's lifestyle choice, he wanted to ask why Kir hadn't tried to keep her in the pack, maybe to teach her more about the life. Had anyone taught her how to actually be a wolf? Because while it was mostly instinctual, there was a lot to deal with if the wolf had grown up in human society and had to learn to hide their true nature. Which apparently Blyss had not been taught.

Hadn't her mother talked to her about coming into her shift? It was a basic fact-of-life talk. They must not be close. He'd not forgotten the gibe the siblings had made about their mother not caring. Stryke was thankful his family was so close. And even though his mother was faery, the mixed blood that ran within his siblings' veins had only fortified their understanding and acceptance of other breeds. There weren't a hell of a lot of breeds the Saint-Pierres didn't associate with.

Except demons. That breed was nasty.

Kir drove a small but sturdy black SUV toward the 9th arrondissement, where the nightclub was located. It was eleven in the evening and he'd warned that the club would be crowded and loud. A good time to sneak around.

"I care about your sister," Stryke felt the urge to say over the low background noise of the talk radio. "We came together in a weird way, but trust me, I only want what's best for her. And I want to do what I can to keep her safe and protect her."

"I get that about you," Kir said, one wrist resting on the steering wheel as he navigated the Parisian traffic. "Do you love her?"

"I've only known her a short time. Love is…big."

Kir nodded knowingly. "That it is. Blyss is a tough person to understand. She's made an odd life choice, but I love her no matter what. She's my blood."

"Do you think she would have chosen differently if,

I don't know, she hadn't such a traumatic first shifting experience?"

"I remember that incident. It did scar her. I wish I had been in school at the time, but I'm ten years older than her and at the time was already out working with the Enforcers. And our mother has never been a hands-on compassionate sort of woman. That incident definitely shaped Blyss into what she is today. I can't say I understand her choice, though. It offends me that she doesn't want anything to do with our breed. And yet, today I stop by her place and discover her latest lover is a wolf. So she can surprise me."

Thinking about how she had surrendered to their spur-of-the-moment food fight, Stryke had to agree. The woman was indeed surprising.

"I don't want Thrash to hurt her," he said. "We need to find the black diamond. And after that, well…"

Kir cast him a glance. "Well?"

"Just well. I intend to head back to Minnesota once I know Blyss is safe. I've been tasked to start my own pack by my father. So…I'm in the market for a wife. But if I had a reason to stay in Paris awhile longer? Well then."

"I get the wife search. I'd love to marry a werewolf, but the only way that will happen around here is usually arranged."

"My grandfather is in an arranged marriage. They are still madly in love."

"Good to hear. I'll remember that should I ever be faced with the situation. I like you, Saint-Pierre. If you have a chance, I'd like to introduce you to my pack. You'd get along with my best friend Jacques."

"That would be cool. I'd like to learn more about the Enforcers. I graduated from the police academy back home, but when it came time to get a job I realized I couldn't do it. Entry level was desk work. I couldn't bring myself to work with humans, even though they surely need the help as much as we do. I want to work with my own kind, protecting them. We need it."

"You could start an enforcement agency back home."

"It's an idea. Might be the thing to help build a new pack, as well. The place is right up there." Stryke pointed out the club with the black metal door.

"Yep. Been inside that club too many times to admit to. But only for a case, never because the skeevy vampire chicks turn me on." He winked and got out of the parked car. The streets were crowded with young human partyers, but Stryke sensed paranormals mingled among the mix.

"The club usually only allows in paranormals," Kir said as they strode toward the doors. "But they admit pretty human women for the vamps to feed on. The humans aren't aware, but then again, some are and return for the bite. Fang junkies."

"When Blyss and I were here the other day it was dead. We didn't find anything, but the scent trail from Hawkes Associates was unmistakable right until I reached the main room inside."

"Then we need to go deeper," Kir said.

The bouncer was different than the one who had let Stryke in previously. The bruiser sporting deadly studs—on his forearms, not his leather vest—looked Kir and Stryke up and down, then nodded and opened the door. Demons could scent out any breed, including humans.

"So the devil Himself owns this place?" Stryke asked as they strode down the dark hallway.

"Don't say that name again," Kir cautioned as they

paused before the main dance floor. "Say it three times and you've invited that bastard for lunch."

"Got it. I think the back rooms are beyond the stage over there." Stryke sniffed. "I can pick out the familiar scent. I don't think they're here. It's lingered that long. Definitely leads back that way."

"Then let's follow your nose. Take the lead, man."

They pushed through the crush of dancers and to the darkened depths that led through the doorway and turned into a maze of dark hallways. When Stryke sensed someone walking toward them, he slipped behind a black velvet curtain and Kir followed. They waited until what smelled faery to Stryke passed and then sneaked out.

Stryke followed the demonic scent he'd originally picked up at the wedding and at Hawkes Associates. It was barely there, but cloying enough that he didn't feel he was wrong. It wasn't difficult to hold the scent either, despite the thump of drums in his heart, and the rush of adrenaline passing through the dance floor had ignited in his system.

When they landed upon a dead-end wall painted with glow-in-the-dark graffiti, Stryke stepped onto a metal plate and jumped, testing the floor. "A door," he decided. "Going down."

Knowing the devil Himself owned the place and finding a door going down didn't sit well with him. Stryke reminded himself he wasn't here to play scared. In fact, he had wanted to find danger here in Paris. And here it was. "Shall we?"

"After you," Kir said with a glance the way they had come.

A steel staircase descended straight down within a tunnel, so Stryke could stand upright, stepping down and balancing himself with his hands against the curved steel wall before him. It was claustrophobic, but he felt cooler air rising from below. After descending about thirty feet, he sensed he was close to landing.

Both men arrived on a solid dirt floor and stood underground in the dark, surrounded by steel walls and an icy chill. The thumping beat from the overhead club was now but a murmur inside Stryke's veins.

"It's been built up," Kir noted. "Most tunnels under the city are carved out of the limestone. Interesting."

They sniffed to take in the surroundings.

"This way," Stryke said, veering left. Kir followed. "Just ahead. The scent grows stronger."

A dim light marked a room that was closed off by iron bars. The bars were spaced so wide that Stryke and Kir were able to slip through them and look about. Everything was dark and either steel or blackened metal. The walls were impressed with markings, as was the ceiling. Looked tribal, or at the least, some definite design. Stryke noticed that the floor featured a geometric design, fitted in the dirt floor with black metal ribbons, that traced to the center of the room—where the silver scepter had been placed in a keyhole that looked as though it had been made specifically for it.

"Why does this remind me of every horror or creature flick I've ever seen?" Stryke commented.

"If that doesn't give you the creeps, check that out."

Kir gestured to the wall behind them. In the dimness beyond closer-spaced iron bars were living beings. In cages. Glowing red eyes peered out at them. Four pairs.

"This can't be good," Stryke said. "They've begun to collect the demons for the sacrifice."

Chapter 15

The apartment felt vast and empty now that the men had gone. It was almost as if each had lifted up his own air and carried it out with him. And the air that surrounded Stryke Saint-Pierre was fresh and new and yet it occupied so much space, Blyss could feel his absence painfully.

As she finished cleaning up the food from the floors, walls and counters, she lamented such strange emotions. What was that about?

She didn't miss men. She used men.

Since her early twenties, when she had decided to live as a human among humans—and knew it would require a certain income as werewolf daughters were rarely taught marketable job skills; yes, the medieval ways still ruled in most packs—she had trained herself to carefully select a man as her lover, someone who possessed esteem, money and who got bored quickly.

Blyss didn't want to become *the girlfriend*. She enjoyed being the lover. Besides, it was dangerous when men started to develop feelings toward her. She preferred to take the jewels, thank them with a sexy weekend and then stride out of their lives.

Until Stryke had pushed her up against the wall and changed her mind.

Everything about the man was nothing she had ever been interested in. And yet it didn't matter to her at all that he wasn't rich. She preferred his down-home sensibility and everyman qualities. It didn't matter that he'd never bring her a five-hundred-euro bottle of champagne. He liked to lick the cheap stuff off her skin. And that was a thousand times more satisfying.

It might not even matter that he was werewolf.

Maybe?

Blyss sat back against the kitchen counter. She'd scrubbed the floor clean. She tossed the sponge in the bucket of dirty water. She couldn't remember when she'd last done manual labor. It should appall her. Yet she could only feel a sense of satisfaction as she looked over the gleaming marble floor.

Leaning forward, she studied her reflection in a beam of moonlight that mirrored the marble surface. What she saw was a woman who tried to wear her mask with perfection so others would never see the ugly creature lurking beneath.

"But he's not ugly," she whispered.

In fact, she was curious about Stryke's wolf. She wanted to see him shifted, both as a four-legged wolf and as the powerful werewolf that walked as a man on two legs. She wanted to smell his carnal desire for her. To feel his power and know his strength. She wanted to be owned by Stryke Saint-Pierre in every way possible.

And she realized what hidden part of her actually felt those desires. Her wolf. It had to be. Because the socialite Blyss Sauveterre, masquerading as a human woman, would never consider a werewolf anything but a foul and disgusting creature.

She glanced around the counter and up the side of the stainless-steel fridge where the iPad hung on a rack; it served as her digital calendar. Less than three days before the full moon. It hadn't been a year since she'd last shifted to werewolf. She didn't need to make the shift this month. But she would be forced to if *Le Diabolique* was not found and she could not hand it over to Ed.

Maybe she didn't need the crutch of the pills anymore? Could she…accept her werewolf?

She shook her head, catching a spill of hair against her palm. "What am I thinking? Just because a handsome wolf has snuck into my heart doesn't mean I need to start thinking crazy."

Because without the pills she would revert to werewolf and would need to shift. Every month.

She pressed a palm over her heart. Indeed, Stryke had found a way inside, beneath the mask and into her soul. She felt him there. Wanted to keep him there.

Which complicated things.

Why was she listening to her heart instead of the exacting, rational, and yes, even conniving, socialite who knew what had to be done to survive?

If she was honest with herself, it felt good to allow her heart the lead. She hadn't done so—well, ever. And she missed Stryke. She needed him here, holding her, kissing her, calling her glamour girl.

So what did that mean?

"I think I'm in love," she whispered.

And the realization hurt something far more fragile than her heart. It wounded her very soul.

They decided to leave the caged demons as they were. They appeared drugged because none tried to fight and speak to them. There was no sign of the diamond. Kir walked around the scepter placed in the center of the floor. They couldn't touch it without something to protect them from the silver.

Stryke pulled off his shirt and wrapped it about the scepter, but try as he might, it would not budge. "It's as if it's been riveted into the floor."

"Leave it," Kir said.

They left the underground demon lair with the intention of tracking, but the scents stopped outside the club.

"We'll check back when we learn more," Stryke said.

"I'll check the database and get back to you."

Instead of having Kir drop him at his place, Stryke said he wanted to check in with Blyss and help her clean because he was pretty sure she might be baffled by the whole cleaning process.

Kir chuckled knowingly and said he'd be in touch. He would check his sources regarding local demon nests and call if he found a lead.

Meanwhile, Rhys called. Stryke answered his phone while standing inside the main door that led to the courtyard before Blyss's building. "Rhys, what's up?"

"Tor has more items that need a pickup. Listen, I know this isn't the glamorous security detail I had offered you, but the work does come up occasionally."

"It's cool, Rhys. I'm glad to help out. Is it something I need to dash off to right now?"

"No, actually Tor wants to catalog the items first.

I told him to give you a call when it's ready. Probably tomorrow."

"Sounds good. More demon stuff?"

"No, this is related to the *sidhe*. Not sure what it is exactly. Are you still tracking the scepter?"

"I found it, but wasn't able to retrieve it. Just got back from following a lead that took us below Club l'Enfer. It was like wandering through the bowels of hell down there."

"Be careful, Stryke. You're treading Himself's territory."

"Yeah, but tell me why the dark bad guy would have an interest in releasing an all-powerful demon from some big diamond? I mean, wouldn't that be competition?"

"Does sound odd. You suspect it was demons who stole both the scepter and the diamond?"

"Ninety-nine percent sure. I tracked their scent both from your office and the wedding. Definitely demon."

"They could be working on their own. Independent of…you know who." As Kir had stated, it was never wise to mention Himself's name more than once. "The only demon I know right now that has any control over the local denizens is Edamite Thrash."

"Yeah, he's oddly involved in all this, but I don't think he stole either of the items."

"He surely sent lackeys."

"Maybe." Then why even press Blyss to bring him the diamond if Thrash had others steal it for him? Didn't make sense. "I've hooked up with Blyss's brother, Kir Sauveterre."

"Ah yes, from the Valoir pack. Good bunch of wolves. They enforce in the city, yes?"

"Yes, they do. Sounds like a cool job. We need to organize something like that in the States. Anyway, I'll wait for Tor's call. Thanks, Rhys. Let me know if you get any ideas about this situation. The clock is ticking. I have a sense it's all going down on the night of the full moon."

"Doesn't give you much time. I should mention, I've a cabin about an hour out of the city you can use on the night of the full moon if you're still in Paris then. Leagues and leagues of forest surrounding it. All private land. You interested?"

"Hell yes. Thanks, Rhys. You've been so generous, I'm not sure how I'll ever repay you."

"You already are, Stryke. Talk to you soon."

He knocked on Blyss's door and opened it, calling out to her. A gorgeous vision in white came running down the hallway. Stryke immediately sensed danger and grabbed her, hugging her against his chest, as he scanned the hallway behind her. Instincts lifted his head, sniffing for danger.

"What is it?" he asked. His heart thundered, yet he didn't sense another presence in the apartment.

"I missed you," she said.

"What?"

He lifted her and she wrapped her legs about his hips as he strolled down the hallway into the spotless kitchen. She'd cleaned up herself? He walked into the living room and sat with her still attached to him.

"What's wrong, Blyss?"

"Nothing's wrong. And everything's wrong." She hugged up to him and tilted her head against his shoulder. "I missed you desperately."

"Is that the part where nothing is wrong or everything is wrong?"

"It's both." She bracketed her hands aside his head

to stare into his eyes. "The whole time you were gone I could only think of you. I didn't even mind the cleaning part. I actually found it rewarding. But my thoughts were on you. If you were safe. If you and my brother were getting along. If you would return to me. You came back to me."

"I wanted to make sure you were okay." And see if she needed help. Which she had not. And she'd been thinking of him the whole time? "You were worried I wouldn't return?"

She nodded. "You've changed my heart, Stryke." She hugged him again, this time tightly. "I think I love you."

"Whoa." While having a woman declare her love for him was an amazing thing, Stryke couldn't imagine she was thinking straight. Must have inhaled fumes from the cleaning spray. "What happened to down with the wolves? I'm pretty sure werewolf isn't tops on your list of potential love interests."

"It doesn't matter to me what you are. Oh, I know this sounds crazy. You don't have to love me back. I just wanted to say it, to feel it on my tongue. And it felt great. It feels right."

"Glamour girl." He tilted his forehead against hers. "I do love your surprises."

"Did you find out anything?" she asked.

Much as he wanted to bask in her confession, Stryke nodded. "Kir and I found a lair. Inside were caged demons. And the scepter. We tried to take the scepter, but it was fixed into a weird mechanism."

"What about *Le Diabolique*?"

"No sight of it. I'm thinking the only way to find that might be to set a trap. Locate one of the twelve demons on the list Libby gave us and sit in wait for whoever comes for it. But even that is an iffy plan. Who's to say the guy in charge will go for that particular demon? Much as I hate to admit it, I'm at a loss what to do. But your brother is looking into his contacts."

"I'm glad the two of you get along."

"Kir's a good guy. He invited me to come meet the pack."

"Valoir is a noble pack that goes back for half a dozen generations. They are good people." She sighed. "If you can overlook my mother. But even she has some favorable moments, I'm sure."

"I don't want to meet anyone from Valoir without you at my side."

"Then I'm afraid that will never happen."

"Hey." He traced a curl of dark hair that tickled along her cheek. She was so soft and smelled like precious things. "I don't want to force you to change or to be something you're not. But you did make an exception for me."

"I have. I think I even want to meet your wolf."

"Really? What have you been smoking, Blyss? Must have been some strong chemicals in those cleaning products. You've had a drastic change of heart."

"I think you got inside me."

"Well." He pumped his hips against her legs. He did have an erection, but that was impossible to avoid when holding her.

"In more ways than the physical," she reiterated. "And I have to face the fact that you might never find the diamond. In a few days the world I've created for myself might forever change. I may have to face my own wolf."

"I'm doing everything I can to stop that from happening, lover."

"And why are you doing that? You, the man who

told me he wants to settle down with a wolf and raise a pack of his own. You can't possibly fall in love with me. And I've told you happily-ever-after is out of the question. Why are you helping me, Stryke?"

Why, indeed? *Did* he feel more for her than lust and adoration? Could he possibly be falling in love with the wrong woman? The one woman who was completely the opposite of his ideal mate?

No. He wasn't stupid. He'd entered into this relationship knowing full well it could never satisfy him. It was a fling. In a few more days he'd leave Paris for home, destined to pine for a werewolf wife who may never become reality.

But until then.

"You deserve kindness," he said and kissed her nose. "And I want to see you happy. Even if that means you'll never howl again."

She tilted her head against his shoulder. "I haven't howled for a long time."

"If you get your supply restocked before the full moon, you won't shift?"

She shook her head.

"So you don't need sex the days before and after the full moon?"

All werewolves felt the compulsion to shift the day before the full moon, the day of and the day following. Generally, they tried to shift only one day a month. The werewolf needed that release. But as well, to shift more often was risky. Living among humans required a delicate balance between their wereself and the animal within. And the only way to calm the inner wolf on the days before and after the full moon was to have sex until satiated. It was a nice bonus.

"I don't need to satiate my wolf," Blyss said. "But I would love to be there to help you satisfy yours."

Score! Maybe he wouldn't need the cottage in the woods Rhys had offered, after all. But there was still the night of the full moon. He had to shift. Stryke would never deny that instinctual desire.

"I'll take you up on that offer," he said. "But tell me this. What if you don't get your pills?"

"Then my wolf will come out, and...I'll have to face it."

He hugged her against him, feeling her tiny shiver. She didn't want that. He would love to see her unleashed and wild. But he knew such a release wasn't in Blyss Sauveterre's nature. If he respected her, he'd allow her to be the woman she felt she needed to be.

He tilted his back against the sofa cushion and closed his eyes. It was nice sitting here with her, holding her, feeling her heartbeats against his chest. Comfortable.

A wrong comfort.

So why did it feel so right?

Stryke woke with Blyss in his arms. They'd crawled into bed with a few kisses, but hadn't undressed because sex hadn't been important. Closeness had been. He must have slept the whole night with her hand clasped in his. Generally he tossed and turned. Last night had been peaceful.

What was up with him and his inability to simply walk away from this impossible woman? He liked her. He needed to remain cautious with her. He understood the reasons for why she did what she did. And that allowed the caution to slip away. He wanted to hold her whenever she would allow it. And snuggle up to her and feel her delicate warmth relaxed against him.

Could he be falling in love? He'd fallen in love a few times. With human women. It had happened quickly, and he'd enjoyed the feeling, but inside he had always known that it could never last. Love didn't have to mean forever. People came together all the time, fell in love and then drifted apart. It was how the world worked. And he'd known from the start this particular relationship had an expiration date.

Sure, werewolves married human. But it took a strong human woman to accept a man who, once a month, shape-shifted into a man/wolf creature and who liked to race through the forest, howl at the moon and even track, kill and eat small animals.

And there were his werewolf's heightened sexual desires. He simply demanded more from a woman in bed. Of which, Blyss had responded beautifully. It was probably because she was wolf. Sort of wolf. Even though she took pills to suppress the wolf, her true nature had to exist within her. There was no changing that.

Was there?

He'd love to bring out the wolf in her. But he didn't want to force her. So that meant he had to accept her as she preferred to be. He could do that. Maybe. Could he? Did he have a chance at a long-term relationship with this woman?

He stroked her hair down her back. Soft morning light glittered on her pale skin.

He suspected even if things did work out with them, it could never last. His home was in Minnesota. Her home was Paris. She'd made it very clear she wasn't up for the country cottage and the kids.

Or the happy ending.

Though maybe one or two kids? They could grow

up bilingual and have the manners of a city slicker yet the instincts and call to the wild.

What was he doing? Already planning children with her? If Blyss could read his thoughts she'd laugh and toss back her gorgeous tousle of hair.

No, she was one classy glamour girl. Wolf or not, she belonged at cocktail parties dressed in fabulous gowns and dripping with diamonds. He could never give her the luxury, of which she expected and thrived upon.

So he wouldn't allow his heart to make the leap. That big leap into love that he knew lingered so close. It would be difficult. He was more suited for difficulties such as facing down demons with claws bared and yeah, even the occasional couch-talk-down with a brother who had just been dumped and wanted to punch everything in sight.

He leaned in and kissed the line of Blyss's shoulder blade through the white blouse. She smelled like a flower, of which he would never learn its name. The whole room smelled like a garden. He wondered if whatever flower it was would grow in Minnesota. If so, he'd plant a whole field for her in hopes to win her everlasting affection.

"Morning already?" she whispered and rolled onto her back.

He kissed her forehead and swept away the hair from her face. She wasn't wearing makeup and her green eyes sparkled as if stars. He liked her natural and soft. Unguarded. She seemed more vulnerable, yet also stronger. Because this was simply Blyss unhampered by the mask of makeup and jewels.

"You're beautiful, glamour girl," he said. "I like waking up next to you."

"Could you imagine waking next to the same person for decades?" she whispered, closed her eyes. "I can."

"I can, too." He turned onto his back, staring up through the windows. Clasping her hand, he held it over his stomach. "I might have to run out to do a job for Rhys today. But if I'm not busy I'd like to hang around here. If that's cool with you?"

"I do have some business at the gallery. Insurance stuff regarding *Le Diabolique*. But that can wait until you leave. I'd offer to make you breakfast and we could have a romantic tête-à-tête, but I suspect there's nothing in the fridge."

"Not after yesterday. I'll run out for those *pains au chocolat* that all the women seem to like. Maybe some chai, too. I miss that stuff. Usually drink it every day at home."

"Tell me about your life back in Minnesota. I don't know much about you."

He kissed her and sat up, stretching out a kink with a twist of his back. "I'll fill you in on all the boring details over breakfast. Mind if I hop in the shower quick?"

"Go ahead. Grab some fresh towels from the closet. I'm going to linger in your warmth."

She spread a hand across the sheet where he had sat. Stryke wouldn't have been surprised if a purr had accompanied her kittenish move.

"You make lingering look so damn gorgeous." He strolled into the closet and at sight of the regimented contents let out an appreciative whistle. "Wow."

"Oh, that's the wrong closet," Blyss called. "The towels are in the other one on this side of the bed."

"No kidding?" He took in the rows and rows—and rows—of shoes in the closet that was as large as a living room. The woman had a serious shoe addiction.

He backed out, the awe setting him slightly off-kilter as he stumbled into the bedroom. "You have a room just for shoes."

She nodded and tucked the sheet up around her smile.

"How many do you own?"

An innocent shrug. "Hundreds?"

Again he couldn't resist a whistle. Women and their shoes. It was some kind of sacred thing he would never understand. Shaking his head, he found the right closet, grabbed a towel and headed into the bathroom.

An hour later, they sat in the living room finishing off the flaky pastries. The patisserie had also offered chai with fresh cream, much to Stryke's thrill. He'd brought some for Blyss, who had never tried it.

"Good stuff, right?" He liked his spiked with extra clove.

"*Exquis.* You've made me a convert from coffee."

"I'll show you how to make it homemade. I have a secret spice blend recipe that will knock you off your feet."

She bobbed one of her crossed legs, the pink marabou-fluffed slipper dusting the air. Totally *Green Acres.* But he wouldn't tell her that. He didn't mind looking at those gorgeous ankles and the pretty things with which she liked to decorate her feet.

"So you wanted to know about my exciting life?" he prompted.

"It has to be more interesting than mine. Trust me, it may look glamorous, but I can only drink so many glasses of champagne and chatter about the latest designer's affair with a supermodel so many times before I want to gag."

"Try chopping wood and digging six-foot-deep holes

in the ground for a fence I've been putting in around my property."

"Don't they have a machine that can do that for you?"

"Sure, but I like the manual labor. And…I've not a job, so it keeps me busy."

"You've no desire to hold a job?"

"Not really. I shouldn't say that. I did attend the police academy. Had big dreams of protecting and serving and all that jazz."

"But?"

"But the idea of starting out behind a desk and answering phone dispatch calls turned me off real fast. And I realized I couldn't be happy wearing a gun at my hip and protecting humans. I'm more interested in working with my own breed. No offense against humans. I get along with them fine. Have to. But your brother's job does interest me."

"Perhaps you could establish an enforcement team back home?"

"Your brother suggested the same thing, and I'm liking the idea. As soon as I get that fence in. Gotta keep the coyotes out of my chicken coop."

"Really? You don't get along with that breed?"

"Not the mangy bunch I've got lurking about the farm. Tried scaring them off with my werewolf one night and they ran, but came right back. Idiots. But I won't trap them. That's cruel. Once I get the fence up I'll hang some bright flags on it and that'll keep them away."

"Living on a farm sounds like a lot of work."

"Probably a lot less work than trying to keep up appearances for the rich and snooty," he commented without thinking. And then he did think. "Oh. Er, I, uh…"

Blyss sighed. "I get it. But rich and snooty is all I know."

"I'm sorry." His cell phone rang. Saved by the bell. An unknown number. "Excuse me. I should check this."

Blyss finished the last sips of chai as he talked.

"Hey, Kir, good to hear from you. What's up? A lead? Yes, I can meet you. Uh, not my place. You can pick me up at your sister's place. See you in ten."

He hung up.

"I suppose Kir is over the moon that I've a werewolf lover," Blyss commented, but she said it with a smile.

"I think he's too polite to make a comment like that. He cares about you, Blyss."

"I know that. I wish I could see him more often, but he has to come to me. I won't go near the pack. So what are you two up to now?"

"Kir has a lead on demon activity. We're going to drive over and check it out. You okay to be alone?"

"Of course," she answered quickly. "But will you call me later?"

"I will." He kissed her and then lingered at her mouth, his lips barely touching hers. "You taste like chai. Mmm, I could drink you. Can we do a date night? After I get back from this, and I might have that thing to do for Rhys, but later, can we do something together?"

"What did you have in mind?"

"I still haven't found time to see the Eiffel Tower."

"How about a dining cruise? You board right in front of the tower, eat and drink as you cruise down the river. Then you arrive back at the tower just as it lights up for the evening. It's a little touristy but I've always been fascinated by the idea of cruising the Seine at night. I'll make a reservation."

"Sounds cool. I'll see you later. Do I have to dress up?"

"A suit might be— Uh, no. Just be yourself." She hooked a finger under his jeans' waistband. "I like you in jeans. Especially when they sit low and show your muscles."

"But a suit would be more appropriate?"

"Those cruises are filled with all sorts, from locals looking for a fancy evening out to tourists in jeans and sweatshirts. I'll even dress down. Nothing sparkly or glittery. Promise."

"I kind of like you sparkly. Make the shoes sparkly, okay?"

"Now, that I can manage."

His kiss wrapped about her heart with a tangible hug. Blyss didn't want the feeling to end, so she followed him down the hallway, lips locked and feet stumbling as he walked backward. Stryke's back hit the front door. Blyss stepped up on tiptoes and tasted him deeply. She never wanted to lose the taste of him.

Her werewolf lover.

Chapter 16

The lead Kir had provided led the men to traverse the sewers of Paris. Stryke shook his head at his incredible luck. He'd seen some seedy parts of the city while here. Guess the City of Love wasn't so romantic once you peeled back its layers. But he didn't mind. The aqueducts were fascinating. He knew they'd been in existence for centuries and was instantly thankful for modern-day plumbing.

They walked along the river, underground, the city above them. The stone aqueduct ceiling arched over this narrow section that was more sewer than actual river, as Kir explained.

"These aqueducts maze all under the city," Kir said, noting Stryke's interest. "And don't get me started on the underground tunnels that twist and twine some seven stories below the city."

"Really? Deeper than the demon lair we found? That's cool."

"There's a whole legion of humans that call them-selves cataphiles, who explore, party and even live be-neath the depths of Paris. Some of the demons who are incapable of pulling on a humanlike glamour also live underground. You don't want to mess with those horns."

"I imagine not. So this is a gang of demons you've heard that are stealing valuable artifacts?"

"We call them denizens," Kir said. "Large groups of demons that follow one particular leader. Like a vam-pire tribe or a werewolf pack. This particular denizen is headed by a wraith."

"Is a wraith actually a demon? I thought wraiths were ghosts or spirits." Stryke ducked to pass under a particu-larly low section of ceiling formed by arched limestone.

Kir came out on the other side and stopped before a rusted iron door that had a big red symbol drawn on it.

"A wraith demon moves like a ghost but it's solid and deadly. It's powerful and wields some wicked tal-ons. No lower jaw, either," Kir added. "Nasty things. So you got any weapons on you? Salt?"

Stryke shook his head and chuckled. What kind of idiots walked into a demon nest unarmed? "You got me, man. I'm so unprepared for this mess I stumbled into in Paris."

"I suspect you probably didn't stumble so much as fell under my sister's allure. You must really like Blyss to be doing this, Saint-Pierre."

"It might be more than that."

"Right. You said you're looking to start a pack. You think hooking up with a werewolf who denies her heri-tage is such a wise move?"

"I know Blyss likes her men rich and *human*. But right now I've got her attention and we're having some fun together. She deserves whatever I can do to help her out of this situation."

"Damn, I wish you lived in Paris. You'd be good for my sister."

"I don't think she'd care for my idea of living in the country. In fact, she's already made it very clear she would not."

"She is abrupt." Kir rapped the door, avoiding the red marking. "This is a demon sigil drawn in..." He sniffed at the red mark. "...human blood."

"Nice," Stryke said with no appreciation whatsoever.

"I think it best if we stay as far from the nest as possible but get close enough to see if we can pick up a scent trail," Kir said. "You'd recognize the scent, yes?"

"Of course. I'm still thinking about our lack of weapons, though. How to fight a demon?"

"Move fast, and if you can help it, don't bite them. Demon blood won't kill us but it is nasty."

"Got it. So are we going to shift?"

"Much as I'd like to, I think it's wiser to keep our wits about us."

"Yeah? My wits are fine when I'm shifted. If we're overwhelmed, I've got your back, but it's going to be in werewolf form. I can promise you that."

"Deal."

"You want to lead the way?"

Kir stepped aside and gestured toward the door. "I thought I'd give you that pleasure since you're the guy with the nose."

"Sure thing." Stryke tilted his head side to side, snapping the kinks out of the muscles. With a shrug of his shoulders he bolstered up his courage.

Thing was, all the courage in the world wouldn't save him from a creature who served a wraith or even the devil Himself. He flexed his fingers, feeling the tingle of his werewolf *right there*. Close, if he needed it. It took only seconds to shift.

"Hey!"

Both men turned to spy a tall, dark-haired man dressed all in black striding down the narrow aqueduct ledge.

Stryke scented him before he recognized the hematite glint at his temples. "Thrash." He fisted a palm and set back his shoulders.

"Dial it down," Kir cautioned as he stepped around Stryke and offered his hand.

Edamite Thrash shook Kir's hand and the two greeted one another as old friends.

What. The. Hell?

Blyss paced in the kitchen, unsure what to do with herself. Something felt off about the diamond situation. *Le Diabolique* had been missing for days now, and the original owner had not checked to reclaim the borrowed property.

In fact, she was baffled why the police and detectives hadn't knocked down her door yet. And then she realized she couldn't quite place a name to the person who had loaned her gallery the diamond.

Where had it come from? Had the owner known it contained a demon? Maybe that person had wanted it to be stolen and eventually unleashed on the city?

Crazy thoughts. But really, when one had possession of a diamond that contained a demon, could anything be more crazy?

"I need to check the paperwork."

And while most of the gallery's paperwork was digitized and accessible from her home computer, this particular acquisition was not in the records. Further weirdness.

So she dashed on some eyeliner and lipstick, slipped her feet into a pair of red leather Jimmy Choos and headed off to the gallery to try to figure out this mess.

"You're working with the wrong side, Sauveterre," Stryke said as he strode up to Thrash and Kir. "This asshole kidnapped me the other day and he's extorting your sister."

"Yeah, about that." Kir punched the demon in the jaw.

"Seriously?" Stryke asked as Thrash shook off the iron-fisted hit with a red-eyed smirk. "So why the friendly handshake? You knew what he was doing to Blyss."

"Ed and I go way back. He's okay," Kir said. "Except when he screws with my sister."

"Hey!" Ed put up his palms to ward off the next imminent hit. "Kirnan, you know I respect Blyss. I would do anything for her. She came to me. We've had this business arrangement for years. I am helping her."

"Helping her?" Stryke wanted to be the next in line for the punch. "If she doesn't pay you half a million by the full moon you've threatened to kill her family. That would be your family too, Kir."

This time Thrash's body soared with the punch that Stryke delivered. The demon's head and shoulders hit the limestone wall and he collapsed in a heap before the men.

Stryke rubbed his knuckles and cast Kir a sidelong glance. "Your priorities when it comes to friendship are questionable."

"I know he's been supplying Blyss," Kir said. "I

didn't realize he was making threats. He's…" The were-wolf bowed his head and said in tight tones, "…sort of family."

"What?"

Kir rubbed his jaw, thinking for a moment as the demon shook his head, attempting to pull out of the bruising punch Stryke had delivered him.

"Blyss doesn't know this," Kir said, "but years ago, when my father was forced out of the pack because he was having an affair with a vampire…"

"Yeah?"

"Me and the old man had a good long talk. He's into more than vampires. Demons are his first choice when it comes to women."

"Don't tell me. He had an affair with Thrash's mom?"

Kir nodded. "Long time ago. We're half brothers."

"Yikes." Stryke didn't know what to say to that one.

"We've been—well, I wouldn't call it friends, but it's something—since learning about one another. We keep each other up on the weird and wacky family we've been meshed into. But we decided to keep it from Blyss. She likes to stay as far away from the paranormal realm as possible. She hates being a wolf. Can you imagine what it would do to her if she learned Thrash was her half brother?"

"Apparently Thrash wasn't going to tell you about the threat to your family. And I suspect family includes you."

Kir lifted Thrash by the back of his shirt and pushed him against the wall. The demon spat black blood to the side. "What's gotten into you?"

"It's *Le Diabolique*," Thrash said. "I need to keep it out of the wrong hands."

"What?" Stryke shoved a hand against Thrash's

shoulder and Kir stepped aside. "Blyss said you wanted to release the demon within the diamond."

"Great Beelzebub, no! That stone imprisons Xyloda from this realm. That demon gets out, I'm finished. I want to keep it out of the wrong hands. I should have never trusted Blyss could handle the snatch. Why the hell did she give it to you?"

Stryke shook his head. "I'm two pages behind you, buddy. This whole affair confuses me. So you want the diamond to keep the demon inside? But right now some demons have both the diamond and the demon scepter. And yesterday, Kir and I found the lair where they're going to perform the release ritual. They've already got demons caged and waiting for the sacrifice."

"Merde." Ed pushed down his shirtsleeves and pressed a thumb to his mouth in thought. His hand, which was concealed by a black leather half glove, revealed dark scrawls on the fingers that looked like tattoos, but Stryke felt sure they were far more evil in nature. "Where was the lair?"

"Beneath Club l'Enfer," Kir said. He met Stryke's castigating expression with a shrug. "Believe it or not, he *is* on our side."

"This asshole had his thugs work me over. Punches intended for your sister. He was going to hurt Blyss."

"I would never hurt her. She's my half sister. I…" The demon shook off what he was going to say. "The pills she takes are expensive, and I do have my own finances to manage. But I had to make the threats to ensure she actually did it. If she doesn't bring me the stone she won't get the pills she so desperately desires. I sure as hell won't lay a finger on any of her family members. Including you, Kir. But without those pills you might have a howling werewolf on your hands in a few days." Ed arrowed his gaze on Stryke. "Bet you'll be thrilled about that, eh, country boy?"

This time Stryke's punch knocked out Thrash and toppled him to the right. The demon's body teetered toward the river. Kir managed to catch his half brother by the wrist as his legs slipped into the Seine.

"I know you're angry," Kir said as he struggled to hold the unconscious demon above water, "but we can work with him. We'll make him pay later for being cruel to my sister, and the threats."

"What? With a brotherly punch? I know how that works."

"Just chill, will you? We can trust him. Right now Thrash is the closest connection we have to whoever might have stolen the diamond. We need him."

"Fine." Stryke bent and reached for the demon's pant leg and helped Kir hoist him onto the cobbled sidewalk. He stepped back and leaned against the wall, catching a palm against his forehead. "If the lair was in the club owned by Himself, why don't we go straight to the source? The devil is obviously behind this. Let's just call him here. The Old Lad, right?"

"Dude, no. Don't say it—"

"Himself!" Stryke called. "We need to talk. Himself!"

"Merde," Ed said as he sat up. "Tell me he didn't say that name three times?"

"You rang?" a sepulchral voice echoed from down the way.

Chapter 17

Before heading into the office, Blyss unlocked the door to the acquisitions closet, which was a small room where she stored all items received before placing them in the gallery. It was built like a safe, with two-foot-thick walls and a digital keypad that was supposed to reset the password every day, which she got updates for on her mobile.

On the night of the Marie Antoinette exhibit, she had slipped in early, replaced *Le Diabolique* with a fake and then placed the real diamond in her desk drawer until she knew she could return later with a dupe. Someone who could carry the diamond out of the museum without a clue.

Stryke was no dupe. But he had, unfortunately, served a purpose. Too well. She never could have anticipated the diamond being stolen from him at the wedding. Or that those who had taken it would be demons.

"Such a mess," she muttered as she stepped into the dark room and flicked on the lights. A Rembrandt sat upon an easel waiting for next weekend's showing. In the center of the room, sitting under a glass case on a pedestal also made of glass, sat...

"Where is it?"

She lifted the glass cube and set it on the floor. Bending before the pedestal, Blyss examined the empty platform, her eye searching for fingerprints. She'd worn black gloves when replacing the real stone with the fake.

Someone had stolen the fake?

"They must have thought it was the real thing. More demons?"

She stood and pressed a hand to her chest. What the hell was going on? And who had gotten into this locked room with no noticeable signs of forced entry?

She turned and inspected the lock and the interior door frame. Pristine. No scratches in the metal sheathing. Her eyes took in the small room from every corner of the ceiling, down the walls and along the baseboards. There were no security cameras. She hadn't felt them necessary in this safe room. A vent near the floor was too small for anyone to access.

Unless they could shape-shift.

Blyss gasped on her own breath. A demon had been here. Had to have been. She sniffed the air, then cursed her inability to detect minute scents that Stryke or any of her breed might do with ease.

Closing the door and marching down the hallway toward the office, she cursed loudly. She did not like losing control. Someone had taken that away from her when the diamond had been stolen at the wedding. And again when stealing the fake.

Alone in the gallery office she paced, hands to hips,

her high heels angrily clicking the marble floor. She couldn't call the police. To report a stolen fake? The last thing she wanted was police involvement.

She had planned this carefully. The event featuring *Le Diabolique* had not been announced to the public because she'd never intended to go through with it. Lorcan was the only one she'd needed to fool. And she had. He hadn't asked after the diamond since the night of the showing.

"This should have been so easy."

Could Edamite be behind this? Then why had he insisted she find the diamond and bring it to him?

No, there must be another faction of demons who were also after *Le Diabolique*. How had anyone, beyond Ed, gotten the information that her gallery was to display the diamond?

She sat before the desk and scanned the acquisitions files for the past few weeks. She had been the one to receive *Le Diabolique*. It had been delivered via courier, from the back of a black Mercedes. Such a private delivery method was often utilized with valuable works that the client trusted only to his closest employees.

The courier had unlocked the titanium case from around his wrist and walked inside the gallery. She'd handed him the bill of lading to sign and had signed it herself. In turn, she had signed a form from the courier and...

"Where did I put that form? I did get a copy. It was a yellow piece of paper and had the owner's monogram on it."

She'd noted the elaborate monogram, but at the time, she'd been so nervous about receiving the valuable item she hadn't taken time to really look at it, to determine what letters were woven into the monogram.

She'd become accustomed to overlooking things. Her expectations for all things fine and luxurious had blinded her to details. She could spot a bottle of Krug fifty feet off, but to really say what the label looked like? No clue. Louboutins were a no-brainer. The red sole! But as for the actual design on the main part of the shoe? Just glimpses here and there.

And a sparkling ten-carat diamond always caught her eye, but the setting was never important.

"I can't find it. Maybe Lorcan hasn't transferred it to the digital files."

Her assistant went through the paperwork every few days. And where was Lorcan, anyway? He hadn't called in sick. He simply hadn't shown up for work. Could he be on a bender? She had suspected him of excess drinking or a drug problem because his eyes were often red and puffy and he always had an excuse for a missed morning.

Blyss dialed his number but the phone didn't ring. Instead she got a canceled-number recording.

"Weird."

She had a sneaky feeling she'd never hear from Lorcan again. Had he been in on it? Who was Lorcan Price? She'd thought him merely human. Could he possibly be a paranormal breed? But what? Thanks to the pills she took, she had no way to sense a fellow paranormal. Was it possible he'd been in on the placement of the diamond from the get-go? Could Lorcan be demon?

Had *Le Diabolique* specifically been delivered to her with the hopes it would be stolen because...

"Why?" Blyss asked herself. "It doesn't make sense. Unless Thrash is involved. But then he would have never needed me to steal it in the first place. I don't understand this."

It was as if someone had expected her to take *Le Diabolique* and wanted to make it easy. And with no police investigation to hamper or bring suspicion, then she got off free.

As did the person who had ultimately arranged for this heist in the first place.

That person had to be the one who sought to release the demon from the stone. Yes?

"Makes weird sense."

Then again, why not simply keep the stone and not go through the process of handing it to her gallery? What if she had never agreed to steal the diamond? This made so little sense!

Blyss grabbed her purse and locked up. She hadn't located any clues here. Instead, she'd found only further questions. And a missing fake. Should she call Stryke? He was out with her brother at this moment trying to track *Le Diabolique*. She couldn't provide him any additional information that would help that search.

She'd wait for him to return and tell him her suspicions.

And then she'd tell him again that she loved him. Because more and more she believed what she'd said almost by accident earlier.

There was something about Stryke's kiss that wouldn't allow her to turn away. To instead seek a man who would offer her riches, vacations or false compliments. She wanted Stryke's kiss. Because it tasted like him. Because it tasted like something fine she could never possess. Because it tasted real.

And more and more, she craved real.

"Who is that?" Stryke asked.

A beautiful redhead in a tight black lace dress strode

toward the three men. She wore heels high enough to make a man jump for mercy. And her breasts vied to escape the low neckline. Well, well.

Kir whistled. "I've always loved blondes."

"Blonde? She's a redhead," Stryke muttered with growing interest.

"Gentlemen," Ed said quietly, and with a distinct warning, as he squeezed the river water from his shirt hem. "That's not a woman. The Saint-Pierre idiot just called up the Dark Prince."

"Ah shit." Kir straightened and looked aside to avoid seeing what he knew was illusion.

Those who looked upon Himself saw an image of their greatest temptation.

"What do you mean?" Stryke asked. "She looks like Blyss, but instead with red hair."

"Now is no time to be racking up brother-in-law points," Kir hissed. "Get a whiff of the guy."

Stryke inhaled, expecting some sexy perfume, and instead got a nostril blast of the worst sulfur ever. Hell. He *had* called up the devil Himself.

Heh. He'd called up Himself.

Now, to get down to business.

"Who the hell are you?" The gorgeous woman stood with hands on hips looking too painfully delicious. Her bright green eyes, framed by lush black lashes, took in the trio. Her tongue dashed out to lick red lips. Everything about her was so wrong. "I know the demon Thrash and Kirnan Sauveterre." Her gemstone eyes fixed on Stryke and her teeth actually glinted, as if in a TV commercial. "But you don't belong in Paris."

"I'm Stryke Saint-Pierre."

"Ah." The woman smirked. "I remember a thing with your grandfather Eduoard Credence Saint-Pierre. Something about his daughter, too. Kambriel…" The name sifted from the woman's lips with such lustful reverence Stryke shuddered.

He'd heard about Kambriel's unfortunate stumble upon Himself after moving to Paris to *find herself*, and how the devil had fallen in love with her and seduced her out of her wits. She'd been lost for months in a trippy sort of head game, a virtual slave to the Master of Darkness, until Johnny Santiago had come along and rescued her.

Stryke needed to keep a cool head when dealing with this Demon of All Demons. And that was something he was expert at.

"Why are you after *Le Diabolique*?" he asked the Dark Prince. "Don't you have enough power in this realm? And why unleash another überpowerful demon to torment the humans? You'll get their souls soon enough."

"Insolent!"

If getting sucker punched by a sexy woman wasn't humiliating enough, landing the wall face-first and feeling his nose crunch was. Stryke swallowed blood, grinned and spun around. But, expecting to face off against a gorgeous woman, he abruptly halted his charge when before him stood Himself in his true guise.

The Demon of all Demons was formed all of black muscles and sinew, towering four heads higher than Kir, the tallest of the three men. His shoulders were as wide and bulky as a Barcalounger. Glossy black talons scythed out from the ends of his fingers, putting all horror-movie villains to shame.

At his temples were huge ebony horns just like a matador's nightmare. The demon's red eyes glowed above a haughty stretched-leather smirk that revealed an imperious glint of fangs.

"Now," Himself said in tones that cut like ice down Stryke's spine. "What is this about *Le Diabolique*? I banished the demon Xyloda into that stone centuries ago. Why do you think I would want to bring that bastard out?"

"Because the lair to perform Xyloda's releasement ritual is set up below your Club l'Enfer," Stryke said.

Himself cast a steaming gaze toward Edamite, who, still dripping with river water, bowed his head and stepped back. "I have no intel, Your Darkness," the demon muttered.

Finding his courage, Kir stepped up beside Stryke. "It's true. We saw the lair. Four demons of the twelve required for the blood sacrifice have already been captured. Surely more have been acquired since we've seen the place."

Himself coiled his meaty hands into fists. Behind him, the river Seine actually steamed, mimicking the dark lord's boiling anger.

"We're trying to stop the release from happening," Stryke said, finding his stance and not fearing another hit from Himself. He was still swallowing his own blood from the punch, but at least he was standing and had his wits about him. "If you're not involved, then tell us who is, and we'll take care of it."

"You'll take care of it?" Himself tilted his head at him, the horns moving dangerously close. One slice from those could take off his head or half his body. "You, a frail werewolf, and his idiot cohorts? Of what value does it serve you to stop Xyloda's release?"

Stryke splayed out his hands before him and offered, "I like my world as demon-free as possible."

Edamite coughed.

Himself sneered. Steam hissed from his black nostrils. But he did not move toward Stryke for another punch.

"So your heroic quest has nothing to do with the tasty bitch who can't decide if she wants to be wolf or human?"

Stryke lifted his jaw. "It has everything to do with Blyss. And she's happy with what she is right now."

"You don't know her very well, boy." Himself eyed Kir up and down and then Ed. "I will not tolerate Xyloda's release. I will end this right now. But the three of you won't escape without proper recompense. I will ensure those who stole *Le Diabolique* are aware of exactly who wished their plot foiled."

Kir and Stryke exchanged looks that said "can't we get a break?"

"That's for the comment about the world having fewer demons," Himself said to Stryke. "If that is all, then, gentlemen, I'll be off."

"I'll go with you," Stryke said, pausing the Dark Prince. "To stop the demons from releasing Xyloda."

Himself tilted his head, considering the offer. "You watch too much television, werewolf. This isn't a supernatural buddy episode."

"Yeah, but I sure as hell wish it was. At least then I'd know a happy ending waited for me. I need to finish what I've started. I promised Blyss I'd take care of matters between her and Thrash regarding that diamond. And until that big black stone is found, it's dangerous."

Himself blinked, and when he eyed Stryke this time his corneas were black around the red irises with a slit of black in their centers. "Your offer amuses me."

The demon king clapped his hands together once,

and Stryke suddenly stood in a dark chamber carved from dirt and limestone. Torches lit the vast space, and when he took in his surroundings he found the twelve cages were all filled. And he wasn't sure what number, exactly, *denizens* equaled, but he guesstimated a good twenty to thirty demons standing to one side of the room, each of them lifting their heads to eye Stryke and Himself.

Chapter 18

Stryke muttered to his demonic cohort, "I'm going to need a weapon."

"How about this?"

Stryke's left arm jerked as a medieval mace suddenly appeared in his grip. The spiked ball must've weighed ten pounds. He gave it a test swing and the spiked iron ball almost sliced his leg open.

"Something a little more modern?" he hissed.

Himself shook his head and grumbled, a rattly death thunder that birthed in his throat. The demonic denizen approached with caution.

A Lightsaber with purple beam appeared in Stryke's hand, startled him on his feet. He swung it and it actually made the noise it should. But seriously? "Are you kidding me?"

"Be specific, insolent!"

"Salt and a blade, if you don't mind."

A pistol replaced the Lightsaber, and in his right hand manifested a long, scythed blade that he felt could take off a demon's head with but a slice.

"Nice." Stryke eyed the closest demon, who sported enough hardware in his nostrils, ears and at his temples to make a punk rocker jealous. "Let's do this."

Stryke's blade sliced through a demon's neck. The head toppled, only to reveal yet another demon standing behind him, snarling its wicked double rows of fangs and swinging the silver scepter—which happened to sport *Le Diabolique.*

"A little help here!" Stryke called.

Himself stood off to the side, by a cage, watching as Stryke had taken out half the denizen. At one point when Stryke had been held down on the dirt floor by a nasty demon drooling some kind of caustic saliva onto his neck, he looked up to see Himself studying his talons most intently.

"I thought you said you had this one!" Himself called back.

"I said I wanted to help! I thought I was doing the buddy sidekick role."

"Ah. Always be specific." The Dark Prince stepped into the fray and with but a slash of talon took out the demon wielding the scepter.

Stryke stumbled against one of the cages. The demon within grasped him around the neck. Pointing the pistol over his shoulder, he pulled the trigger. Loaded with salt rounds, it hit its mark. He felt the demon scatter into flakes behind him.

With a clap of his hands over his head, Himself stomped the floor. All standing demons dispersed into flakes of red-ember ash. Demon blood spattered

Stryke's face and body. The room went black with the shrapnel. Stryke took aim at one demon standing near the doorway and fired the pistol. Right on target.

Himself turned and nodded acknowledgment. "Good one."

Stryke returned the nod. "Are they all gone?"

The devil swept his hand over the piles of demon ash, and from beneath rose the scepter. And in the center of the room, up popped *Le Diabolique*. Himself snatched both. The scepter, he pointed toward Stryke.

"You want this for a souvenir?"

"I think I'll pick up one of those flashing Eiffel Towers when I get topside, if you don't mind."

"Suit yourself. This is mine." Himself eyed the diamond in the murky darkness. His crimson eyes glowed brightly. He popped the diamond into his mouth and swallowed.

"That's going to give you nasty heartburn."

Himself's chuckle didn't touch levity. "One so heartless as I need not worry. But to show I'm not all treacle and brimstone, I do thank you for alerting me to this anomaly, Saint-Pierre. Ask for one thing and I shall grant it to you."

"Like a wish?" Stryke scratched the back of his head where he was pretty sure demon blood had changed his hair color to black. He eyed the Dark Prince warily. "Are you for real?"

"I invite you to act as my sidekick and you still question me?"

Stryke shrugged.

"I've not the patience for your dally."

Stryke didn't want anything the devil could give him, olive branch or not. Although…

"Can you give me something to make a werewolf completely human?"

Himself actually rolled his eyes. "The woman again? You don't know her very well."

"So you've said. That's what I want," Stryke insisted.

"Very well." Himself gestured dramatically with a sweep of taloned, black-muscled hand, and a glass vial appeared in his grasp. He stretched his arm out over the vast piles of demon ash and the fine particles streamed upward, filling the down-turned vial. A cork stopper appeared in the vial's neck. Black wax melted about the rim. "Here you go."

"This is filled with freaking dead demons." Stryke caught the murky vial. A shake revealed the contents had turned liquid. Of a sudden the contents within the vial glowed red. "What the hell?"

"What is it they say in this abominable realm?" Himself said. "Have a nice day!"

The demon dispersed into ash that then swirled into a black smoke that followed the steel-walled aisle, which led up to the nightclub. And of a sudden Stryke wobbled, arms out to his sides, to catch himself from falling into the Seine.

Kir grabbed him by the front of the shirt and tugged him upright. "That didn't take long. What happened?"

Stryke stood in the aqueduct. No demons. No cages. No devil. Guess his job as sidekick was now officially over.

Edamite peered over Kir's shoulder. "Nice," the demon said from behind them. "Thanks to you, I'll have a gang of pissed-off demons on my ass. Good going, wolf."

Stryke spun about, catching Ed by the throat and slamming him against the stone wall. "I just did what you've been trying to do in a half-assed roundabout way with no success. I went straight to the source. And together we creamed those demons' asses, and the Dark Prince ate the freakin' black diamond. So now you've got what you wanted. No one is going to release Xyloda from the stone. And you're going to do as you promised for Blyss. She owes you nothing. You don't ever speak to her again."

Ed raised his hands up by his face. "The deal was if she brought *Le Diabolique* to me she could have her pills. I don't have the stone."

"But you've the same results."

"Do as he says, Ed," Kir said from over Stryke's shoulder. "Or you'll have to answer not only to Stryke, but as well, me."

Ed fisted the air. "Fine! The things I do for family." He nodded toward the vial Stryke held. "What's that?"

"It's for Blyss. She doesn't need your damn pills anymore. So I don't care if you are her half brother. Stay. The hell. Away from her."

"Did Himself give you that? Is it for Blyss?" Kir asked.

Stryke stuff the vial in his front jeans pocket. "It'll do for her what the pills have done. Only permanently."

"You really want your girlfriend to keep denying her true nature?" Ed blurted out.

Stryke slammed Ed's head against the wall. "None of your damn business, demon."

"Actually, it—"

Stryke growled at the man, and he ceased protest. He turned and strode away, not caring if Kir followed. The deed had been done. The Old Lad would not have another powerful demon running amok on his turf. Of course, Stryke had no idea what to expect from the demons when they discovered who had narced on them.

"Bring it," Stryke muttered. "I want to smash in some demon skull."

"Then you'll need weapons," Kir said as he joined Stryke's side.

"I've got a salt pistol." The thing was still tucked in his waistband. Must have dropped the scythe in the chamber. "You didn't stay behind to talk to your brother?"

"Drop it, Saint-Pierre. You'll never understand how family ties can forge relationships. All may look peachy right now," Kir said, "but you'd be wise to arm yourself. And stay close to my sister."

"That I can promise I will do. I'm heading there right now. We've a date."

"Oh yeah? Somehow I suspect the demon-blood look is not going to go over well with my sister."

Yeah. He'd better head home and shower first.

Stryke's cell phone rang. "Hello?"

"Can you do a pickup?" Rhys Hawkes asked. "In an hour?"

"As soon as I can get to a vehicle I'll be there. Same place?"

"Yes. See you then."

"You're not going straight to Blyss's place?" Kir asked as they landed the surface and the bright evening sunlight made them both blink. "I said you need to protect her."

"I have a quick job to do for Rhys Hawkes. I'll get to her within two hours. You can go check on your sister, you know."

Kir glanced back down the tunnel they'd come from. Stryke suspected he had unfinished business below.

"When you talk to the demon you be sure he keeps his promise to stay away from Blyss."

Stryke wandered off in the direction of the Île Saint-Louis. A half hour later he'd showered, decided the salt pistol was a good accessory to carry with him and headed out to meet Tor for another pickup.

Blyss stood in the shoe closet vacillating over the crystal-laden Louboutins or the black velvet Viviers with the diamonds on the toes.

As a wolf, she'd ruin these precious things. If she shifted all the time, her hair would be a mess. She'd have to shave too often. Her fingernails would be ragged. She'd be a disaster.

Yet if she was a werewolf she could sense Stryke, go for a run in the forest with him. Have werewolf sex with him— What would that be like? Messy. Wild. Weird. Amazing?

She sighed.

"What to do?" She traced a finger along the Louboutins. "I love him. But do I love him enough to change for him?"

Tor presented yet another curious device to Stryke in a wooden box shaped much like a bread box.

"Is it going to jump out at me or otherwise attract demons?" Stryke asked, keeping his hands to his chest because he wasn't too eager to open the box after the surprises he'd found.

"It's *sidhe* related."

"Faeries? So what's inside? A bunch of twinkly dust?"

"Actually, it is." Tor opened the box top and tilted it toward Stryke. Inside, the contents sparkled madly.

"It's the remains of a dryad. Can be used in magical spells, alchemical potions, and various rituals and/or occult ceremonies. Lots of power in this purple stuff. Tell Rhys to keep it under lock and key."

Stryke accepted the box with some apprehension. "All that from a bunch of glitter?" He shook his head and whistled. "The things a guy learns. My brother Kelyn…" He suddenly had a desperate thought. "Is this what will happen to him when he dies? He's faery."

Tor shrugged. "I'm no expert on the *sidhe*. Probably. Who knows? How'd you manage a faery in your family?"

"My mother is faery." And then, wanting to see the man's reaction, he said, "Grandpa is a vampire."

"Is that so?" Tor's brow arched.

"He'd never do a thing to attract attention from the Order of the Stake," Stryke clarified. "He fights the good fight. Actually keeps his eye on the local packs who believe they've a right to pit vampires against one another in the blood games."

"Ah. Creed Saint-Pierre. I've heard of him. Good blood."

"Indeed." Stryke tucked the box under an arm. "So that's it?"

The keening wail of something like an insect prompted both men to look toward the heavens.

"Ah, *merde*," Tor muttered. "Demons."

Chapter 19

Stryke saw the demon's face as it leaped and soared toward him—missing the lower jaw. It was one of those nasty wraith demons. Now was no time to bemoan the thing's lack of polite introductions.

Delivering an undercut up into the creature's open maw, he sent it flying up and bouncing over the top of the van.

Tor dived into the back of the van. "I got something!" the Brit called.

"Just stay inside!" Stryke yelled as he bent to avoid the next wraith. Its talons cut through his short hair, sending a chill down the back of his skull. "I got this!"

Pistol in hand, he swung back his shoulder and eyed his periphery. Tor was digging around inside the van. One wraith climbed like a spider over the top of the van, the other—

He smelled the sulfur and turned to catch the demon

square against his chest. They both landed on the cobblestones. Stryke kicked up his knee, but didn't land any particular body part. He grabbed for hair. There was no hair. Something viscous dripped onto his chin and neck. It was coming from the bottom half of the demon's face, which wasn't there.

"You ugly—"

The demon's screech drowned out his oath. And when it spoke the voice was garbled and bubbly. "You sent Himself after us."

"You bet." The Dark Lord had warned he'd let those who wanted the diamond know whom to blame for Himself's discovery of their plot. That was fast. "But if they could only manage to send two of you…"

"We are diversion," his attacker garbled. A swipe of its talons cut across Stryke's collarbone.

Stryke shifted his hand, calling out his claws, and returned the slash with a hearty swipe that cut through the demon's chest and face, rendering it to a goopy, sputtering corpse. He rolled out from under the mess as it collapsed and looked up in time to see Tor dragging what looked like a chain saw down the center of the other demon. But there was no mechanical noise, save for the demon's screams.

The demon dropped in a messy pile and Tor stepped back, wielding the chain saw proudly.

"What is that thing?" Stryke asked, jumping up and leaping over the piles of demons. He shoved the pistol into the waistband of his jeans. "Looks like a chain saw, but it's silent?"

"Yep, it's modified. Easier to sneak up on the enemy that way. Picked this up from a witch years ago. It's especially helpful when attacked in the city and you don't want to draw human attention." Tor cast a glance around and landed on the desecrated demon. "Salt rounds?"

Stryke patted his hip where the pistol grip stuck up. "Yep. But it was more satisfying to take the thing out with a talon."

"I bet. Good thing no one spilled the faery dust. But I've still a sticky mess to clean up. Demon blood. It clings like tar."

"Aren't there people you can call for that?" Stryke knew there were those who specifically answered the call for cleanup after a paranormal being was rendered dead.

"I'm that people." Tor set the chain saw in the back of the van and grabbed a white hazmat suit from a hook on the interior wall. "When necessary, I can clean a crime scene in twenty minutes flat. This mess? I'll be finished in ten. A vacuum cleaner will do the job nicely. What do you think they were after?"

The question hit Stryke hard. He knew the answer to that one. Unfortunately.

"The wraith said something about a diversion. Hell. Blyss. They might be after her, as well." He grabbed the wooden box full of faery dust. "I gotta go." Turning and racing around the side of the van, he paused and backtracked. He tapped the chain saw. "Mind if I borrow this?"

"Go for it. Uh, and if you need cleanup? Give me a call."

"Thanks, man!"

Stryke landed in the driver's seat of the car and tossed the wooden box aside along with the chain saw and the pistol. Bringing up the GPS on his phone, he hoped to find his way to Blyss's place before it was too late.

* * *

By the time Stryke landed in the lush garden courtyard before Blyss's apartment, the scent of sulfur filled his nostrils. Chain saw ready—and so strangely quiet—he sneaked up behind the demon who strolled through the hedgerow toward Blyss's front door. He stepped quickly.

The demon turned toward him. Same missing lower jaw. A wraith.

Stryke winked. Then he dragged the chain saw down the demon from head to gut. Black blood spattered him and the wall outside Blyss's door. But remarkably, the demon didn't shriek. If the neighbors had been watching… He glanced about. Curtains before all the windows.

"Paris. Whoda thought the city of love would be teeming with nasties?"

Tugging out his cell phone, he dialed up Tor. He could be there in fifteen minutes.

Stryke knocked and tried the door. It was open, so, leaving the chain saw dripping with black blood outside, he slipped inside the foyer and closed the door as Blyss's arms wrapped about his neck.

He turned to catch her kiss. "You're happy."

"Because you're finally back. Oh. You smell like…" She tugged him down the hallway and into the kitchen light. "You have black stuff all over you. Demons?"

"Had a bit of a snag with a pickup for Hawkes Associates but it's all good." And before that? She didn't need to know.

"Is it?" Her green eyes watered and he could read her apprehension in the wobble of her lower lip.

"You bet it's good because I'm here now and you are

one gorgeous bit of glamour girl. Did you make dinner reservations?"

"I did. Really? It's…good?"

"Yep." He hugged her. To tell her the truth would only worry her more.

"I think I have a shirt for you to borrow."

Stryke followed her into the bedroom and tugged off his demon blood–soaked shirt while Blyss disappeared into the clothes closet. "Do I want to know how you always seem to have spare men's clothing?"

"Probablement pas!" she called out.

He didn't know what that meant but guessed she'd told him to mind his own beeswax. He wasn't willing to explain about how his day went either, so he'd leave it at that. As far as Stryke was concerned, Blyss no longer had anything to worry about. Her world could return to normal. Or however she defined normal.

And he…well, he'd take each minute as it came and hope for the best.

Heading into the bathroom, he washed his face and squeezed the demon blood out of his hair.

Blyss sipped the white wine and admired its quality. Normally she would send back anything that wasn't exquisite. This wasn't even close to divine, but it sufficed. She hadn't expected much from this river cruise. Thus, her expectations had been wildly exceeded. She sat across the table from a handsome man who only had eyes for her. He wasn't even watching the landmarks they passed by as their boat cruised down the Seine.

"You're missing all the good stuff," she said to Stryke, who finished his salad.

"The good stuff is right in front of me. And I'm not talking about the food. You look amazing tonight."

She wiggled on the chair and touched her hair. She'd pulled it back into a chignon and tucked a diamond clip above her ear. She'd almost gone with the black silk dress but at the last minute had switched to a light pink, airy, summer chiffon dress with matching Louboutins covered in pink crystals. *Keep it simple,* she'd coached. Yet one must always include sparkles when possible.

"You clean up nicely, as well," she said. "Your jeans didn't get any blood on them?"

"Not that I noticed." He tugged at the borrowed tie— so she had a few men's shirts and ties in her closet—and Blyss again noticed the bruise on the side of his neck.

She'd wanted to ask him about his afternoon and the very obvious smell of sulfur on him when he'd arrived, but when he'd come out of the bathroom mumbling something about both of them having secrets to keep, she'd let it go.

Of course, she didn't want to keep her secrets anymore. She had to tell him about the missing fake, but right here on the crowded dining boat was not the place.

The waiter stopped by and served them coq au vin with steaming rosemary bread, and slipped away as quickly and silently as he had appeared. The evening was dusky, though the city lights shone along the shore and glittered on the river, vying with the bright beam of moonlight that dashed across the waters.

"Things didn't go well this afternoon with my brother?" she asked.

Stryke tilted back the remainder of wine, then poured another full serving before leaning forward, checking around that the other diners were all busy chatting and oohing and aahing over the sights, then said, "I called out Himself."

Blyss gasped.

"I know," he rushed out. "Not the sharpest knife in the bunch, this country hick from Minnesota. But at the time it seemed like the quickest way to get to the end point. We've been trying to find the demons who stole *Le Diabolique*. If the lair was found beneath the nightclub, then I assumed he was involved. So why not go directly to the source? But get this. It was news to him."

"Stryke." She placed a hand over his. "I have to tell you about what I found, or didn't find, today while searching the gallery records for info about *Le Diabolique*."

"I wish you wouldn't have gone out. It's dangerous right now, Blyss. That demon by your— Er. Forget it. I'm still worked up over this afternoon. I don't think you have anything to worry about anymore. We talked to…you know, the big dark prince. He didn't want Xyloda released either. So…we took care of it."

"Really? Wait. You said 'we'?"

"Yeah, me and the dark prince are tight." He chuckled and rubbed his jaw. "Kidding. I am so not friends with you know who. But it's over, Blyss. You don't have to worry anymore."

"Then that clears up almost everything."

"Almost?"

She sat back against the chair, no longer hungry. It was amazing that Stryke had found a way to ensure the demon never be released from *Le Diabolique*. That negated her worries about the missing fake. Because it was worthless to whoever had taken it, anyway.

But what was she to do about Edamite Thrash and her very obvious missing supply? The full moon was in two days.

"There's still Ed," she said softly.

Stryke stood and took a step around to squat beside her chair. He clasped her hand and kissed it. His touch always lured her heartbeats to a slower, more relaxed pace.

"We ran into Thrash today," he said. "Your brother has— Well, that's for him to talk about with you. Suffice, Ed's problem was solved today. He actually wanted to ensure the demon was never released. Can you believe that?"

She could actually. There was something about Ed that wouldn't allow her to label him *full-blown villain*.

"Thrash is satisfied," Stryke said. "He's not going to bother you anymore."

"But he's— Stryke, he is my supplier."

"Yeah, about that. I've a surprise for you. It'll give you the human life you want."

"I don't understand."

"I want to hold off on the surprise. I'll explain it all later." He stood and bent to tilt her face to look at him. "You're going to be fine."

And he kissed her softly and lingered there, as if they were the only two on the boat. He was the only sustenance she needed, and she wanted to tell him that to show him how much he meant to her. But he stood and slid around to sit again. He forked in some chicken and smiled widely. The hero had saved the day. A job well-done, indeed. And she had done nothing to deserve such a favor.

"Thank you" was all Blyss could manage to say without crying and smearing her mascara and turning into a perfect mess. "I love you for that."

He winked at her. "Tomorrow night is the night before the full moon."

"Is that so?" She sensed his teasing tone and wanted to go with the playful mood instead of sinking into the worry that had been niggling at her calm. "I hear your sort require a lot of sex to satiate the need for…" She looked aside before leaning closer and whispering, "…your wild to come out."

"True. Very true. Did I mention that Rhys Hawkes has given me the key to his country cabin for the next few nights? I was thinking of heading out there tomorrow night. Call it a vacation away from my vacation. You interested? Uh, I mean, for tomorrow night. I won't ask you to come along with me on the night of the full moon."

She lifted her goblet and he met hers in a clink. "I'm in for tomorrow night."

The dining boat docked below the Eiffel Tower. By the time they'd climbed up the concrete stairs to street level, the tower twinkled madly with hundreds of thousands of white LED lights and the crowd clapped and cheered.

"Wow." Stryke clasped Blyss's hand and walked toward the massive Iron Lady, head tilted back to take it all in. "This is incredible. I suppose you've seen it so much it doesn't even register on your awe scale."

She snuggled next to him and kissed his jaw where the stubble tickled her mouth. "I've never seen it with you. That makes this a special moment. Come on. Let's stand underneath it."

"Cool. Can we go to the top?"

"Sure, if you want to wait in line."

He stretched his gaze to follow the line that marked around two sides of the tower base. Easily four hundred people waiting, even at ten at night. Probably hours before anyone got to the top.

"Seriously? That's the line?" he asked, his eyes falling to her shoes. "I think I'll pass." He eyed the underside of the tower. His hand clasping hers, he wandered to the left, then stepped back a few paces. "Right here. We're dead center underneath this monster."

"I think you're right." She tilted her head back and looked up into the intricate iron lacing that designed the monument. Exquisite artwork. She was thankful this monument had not been torn down, as was the original plan when it had been built merely as part of a grand exposition in the late 1800s. A breeze brushed the pink chiffon against her legs and tickled through her hair. Never had she felt so light.

"Can you imagine what it was like to build this thing?" Stryke asked. "I mean, what was it, the nineteenth century? No advanced technology. Probably no cranes to hoist up the heavy pieces. Amazing. Come here."

He sat on the ground and patted the concrete beside him.

Blyss tugged at the hem of her pale pink skirt.

He tapped the toe of her shoe. "Yeah, Sparkles, you're going to get a little messy again." He winked, and her heart fluttered in response.

She sat beside him and together they lay back and admired the tower while tourists wandered around them. The night was bright and bustling with people, but Blyss felt the world slip away and in that moment she and Stryke were the only two that existed.

He pulled her hand to his mouth to kiss it, and she nuzzled her head against his shoulder. Who cared if her dress got dirty or her shoes scuffed? All that mattered was she was exactly where she wanted to be right now. Next to a man who had teased her out from behind the mask.

Yes, she felt vulnerable to think that. Because she had let down some of the glamour and just wanted to be with him. Simple. Nothing complicated.

But everything right. Or as right as it could be. Because indeed, she was light.

She wondered if she would ever get a refill of pills from Edamite. Were things settled with him? Not hardly. If not, she would remain the same breed as Stryke—forced to accept her werewolf—but she could never be the woman he desired because she'd always regret her lost humanity.

She wanted to be everything for him.

"What are you thinking about?" he suddenly asked.

"Besides that I hope no one steps on us?"

"Yes, besides that."

"I think I'm lucky that I chose you that night at the gallery. I'm sorry for all the horrible things that have resulted because of that choice. But for all the good, I am thankful. And you are the good."

She twisted up to kiss him, and there beneath the Eiffel Tower, oblivious to the world, they made out like teenagers.

Chapter 20

Once at home, Blyss unzipped her dress as she walked down the long hallway, through the kitchen and veered toward the bedroom. Stryke followed. He'd kicked off his shoes by the door. He tugged the shirt over his head in the kitchen. By the time he'd reached the bedroom door, the zipper on his pants was open.

Blyss stepped out of her dress. Clad in pink lace bra and panties, she wandered toward the bed. She stood there, bathed beneath the moonlight, her fingers gliding along her pinned-up hair.

"Let me watch you take it down," Stryke said in a desire-tinged voice that hardened her nipples in anticipation.

She pulled out the diamond clip and slowly unraveled her hair from the chignon. It tickled across her shoulders and down her back, but knowing her lover watched made the move intensely erotic. Gliding her fingers down her sides to her hips, she tugged at the panties, slipping them down a bit...

She turned to find Stryke leaning against the wall, his gaze fixed on her. He nodded, and she wiggled the panties down and dropped them to her feet, where she stepped out of them, her Louboutins clicking the marble floor.

Turning, she toyed with the snap between the bra cups. She walked toward him, lowering her lashes in a teasing glance. Once unclasped, she quickly peeled aside the cups, flashing him, then as quickly held the lacy bits over her breasts.

"You think so, huh?" He gestured she come closer. Oh, that knowing smile! "I want another peek."

Blyss stepped closer. "Say *s'il vous plaît*."

"What does that mean?"

"Say it, and you'll know."

"See voo plate."

"Oh, darling." She stroked his cheek, following the line of the soft stubble. "Your French is terrible."

"Guilty. But I don't need words to please you." He drew his fingers up her thigh and over to her mons, where he moved lower, deeper.

Blyss sucked in a breath. She tilted her head and closed her eyes at the delicious sensation of his finger entering her. He turned her chin to face him.

"Look at me, glamour girl." Now he slicked over her clit slowly, achingly. "Don't look away."

In his eyes she found an intensity that would have made her wolf howl with delight. It certainly made the woman she was shiver and coo.

Hands still at her breasts, she released the lacy cups and then caressed them while Stryke coaxed her body toward release with his fingers. The focus in his eyes heightened every sensation. It was difficult to look at him, and yet she couldn't look away. That would be a betrayal, a refusal to give him all that she could. And she wanted to. She needed to.

Tomorrow night he would need her to satiate him. And she would do that. Because he could touch her very soul. And she never wanted him to stop.

Gasping as the hum at her loins began to ripple outward, gripping her muscles and promising exquisite release, Blyss moaned and tilted her forehead against Stryke's.

And as she came, she whispered, "I'm yours."

He wanted to melt into her. To kneel before her and worship her. To tie her up and keep her only for him. To set her free and watch her spread her wings. He wanted to never forget the feel of her body shuddering against his as she came. And he must never forget the sound of her whimpers and the clutch of her fingers against his shoulders as the tremendous release captured her.

He didn't want to share her with anyone else. Ever.

Be damned his plans to leave Paris with fond memories of an amazing fling. He wanted to make this woman his. His bondmate. Maybe even his wife.

Yes, even if she chose to live life as a human as opposed to the true wolf she could be. Stryke couldn't see any other way to keep her. So he'd surrender his need to love a werewolf, to love and raise the big family. He'd sacrifice it all for Blyss. Even the pack.

"Let me love you," he whispered in her ear as she shivered against him. "Always."

"Yes. *Jamais.*"

"No one else," he said as he lifted her and carried her to the bed. "Only me."

She pulled him on top of her and pushed down his boxer shorts. "Only you. I don't want any other man, Stryke." She kissed him and then pushed him to roll onto his back so she could straddle his hips. "I don't want any other wolf."

Dipping her head, she licked down his stomach and then took his erection into her mouth. He raked his fingers through her luscious hair and followed her rhythm as her head dipped up and down. She devoured him, nipping gently and then laving him from tip to root.

As he rode the wave of orgasm she clung to his body, her heat insane and the stroke of her fingernails over his skin only prolonging the pleasure. Finally he exhaled, his energy spent and his body lax.

He'd meant it when he'd asked her to love only him. He'd worry about real life—the fact he didn't even live on the same continent as her—in the morning.

Stryke woke to the patter of the shower in the bathroom. Lavender permeated the room. Combined with the lingering tendrils of Blyss's flower perfume, it made for a heady atmosphere. He sat in the queen's chambers, her willing subject, waiting for her beck and call.

With a smile, he got up and pulled on his pants. The glass vial the devil Himself had given him dropped to the floor. He'd almost forgotten about it. After they'd returned to her apartment—well, his mind had been elsewhere. And over dinner he hadn't wanted to spoil the romantic mood.

"She'll be pleased."

And for a moment Stryke struggled with tossing the vial outside in the nearest garbage can, thus forcing Blyss to face her werewolf. She'd never have to know he'd held a definitive fix for what most bothered her.

He rubbed a palm over his face and shook his head. "She's gotta do what she needs to do to be happy."

Because he'd decided last night that he could be happy with her no matter what. Really, he could.

Mostly. He chose to ignore that niggle of doubt that said perhaps his happiness wasn't worth the effort of tossing the vial.

He clutched the key to Blyss's happiness.

The shower stopped. Blyss's humming made him smile. But too quickly the smile slipped away. He shook the little glass container. Just demon ash? Or something so powerful even he would regret ever giving it to her?

"Morning, lover."

He turned and held out the vial toward Blyss. Because if he didn't do it now he'd lose the courage.

She wore a sheer black robe that did not hide the gorgeous body beneath. His eyes veered to her breasts, and even as she took the vial, he pulled her to him and bent to bite gently through the sheer fabric at the full swell of her breast.

"What is this?" she asked.

"From Himself."

"What?"

And for the first time he considered that what gleamed red inside the glass vial was devil magic. The darkest form of magic in existence. Did he want to let Blyss take her chances with it?

He had no right to deny her.

"The Dark Prince offered me anything I wanted after I'd told him about the missing diamond and we…" Nope. Wasn't necessary to detail his adventures as Himself's sidekick. "I asked for something that a werewolf could take to become completely human."

She clutched the vial against her chest. "Really? But that's… Wow. But what about you?"

"I don't want a thing. My needs are simple. And this way, if you drink the stuff, it's permanent. You'll never have to deal with Thrash again. In fact, I told the asshole to stay the hell away from you."

"You always think of me. That's so…" She gasped. "Thank you, Stryke."

"You deserve whatever makes you happy."

He kissed her. And her lips tasted bittersweet. Suddenly life tasted the same.

He could do this. He wanted to do this. With Blyss.

"You going to take that before I push you onto the bed and make you messy again?"

"Yes, sure. I'll be right back."

He winked and strolled away, wincing as he imagined her pulling out the cork stopper and tilting back the vile concoction. He'd found the wolf he had hoped to find to make him happy.

Too bad she couldn't face that truth.

It was afternoon when Stryke kissed Blyss and bid her *au revoir*. He intended to pick her up and they would then drive out to the country cabin Rhys Hawkes had loaned him for the weekend. Blyss wanted to pack a few things for the day and he was going to the apartment to grab some things, as well.

She closed the front door and realized with a start that she'd forgotten to tell him about the missing transfer records for *Le Diabolique*. And the missing fake. Not that it mattered anymore. She now had the key to making her life exactly as she wished it.

She wondered if Edamite had forgiven her debt to him. Because she did still owe him the five hundred thousand for this past year's supply. And since when were Ed and Kir friends? She vacillated over giving her brother a call, but the glass vial on the counter called to her.

Tomorrow night was the full moon. When she stopped her pills once a year for the shift, she usually stopped taking them the day before. So today would be appropriate. But it had been only ten months since she'd shifted. She didn't need to do so this month.

The contents of this vial would forever make her human? That was all she desired. She teased at the cork stopper, which was sealed with black wax. She ran her fingernail along the wax, but didn't press hard enough to crack it.

She set the vial on the counter. She'd tuck it in her bag and take it along to the cabin. Right now she had to find something in her closet that could possibly be worn in the country. In a cabin. In the middle of nowhere. That probably didn't even have internet.

"I wonder if there is even plumbing?" She shuddered to consider they could be going rustic tonight. "I hope Stryke realizes the sacrifice I'm making by roughing it. This may be harder than facing my werewolf."

Now, what sort of shoes did one wear to venture into the country?

Chapter 21

Rhys had loaned Stryke an Audi coupe and the keys to a country cabin. The man's kindness was impressive. And they weren't even related, only by the new distant ties that Stryke's aunt had forged with Rhys's grandson, Johnny Santiago. Stryke had yet to meet Rhys's wife, Viviane.

Viviane, a vampire, was supposed to be crazy. Apparently in the eighteenth century she'd been buried alive in a glass coffin by a nasty vampire, and Rhys had only found her two hundred and fifty years later. That would be enough to drive anyone crazy. And talk about holding the romantic torch for over two centuries? Cool.

He glanced at Blyss, who followed the streaks of rain that beat down the car windows with a manicured fingernail. A downpour had rolled into Paris as they'd exited the city periphery and it was difficult to see driving along the dark country roads. Blyss's lips curled into a smile.

"What are you thinking about?" he asked as he slowed the vehicle to follow the GPS's blinking directions to turn. He had to keep an eye on the screen because the French instructions could not be adjusted to English.

"About all the sex I'm going to have with you tonight." She shot him a flirty shimmy of shoulders and a wink. "I've always wanted to have sex in the rain."

"Even this monsoon? Maybe we can find a place on a porch or under an overhang. Wouldn't want you to muss your hair."

"Oh, please. You like me messy."

"I do. I'd love to lick more food off you too, if you want to make that happen."

"All I've brought along is wine, cheese and bread. I suppose I should have packed more if you intend to stay the entire weekend."

He planned to bring her back to town tomorrow and then drive out to spend the full moon by himself. He'd shift, and all would be well with his werewolf.

"I'll pick up some food when we return to town. Rhys did say there was meat in the freezer and some stock in the cupboards. I guess he owns a handful of properties in and around Paris. This cabin he mostly lets friends use. The man is generous."

"Half wolf and half vampire, right? I couldn't imagine having a hunger for blood."

"One of my brothers has such a hunger. Blade is faery and vampire."

"Quite the mix. Has he ever bitten you?"

"Once, when we were teenagers. It was more a tussle kind of thing. But he spat it out and walked away. Blade is kind of…intense. He's the black sheep of the family if there ever was one. Been through a hell of a lot."

"Handsome, too," Blyss commented. "But everyone in your family is attractive. Your sister's hair was pink."

"Because she's half faery. Make that *faery* now. She sacrificed her wolf because there was something wacky going on with her body. Her two sides were fighting one another, so she had to choose one over the other."

"Living among humans, I've forgotten all the interesting situations and people our breed encounters. I confess the wedding made me nervous."

"I sensed that."

"I've completely forgotten how to be a werewolf. Not that that's a bad thing."

"You said you shift once a year?"

"Yes. It hurts. I don't like it."

"It actually physically hurts you?"

"Yes. Probably because I don't do it often enough. I know it's not supposed to be painful."

"I love shifting," Stryke said. He slowed, noting their destination was a mile ahead. "Great way to stretch the muscles and invigorate my whole system. I bet if you did it more often it would stop being painful."

"Probably." She tilted her head against the window. She didn't like talking about it, so he'd leave it be. For now. Because even if he thought he could overlook her weirdness, he knew, in his heart, the bigger discussion was necessary if he meant to think long-term about their relationship.

"There's a light ahead. Must be the place. Rhys said the garage is separate from the house, so we'll park and then you'll have to dash through the rain."

"I can handle a little water."

The car headlights beamed onto the garage door. Stryke found the door opener and pressed the button. Inside the three-car garage sat a four-wheeler and a couple of mountain bikes. Once parked, they got out and he retrieved their bags from the trunk. Blyss had packed a large suitcase for her one-night stay. He wasn't even going to question. Not after stumbling into the shoe closet.

Standing inside the garage, they assessed the hundred-yard walk from there to the house. Grassy and muddy and slick from the rain, the land rose to an incline closer to the house.

"I'll run these up to the house, then come back and carry you," he suggested.

"You don't think I can walk on my own?"

"Not in those heels and that mud. Unless you want to give it a try?"

She tapped her heels together. "I'll wait here for my knight to come rescue me."

"I like the sound of that. Give me a few minutes." He grabbed the suitcases. "I'll be back."

Blyss leaned into the mist that sifted into the garage. Cool on her nose and lips, it made her smile. Or probably the smile was because she was to spend the night in a romantic cabin with the man with whom she had fallen in love.

She pulled off her shoes and clutched the heels with one hand. "Manolos for a cabin adventure? What was I thinking?"

Should have worn the riding boots and a comfortable pair of jersey leggings. But she felt wrong when not wearing a dress. It was her uniform of sorts. A dress was feminine and sexy and so not rough and wolflike.

Ah, well, she didn't intend to stay dressed long.

"Whoa!" Stryke slid down a slant of dirty land and caught himself by slapping his palms against the garage door wall. "That mud is slippery. The cabin looks amazing. There's a fire started and everything."

"Really?"

"It's an electronic fireplace. I think Rhys sent a maid in to gussy up the place for us. Very cool. As for getting you up to the cabin, you are going to get wet."

She tugged him to her. He was soaked to the skin and smelled like wild spring. "Doesn't take much to get wet around you, *mon amour*."

The man beamed and he leaned in to kiss her, crushing his wet clothes against her body. She couldn't complain. Tonight, she was in for the whole messy adventure.

Stryke swept her into his arms. "Ready?"

She tucked her shoes against her chest. They were going to get wet, but there was nothing she could do about it. Thank goodness they were patent leather. "Ready as I'll ever be."

He dashed out into the rain. Cold, pounding, it beat about them as he seemed to be racing directly into the storm. A few times his footsteps slipped. His body wobbled, but he maintained balance. Eyes closed against the downpour, Blyss clung to his wet shirt and biceps. They were halfway to the cabin when a big splash of muddy water preceded Stryke's shout. This time when he wobbled he went down.

Blyss fell out of his arms. The shoes flew. And she landed on palms and knees in thick, slippery mud.

"Ah shit, I'm so sorry!" But the chuckle that followed didn't jibe with Stryke's apologetic words. "Told you it's slippery out here. Blyss? Are you okay? You're not hurt?"

"I'm… I don't know." Kneeling there, she tried to get her bearings. Her fingers curled into cold wet mud.

Something gritty irritated her knees. She tasted dirt in her mouth. And her precious shoes were not to be seen. "This is horrible."

"I'm sorry, sweetie. Let me lift you carefully—"

"Back off, wolf." She shoved a muddy hand at him, landing on his face. She hadn't intended to do that. Didn't want him to think it a slap. "Oh, no, I didn't mean…"

And then something shifted inside her. The pristine, primped socialite fell off her pedestal and landed in the mud—and laughed. She lowered her head and curled her fingers deeper into the mud and laughed louder.

"Really?" Stryke sat and wiped at the mud on his face. "You think that was funny?"

"*That* wasn't funny." She grasped at the oozy mud and flung a wad at Stryke's chest. His stunned expression was exactly as she'd intended. "But that was."

"You think so?"

He raked up a slosh of mud and trailed his palm along her bare leg to her thigh. It didn't feel any nastier than the cold rain or the gritty mud beneath her knees. Blyss shifted in an attempt to shake his touch away, but her knees slid and her shoulders went down. She landed her back in the mud.

And Stryke landed on top of her, hands to either side of her head. Mud from his cheek spattered her nose and lips. She spat it out and cried out in disgust.

"Too late now, glamour girl. You're going to get messy."

"I already am!" she pleaded as his muddy hands moved over her hips and up to her breasts, where he pulled down her dress and caressed her bare skin. The cold shock of his touch tightened her nipples and the slip and slide of their bodies in the mud made their dalliance more fun than she would have expected.

"You're merciless," she gasped, but followed with a wad of mud to his neck. It oozed down his shirt, which he pulled off and tossed aside.

The sight of his bared muscles dripping clean with rain enticed her. She kissed his cool/hot skin and gently tugged his nipple with her teeth. "Mercy, you are beautiful."

His hand slapped her thigh and slid up under her dress, lifting it to expose her panties, which were soaked in mud. The ooze between her legs was not the sexiest feeling, but the roaming hands that lifted her to sit atop his thighs were.

She kissed his muddy mouth and tasted dirt and rain and summer grass. Definitely a unique taste experience, and the intensity of his want would not allow her to stop.

"You know," he said as he kissed down her chin and to her neck. "There's something about you getting all messy and horny at the same time. When you let down your defenses you get wild."

"You like me this way."

"I love you this way. Wild and unrestrained. You don't care what others think of you or what you look like. It's sexy."

"It'll be even sexier if we can make our way to a shower. I'm beginning to feel the mud creep into places I'd rather not feel it."

"There's a shower right inside the back door. It's like a mudroom."

"Well named."

"Right?"

"I never thought I'd ever have the need for something so terribly named as a mudroom, but I am at your mercy."

"Come on." He stood and grabbed her hand to pull her up. She claimed her muddy shoes in the process. "Sorry, but the rescue mission was a complete failure." He stroked a hank of wet, muddy hair from her cheek. "Forgive me?"

Blyss shook her head and held the shoes out at a distance. "Never. I like what you've done to me, Stryke. And despite the mud, it feels good. Unrestrained, like you said. Do you think it suits me?"

"It's an odd fit, but you know what? It does suit you."

And he swung her up into his arms and this time made it to the house without another slip.

The mudroom lived up to its name. After they'd showered and Blyss had headed upstairs to the bedroom to unpack, Stryke wiped down the tiled walls and made sure they didn't leave too much of a mess for Rhys.

Out in the homey kitchen that featured open shelves, log walls and red-checked curtains, he found a basket laden with fruit and wine and a welcome note that clued him there were fresh towels in the bathroom and sheets on the bed. Wine chilled in the fridge. The note was signed by a maid service. Nice.

He could get used to living the high life. An apartment in Paris and a country cabin? Toss in a gorgeous girlfriend and what more could he ask for?

Blyss's purse sat on the counter next to the fruit basket and it was open. He spied the cork stopper in the top of the vial he'd gotten from Himself. His heart dropped in his gut.

A *werewolf* was what more he could ask for. But he'd

resigned himself to accepting Blyss for what she wanted to be. She accepted him, country hick that he was.

Blyss wandered into the kitchen wearing her sheer robe and fluffing her wet hair over a shoulder. "All the mud gone?"

"Mostly," he reassured her, turning to embrace her and kiss the crown of her head. "Nice place, eh?"

"It is. Not so backwoods as I'd anticipated. Which is a relief. I want to sit in front of the fire. How about some wine before we tame the beast?"

"The beast? Is that what you think of a guy's were-wolf?"

"Well, it is your more beastly side, isn't it?" She trailed her finger down his bare chest. He wore but a towel around his hips. "I'd like to tame it."

She wandered into the living room and toward the fire. Firelight danced through the sheer robe silhouetting her slender frame.

"Taming sounds good," Stryke muttered.

He quickly located a corkscrew and opened a wine bottle. Pouring Blyss a goblet and bringing the bottle along for himself, he joined her on the thick white carpet before the fireplace. It was an electronic fire, but it put off some good heat and was probably safer. Though he did miss the smell of smoke and burning logs.

Blyss tilted her goblet against the bottle he held. "Here's to taming your wolf."

Stryke howled, releasing a long and randy call. "Give it your best shot, glamour girl."

"I think I'll start right now." And she tugged the towel from his hips and bent to kiss the head of his extremely hard erection.

Chapter 22

The sun was out. The rain had stopped. The surrounding forest glittered as if it was Faery. Keys in hand, Stryke was prepared to drive Blyss back into Paris when she descended from the upstairs bedroom wearing a sundress and no shoes. Hair darker than the black diamond that had caused him so much trouble spilled loosely over her shoulders and she floated up to kiss him.

"Good morning, *mon amour*."

"Uh, good morning." His sight lingered on the rise of her breasts peeking above the cheery yellow fabric. "You're looking so not ready to head back into the city."

"You want to be rid of me so quickly?"

"Hell no. But I thought… It is afternoon already, Miss Layabed."

"Do not mock my beauty sleep."

"Wouldn't dream of it."

"So…" She sidled up alongside him. She pulled her purse across the counter and sat on a bar stool to sort through whatever it was women kept inside those sacred caches of femininity. "What if I've decided to stay the night with you?"

Stryke couldn't help but gape. The implications should she stay…

"You do understand I'm going to be out running around in the forest tonight? In werewolf form."

She nodded, then pulled out from her purse the glass vial with the black wax seal and placed it on the counter between them.

Stryke bent to peer into the vial at eye level. The red liquid filled it to the top, which didn't make sense. He averted his gaze to Blyss, who nodded in agreement to his unasked question.

"You didn't drink it?" Standing, he stretched his arms along the counter and again eyed the devil's gift. "But that means…"

"I, uh…" She fluttered her lashes and looked aside sheepishly. "…was thinking maybe we could go out together tonight?"

"You mean as wolves?" He straightened. Smoothed a palm down his abs. Scratched his head. "But, Blyss, you said you only have to shift once a year, and that shift wasn't due for a few more months. You don't need to do it. Drink the potion and you'll stay the way you desire."

"I want to do this, Stryke. As painful as it will be to shift, I want to race alongside you and know what it's like to be in the presence of another wolf. A wolf that I can trust. Is that okay?"

"Okay?" He swung around the counter and pulled her into a hug. "That's better than okay. But are you sure?"

"Positive. I can drink the stuff tomorrow and get right back to where I prefer. But for tonight…I want to do this for me, but I also want to do it for you. Will you let me?"

"I can't wait until moonrise."

Stryke lowered the strap on Blyss's sundress, inhaling her sweet flower perfume as the fabric skimmed her skin. The dress dropped to the summer grass and tickled his bare toes. Naked, she shivered. He sensed it wasn't because she was cold, but rather nervous. The night was sultry and warm, a perfect evening to go skyclad.

That she wanted to shift to be with him as wolves was incredible. But he didn't want to force her to do anything to please him.

He'd already stripped away his clothes in preparation to shift. The summer breeze felt great on his skin, and his erection—unpreventable when standing so close to Blyss.

Now he bent to study her gaze. "You sure?"

"Very sure." She touched his abs and he hissed at the erotic flutter that shivered through his system. "But I don't want you to watch me shift. I don't want you to see me in pain."

"Blyss, if it's going to hurt you—"

She kissed him, stopping his protest. Her mouth was a gift he could never refuse. So sweet and soft. Priceless.

"It only hurts until I'm shifted," she whispered. "Maybe you could go on ahead and wait for me to follow after you?"

"I can do that." He respected her need to protect herself when likely she felt most vulnerable. "But if at any time this feels wrong to you, shift to *were* shape and we'll head back to the cabin, okay?"

"Your werewolf needs to howl at the moon, and I'm going to howl alongside you. Shift, lover. Let me admire you. Then run along and wait for me."

He kissed her, tasting the wine they'd imbibed earlier. The afternoon had been spent on the floor before the fireplace making love, lying quietly beside one another, snoozing a bit. It felt great to hold Blyss and think about spending the night together as wolves. And while he didn't want to know how painful the shift was going to be for her, he also wanted to experience her wild if she was willing to show it.

"I'll wait for you up on that rise in the forest about half a mile north." He pointed in the direction. And then he turned his focus inward and allowed his wolf to take control.

The shift was an exquisite exercise in muscle control and internal command. His bones shifted and shortened. His musculature stretched and snapped to conform to the smaller wolf shape. Fur grew out from his pores and his head changed the most, the maw growing long and his canines lengthening.

When finally he stood on four legs, Stryke was aware of the human female who stood before him. She smelled familiar and a little like a wolf. He knew she was his, but in his wolf mind he had no name for her. What he did know was that he should move along and wait for her elsewhere.

As she bent to stroke her fingers through his fur, he bowed his head and licked at her knee, her leg, the tips of her fingers. Tasted familiar. Tasted safe, like his own.

"I'll be right there" was what the sounds coming from her mouth formed, though he didn't understand them.

Stryke scented a rabbit not far off and his ears swiveled, picking up the movement of dozens of smaller creatures scampering about the earth and within the thick forest undergrowth.

He yipped and dashed off in pursuit of the adventure that could result in a tasty meal.

"That is one gorgeous wolf," Blyss whispered as Stryke loped off into the forest.

His fur was variegated in shades of brown, black and blond. He'd stood high to her waist, and he carried his thick tail proudly upright. A natural pack leader, if there was one.

Blyss had always considered the wolf as repellent as dogs and other animals she didn't want to get too close to. Yes, she had grown up among wolves. Had been accustomed to her parents wandering outside in wolf form, besides having some friends who had already come into their werewolf. Her disgust hadn't developed until her own shift had so awkwardly and devastatingly introduced her to ridicule.

But she was safe here with Stryke. And a giddy hum within her core urged her to crouch on the ground beside her discarded sundress. She wanted this. She needed this.

Closing her eyes and summoning the inner ability to shift, the first painful reactions crackled in her bones. She gasped, her fingers digging into the wet grass and dirt. It wasn't too late to stop. *Keep going. You want to be with him.* Her spine curved unnaturally upward, burning the pain along her length.

She cried out, yet continued. Bowing her head to the ground, she tensed her jaws as every muscle seemed to snap in on itself and tug her skeletal system into a bunch. Flipping onto her back, she released all human thoughts, and as fur covered her body and her legs kicked at air, the wolf whined at the horrible pain.

Finally, the shift was complete and the wolf shakily stood on all fours. The pain had ceased. No one around to fear. To point fingers. She was safe.

She sniffed the air, taking in the lingering scent of what she knew was her partner. And of a sudden, her tail wagged.

The moon was high and full.

The night called to her wild.

The wolves found one another, bumping noses and licking one another's maws in greeting and respect. They nudged their noses against ears, head and body, scenting one another, showing love and care.

Then Stryke dashed off through the forest and Blyss followed close behind.

They chased a rabbit and then a red fox. A few mice were sacrificed in playful dally. The wolves paused near a rocky outcrop and basked in the moonlight, Stryke's head resting upon Blyss's furry flank. And they were taken by the need to mate, and did so, howling their connection to the moon.

They woke on the porch before the cabin, both naked in human *were* form. Moonlight glanced through the oak and maple leaf canopy, dazzling across their skin. Stryke plucked a strand of grass from Blyss's hair and kissed her deeply. She curled up against his body, not being able to recall the pain of the shift, but remembering clearly the freedom and joy she had felt with her lover in their four-legged forms.

"Thank you," she whispered. "For making it so easy to trust you."

"You make a great wolf, glamour girl. I'm pretty sure we had sex."

"I think it was awesome. But you didn't let your werewolf out."

"The night's not over yet. I'll have to give the werewolf reign or it'll be on me all month to do so."

"I wouldn't miss it for the world."

"Really? You going to wolf out with me again?"

"Think you can handle my werewolf, big boy?"

"Bring it."

"Will I…? Will we…?"

He guessed what she couldn't quite put into words. He shouldn't be surprised no one had ever taught her the ways of their breed.

He nodded. "When a werewolf comes upon another of his breed, like a gorgeous female werewolf, he'll feel compelled to mate with her."

"And mating in werewolf form will bond us?"

He clasped her hand. "I don't think either of us is ready for that. Especially not when you've that vial of red stuff sitting inside on the counter. Why don't I head out on my own?"

She nodded. And Stryke exhaled in relief.

Disappointed? Hell yes. He'd love to bond with her. But no, he wasn't prepared to commit to a woman in werewolf form and then forever lose her to the humanity she craved.

He kissed her. "Go inside and snuggle before the fireplace. I won't be more than an hour."

"I'm sorry—"

He kissed her again. "There is nothing to apologize for. I know you. I accept you as you are. Okay?"

"I love you."

"I love you, too."

* * *

Morning woke them on the rug before the fire. Stryke had gone out and when he'd returned to the cabin had found Blyss sleeping. They showered together and made love.

Now he turned off the lights in the cabin and checked the fireplace one last time. "All hatches are battened down. You got your purse?"

"Yes."

"Don't forget that vial. It's sitting by the sink."

"Thanks. I'll drink it when I get home. I'm enjoying being able to smell everything turned up to eleven, and I never realized how improved my sight is when I let the wolf out."

"You still think I'm sexy now that you can see better?"

"You're even sexier." She kissed him quickly but took a moment to rub her cheek against his stubble. "Mmm... You're a combination of handsome, sensual and sexy eye candy."

"I don't know what to say to that."

"I'm crazy about you, Stryke. Take it for what you will. Let's stop and pick up some breakfast along the way, yes?"

"Way ahead of you. I'm craving eggs and bacon. Do they make that here in France?"

"A Croque Madame would be delicious."

"A crock of what?"

Blyss giggled. "I did see a McDonald's when we were passing through the suburbs."

"Sausage McMuffin, I'm coming for you!"

The drive-through McDonald's gave Stryke hope that the Europeans had a bit of redneck in them, after all. If he could park the car and shove down some processed food and a tall Coke he was happy. Blyss even took a bite of his sausage-and-egg sandwich and declared it tasty—but now sipped orange juice. Ah well, one did require a certain palate to appreciate the greasy goodness of fast food.

Stryke's thoughts wandered beyond the buzz of traffic zipping by on the ring road. He'd encountered danger in Paris, as he'd hoped for, and had defeated all threats to Blyss. But the thing with Tor and the wraiths the other day wouldn't leave his brain.

"This diversion thing is gnawing at me."

"Diversion?"

He confessed, "The night I showed up at your door with demon blood on me, ready to go on the boat cruise? I'd just killed a demon outside your door."

"What?"

"Earlier, when I met with Tor to pick up some faery dust, we were hijacked by a couple of demons. Only they said they were the diversion. Which is how I guessed you might be in trouble and headed immediately to your place. Caught a demon outside your door."

"Why didn't you tell me that?"

"Wasn't necessary." He balled up the food wrapper and tossed it in the open paper bag on the backseat. "I took care of it. But now that I think of it, if they weren't after me, but instead you, why? Why are demons still after you even knowing you no longer have *Le Diabolique*? What do you have that they want?"

Blyss shrugged. "I have no idea. I've sold all my jewels to pay for the pills. I have nothing of value save this diamond pendant." She tapped the necklace. "Well, and my shoes. But I don't think…"

No, the glamour girl could never part with those precious beauties.

"Think, Blyss. Do you have any friendships or business deals, anything, with demons beyond Edamite?"

"No. Not that I know of. I mean, I could be standing right next to one and I'd never know."

"Right. The pills." He tilted his head against the seat. "Who works with you? Who have you dealt with that might have something against you?"

"No one that I can think of. I'm a socialite. I don't make enemies. I, well, I make love. Except…"

"Yeah?"

"I haven't seen Lorcan in days. You met my assistant. I hired him six months ago. He's always been very attentive and suddenly he's gone. And I was going to tell you about the missing paperwork, but then when you found *Le Diabolique*, I figured it no longer mattered."

"What missing paperwork?"

"I have no records of receiving the diamond. No clue who it came from."

"And your assistant is up and missing?"

She nodded. "Do you think he could be in trouble? The demons could be after him?"

Stryke rapped the steering wheel with his fist. "Whatever it is, I'm inclined to suspect someone out there thinks you have something and they want it."

"I don't have anything. The only thing I took from the gallery was *Le Diabolique*."

"Right. And if demons are still after you, it makes me guess you would have something they want. Demonic."

"Do you think…they want to get rid of me?"

He caught the wobble in her tone and clasped her hand and pulled it to his mouth to kiss. "No, I don't think so. I may be blowing this all out of the water. It's done. *Le Diabolique* is safe and sound in the— Er, wherever the Old Lad has it." Which was in his gut. "And the ones who tried to take it have already had a swing at me and failed. But the missing assistant does bother me."

"It could be Edamite," she decided.

Stryke winced to recall what Kir had told him about Edamite being their half brother. The demon had said he would never harm Blyss. Threaten her, sure. Could he trust the demon had been speaking truthfully?

Hell, if Ed had wanted Blyss out of the picture, he would have succeeded with that task by now.

"You should have a talk with your brother about Ed sometime," Stryke suggested. He navigated the car down the street, heading toward the busy 1st arrondissement, where Blyss lived.

"Why?"

He shrugged. "Just think it would be a good idea. Ed is...more on your side than you know."

"Well, why don't *you* tell me?"

He winced again. Bad move. He didn't want to get stuck in the middle of a forced sibling reunion or rivalry.

"There's your street," he said, relieved for an escape. He pulled before Blyss's building and they strolled through the courtyard. He paused before the door, her suitcases in hand, and sniffed.

"What is it?" she asked as she punched in the digital code.

"Thought I smelled demon. But it's probably leftovers."

"Leftovers?" Blyss wrinkled her nose and did an assessment of the door, wall and ground around them. Tor had done an excellent job of cleanup, Stryke noted. Not a spot of demon blood that he could see.

"Can we go in? These suitcases of yours are heavy."

She cast him a doubtful look before crossing the threshold. So it had been a stupid excuse. He could heft a dozen of these bags and not feel the strain in his muscles. But it wasn't necessary to give Blyss all the bloody details. He'd taken care of the threat. Story over.

Her heels clicked down the hallway, and he followed the sexy sashay of her hips, clad in a narrow yellow dress that hugged all her sleek curves. The swing of her long hair across her shoulders made his mouth water, and he set down the suitcases and went in for the kiss—

"Ahem."

Stryke twisted to spy a strange man in a pink suit standing in Blyss's living room.

Chapter 23

"Lorcan."

Stryke stepped before Blyss, keeping her from approaching the assistant, who stood by the white couch, hands at his hips, the smile on his face as forced as a thief's entry.

"What are you doing here?" Stryke asked. "Do you always break into your employer's home?"

"I came to apologize." Lorcan paced to the side, putting himself a little closer to Blyss, so Stryke was forced to move slightly aside. "I took *Le Diabolique*. I was desperate."

"Oh, Lorcan, but it was a fake."

"Blyss." Stryke was not sensing the man had come to beg forgiveness. Something about the tension in the fisted hands at his sides and the faint but distinct red glow in his eyes. "He's demon."

"Aren't you the clever one?" Lorcan suddenly

dropped the contrite act. "And her." He drew in a breath through his nose. "You're smelling rather wolfish today, Blyss. You finally decide to drop the lie and come clean?"

"What do you know about me, Lorcan?" Blyss asked. Stryke clasped her hand when she stepped up to stand beside him. "Who are you?"

"I've been living among the bloody humans for months in wait of the perfect means to finally gain some power in this city. I need control. More power than Edamite Thrash holds over the local denizens. My denizen was this close—" he pinched his fingers together before him "—to releasing Xyloda. And then the Lone Ranger of Werewolves comes riding in with Himself as his sidekick and spoils all my hard work."

"You were the one after *Le Diabolique*?" Blyss said on a gasp.

"It's gone," Stryke said firmly. "So you can either take the easy way—leave and never return, or…" He flicked out his claws. "…you can do it the hard way."

"I mean Blyss no harm," Lorcan hurried out. "I've seen the error of my ways. I want you to take me back, Blyss. I need the job. I've ransomed my hopes of defeating Thrash at his own game. What do you say? Let bygones be bygones?"

Blyss glanced up at Stryke. He shook his head. No way the demon was telling the truth. "He sent his henchmen after you. They would have killed you."

"Oh, no," Lorcan said. "I don't think I could have killed Blyss. At least, not until I'd learned where *Le Diabolique* was."

Blyss shook her head. "Get out." She stepped forward, gesturing toward the door down the hallway, and in that moment in which her body was positioned slightly closer to the demon than Stryke's, Lorcan grabbed her by the arm and wrangled her into a choke hold.

Stryke growled.

"Come one step closer," Lorcan warned, "and I'll crush her throat." He eased his fingers about her slender neck. "I want the diamond! You were the last to see it. Take me to it, and only then will Blyss be safe."

The bastard didn't know whom he was dealing with. And he would not allow this fool one more moment of contact with his woman.

"Nope." Stryke swept a hand aside Blyss's neck, pushing her away, while at the same time, he brought his other clawed hand down across Lorcan's chest.

The demon screamed, clasping at his chest. Blyss stumbled against the wall.

"I don't make bargains with idiots," Stryke said as the deep cuts in the demon's chest crackled and formed into black crystals that then moved over the pink suit as if eating the creature alive.

Lorcan's body crystallized, burning away the suit, and dispersed across the white marble floor.

Stryke shook his hand and his claws retracted. He grinned over the pile of demon ash. And then he noticed Blyss shivering and balled-up by the wall. He dashed to her and took her in his arms.

"Sorry you had to see that."

"He deserved it. He would have killed me and you."

"You really believe that?"

She shook her head. "No, I don't. You would have protected me, no matter what. He was no match to you. Thank you."

She buried her head against his neck and clutched him tightly. But she didn't cry. Instead, Stryke thought he could feel her strength permeate his skin and bones, and he inhaled her natural wolfish scent. This woman was strong and brave, and she was more than a simple glamour girl.

"I love you, Blyss. Nothing in this world will come between me and that love. I promise."

"You make it sound like forever," she whispered.

"I want it to be forever."

She looked up at him, her green eyes blinking back tears. "Really?"

"I love you. No matter what. Wolf or human. I'll love you."

"I love you, too. No matter what. But you know what would make me love you even more?"

"Tell me. I'll make it happen."

"Help me clean up this demon mess?"

He laughed and she joined in, and in the middle of retrieving the broom and dustpan and trying to avoid all the black crystals scattered across the marble floor, Stryke's phone rang.

"Rhys, I'm not sure. I'm in the middle of something with Blyss right now. Huh? Oh, no, not that." He winked at Blyss.

She swept the demon ash toward the dustpan. "Go. I've got this."

"I shouldn't leave you."

"Why? Do you think there's still demons out there who want to harm me?"

"No, I just…"

"I'll be fine," she offered. "Go. Come back to me when you can. I'll be thinking of you."

Stryke kissed her long and deep and then glanced to the pile of demon ash. "I should clean that up for you first."

"No." She pushed him down the hallway. "You know I've been testing my domestic skills lately. This'll be fun."

"Seriously?"

"Stryke, you're needed."

"And it feels like you're trying to get rid of me."

She kissed him again. "Never. I'll be waiting for you in bed."

"I'll hurry back."

Closing the door behind her lover's retreat, Blyss let out a huffing exhalation, then charged into the bedroom and landed on the end of the bed, breathing heavily.

Her spine shifted. Her skin crawled. She moaned at the tendrils of pain that crossed her skin.

"Shit," she hissed, and then her body began to shift.

Stryke had used Rhys's name when holding the phone conversation before Blyss, but that had been a ruse. He had been thinking quick on his feet and hadn't thought it necessary, or wise, to reveal to her who was really on the other end of the line.

Now he shook Edamite Thrash's hand and the demon nodded he follow him down the aqueduct toward the rusted door they had visited previously.

Yeah, he'd shaken the guy's hand. Much as he'd never admit it out loud, Stryke was okay with Thrash. He wasn't okay with how he'd threatened Blyss, but he did believe he would have never gone through with those threats. And the demon had only been trying to keep Xyloda from being released upon this mortal realm.

Something all right about that goal.

Ed stepped through the open doorway, bending as he led Stryke down a tunnel that was all of limestone.

Despite the river outside, Stryke swallowed harder the deeper he walked, for the dry air seeped into his lungs.

He was hit by an intense sulfur scent as the tunnel opened into a vast cave. Ed spread out his arms before the empty room. "Wanted you to know that matters have been dealt with."

"I don't understand." He traced his gaze along the walls and up and around the curved ceiling and finally across the floor— Ah. "That looks like a hell of a lot of demon ash."

"I, and my team, slaughtered Lorcan's denizen."

"Nice. How'd you know it was Lorcan?"

"One of his lackeys came to me this morning. I thought you'd appreciate me taking care of the riffraff."

"I do. Wish you would have called earlier, though. Lorcan was waiting for us in Blyss's apartment."

"Merde."

"He's ash."

Ed smirked and met Stryke's fist bump. "I like you, Saint-Pierre."

"Yeah, well…" Stryke sighed.

"You don't have to say it. I have my own way of doing things. But know I would never harm Blyss or her family. Er, my family."

"I get that. But Blyss still owes you money."

"I'll be fine. Are you going to take care of her? She needs you."

"Not sure Paris needs me, and she doesn't need Minnesota."

"If it's love you should go for it. Not often that comes into a man's life."

"I'll take that into consideration. Thanks, man. I need to get back to Blyss. Left her to clean up Lorcan's ash."

"Blyss does housework?"

"Wonders never cease, eh?"

* * *

The doorbell rang and Blyss sat up on the couch. The soft white wool blanket she'd wrapped herself in slipped from her shoulders. She eyed the turned-over coffee table and hastily righted it, setting the books back on top. Cruising through the kitchen, she picked up a tattered magazine and tossed it in the trash.

She glanced about. She'd picked up most of the mess earlier and had swept up Lorcan's remains. *After* she'd come back from the shift to wolf. The new mess had been from her wolf.

She hadn't been able to control the insistent need to shift. The wolf had come upon her so suddenly it was all she could do to keep from screaming at the pain and alerting her neighbors. Thank the goddess the wolf had been contained within her apartment and hadn't tried to get out through a window. She'd been able to come back to human form only fifteen minutes ago and had collapsed on the couch in tears.

Now she checked her face in the refrigerator door glass. She hadn't time to put on makeup earlier—no streaked mascara or smeared lipstick. Her hair needed combing, and other than being naked beneath the blanket, she looked…

"Like hell. He'll never believe me. But I can't tell him. Not yet."

Because she had to be sure. She didn't want to get his hopes up. Or hers.

Stryke rang the doorbell as she swung the door open and leaned out to kiss him. She pulled him inside by his shirtfront, still kissing him and hoping to distract him from asking the obvious questions.

"Mmm, you are happy to see me."

"I am." She tugged him down the hallway.

Stryke slid onto the stool before the counter. "You're wearing a blanket? What do you have on under there?"

"Nothing." She tugged the blanket a little closer. Not feeling the sexy vibes at the moment. "I showered and then lay down for a bit. I, uh, think the weekend tired me out. I was going to get dressed and then you rang."

"You don't have to get dressed. I like you au naturel."

"You like me any way but all dressed up and— Stryke, you used French. You're learning, *mon amour*. So what's up? Everything go well with Rhys?"

"Yep. Another job done all tidy and swept under the rug. And speaking of sweeping… You need me to sweep up a demon for you?" He glanced over his shoulder into the living room.

"No, I got that. Though I've still some cleaning to do. Don't look at the mess."

She cringed at sight of the lamp hanging off the chair arm.

"But how did it get so—?"

Blyss tugged Stryke toward the bedroom. "Come and help me pick out some clothes and shoes."

"Shoes? I have no talent for shoes, glamour girl."

"Sure you do. Just sit there." She pushed him onto the bed. "And I'll model for you." She headed into the shoe closet, glad to have diverted him from the mess out in the living room. The man was keen on picking up the details and sensing when all was not right.

He'd have to go back that way sooner or later. How many pairs of shoes could she model before he figured something was up?

Once inside the closet she felt the strange tug across her shoulder muscles. Hell, the feeling wasn't strange; it was too familiar.

"Not again." She clasped the lip of the closest shelf

and breathed shallowly as she concentrated on the sudden twinges to her muscles. Sure sign of an imminent shift. And focusing on the sweet pair of candy-red Viviers wasn't helping to distract one bit.

"I suddenly have the desire for some champagne!" she called out.

"Uh..." Stryke said from the bedroom. "Okay. I'll get some from the fridge."

"All out! You'll need to run to the wineshop down the street."

"Seriously?"

Tensing her gut and clinging desperately to the door frame, Blyss forced on a smile and brushed back the hair from her face. She strode to the closet doorway, blanket clutched before her chest. "If you bring the champagne, I'll find it very difficult to get dressed so quickly."

His eyebrow lifted. That sexy know-it-all smirk curled.

Even as she felt her spine twitch, she ran her tongue teasingly along her lower lip. "I want to celebrate us," she managed to say. "All night."

"The woman has a plan." Stryke stood and approached her.

She put up a palm. "No kisses until you bring the champagne. I'll be waiting." She tugged off the blanket and tossed it at him. "No touching until you get back."

Her fingernails dug into the door frame on the closet side. He couldn't see her fighting the shift.

"Deal." Stryke tilted a wink at her and strolled out of the bedroom.

Chapter 24

Champagne in hand, Stryke picked up his pace down the cobbled street. It had taken an inordinate amount of time in the wineshop. A two-for-one sale had brought out the French in hordes. And his inability to speak the language had probably made him miss his chance at the register more than a few times. And then there was the spry old woman who had pushed past him with an armload of vino.

Ah well, he'd survived that debacle. And now a gorgeous, and naked, woman waited his return. A woman he had promised to love no matter what. He couldn't wait to snuggle up to Blyss beneath the sheets and drink the champagne from her lips.

Rounding a corner, he was roughly shouldered by a teenager running by. "Hey!" But Stryke didn't pursue because a scream alerted him. "What's going on?" he asked a passing tourist who screamed and clutched his child's hand.

"A monster!" the man said in frantic gasps. "It's a big wolf!"

Heart dropping like a stone, Stryke picked up his pace. A big wolf? Monster? It couldn't be. Not in this city crushed from building to building with people. Suddenly he saw the wolf run across the street and down a narrow alleyway.

Not a wolf, but a werewolf.

A handful of teenage boys followed, curiosity killing their sense of safety.

"Shit." It couldn't be. Could it? "Blyss?"

He'd not seen her in werewolf form. And she had taken the elixir, right?

"Please let her have taken the elixir."

He hastened into a run and rounded the corner, racing up behind the young men. Shoving them out of his way, he pushed hard enough to knock them over, but not break bones. "Stay the hell away!"

"But, dude, it's a werewolf!"

"Movie costume!" Stryke called back.

Ahead, the werewolf howled, obliterating his claim to it being a fantastic movie prop. No werewolf with a sense of self-preservation would ever shift in the city. And if so? They certainly wouldn't run around frightening tourists and inviting the police, or worse, animal control with a tranquilizer gun.

It could be Blyss. Hadn't she taken the elixir Himself had made for her? Did she fear its dark origins? Or had she simply forgotten?

No, that was out of the question. Foremost in Blyss's heart was keeping the illusion of normality that she'd created over the years. Drinking that vial would have been a quick and easy fix. He didn't understand.

Yet she'd pushed him out to get the champagne. He

hadn't thought much about it until now. It had been weird, as if she'd wanted to get rid of him. But why? To shift?

"Can't be her," he muttered and pushed harder to gain on the wolf.

They'd entered a residential area. Overgrown shrubbery demarcated some yards. A quiet neighborhood. Not the optimal place for a crazed werewolf to roam. Of course, no place was, unless it was out in a vast forest far from humans.

Just don't howl again, he thought.

The sound of a police siren trilled behind him. A long way off. He couldn't know if it was because of the werewolf—what sane police dispatch was going to answer a call to pursue a werewolf?—or probably it was headed out on a routine call like a burglary or traffic violation.

This had to be the first time Stryke wished for burglary in answer to a multiple-choice question. Because he knew in his heart the werewolf was Blyss. He sensed her now. Could smell her essence. His own wolf stirred in an instinctual need to catch the wolf it recognized as one with whom he'd mated.

The werewolf veered left. Stryke made a quick turn, hoping to head off the wolf. He pushed through a tangle of vines, and seeing the hip-high shrub that delineated a backyard, he leaped and jumped over it, landing deftly on the ground. Realizing the champagne bottle was still in hand, he abandoned it and picked up into the run again. He could hear the wolf's breathing now and sensed it had slowed pace. Pausing to mark the area, determine where next to go. Or perhaps even slowing to rest, take in the surroundings. Seek shelter.

Sneaking under a high-trimmed willow tree, Stryke

sighted the sleek black werewolf, who entered a small garden shed without a door. He eyed the house. He saw no clues that residents were inside. The overgrown garden and a couple of plastic bags of garbage sitting on the back stoop also alerted him that perhaps they were gone.

He raced to the shed, and when the werewolf turned to slash its talons at him, Stryke realized he wasn't going to win this one in human form.

Quickly, he shifted, unzipping and shoving down his jeans as he did and tearing off his shirt. The shed was probably ten-by-ten feet square and empty, save for a rack on the wall that held a rusted old bicycle.

The werewolf lunged for him again and pinned him to the dirt ground just as his werewolf fully formed. The werewolves struggled briefly, but Stryke's wolf was able to easily subdue the other, who wasn't so much fighting as acting in self-defense. He sniffed the female and sensed their connection, and as much as the wolf in him wanted to mate, his *were* side pulled more strongly.

Safe was the feeling he knew he had to share. The werewolf needed to feel safe.

Stryke shifted back to *were* shape, clutching the other as she also shifted. They came to *were* form together, lying on the shed's cool dirt floor. Blyss shivered in his arms. She startled and scrambled closer, frantic pants huffing across his chin.

"It's okay, sweetie. I'm here." He pulled her onto his lap and cradled her head against his chest.

"How did I get here? Where are my clothes?"

"You shifted to werewolf shape."

"Mon Dieu."

Why the hell this had happened, he couldn't begin to guess. But now was no time for questions. "Let me take you home."

She nodded and clutched him tighter. "Please."

"I'll get dressed. Then I'll find you something to wear."

He hated leaving her alone and shivering in the shed, but he couldn't walk through Paris with a naked woman in his arms. His jeans had survived the shift. Mostly. One leg was ripped down the inner seam. Nothing he could do about that.

Walking around back of the house, he determined no one was inside, and while he wasn't an expert at picking locks, he did find a low sash window that wasn't locked. And he wasn't sure how much time they had before a curious human found them. Jiggling the wooden frame, he was able to push it up and climb inside.

Elderly people had to live here because he couldn't find anything more suitable than a long, floral robe for Blyss to wear. She didn't complain as he helped her dress.

In fact, she remained quiet, her head bowed. The shift had been unexpected, he decided. She was as freaked about it as he.

"Let's go," he said and swept her into his arms.

Once back at her place, he ran a bathtub full of hot water and helped her get in.

Stryke brewed some chamomile tea he found in the kitchen cupboard. He'd left Blyss to soak in the tub. She had clung to him all the way home, but he'd sensed her need to clean up and pull herself together. To be by herself. He couldn't fathom why she'd been out and about as a werewolf, but he sensed it hadn't entirely been her fault.

Had something gone wrong with the potion Himself had provided? Maybe it was faulty? He should have never accepted a boon from such evil. He blamed himself for anything that may go wrong with Blyss because of the elixir.

And yet, were he a pack leader and had it been one of his pack members who had exposed their breed to the public, he would surely reprimand the wolf. A beating, perhaps from the pack, a show of authority. A female he would assign a less severe punishment.

Could he command a pack and delve out the punishment when the rules were broken? Yes. Because the rules kept them alive. Blyss needed—well, she needed to be human. It was what worked best for her.

What would a pack think if he had a human wife, but also knew that she had been born wolf? That she denied her heritage. It wouldn't go over well. And he would never ask any wolf to accept her as part of the pack family.

He didn't want to lose Blyss.

Did that mean he'd never have a pack? He couldn't let his father down. Or himself. Which meant the next conversation he had with Blyss would prove the toughest ever.

The tea was mixed with a touch of mint, and the cool scent tingled in his nose. He'd made himself a cup, too. The sun had set. Moonlight beamed through the glass ceiling.

Sighing, he picked up the cups and wandered into the bedroom. Blyss sat on the bed, a sheet pulled up about her breasts. She hadn't dressed. She thanked him for the tea and sipped. Earthy scents infused the room.

He wasn't sure how to start the conversation, so he crawled up beside her and nuzzled his face into her hair. She smelled like the exquisite socialite he'd first met in the gallery weeks ago. But her delicate, shivering frame felt defeated and small. As if something had stolen her hope.

After a few sips in silence he made a stab at the truth.

"Blyss, you haven't drunk the red stuff, have you?"

She shook her head, lowered her lashes.

"Is that why you shifted?"

"I think so. I didn't shift on purpose. It came on me so suddenly. I, uh… Earlier today when you were away helping Rhys, I shifted to wolf without volition, as well. It's why I pushed you out of here so quickly when I felt it happening again."

"I did get a weird feeling about that."

"I'm sorry."

"Why don't you drink the elixir and stop it? What happened was dangerous, Blyss. Not only to you but innocent humans. A fully shifted werewolf should not run through the streets of Paris."

"I know, I know."

He traced her cheek, toying with a curl of darkest hair. "I thought you wanted to be human more than anything?"

She stretched her shoulders back, sitting up straighter. The sheet fell away. She was so beautiful beneath the moonlight. He decided this apartment, with the windows in the ceiling, must have been crafted with Blyss in mind. Like a star upon a stage, she was a true glamour girl.

"Things have changed," she said so softly he had to lean forward to hear, and that was saying a lot considering his wolf hearing could pick up a mouse running across wet summer leaves half a mile away.

He took her teacup and set his and hers aside on the nightstand, then clasped her hand and waited for her to explain. For the longest time she held his gaze. Her bold green eyes captured him, teased him, touched him. Revealed her vulnerabilities. For the first time in his life, he could feel tears well behind his eyes.

So this was what it was like to love someone so much that their pain became your own?

Yet beyond her pain he sensed something brighter. Perhaps even hopeful.

"I didn't take the elixir because I thought I could give the werewolf a test-drive," she said. "Maybe try it on and wear it awhile. Get a feel for, well…myself. A lot has changed since that first horrible shift. My life is something I've created down to every last detail, but…" She touched his lips and smiled. "Is the life I've made really the life I was meant to have?"

He kissed her fingertips. She was the only one who could answer that. Hell, he had no clue because he was still making his own life. And he liked the way it was going so long as it included Blyss.

"I figured I could give it a month or two," she continued. "I'll always have the elixir. I can take it at any time. I want to do this for me, but as well, I want to do it for you. I love you, Stryke. And I never felt closer to a person than during the time we spent at the cabin. You make me want to embrace something I've always denied."

Her words were sincere. He believed that she believed what she said 100 percent. But could the glamour girl exist alongside the werewolf? He didn't want her to sacrifice any of the fine things and the lifestyle she had come to love for him.

Because loving him was as far from fancy shoes and diamonds and Paris as she could get.

"Tell me you'll support me," she said. "Please?"

"Blyss, I'm behind you 100 percent. You want to try

on your werewolf and take it for a spin? I've got your back. As well as your pretty little tail and those gorgeous claws. But will you promise not to take the werewolf for a run in the middle of Paris during the height of tourist season?"

"That's the one small problem. I can't seem to control the urge to shift. It just…attacks me. I wonder if there's a transition period? I hope that's what this is, because if I can't control my wolf then I might as well drink the Kool-Aid right now."

He stroked her hair and chuckled. "The French have Kool-Aid?"

"Something similar. But will you help me? If I shift again, I don't know what will happen. The wolf I can keep contained in the apartment, but my werewolf is another story."

"Maybe we should head out to the cabin for a couple more days?"

"Can we? Would Monsieur Hawkes mind?"

"I'll give him a call." He kissed her, intending for it to be quick, but Stryke got lost in the sweet taste of his future, and he pushed Blyss back into the pillows and caressed her breasts. "Mmm, I suddenly have the urge to mess you up, glamour wolf."

She propped up on her elbows and pressed a finger over his lips. "You called me glamour wolf."

"That's what you are. You okay with that?"

She nodded. "Very."

A month later, Stryke still hadn't left Paris. And Blyss was over the moon about that. Rhys Hawkes had offered him a permanent job at Hawkes Associates, which he was currently considering. But Blyss knew his home in the States called to him. There was where his family lived. It was where he had made a life, as small and comfortable as it was. It was where his future as a pack leader waited.

And she wanted him to have that future.

As well, Stryke considered the idea of starting an enforcement team such as Kir was a part of. He'd spent more time with Kir and had gone out with the Enforcement team to observe. He always returned to Blyss in a great mood, rambling on how he intended to institute the ideas and procedures when he got back home.

He'd made plenty of friends and gained family here in Paris. But he missed his brothers and sister and his home.

Blyss sensed his heavy heart, and now as she wandered through her apartment, crossing the clean white marble floor and landing in the living room beneath the skylights, she sighed.

Was this her home? Or was it a stage she'd created to suit her desire to live a life as completely opposite of that which her wolf demanded?

Werewolves lived in the city. It wasn't an odd thing. They could even own galleries and host elaborate parties and socialize and own closets full of expensive shoes. She knew that because she'd been doing it for a month.

The wax-sealed vial sat in the medicine cabinet, waiting her complete abandonment of this new lifestyle. Yet it wasn't so different. She'd gained control of her wolf after a weekend at the cabin. It was as though her wild side had jumped forth after being suppressed for all those years. It wanted out and needed to run free. So she had let it out and had spent more time in wolf and werewolf form than in *were* shape.

She and Stryke had been cautious not to bond as

werewolves, though. He said it was something sacred, something he would only do if and when they decided that they were the only one for the other. He'd not used the word *marriage*, but Blyss understood. He was old-fashioned that way.

When two werewolves mated, they bonded for life. It was a serious deal. And yet she entertained doing just that with Stryke. She loved him. She wanted to be with him forever.

But his forever tugged him away from Paris. Could she leave the city in which she'd grown up? The city that was as much a part of her soul as her breath?

She'd already made the decision to travel to the States for a few weeks with him over the winter holidays to meet his family. But once there, would he want to stay? Could they manage a life together yet perhaps live in both places? What about a long-distance relationship?

When she'd only recently thought her biggest challenge was accepting her wolf, now she was surprised by the difficulty she faced in merely leaving a city. Her home.

"Come here, glamour girl."

She settled onto the sofa on her lover's lap. His hair had grown since he'd been here and tufted over his ears.

"You have a fancy shindig tonight?"

The gallery, which she was considering selling, was showing a series of Mucha lithographs this evening. Her presence was required, though she trusted her new assistant—Lisa, a human girl from New York City just out of college. She had been vetted by Stryke as human, when she'd introduced the two and he'd surreptitiously sniffed her out. Lisa could handle it. But Blyss did still enjoy the socializing.

"You want to come along?" she asked.

She didn't miss his wince. "How about I head out to the cabin and wait for you? Full moon tomorrow night."

"Sounds like a plan. I'll even pack proper country clothing this time."

He'd spent hours browsing the jewelry shops, looking over every diamond ring, nodding as the salespeople wanted to show him yet another stone in a different cut, or clarity. Or how about a few more carats for the lucky girl?

After two days of shopping for a ring with which he could propose to Blyss, Stryke had given up. Because he realized no diamond could ever satisfy her. Sure, she was all diamonds and moonlight now. He loved his glamour girl when she followed him out to the forest, dropping her pretty silk dress without a care and leaving the diamond on top of that. And then her wild overtook and the moonlight reigned.

No precious stone could ever show her exactly how much he adored her. How much he admired her for bravely accepting her wolf. Or how much he loved being with her.

So when he paused before a shop that sold funky yet modern clothing and jewelry, his eyes landed on a simple ring in the window display. He pressed his palms to the window.

"Perfect."

Chapter 25

Stryke navigated the long country road that wound two miles through a thick forest of pine trees and bare-branched elms to his parents' property. The whole family would be waiting, and he was nervous for Blyss.

Sure, she'd met his brothers and sister briefly at the wedding last summer, but that had been different. Now he was presenting his bondmate to his family. The woman with whom he intended to spend the rest of his life. The woman who wore a wooden engagement ring on her finger because she loved him and wanted to be with him forever.

Okay, so he was nervous, too. He wanted his family to like her. He'd explained everything to his mother over the phone about how Blyss had denied her werewolf for years, and how she only recently embraced her heritage. Surely that news had circulated among his siblings.

It was Malakai Saint-Pierre, his father, from whom

he most worried about getting the seal of approval. If his father didn't like Blyss, then she was out, plain and simple. And while he loved Blyss, he respected his father and would likely have a tough decision to make should the pack principal give the thumbs-down. But he couldn't imagine anyone saying nay to Blyss.

As well, when the New Year turned, Kai intended Stryke should make his new pack official by choosing a scion. Trouble wasn't at all bummed that the family pack was being dissolved; he intended to start a pack on his own. But not until he'd thoroughly sown his wild oats. And that guy had a lot of them.

Blade had said *no, thank you* to scion. Kelyn would make an excellent right-hand man but Stryke would give it more consideration. With luck, Blade would change his mind.

He stroked Blyss's cheek now and she smiled at him.

"Pull over," she said and turned on the seat to sit up on her knees.

"We're almost there, glamour wolf. Half a mile—"

"Please?"

She must be as nervous as he was. A few minutes to take a deep breath and chill was a good idea. He shifted into Park and they sat in the Ford truck, the engine idling, the radio quietly broadcasting a country tune.

"They will all love you," he reassured her. "But never so much as I do."

"I'm not worried." She crawled over and straddled him in the tight confines of the cab. "Are *you* worried?"

"My dad's the tough one," he said. "But I know he'll love you."

"It was a good idea to come here for Christmas. I'm already in love with your state after seeing all this snow."

"You may be the only one who has ever made such a confession."

"Well, I don't have to shovel it. And so you know, I will never shovel snow or do the manual labor in this partnership."

"Wouldn't dream of letting you lift a pretty little finger to do anything but this." He took her hand and kissed her fingertips, one by one. "Sure you don't want a diamond engagement ring?"

"Never. This one is perfect. It's you, wrapped around my finger. I adore it." She leaned in and whispered aside his ear. "I want to give you your Christmas present now."

"Really? You got me something? Blyss, you shouldn't have. Us together is all I want for Christmas."

"Then you don't want this?" She took his hand and placed it over her stomach, which was softly swollen beneath the thick sweater she'd bought yesterday in town at the local thrift store.

"What, sweetie?"

She tilted her head at him and told him to close his eyes. "Now," she said, "concentrate on what you feel. Can you feel it?"

Stryke slid his hand across the soft pink sweater. He could feel her warmth radiate out and into his skin. And beyond the subtle hum of her sensual being, he picked up...

He flashed his eyes open to meet her expectant gaze. "Really? I think I feel a tiny heartbeat."

She nodded. "Our family is already growing."

"Blyss, this is amazing. Really? I'm going to be a daddy?"

"And a very fine dad you will be. We'll raise our family here, in the place that makes you most happy, sending them off to school in the fall and winter, and then in the summer we'll vacation in Paris. Can the pack handle that?"

"They'll handle whatever their leader says they can. You've got great plans. You really think you could live in Minnesota?"

"So long as the summers are in Paris and my shoe closet can be shipped back and forth."

"Why not keep a shoe closet here and one in Paris?"

"I adore you, *mon amour.*"

He bent and hugged his cheek against her tummy and tried to listen for the tiny heartbeat. Detecting it, Stryke smiled. "This little one is going to love his were-wolf mommy."

* * * * *

THE VAMPIRE'S FALL

Chapter 1

It wasn't often Blade Saint-Pierre walked through the Darkwood without a purpose—or a weapon. Tonight he'd craved the exhilaration of awareness that always accompanied such a venture. Instincts on alert and every muscle in his body strung tightly, he closed his wings against his back as, barefoot, he strode toward the clearing that opened to a mossy bed edging a stream.

A dark forest of no return, the massive acreage edged his property. The Darkwood was a no-man's-land that was principally Faery, but as well, a place for all breeds to congregate. It provided respite for those who could not walk amongst humans. A wayside stop for those paranormals traveling this realm that wished to take a breath before meeting the challenge of humans.

No humans dared enter the forest, for rumors told it was haunted and that the former residents of Blade's property—the original 1910 mansion had been razed—

had killed themselves after hearing voices tell them to cut out their hearts.

Great rumor, Blade thought. It helped him maintain his privacy. It wasn't at all true. But it worked for him. Though he respected the boundaries of the Darkwood and only entered it with a certain reverence and much caution. Even then, he only stayed so long as his comfort level allowed.

Rumors told that people went into the Darkwood and they never came out. Deer, squirrels and wildlife? They didn't exist within the dark thickness of evil that formed the murky wood.

Blade smirked as a squirrel scampered past him, its goal, the stream. And at that reminder that all was not as it seemed—or was rumored to be—he let down his shoulders and knelt on a mossy stone, pressing his fingers into the thick, verdant frosting. For the moment, he connected with it all. The grass, stones and trees. All creatures small and large whose heartbeats he could sense. The atoms that formed his body were the same atoms that formed nature, the very air, earth and flora.

How blessed was he?

You are alive. You have survived. Move on, yes?

He was trying.

While principally considered vampire, Blade had also his mother's faery genetics coursing within his system. His black wings were not so faery-like, and the leathery edges were serrated and sharp, as if demonic. He didn't mention his faery side to others. It was his dark beast, which craved unnatural tastes, such as demon blood, that others knew about—if they knew at all.

Blade honored all of nature's creatures, including those breeds considered monsters by humans who would believe in myth. And yet, he hated demons. That a part of him looked similar to the creatures disturbed him. His wings shamed him and defined him as different. And different amongst the varied species was not always a saving grace.

Such a difference had attracted cruelty to his life.

He'd kept to himself over the past year. To the point that his brothers and sister had begun to call him a hermit. The quiet one.

He'd always been quiet. More in tune with nature than with what was going on with the human realm. The cruelty that his difference had attracted? He'd suffered torture a year ago. And following that, he had hidden away. Not wanting to show his face, his scars, to anyone. Not wanting to put himself out in a world that could attack at any moment.

For if attacked, he would retaliate.

He didn't wish to harm others. Unless it was necessary.

He'd almost mastered the hermit role until last month when an old man filling his rusty 1970s Ford at the gas station had asked him if he'd any carpentry skills. Reluctantly, Blade had nodded and stepped outside his self-imposed prison of comfort. He'd been helping the elderly with small projects in and about their homes for a couple weeks now, and…it did feel good.

Life was beginning to look up.

At the sound of something heavy lighting onto the moss behind him Blade tilted his head. He smelled no odor out of the usual, yet his skin prickled. He should be able to pick up most scents. He rose to his six-feet-four-inch height, and with a stealthy twist, turned to stare into the cold white irises of a man with equally pale skin.

From the Darkwood? Most likely. The man looked human, save for the diagonal scars over each temple, which resembled gills, but no breath opened and closed the slashes. His brows were as black as his hair and clothing, which blended him into the night. His pale face, neck and hands were the only things remarkable; the pinpoint blue glow that seemed to radiate from around his irises especially stood out on his face.

"Blade Saint-Pierre," the man said in tones that slithered with a sharp silver edge. "I am Sim."

"What are you?" Blade asked, stepping up closer and thrusting back his shoulders. He unfurled his wings and they stretched out boldly behind him.

"Nothing so spectacular as a winged vampire," the man said with a glance to take in the imposing wingspan. "I have an offer for you."

Blade inhaled through his nostrils, frustrated that he couldn't scent the man. Which meant he was not one of the many species he could instinctually sniff out. But for every breed with which he was familiar, there were so many more he could not scent.

The curiosity wasn't demon. That scent always put up Blade's hackles. And that small detail was the only thing that stopped Blade from sweeping forward a wingtip and slashing it across the stranger's long pale neck.

"I can move much faster than your feeble mortal realm allows you," the man warned, seeming to sense Blade's defensive thoughts. "You do not know me, but trust me, you've no reason to fear or consider me enemy. In fact, what I want of you will give you such satisfaction that your faery will delight in the riches."

"I don't need money," Blade countered. "You know nothing about me."

"Not monetary riches but rather such that feeds your very soul. I know you crave demon blood, fanged one."

Blade's fingers twitched for the knife he'd left back home. He'd not revealed to anyone his insistent craving for demonic blood. It had developed during the torture a year ago. His family members would be appalled to learn of his new habit. For a man without a vast network of friends, their opinion meant everything to him.

He remained before the scentless curiosity, willing to hear him out.

"The demonic ranks are growing in the area," Sim stated, clasping his pale hands before him. "I want you to annihilate them."

Blade chuckled.

"You laugh as defense, vampire. Foolishly so. You have the desire to do as I request. I know you have been humiliated and crushed by the *mimicus* denizen. I offer you the chance to bring them all down. Cleanse this realm of the demons who dare to tread amongst humans before their denizens populate into rages."

A *denizen* was a group of demons, much like a vampire tribe. When their numbers increased or the denizens joined forces they were termed a *rage*, vast quantities of the merciless bastards.

The man was playing it dramatically, and that made Blade wonder if he was mentally unbalanced, or if it was just his manner. It wasn't every day he met a dark stranger in a haunted woods who asked him to slay denizens.

But he did have one thing right—beyond the insistent craving for demon blood, even more fiercely, Blade craved vengeance.

But he was no assassin. Not without good reason.

And he had begun to step toward the light. To do

good. He strived to avoid making the same mistake twice.

"No," Blade stated simply. He folded down his wings and took a step back off the mossy rock, putting himself a head below Sim's stance. "The way to redemption is not through violence."

"It doesn't concern you that the demons will soon take over? They will torment humans and paranormals alike."

"Where's your proof? I've lived here all my life. There are demons who live amongst us, sure. But not in numbers so great as a rage."

"You'll simply have to trust I know of what I speak."

"I do not blindly offer something so valuable as my trust." And Blade walked around the man and into the woods. "Get off my property!" he called back.

"The Darkwood belongs to no man." He heard the quiet reply. "You will change your mind. I can wait. But not for long."

Blade started to run. Flapping his wings, he soared up from the ground. He dodged a ghostly wraith that lived within the forest, but which would never leave.

Kill all the demons? Sounded like a dream. But Blade was trying to turn his life around and be less violent. And he could do it.

If he could get beyond the need for revenge.

One week later...

Zenia parked the olive-green Chevy truck at the end of the block where she'd been hit by the bus. Hopping out, she skipped across the grassy road verge to the sidewalk. A wind-strewn newspaper lay on the ground, and she recognized the faded ad she'd seen a week earlier.

A pharmaceutical ad touted something called Zenia. A word she'd liked so much she'd taken it as her name. It conveyed mystery. Just like her.

Which was about the only thing she did know about herself. That she was a mystery. The term used to describe her condition was *amnesia*, and she had it. And it had started in this neighborhood.

The street and houses were quaint. A smooth, narrow sidewalk stretched before neat yards, and most of those yards were fenced with white pickets. Bright yellow marigolds, pink-and-white roses and orange zinnias bloomed in profusion. Butterflies and bees fluttered from bloom to bloom.

The bus must have been cruising this quiet neighborhood so slowly that if someone had been hit by it, they wouldn't have sustained a serious injury. And the bus driver may have never noticed the casualty.

Zenia strode down the sidewalk, a long floral skirt flitting between her legs. Her pink T-shirt was encrusted with rhinestones in the shape of a heart. She loved anything that sparkled. That much she did know about herself.

Summer sun warmed her skin and she flipped her long, midback hair over a shoulder. She brushed at an insect that briefly landed on her arm, and took note of the faint design on the inside of her elbow. Barely there, it looked as though someone had taken a white marker and drawn an arabesque. It was also on her other inner elbow, and had faded, but perhaps still needed a few more showers to completely wash away. It resembled the mehndi designs she knew were a Vedic custom in India.

How she knew about that baffled her. She seemed to know quite a bit about many things—except personal details. Had someone drawn these marks on her?

Or perhaps she'd scrawled it during a lazy afternoon doing…what?

She wanted to know what she'd done in life, if only so she could resume doing that for survival. It had been a week since the accident and she had no money, had stolen clothes from a donation box on a street corner, and had only managed a handful of meals by chatting up lone men in the local diners and then dashing before they could ask her out.

And while remembering who she was would be terrific, perhaps she didn't know for a reason?

Weird thoughts. But what else was there to think about?

A lot actually. Everything. From the solid feel of the sidewalk beneath the pink flip-flop sandals she wore to the warmth of the air embracing her shoulders. The sensory details were immense in this world. And it was almost as if she was experiencing touch, sight, smell and sound for the first time. There, a bird chirp sounded like a song she must know the words to, but unfortunately had—like her identity—forgotten.

Forgetting was frustrating. So she had returned, determined to trace her steps to learn where she had come from and what she had been doing before the accident.

Zenia stopped walking. A warm sensation blossomed in her chest. A visceral feeling of memory. She studied the pink, two-story house in front of her. White paint decorated the window frames and front door as if it were a confection under glass at a bakery. It looked familiar.

She walked up to the picket fence and darted her gaze over the yard, which was overgrown with brushy emerald grass and dotted with yellow dandelions. It smelled lush and wild. Didn't look as though anyone lived on this lot. Did *she* live here?

"I walked through this yard," she said with definite knowing.

She turned and eyed the street. The bus stop sign was thirty yards to the left, and the grass around the sign had been worn to dirt where she assumed people waited while sipping their morning coffees. "And there is where I got hit."

Turning and wandering into the yard, she had to lift her skirt so that she didn't get tangled in the long grass. Had she been walking out from behind the house? She could see an open backyard. No trees. And beyond that a field stretched quite a distance before it ended at a forest's dark, jagged tree line.

Paralleling the side of the pink house, she walked around to the back and let out a gasp when someone stepped right in front of her. The woman couldn't be younger than ninety, and her posture curled her spine forward so she had to lift her head to look up at Zenia. She smelled smoky. And a little too ripe for Zenia's heightened senses.

"I'm sorry," Zenia said, stepping back a pace. "I didn't mean to trespass. I'm trying to track down a path I took a week ago. Would it be all right if I walked through your backyard to that field?"

"Never seen you before, young lady. Why would you walk through my yard?"

"I don't know. I've lost my memory. I'm trying to piece things together, and I recall walking from back here. Maybe even through that field. Though I'm not sure why I would be in a field. I won't do any harm to your property. I'll walk straight through and on to the field."

"Very well. You go find yourself. And I'll go, uh… find myself."

The old woman gestured dismissively with a swing of her arm then made a surprisingly hasty retreat into her house through the back door.

"Yes, find myself," Zenia muttered. "But out in a field?"

And the old lady needed to find herself? Curious. But old people were some kind of curiosity, for sure. If not badly in need of a shower.

Zenia strode onward, her sandals stomping down the grass until she landed on the soft black earth of the freshly plowed field. Didn't feel familiar to walk across the uneven surface. Hmm…

"This is the closest I've come to finding myself. I won't give up."

She walked onward.

Blade Saint-Pierre shoved the Craftsman toolbox into his truck box and pushed up the creaky metal gate to close it. He'd helped old man Larson fix the trellis that had come detached from the back of his house. Squirrels had been nibbling at the trusses. Now it was secure and the violet morning glories that reminded Larson of his dead wife, Gloria, showed through his bedroom window.

These neighborly fix-it stops were fast becoming an enjoyable way to spend the day for Blade. It made him feel better to help someone he didn't know. But he was sure it would never counter all the guilt that weighed down his heart. It certainly wouldn't grant him redemption.

But neither would slaying a rage of demons. He

hadn't seen the stranger, Sim, since that night in the forest a few days ago. Probably for the better.

Opening the driver's door, he paused to eye the stunning beauty walking down the sidewalk on the opposite side of the street. He'd not seen her in Tangle Lake before. Blade had seen a lot of pretty women pass through this tiny Minnesota town. Most visitors hailed from the big city. Some liked to do an antiques run through the smaller towns along the highway that stretched from the Twin Cities north to the shipping harbor of Duluth.

So he was unusually curious about this beauty who looked as out of place as a demon in a salt factory.

Long red hair spilled down her back. He wouldn't exactly call it red, more like copper that caught the sun in glints much like polished metal. Her skin resembled creamy caramel. A flowery skirt flitted between long legs as she strode the sidewalk, her attention taking in the house fronts and tidy yards. A faded T-shirt with an obvious hole at the back hem topped off the bohemian look. She scampered through an overgrown yard, which Blade wondered if he should offer to mow the lawn. Could be a hazard to an elder person trying to navigate the long grass.

He observed the sexy bohemian chick speak to an elder woman who seemed a bit too spry as she bounced back into her house. Blade could see the old woman's shadow through the front window that wasn't obscured by drapes. He kept her in peripheral vision while he satisfied his need for beauty.

The woman in the skirt scampered toward a dirt field. Did she have something to do back there? It was a big empty expanse. And across the stretch of black dirt was forest, which, after dozens of acres, backed up to Tangle Lake. Maybe she owned a strip of the black earth and intended to plant a garden? It was a little late in the season for that and she hadn't any gardening tools on her.

An odd commotion inside the house made Blade turn his attention to the front window. The old woman's silhouette was…changing. One moment she stood hunched, her head hanging and shoulders curved forward and down. The next moment, she'd grown another head. And another.

Instincts kicked in and Blade tugged out the silver bowie knife he kept stuffed in his combat boot. He closed the truck door. He knew better than to doubt his instincts.

The silhouettes in the house were now three separate entities, and big, and…

Blade sniffed. A faint trace of sulfur curled into his nostrils.

"Demons," he muttered. "I do hate demons."

Chapter 2

Running along the side of the house, Blade veered around the corner and toward the back door, noting that the woman with the copper hair stood three hundred yards away in the field, her back to him. Unaware of the weirdness brewing within the house. Or so he hoped.

He opened the door and dodged to avoid the slash of obsidian talons. Pulling the door shut behind him, Blade hoped to keep the demons contained. And the beautiful woman safe.

The threesome of demons growled and spat at him, and lunged. Blade leaped to the top of a laundry machine, and jumped, flipping in the air and landing behind the nasty trio. Bowie knife at the ready, he defied them with a come-on gesture of his fingers.

"Are you the rage Sim spoke about?"

In a rare pause from attack, the demons glanced at one another. Black-hooded red eyes blinked. It was obvious they knew nothing about what he'd just asked. And really, a rage of demons would blacken the sky with their numbers. These three were barely a denizen.

"Is the woman one of your own?" he asked. He knew some demons could take on human form, many of them, actually, but he doubted the woman in the field had anything to do with this bunch.

"She is ours," one of them hissed. "Keep away!"

"I don't take orders from demons." He twirled the knife and caught it, blade pointing toward the speaker. "Want to try asking nicely?"

The next hiss was accompanied by burning spittle that sizzled on Blade's wrist. Wrong move.

The best way to kill a demon was with a blast of salt to its black heart. Blade did have a salt knife, but rarely carried it. In lieu of salt, he'd have to do this the old-fashioned way.

Leaping to the left, he feinted right, ducking to avoid attack. With that demon occupied in missing him, Blade slid under a groping talon and stood before Thing #2. He jammed up his knife, catching it deep in the rib cage of the surprised demon. A knife wound wouldn't take out a demon. Unless it was more than a wound, and the weapon had been warded against demons. Dragging the blade upward, he cut open the creature from gut to throat and flung its spasming body aside to scatter in a spray of black ash.

Grabbed by the shoulders, the creature's talons pierced his skin. Blade growled, and slashed blindly, feeling resistance and tasting a spatter of black demon blood. He lashed out his tongue, even as he bent to fling the one on his back toward Thing #3. The taste of blood frenzied his faery's wicked craving. His fangs descended as he snarled. He tightened his grip on the knife.

"Now I'm angry," he muttered.

Standing tall, Blade turned to face the two, who actually cowered at the sight of the vampire with black blood dripping from his mouth.

Charging, he continued his assault. Catching one demon about the neck in a clothesline, the other demon he stabbed with the knife. He gouged his hand upward, tearing the warded steel through the shrieking demon. As the blade tore out of viscera, he curled his hand around to land the other thing through the skull. Both demons scattered in ash behind him.

Blade licked the side of his hand, coated with black blood, and growled in satisfaction. Nasty stuff, but it hit him with a jolt of power and comforting darkness. And that was an irresistible high. Mmm… He could feel it move down his throat. Delicious strength shimmered in his muscles. His wings trembled for release, to allow the wicked blood to course through their very structure like cocaine to an addict's soul.

"Hello?"

Kicked back to reality by the female call from outside the back door, Blade shook his head and stopped his wings before they could unfurl. Right. *Keep your head, buddy.* He shoved the knife down the side of his boot and stepped out the door and marched across the unkempt backyard. The woman in the long skirt strolled toward him, oblivious to what had just gone down inside the pink house.

Demons didn't follow humans around. Not that he was aware of. And the woman had purposely gone to this one; he had seen her speak with it. Had she known it was demon? And if so, what was out in the field that the demon had directed her to?

Blade wiped the blood from his mouth and retracted his fangs. The woman's face brightened as she neared, and she lifted her long skirt to run toward him. "Hello! Do you live in the house? I didn't find what I thought I would find—"

Blade grabbed her by the upper arms and growled. "What are you?"

The man's grip was too firm, Zenia thought. He actually looked angry, his dark brows narrowed, and the sun shone on his hair, bluing it around the one eye that was visible. A fathomless, gray eye. He had seen tribulation. Zenia knew that with certainty, as she knew so many odd facts.

And he was sexy. Devastatingly so. His broad chest stretched a charcoal-gray T-shirt in ripples, and thick veins corded his massive biceps. Combine his remarkable physique with a handsome face and he was the complete package.

Yet he did not relent his strong grip. Zenia struggled and finally managed to squirm out of his pinching grasp.

"What am I?" she asked, stepping back a few paces from him. "What do you mean? I'm a woman. A human. You think I'm some kind of alien?" She looked over his shoulder and noted the back door of the woman's house hung open. "I should go up and close that door for her. She probably forgot. She's old—"

"Don't go near the house." He gripped her by the arm, and again Zenia shoved his chest and struggled. She stumbled in the long grass and he helped her to stand. It was all she could do to step away from him without falling again.

"Who are you?" she demanded with an impertinent lift of chin. "You don't live here. If you did, you might have taken care of the yard for your grandmother, or whoever she is to you."

"She's not my—" The man gestured a wide splay of fingers toward the street. "I was working across the street and saw you two talking. I just— I don't need to explain myself. I asked first. Who, and what in particular, are you?"

Zenia crossed her arms and looked the man up and down. Dressed all in dark clothing from his loosely laced Dr. Martens to the black jeans and gray T-shirt, his muscled arms gave her pause, as did his broad chest. But the long black hair with a weirdly blue sheen to it screamed goth. Goths were skinny and morose. This man's physique said, *I work out*—a lot.

"Well," she provided, "I'm certainly not an alien." Of that she was aware.

The nerve of the man. He hadn't even offered a friendly how do you do. Perhaps this neighborhood wasn't as friendly as she'd originally thought. And for as much as she enjoyed the view of him, she did know not to trust a complete stranger.

Zenia marched past him and up toward the house. He passed her and slammed the door shut, stepping before it as if to guard the contents. His anger was so palpable she felt shivers trace her arms. But it wasn't warning enough to make her run away from the guy.

"I didn't find anything here," she offered, hoping to appeal to his compassionate side. If such a thing existed. "This is where I came walking out and into the street before I lost my memory. I feel as though I was walking in from that field, but I haven't a clue what I was doing out there. It's just a bunch of dirt."

"What the hell are you talking about, lady?"

"I, uh…" She raked her fingers through her long hair and splayed out her hand uncertainly before her. When she noted the cream-colored markings inside her elbow, she slapped a palm over them and offered with a shrug, "I have amnesia."

This time when he raised his hand, perhaps to clutch her again, she flinched. That paused him. He put up both palms facing her, placatingly. And Zenia sensed whatever it was that had made him so tense and angry settled. Just a teensy bit.

"I'm sorry," he said. "I shouldn't have grabbed you like that. There was a commotion in the house while you were wandering in the field. I don't think you should go inside."

"What's wrong with the old lady?" Zenia bobbed on her toes in an attempt to see over his broad shoulder and through the window near the back door. "Is she okay?"

He narrowed his gaze on her so intently that she felt as if he'd physically touched her. Over the heart. And she suddenly wanted to know that touch for real. She'd not been touched by a man before. Maybe. She couldn't remember if she had. Oh, woe, if she had not.

"She's…been better," he offered.

Arms sliding defensively across her chest, she studied his eyes again. Both of them now, for his hair blew away from his face. A curious gray and some fleck of brighter color. Violet? They had softened, though she could see the sharpness in them as if a cut to her hope for his kindness.

When he asked, "Did the Darkwood denizen send you?" her mouth fell open.

Because Zenia knew what a denizen was. Yet that knowledge startled her. Why did she know the word for a group or gathering of demons?

Because there are demons in this world. As well as angels, vampires, witches and other things most didn't believe in.

Did she believe in them? No, such things were mythology. Fantasy bred into wild stories designed to entertain the masses. Which made this guy, as handsome as he was, some kind of wacko.

"I am not a demon."

She turned to march around the side of the house. She wasn't going to find what she was looking for here. And most especially, she did not want to deal with a crazy man. Even if he was the most remarkable specimen of male she'd seen. Ever.

A hand grabbed her by the arm, halting her near the picket fence that hugged in the front yard. "Yet you are familiar with the terminology?"

She shrugged. Annoyance felt new to her, and she didn't like the feeling so she tried to look beyond it. Was his hair so black it gleamed blue? When the sun shone on it, it appeared blue. Kinda cool. She wondered if it was as soft as it looked.

Oh, Zenia, do not let his good looks distract you!

"I know a lot of things," she offered when he gave no sign to leave her alone. "Except who I am."

"So then how can you be sure you are not a demon?"

Zenia slammed her hands to her hips. "Are you for real? Demons are myth, buddy. Stories. Fantasy. I think it's time I got some facts from you. Who are you?"

"Blade Saint-Pierre." His shoulders stretched back proudly, yet his eyes remained dark. Uncertain? "I live on the outskirts of Tangle Lake. I was helping Mr. Larson across the street fix his trellis." She followed his gesture to the yellow rambler across the street and spied the climbing purple flowers on the side of the house. "And who are you? Oh, wait, you don't remember."

"Zenia," she offered with a lift of her chin. "It's the name I'm using until I learn my real name. And I'm quite sure you and your weird fantasy ideas will be of no help to that quest, so if you'll leave me alone, I'll be on my way. Do not follow me!"

Stalking away from the man's accusing stature, she strode through the long grass toward the sidewalk. Her truck was parked down the block. Feet shuffling quickly, she landed on the sidewalk and did not look back. A weird feeling that she was rushing forward, walking toward knowledge, flittered into her brain, and as quickly, fluttered back out.

And yet…it had been a *familiar* feeling. She'd felt the very same when she'd been walking this sidewalk previously. Before the bus had changed her destiny.

Destiny?

Hmm… It felt right to think that. At least, nothing in her being screamed, *No, you're on the wrong path.* Interesting. Maybe she had gathered a bit of her memory by retreading her footsteps? Albeit, memory she didn't know how to decipher. A quest for knowledge? It meant nothing to her.

The man followed so close behind her she could hear the trod of his boots on the concrete sidewalk. His name was Blade? Interesting name. Sharp and dangerous. It certainly matched his demeanor.

And he was stalking her.

"I have a weapon!" she called out, and scrambled for the truck keys in her skirt pocket.

"I'm not going to hurt you," he said firmly.

"Says the serial killer before he dumps the girl in the pit," she called over her shoulder.

Where had she mined such macabre information? It was frustrating to Zenia that she knew things—weird, odd things—and yet, knew nothing about herself.

"A knowledge walk?" she whispered as she neared the truck. Her stalker's black truck was parked across the street from it. The truck bed was loaded with lumber and tools. So he'd been telling the truth about helping the old man. He earned trust points for doing a kind thing. Right?

"I need to make sure you are safe," Blade said as he strode beside her, intent on not leaving her alone. "If you're not from around here, and you don't remember anything, you could be in trouble."

"I appreciate that," she said, still walking. "Really. Kindness of strangers, and all that. But I don't know what I have to worry about. Wait. The old lady. I should have checked on her."

"She's...fine."

"You said that with a pause. As if maybe she's not fine. As if maybe you've just murdered her."

He managed to overtake her rapid steps and stop before her on the sidewalk, planting his boots and slamming his fists akimbo. "Will you quit with the serial killer bit? I didn't kill...the old lady. She wasn't in the house when I went in there. I promise. There were others inside. Others who mentioned you."

"Me? Really?" She turned at the hip to eye the pink house, then swung back to Blade. She had to tilt her head to meet his gaze; he was a tall one. "Who were they? They must know me. Maybe they can tell me who I am."

"They were demons."

He said it without a smirk or a wink. And that pulled the cord on Zenia's freak-out alarm.

She shoved the guy away and ran toward her truck. Keys in hands, she opened the door, slid in and started the ignition. She'd be damned if she was going to talk to him one moment longer and risk his kind of crazy.

"Demons?" she muttered. "Talk about attracting a weirdo. I'll have to return later, after he's gone. If someone in that house knows about me…"

She shifted into gear, and rolled quickly by him. He waved, but it was more of a dismissive gesture. In the rearview mirror, she saw him get in his truck and turn it around on the narrow street. She quickly turned at the intersection, hoping to lose him.

"Demons," she whispered again. "Can't be. No. I won't believe it. He's a crazy madman that I was lucky to get away from him. This is bad." She pressed a palm against the thumping heartbeats under her rib cage. "Really bad. Now I've got to shake a serial killer. I don't want to die. I can't die. I don't even know what name they'd put on the tombstone."

The image of a fresh grave made her miss the next stop sign. A shout alerted her to the pair of teenaged girls who had stepped off the curb, and now shook their fists at the truck.

"Oops. Sorry! Concentrate, Zenia. You don't want to be arrested for murder."

She glanced in the rearview mirror. The big black truck still followed.

"But who might be more guilty of such a heinous crime?" she muttered to herself.

He'd said there were others in the house who had asked after her. What had happened to the old woman?

Chapter 3

She was the prettiest woman in Tangle Lake. Demons wanted her. And she had amnesia.

Blade had discreetly followed Zenia to the Blue Bass, a dive bar nestled at the edge of town. So the tail hadn't been as discreet as he'd hoped. Not easy to be covert in a small town with only two main streets. It was nearing eight in the evening and he suspected she had tried to give him the slip, but again, one of the hazards of a small town was lack of privacy.

Normally, he was not a curious man. That was his brother Trouble's mien. But it wasn't every day he watched a sexy woman tread about in a dirt field, and then had to slay demons to keep them from going after her.

He wanted to know where the demons had come from and why. And if she thought to use an amnesia defense to cover her knowledge then she'd better think again. She had to be hiding something. If a person had amnesia, shouldn't they not operate a motor vehicle, avoid drinking in a bar and most likely be lying in the hospital?

Yeah, she was definitely pulling something over on him. Yet if there was a slight chance she was on the up and up, he sensed she wasn't safe.

He entered the bar, and stood by the door to take in the yawn of an establishment paneled in rough-cut timbers and decorated with fishing rods, neon beer signs and the mascot stuffed bass with the milky white eyes. At the bar, Zenia ordered a beer. She didn't fit in this redneck outpost. She looked more like a wine kind of gal.

Currently, she held her own against Brock Olafson, the town asshole. The guy had been divorced twice, owned a tanning bed—which explained his weird orange leathery skin—and never slowed his Hummer for a stop sign unless he sighted a black-and-white nearby.

Asshole was trying to pick up the pretty woman. Blade's fingers had curled into fists the moment Brock sat down next to her. He held his jaw soft, not tense. Years of practice had allowed him to remain calm while holding within the roiling need to attack. It was never wise to attack. At least, not with human witnesses.

On the other hand, if a man opened the door of a house and was greeted by three demons, by all means, attack.

Brock slid his hand up the back of Zenia's T-shirt. She slapped at him and shifted over to the next bar stool. Blade could hear her politely say, "Leave me alone. I just want to finish this drink in peace."

"I'll buy you another," Brock said, shoving thick fingers over his short blond crew cut.

Before the asshole could slide onto the vacant bar stool, Blade pushed his palm onto the bar between the two of them. The bartender nodded at Blade and poured him a shot of Krupnik, a honey-sweet vodka the owner kept in stock for him.

Brock stepped away from the bar, muttering something about weirdos under his breath, but Blade kept an awareness of the man's location in his peripheral vision as he tilted back the shot.

"Despite his rudeness, he did pin you correctly," Zenia said and sipped her beer.

"How's that?"

"You're a weirdo. And I'll ask you to leave me alone just like I did the other guy."

"Sorry," he said, and pushed the shot glass forward. "Did I interrupt something promising?"

She snickered and when she looked at him, he was momentarily fixed to her green eyes. She was so exotic and colorful, this memory-less woman who didn't seem to belong, no matter the setting. And she smelled like the long grass and flowers he'd followed her through but an hour earlier. Blade lost track of Brock.

"Thanks," she said. "But you can leave now."

He sat on a bar stool and propped his elbows before him. "I'm not a weirdo," he offered.

"You accused me, a person you don't even know, of being a demon. Your hair is blue. You look like a goth. And you followed me here like some kind of serial—er, stalker. In my book that's considered weird."

The bartender poured another shot for Blade. He swallowed the vodka with a wince. Good stuff. He had a difficult time getting drunk. Blame it on his genetics. Being vampire and faery did come in handy when he wanted to hold his liquor. The only time he got drunk was when drinking from someone who had consumed whiskey. Whiskey-spiked blood always went straight to his head.

"It's black," he offered regarding his hair. "The neon light from that sign over the bar makes it blue."

"If that's your story. But I did see it in the sunlight. It's blue."

It wasn't. Well, it sort of was. It was the faery in him. It sheened his black hair blue. It was a damned sight better than the pink that donned his sister, Daisy Blu's, head.

"And yours is copper," he offered. "Like a precious metal that someone steals to hock for as much cash as they can manage. It suits you. Looks great with your skin tone. Sorry." He shoved the empty shot glass toward the bartender. "I don't say things like that to women—"

"You mean compliment them? Are you flirting with me? Trying to pick up a demon?"

She was going to work that one until he surrendered. So he would. But only because she was pretty.

"Listen, can we start over? I'm Blade." He offered his hand to her and she stared at it. "I live about ten miles out of town near the Darkwood."

"That sounds…dark." She smirked and he wondered if she might be a little tipsy. But when she took his hand and shook it, he felt a good firm clasp warm his fingers. "Zenia. No last name. At least, not that I recall. I live nowhere, or probably somewhere. But you know, Amnesia Chick."

"So, Zenia, who is only recently Zenia, what's up with that? Did you used to be Martha or Gertrude?"

This time she laughed out loud. Blade heard Brock's huff on the other side of the pool table. The asshole tossed a dart at the board nailed on the wall—and missed.

When Zenia looked at him now he decided she was assessing him. A better risk than Brock? He should hope so. And then, he knew he was not.

"For all I know, I probably could have been Gertrude," she said.

"You don't look like a Gertie. The hair is all wrong. Gertrude likes curls and something shorter. Maybe even a blue rinse."

"You could be right. Okay, so weirdness aside, I like you, Blade." Her long dark lashes fluttered with a look over his face. "I'll reserve judgment on your weirdness quotient until I get to know you better."

He was about to say that she would be better off not liking him, but instead he simply smiled. A rare thing for him. Just ask any of his brothers or sister. The dark silent one put people off with his stoic expression. And for good reason.

He'd learned that keeping his head down was best for all. And yet, his surprising curiosity for this woman demanded satisfaction.

"No memory?" he asked. "How did that happen? Or do you know?"

"I think I only lost personal stuff. I know things. It's as if I know crazy stuff like Russia's population is almost one hundred and fifty million. The main ingredient in miso soup is dashi. And it would take the average person about eighteen months to traverse the wall of China. But I don't know my name, who I am or where I came from. That's why I'm here in Tangle Lake. I was hit by a bus in front of that old woman's house."

Blade was about to order another shot when he paused. "Seriously? Hit by a bus?"

"Yes. I was walking out of a yard—probably that old woman's yard—and onto the street, and—bam! No memory of my life after that."

"So you woke up in the hospital? They must have taken you to Unity. Closest hospital from here."

"No. I, uh, stood up and walked away." She offered a sheepish shrug. "Never saw a doctor."

Blade put up two fingers when the bartender tilted the vodka bottle over his glass. This information was worthy of a double shot.

"It's been a week," she said. "I thought about going to the police, but—I don't know, something inside me said they wouldn't be able to help. So I hitched a ride into the Twin Cities and have been staying at homeless shelters, trying to make some cash to survive. A girl's gotta eat, you know?"

"They have homes to stay in for people who have amnesia. Maybe." What did he know? "If they don't exist, they should. You should see a doctor."

"I'm fine." She bent her head and brushed aside her hair with a curl of delicate fingers over her ear. "I know it sounds weird, but I think the bus sort of…nudged me to pursue a different life. When it hit me, I was flung against the street pole and banged my head. Had a bruise right here." She tapped her temple. "But that faded within a few hours."

A hit that could take away one's memory had to have left a big bruise. Blade had a hard time believing it had faded so quickly. There wasn't a mar on her skin. Another reason to doubt her story. And she could be allied with demons. What game was she playing?

"So here I am." She narrowed her gaze on him. "Do *you* know me?"

He had to chuckle at that hopeful question. "Never seen you before."

"I had to ask. I'm not sure if I'm from Tangle Lake. Everywhere I've been no one seems to recognize me. Friendliest person so far has been that asshole behind us tossing the darts."

"Name's Brock Olafson, and you should stay away from him if you value your safety."

"Thanks. I got that 'stay away' feeling from him." She sipped the beer and wiped off the foam moustache. "I thought visiting the scene of the accident would make something click in my brain, you know?"

"Well, if you want me to hit you upside the head…?"

"Does that work? The knowledge I have on that is it's mainly been used in children's cartoons and tear-jerker love stories."

"I was kidding. So were you hoping asshole would pay your tab?"

"I, er…" She shrugged and focused on her drink.

Blade tugged out his wallet and laid enough cash on the bar to cover his and her tab. "On me," he said. "If you don't have memory, you must not have a job."

"Nope. Not that I know of. There could be a cubicle that's empty right now. Is the whole office wondering where I am? Do I have a big project due any day now?"

She didn't look like a cubicle drone, but Blade couldn't decide what kind of work she might have done. Her exotic coloring and flowing clothes hinted at a bohemian nature. And those sorts were usually musicians and artists. Maybe?

Why not go to the police? Her story just didn't jibe.

"If I can ask, how do you survive?"

"I spent a couple days hawking raspberries at a farm

stand just off Highway 35 and earned enough to eat on. And I have the truck."

"You remembered you own a truck?"

"Uh, no. It was running and no one was using it, so…" She winced and tilted back another swallow of beer.

She'd stolen a truck. Blade was impressed. Pretty *and* devious. The woman had survival skills, that was for sure.

But she'd been hit by a bus and had stood up and walked away? Was she something beyond human? If her story was the truth, she had to be. He didn't scent his own species on her. He could also scent when were-wolves or demons were around. Faeries were a challenge.

He got nothing from her. Just plain human. A human who had attracted a shifter demon who had claimed she was their own.

"You're not afraid the cops will remind you that you don't own a truck?"

"I'm not sure what fear is, actually." She offered her hand again to shake. "I should get going. I'm tired. It was nice to talk to a kind person for a while. Blade Saint-Pierre, right? Maybe we'll run into each other again?"

"I'm in town a lot." He almost offered his services if she needed anything, but…he'd learned his lesson with pretty women. They were nice to look at, touch and make love to. But getting to know them and caring about them? Wrong, just wrong. "See you, Zenia."

She strolled out of the bar with a wave to him. And Blade remained to keep an eye on Brock.

A knock on the truck window woke Zenia from the first tendrils of sleep. She sat up on the front seat, knocked her foot on the steering wheel, swore and spied the dark-haired man peering in at her.

"Blade."

After talking with him in the Blue Bass she'd assessed that he was a nice guy who had the compassion to worry about a complete stranger. But here he was again. And her heartbeats picked up pace. What made her believe she had any skill at reading another person's intent? As she'd once suspected, had she gained a stalker?

She sat up to open the door, but paused. It was close to midnight. She had parked in an empty parking lot beneath a streetlight. A city park paralleled the lot, but no residential houses or businesses were nearby. It had seemed a quiet place to sleep through the night, but now her caution rose.

He hadn't tried to touch her, as had the other creep in the bar. But something about this man was dark. Mysterious. And now the hairs on her arms prickled.

She turned the key backward to the accessories position, then lowered the window down two inches. "Yes?"

"You sleeping in your truck?"

She nodded. Wished she had an iron pipe, or even a wood bat.

"This is going to sound strange," he said. "It might even put up your weirdo alarms again."

"I haven't completely lowered them, so give it a shot."

"You're welcome to park on my land tonight. Uh, it might be safer. Unless you don't mind taking your chances with Brock." He turned and cast his gaze across the parking lot.

Zenia followed his gaze and there, across the street from the lot, idled a big yellow Hummer rimmed in chrome. She couldn't see inside the cab, save for the glimmer of burning cigarette embers.

"Is that the guy from the bar?"

Blade nodded. "I've been watching him watching you for about an hour."

Zenia clutched her arms over her chest. "You've been watching me a lot today."

"Sorry. Seems as though you need it. This is not what I normally do. I mean—"

"Stalk women?"

He nodded and shrugged. It was a sheepish kind of move that settled her worries. She wanted to trust him. She would allow herself to trust him.

"Where do you live?" she asked.

"Ten miles north of Tangle Lake. It's secluded. Brock won't follow you there because he's afraid of me. We had…an altercation a few months back. But then, if you follow me, you do risk leaving the safety of town."

Yikes. When he put it that way. And yet, as strange as Blade was, Zenia sensed the other option would see her struggling with the man across the street not long after Blade left.

"Maybe," she said.

"I'm heading back to my truck. You can follow me if you want to. The drive is down a long forested road, just so you know. You can park in my driveway. Lock your doors. I won't bother you. You have my word."

"I don't know if your word is good."

"That you don't."

Was it fair or even rational to give him points for honesty?

"So you think you need to protect me from demons or something?"

"Beyond the very human Brock?" He shrugged.

"You never know." Blade shoved his hands into his front pockets. "Your choice, Zen."

And he strode off toward the truck that Zenia now saw was parked down the street. A bowlegged stride moved him swiftly, as if a shadow in the night.

Zenia scrambled into the driver's seat and turned on the ignition. When Blade's headlights blinked on and slowly drove past the other man's truck, she made a snap decision and shifted the truck into gear.

Chapter 4

Zenia woke with her name zinging between her ears. Except it wasn't the way she had chosen it. Blade had called her Zen last night. She liked it. It sounded like the man had made the name his possession when he'd said it. And that didn't bother her at all.

But did she feel Zen right now? Hard to tell. She wasn't sure what to feel. She was a woman out of place. Did she have a place to return? Was there a house or an apartment waiting for her to push a key into the lock and resume her life? She hadn't a key, a purse or any identifying materials on her after the bus had hit her.

Only that weird tin circle.

She glanced at the flimsy circle she'd hung around the rearview mirror. She'd been clutching it after coming to a stand against the street pole. In that moment, she'd almost tossed it aside, but she'd felt an intuition to keep it. For some reason. Curious.

Had it anything to do with the destiny she felt she tread? For the undeniable feeling that contacting the police would not be wise? Was it a true feeling or was it that she thought she should have a goal or reason for existing so *destiny* was a good fill-in-the-blank answer?

Sitting up, she pulled her knees to her chest and bowed her head to work out the kinks from sleeping across the stick shift. A knock on the driver's window startled her. A swath of dark hair reminded her that she'd had the audacity to follow a complete stranger out to his property last night. She'd parked at the end of the driveway closest to the highway just in case she'd needed to make a quick getaway. He'd been good to his word. Hadn't bothered her.

Until now.

Zen hit the window control and lowered the glass. The scent of steaming coffee wafted into the truck interior. Never had anything smelled so good.

Blade handed in a black mug. Steam rose from the liquid surface. "Just brewed it. Extradark. Hope you take it that way."

She'd take any offering of food or drink no matter the strength or weakness. Thank goodness he'd paid for her beer last night. That left her twenty dollars in her pocket—left over from selling raspberries—and a half-full gas tank. It was terrible not to know who she was. But not having the funds to rent a room or pay for a hot meal? She would have to look into that home for amnesiacs he'd mentioned if she didn't figure her life out, and fast.

"Thank you." She sipped the brew. It kicked her. Hard. "Whew!"

"It's called Death Brew for a reason," Blade offered. "Have a good night's sleep?"

She shrugged. No one named Brock had tried to break in and attack her, so she figured that was as good as it got.

"Here's the deal," Blade said. "I'm heading into town in an hour. Got some work to do for a couple of nuns. If you want, you're welcome to use my shower before I leave."

"Really?" She hadn't showered in days. Had begun to wonder if her hair would ever see a comb again. "I'd like that."

"Cool. Just me and Oogie live out here in the barn. If my cat likes you, I like you."

"Then here's hoping I pass the cat test."

The eerie, hairless black cat hissed and arched its back as Zenia landed at the top of the stairs leading to the loft level of the big barn. The lower level was a wide-open garage littered with vehicles in all states of repair. This was the living quarters. Vast and open, it felt modern and airy, not at all barnlike.

Blade, who had led her up the stairs and directed her to the left for the bathroom, peered out from around the stainless-steel fridge at his cat, which was poised on the back of a green-and-blue-plaid couch. Blade glanced at Zenia, who had frozen at the top of the stairs, clinging to the backpack strap she'd tossed over her shoulder. Then he eyed the cat, who had arched up its back so high Zenia thought it might fold in half.

"Guess I failed the cat test," she offered.

"Oogie?" Blade knelt and called to the cat. "What's wrong, buddy?" He tilted his head at her and she felt as if his look peeled back her layers and zoomed right to her oozy core.

If only it were so easy to learn who she was.

"Who *are* you?" he asked. Yet again.

And yet again, she had no clear answer.

The cat leaped into his arms, and the man stood, stroking its wrinkled suede-like head. "Oogie likes everyone."

"Obviously I'm not everyone. And that's the big question, isn't it?" She rubbed her arms, though she wasn't cold, just frustrated. And it had taken a cat to nail that frustration to the wall. "Who am I?"

The cat hissed at her.

Zenia flinched. "Uh, do you want me to leave?"

"No. Shower's that way." He nodded toward the hallway. "Oogie and I will talk. You have to walk through the bedroom," he called as Zenia made her way down a short hallway. "You'll see the bathroom door once you get in there."

Overlooking the cat's defensive reaction, she glided into a dark room that was lit by the sunlight beaming through a window set into the slanted roof.

Her gaze swept over the unmade bed. Black rumpled bed sheets. Cozy, in a manly way. Beneath her flip-flops, the floorboards were wide unbleached timber, as were the walls and slanted ceiling. Overall, a darkly clean, yet rustic decor. Just like the man.

And yet, he'd sweetly cuddled that ugly cat. Surprising to see such a big, intimidating man handle a tiny beast so gently.

Veering into the attached bathroom, Zenia was thankful it wasn't all black. In fact, bright white tiles decorated the floor and walls, and though small, the gleaming shower looked inviting through the clear glass door.

She closed the bathroom door and set down the backpack. She'd raided a clothing donation box one night and found a sack of folded clothes that didn't smell. Freshly washed? She could hope. And they'd fit, so she'd taken the whole bag and the canvas backpack that had been stuffed under a pile of smelly gym shoes.

Stripping off her clothes, she caught her reflection in the small shaving mirror above the sink. It was too small to see her whole face so she bobbed to get a view of her condition. Her hair begged a good combing and dark shadows curved under her eyes. She so needed a good night's sleep and...to know.

"Who are you?" she repeated Blade's question to her reflection. "And why the hell were you able to walk away after being hit by a freakin' bus?"

She'd sensed his utter astonishment when she'd told him that. At the time she hadn't thought anything of it. Could have been the adrenaline racing through her system. Shouldn't she have a broken bone or even come away with a bruise or gash? She'd not even bled!

But instead of panicking, she'd been thankful. And that was about all she could do, wasn't it? Live day to day, grateful that she had clothing and a vehicle.

Stepping into the shower, she adjusted the water temperature and said thanks for the kindness of strangers. And then she had the thought that she should have locked the bathroom door behind her.

Blade stood outside the bathroom door, his fingers glancing over the clear glass knob. On his bed sat his pet of thirteen years, the feline's hairless black ears tilted backward and gold eyes wide. Oogie generally liked people. Though, he did tend to get his hackles up when demons were around. Full-blooded demons. Recognizing the *mimicus* breed of demon that could mimic other species had given Oogie trouble.

Don't think about her. Just forget.

Forgetting was what he most wanted to do. But the memory of her had etched itself into his soul. And no amount of charity work was going to rub it away. Not even moving a heavy stone fountain into a garden for a couple of retired nuns.

Blade shrugged at Oogie. "What do you think?"

Oogie's ratlike tail flicked with annoyance.

"She seems harmless. She doesn't even know who she is."

Which didn't necessarily render her harmless. She could have forgotten she was some kind of assassin. Or maybe she was a real good liar.

He was jumping to wild conclusions. Zen was simply a pretty woman who had had a bit of bad luck. With a bus. And demons. Though she seemed genuinely unaware of the demonic trouble.

A stolen truck and no home or belongings? Had to be tough. She couldn't sleep in her truck every night. But he wasn't prepared to offer her a place to bunk down, either.

That way lay madness. Been there, done that. Wasn't about to wear the T-shirt.

But she was a curiosity to him. And her looks were exotically appealing. She couldn't be from around here, Land of Ten Thousand Lakes with hoards of Scandinavians who were whiter than white and had the tendency to mutter *uff-da* to express everything from annoyance to excitement.

Maybe she hailed from the more culturally varied Twin Cities? Had to. She could be a professional, or even a model or an actress.

Why not go to the police? They must have a way of searching for a person without a name but rather a picture. If she was a registered driver her license would be on file. Name learned. Problem solved.

For the most part. Simply learning her real name wouldn't automatically restore her memory. Had to be tough not remembering a thing. She could have family. Friends. A husband.

Blade made a note to check her finger for a wedding band. He didn't want to step on another man's territory. Not that he was stepping. No, he was just helping a needy soul. It's what he did, apparently.

"Come on, Oogie. We can't sit out here like a couple of stalkers."

The maxi dress with bright yellow-and-blue horizontal zigzags was a bit loud, but it felt comfortable and wasn't too low cut. She did have nice, full breasts though, so revealing a little cleavage wasn't going to kill her.

Zenia fluffed out her wet hair, and then borrowed Blade's comb, which lay on the edge of the white porcelain vanity. A search in the small cupboard beneath the sink didn't spy any hair products. And she didn't want to check the drawers in the bedroom. Who knew if Oogie, the attack cat, might come after her?

After hanging the towel she had used to dry over the shower door, she shoved her dirty clothes in the backpack and headed down the hallway. Lured by the delicious scent of pancakes and maple syrup, she got right up to the kitchen counter, dropped the backpack, then veered toward the double cathedral windows at the end of the living area.

The old barn had obviously been restored and the windows added. They looked as though they belonged in Notre-Dame in Paris. And for some reason, she felt as though she'd been in the French city, though briefly; long enough to claim familiarity with the medieval cathedral. No color filled the glass sections that gently curved to a peak at their pinnacles. It gave the windows a clean, modern look. Very suitable for a man's home. In a barn. It was an interesting choice, but again, seemed to match Blade's no-frills, rough demeanor.

"They are so beautiful," she said of the windows, then flinched when she heard the hiss behind her.

"Oogie!" Blade tossed a red stuffed mouse down the stairs that led to the garage below. "Go play with your mouse."

The cat cast her a discerning look, then dashed off.

"I'm sorry," Zenia said. "I don't know why that thing doesn't like me."

"Oogie is a cat, not a thing."

"Yeah, but it looks like a rat. Why doesn't it have any hair?"

"He's a Sphynx."

"Oh, right. I know those breeds are hairless and require special care. Does he wear a sweater in the winter?"

"Actually, he does have one with a skull and crossbones on the back. Got a problem with that?"

She approached the kitchen counter and slid onto a stool. "No. Sorry, I seem to offend at every turn. I should leave. You've been more than kind."

"Not until you eat." He placed a plate stacked with pancakes before her. Beside that sat a coffee cup steaming with dark brew. "You like maple syrup?"

"I…don't know."

"Right." He tapped his temple. "But you do know about Sphynx cats. Interesting."

She dug into the pancakes. Mercy, but it had been

days since she'd eaten a decent meal and not a candy bar or bag of Doritos that she'd gotten out of a vending machine. Her aching stomach growled with glee.

"So your bedroom is all black," she stated between bites. Ah, hot food. And it smelled so good. And tasted even better.

Blade stood across from her by the stove, arms crossed and one hand wielding a spatula. He was noticeably not eating. "That it is."

"And you're all into the dark look yourself. Is that called goth?"

He made show of looking down the front of his black T-shirt, stretched tightly across muscled biceps, black jeans and, well, his feet were bare. "For a chick who's lost her memory, you're very judgmental."

"And you are being sarcastic. I do know what sarcasm is."

"Good for you. I'm not a goth. I'm just Blade. You find everything you needed in the bathroom?"

She touched her hair. "I borrowed your comb. I hope that was okay. You can't imagine how good it feels to be showered and reasonably groomed. My hair must have looked horrible before."

"It's gorgeous," he said quickly. And then he turned and made a show of checking that the griddle was turned off, mumbling as he did so, "I mean, it's fine."

Zenia brushed the wet locks over her shoulder, but couldn't hide what felt like a blush. "So what do you do, Blade? You said you were running into town? To your job?"

"I do some fix-it work for the locals here and there. Got a quick job for a couple of retired nuns who are designing a water garden in their backyard. And I work with my brother, Stryke. He's, er…leader of a…group."

She sipped the hot coffee carefully, trying to figure out what he wasn't willing to say. A group? Of what? People? For what reason? But she wouldn't ask. Whatever he wanted to present to her, she'd take, and anything he didn't want her to know was fine, too.

Should she be more curious? She had enough problems of her own to worry about. And she wanted to move over to his good side, maybe even befriend him. She could use a friend. Where were her friends? Were they worried about her? Had they called the police?

"Stryke is building a compound for…his work," Blade offered. "I'm his second-in-command. It's family stuff."

"Sounds important. Do you think I have friends?"

The man shrugged. "Not sure. But you're not wearing a ring."

She studied her hands. The fingers were long and slender. "I must not wear jewelry." That seemed sad. One should never forego a chance to sparkle. "I should have a couple of rings. I like sparkly things. Why did you notice the absence of a ring?"

"It's nothing," he said again, taking great interest in the griddle.

"These pancakes are delicious," she said. "I'm trying not to devour them, but it's not working."

"Devour all you want. Griddle is still hot. I can make up more fast."

"No, I think five is more than enough. Though, I will take a refill on the coffee. I figure it's the last good meal I'll have for a while. Aren't you going to eat?"

"I did when you were in the shower. So you're sleeping in your truck and I'm going to assume you don't have a lot of cash."

"Twenty bucks." She shrugged. "I'll figure something out."

"There's an inn at the edge of town where you could stay. Family owned. I don't think it's expensive. It's got a big red cock out front."

Zenia sputtered on a sip of coffee. "A what?"

His smile was slow but genuine and it warmed her all over to finally see some levity from him. His eyes were all kinds of sexy now.

"The inn is called The Red Rooster. There's a giant iron rooster sculpture on the front lawn."

"I see." But looking for an actual red cock may have proved more interesting. "How much you think they charge a night?"

Blade opened a drawer beside him, took out a roll of bills and set it on the counter before Zenia. "That should help you out a bit."

A bit? Her jaw dropped open. The tightly wound block of greens looked as though it could bankroll an entire building project.

"Oh, no, I can't." But she couldn't stop from grabbing it and testing the weight of the roll. They were hundred dollar bills. And there had to be a couple dozen of them rolled up. "This is… No. I don't know how I'd ever pay that back. I'm good with sleeping in the truck and eating Doritos. I like the cool-ranch ones."

"It's a gift. I can afford it."

"You don't even know me."

"That's the best kind of gift. It makes me feel good to give. Maybe it will even tilt me out of the guilt column I've been stuck in. Will you let me have that good feeling?"

"I uh…" She set the roll beside the plate. It would certainly come in handy and definitely pay for a month or more at a cheap inn or hotel. And she could really use a hot shower every day. And maybe even new clothes. And some sparkly rings for her fingers.

The guilt column? What had the man to feel guilty about?

It was none of her business. If he was trying to buy some redemption or whatever, far be it from her to get judgmental, as he'd suggested earlier.

"Okay," she said. "But what will I owe you? Besides all this cash?"

"You think I expect something from you for that money?"

"You're a man. If I know anything about men it is that they generally do not give things to others without expecting something in return. And you, being handsome and single, and me being, well—whatever and whoever I am—maybe you want *something* from me."

"Something." He leaned forward onto the counter on his elbows and his hair fell over one eye. He rapped the counter. Considering what his terms would be?

"I don't want to give you sex," she suddenly felt the need to say. "I mean, I don't know you very well. So if that's the condition, then I'll leave without this." She pushed the roll toward him.

"If I'd wanted to have sex with you, Zen, it would have happened last night."

"Oh."

So that meant he wasn't interested in having sex with her? Because the guy was ten kinds of handsome. And—didn't he find her attractive?

Why that thought? She wasn't curious about having sex with him.

Maybe a little. Oh, mercy, to imagine that blue hair

falling over her face as he kissed her and those rigid abs brushing across her stomach…

"I want to help you out and make sure you're safe."

As he seemed to do with the locals. Helping nuns? Despite his dark-and-dangerous appearance, the man must be a pussycat at heart.

"Okay." She clasped the money roll. "Can we be friends?"

Blade abruptly straightened and crossed his arms again. "I don't do the friend thing with women very well."

"I see." A wad of cash and a don't-let-the-door-hit-you-on-the-way-out. Never mind the guilt column, this guy was still occupying the weird column. "So this is it, then? I indulge in your tasty pancakes and then take the money and run?"

"Yep."

Her heart fell, but she kept her shoulders straight and didn't show her disappointment. "That's cool. I've over-stayed my welcome as it is. Got some memory tracking to do." She grabbed her backpack and stuffed the money in it. Holding out her hand, she shook his. "Thanks for everything, Blade. Blessings to you."

"Stay away from Brock Olafson," he called as she headed down the stairs.

She would. But it was too bad Blade didn't want to be friends. She could really use a friend right now. This being-on-her-own thing was for the birds. Whoever she was, she was probably a person who thrived on the connection with others.

Which was why it felt as if she was walking away from the best thing to ever happen to her as she took the stairs downward.

Chapter 5

"Uh, Blade?"

A wave of relief fell over Blade when he heard Zen calling from the bottom of the stairs. She hadn't left.

And what was that about? He didn't care if she left and never returned. He'd told her he didn't want to be friends. Had given her enough cash to survive a few months on her own. Add another tally in his charity column. End of story.

"There's a police car at the end of the driveway," Zen called up. "The officer is looking over my truck."

"Ah, hell. They must have gotten a stolen vehicle report. Get back up here. I'll go out and talk to him."

He passed her on the stairs. The skim of her hair across his biceps felt like silk on his skin. He wanted to feel it brush his lips, to draw in her scent and—

Blade forced his thoughts back to the dire situation. "What's out in the truck that belongs to you?"

"Nothing. All I own is in my backpack," she said, patting the backpack she held before her. "Not as if any of this stuff is mine. Fingerprints?"

"Yeah, well, maybe that would be a good thing? If they traced your prints there could be a chance you'd know who you are."

She shook her head and studied her fingertips. "Not sure about that. I don't want to go to jail. I was just borrowing the truck. You think they'd believe that?"

"Nope. Stay. I'll handle this."

She nodded and he waited for her to reach the top step of the stairs before heading outside.

Earl Smith was a local cop who knew his family. Of course, Smith didn't know the Saint-Pierres were werewolves, vampires and faeries. He thought they were just regular folk that tried to fit in, save when Trouble got rowdy and a bar owner called to have the police escort him home. Blade was sure Trouble knew all the officers and deputies within a thirty-mile range by first name and badge number.

"You're at the wrong place, Earl," Blade said to the lanky man who was probably twice his age and half his weight. "Trouble lives east of town."

"You know where this truck came from, Saint-Pierre?"

Fortunately Zen hadn't driven all the way up to the barn, and had parked near the end of the short drive.

"Wasn't here last night when I got home. First time I've been outside today, Earl." Blade rubbed his jaw and walked up to peer into the cab of the truck. As Zen had said, it didn't appear as if any personal belongings had been left inside. The key was in the ignition. "Hell, I didn't even hear it drive up." He laid a hand over the hood. "Engine's not hot. Must have been here awhile. Who's it belong to?"

"It was stolen from a parking lot in Fridley about a week ago. Got a tip from Brock Olafson—we have breakfast at the Panera every now and then—that I should probably check your place."

"That's odd. How would Brock know about a truck I've never seen before? Maybe he had something to do with it being here."

"I, uh, hmm…"

While Earl gave that one a good think, Blade glanced up toward the kitchen window. Zen's face ducked out of sight.

"I don't know what to say, Earl. You know I wouldn't do such a thing as steal a truck. I have enough of my own in the garage."

The officer straightened and hooked his thumbs at his belt loops. "Mind if I take a look?"

"Inside the garage? Sure thing."

Blade led him toward the barn where the entire ground floor had been converted into a garage for his fix-it projects. Best thing to do was play along. He'd not asked for this trouble, but for some reason, he was damned good at extricating himself from sticky situations.

It was a talent he'd gladly surrender if only everyone would leave him in peace.

By the time Blade returned to the loft, Zen had watched a tow truck haul away the vehicle she had borrowed. Okay, stolen. The keys had been in the ignition. How else to get around while she was trying to figure herself out and had no cash whatsoever?

Was that it? Had she been a thief before losing her

memory and the criminal act was so ingrained that stealing a truck hadn't given her a moment of guilt?

Blade topped the stairs and veered toward the kitchen, where the coffee machine blinked in wait. He inserted a coffee pod and leaned over the machine, his back to her. Zen could sense his irritation. He was still barefoot. Her worry vanished as she studied his feet. They were sexy. Seriously. Those dark jeans slouched over his feet, the hems torn and worn from treading without shoes. It was so animal, in a sensual, easygoing kind of way.

And he had once again saved her butt, this time by diverting the police from her. Because there was just something about not going to the police that made sense. And she was going to call that intuition about the life she couldn't remember.

"Sorry," Zen offered. "Guess I'm not making a fast getaway now like I had planned. Are you in trouble?"

"No. But the local police will certainly be keeping an eye on me for a while. Earl left convinced it was a joyrider who had abandoned the truck here. Why they hadn't driven it into the woods and trashed it was beyond Earl, but he'll dust for prints. I told him to keep me in the loop if he gets an identification."

"Thanks. I think. If they come up with my prints, will they arrest me?"

"Probably." He removed the full mug and turned to face her, sipping slowly. "And why not go to the police?"

She shrugged. "Doesn't feel right. Not part of the destiny."

He raised an eyebrow.

Zen shrugged again. Because really, the words had just come out; she didn't have a clear reason for them. "Don't ask me to explain."

"Uh-huh." He tilted down a few sips of the hot brew. "If you say so."

"So it's as easy as that?" Zen asked. "I tell you not to ask questions and you don't. Whew. You must have a heck of a closet filled with your own skeletons."

He smirked and approached her, laying his hand over her heart. Zen flinched but didn't want to pull away from the surprising touch of his big warm hand over her breast.

"What are you—" It didn't matter what he was doing. She just didn't want him to ever stop.

"Your heart is racing," he said.

"Well, duh. A handsome man is touching my boob."

He flinched away at that statement. Shook his head. "Sorry. Just wanted to know if you were for real."

"I am real. I'm standing right here. What doesn't look and feel real to you?"

"The whole not-knowing-things part. You can tell a lot about a person by measuring their heartbeats. Just thought I'd give it a try."

With a nod he turned and pulled out another coffee pod and set it in the machine to brew.

"All righty, then." Zen sat at the counter, more confused about the man than ever. So her heartbeats were fast. To be expected.

And what did she have to do to get him to touch her like that again?

There was something about this woman that was accepting and open, Blade thought. But also too damned curious. Dare he tell her what he'd encountered inside the house while she had been wandering about the field? That would then lead to a discussion on how he was familiar with demons, and…

Destiny?

There was certainly something *other* about her. But Blade wouldn't necessarily label it destiny. Whatever that meant. When he'd laid his hand over her heart it had felt sure and strong—and fast. His sensory perception of other paranormal beings was excellent. Vampires he could tell by touch. Vamps gave off the shimmer, a knowing tingle. Werewolves were a scent thing. And faeries were a more difficult tell, even though faery blood ran through his veins, but some were just…bright. And that wasn't a glow but rather a feeling he got.

As for witches, he felt a twinge in his spine when near them. Demons gave off a sulfurous scent and they generally had a difficult time hiding their red eyes.

He met Zen's eyes as she sipped the coffee. Hers were blue.

"Yesterday they were green," he said suddenly, leaning forward to closely inspect her irises.

"What?" She met his gaze, and then shook her head. "Listen, after your emphatic statement that we could never be friends, I find your gazing longingly into my eyes a little befuddling, not to mention the free feel you just took."

"They've changed color."

"What? My eyes? No, they're still—" She touched her cheek below her eye. "I guess I've never given them a good look in the mirror."

"Yesterday the color resembled emeralds. Today they are azure. Not red."

"You're hanging on to that theory, eh? Demons have red eyes. Or so the mythology states as much."

"Zen." Blade set his coffee mug on the counter and leaned forward. "That old lady back at the house where I met you? She wasn't old or even a lady."

"Sure she was. I spoke to her. Told her I was there to find myself. Though she did say something odd about finding herself. If she wasn't an old woman, then what was she?"

"What you saw and spoke to was her human facade. I saw her shift into three demons. And then I slayed them."

Tapping her fingernails against her mug, Zen surprised him in that she didn't protest or stand up and dash off. The woman was reading him, delving into his words to glean their integrity. Trustworthy? Always. Upstanding? Rarely.

"What kind of demons?" she finally asked.

"I don't know." He narrowed his gaze on her. She wasn't running. And asking questions was a good thing. Right? "The standard nasty-assed terrors that disperse into black dust when I draw my blade down their sternums."

Zen clutched her chest and made a gagging face. "And you think *I'm* one of them?"

"No. Maybe."

She gaped at him.

"I don't know. But I do believe they were after you. When I was in the house, one of them said something like 'she's ours.' You're really cool with this conversation? Because most humans would not be."

"I haven't decided yet. I know demons exist. In mythology. As do bazillions of other breeds and species. But they are fiction, Blade. You do know that, right?"

He sighed. The conversation about paranormals was never easy, and he didn't have it with humans unless it was absolutely necessary. Something about Zen made him believe this was a necessary conversation, so he decided to jump in with both feet and hope she didn't freak.

"Demons are real, Zen. As are all other creatures of myth you believe are fiction. If you don't have your memory, what makes you think your beliefs are real? That they have merit? Maybe you only think you don't believe in mythological beings?"

She opened her mouth to say something, then paused. He had even confused himself with that question.

"I know some things," she insisted. "As you seem to believe you know things. So I'll play along. Say demons do exist. And you, apparently, are aware they exist. What does that make you? Are you some kind of creature, Blade?"

The million-dollar question. And she couldn't hide the smirk of laughter that niggled at the corner of her mouth. But he wasn't going to lie to her. Because to shuffle around the truth wouldn't get him anywhere. And after slaying three demons he felt as though he'd become involved in something. A something that demanded he pay attention for Zen's sake.

"Vampire." He sipped the coffee and set it down. He ran his fingers through his hair and offered a tiny smile. He wouldn't mention his faery half. That would only complicate matters.

He waited for Zen to digest his confession, and expected a calm reaction, as she'd displayed thus far. So when she stood abruptly and grabbed her backpack, nearly knocking the coffee cup off the counter in the process, he knew he'd gone too far.

"Quit playing with me," she said. "I need help and I need answers. Not some idiot who thinks he can one-up the town asshole. Brock may have been the better choice last night."

And she marched away from him and down the stairs.

Blade leaned over the sink and watched through the small window as she stopped halfway down his gravel driveway. She realized she no longer had a vehicle. The town was ten miles south. Would she make the walk? In a long dress?

Or would she come back inside and ask for his help? She hadn't asked for his help thus far. And yet, he had willingly offered, and had gone above and beyond by giving her the roll of cash.

What was with that?

Normally Blade Saint-Pierre stood off and to the side, in the shadows. He didn't call attention to himself. He didn't like confrontations. Nor did he engage in small talk and friendships. It was easier that way. The unseen were not challenged, or tortured.

Too late for that, eh?

Yet he wanted her to see him for reasons that baffled. Of course, asking her to believe he was a vampire was out there, even for the smartest and most open-minded of humans.

After shuffling down the stairs, he headed out to his truck—he did have the appointment with the nuns— and smiled to himself. Zen would have a much longer walk than she anticipated.

He was following her, so Zenia picked up her pace, determined to make it to town before he could stop and once again offer her help. She didn't need help from a wacked crazy who believed himself a vampire. What role-playing nightmare had he gotten lost in? Didn't boys generally give up that stuff when they left their teens?

But it was a long walk. And he must be driving five miles an hour. Superobvious follow. Yet when his truck pulled in front of her to make a right turn, and his passenger-side window rolled down, it took all her strength not to rush up to the truck door and see what the handsome man had to say.

Arms crossed and posture stiff, Zenia stood at the road's gravel edge. The sun was high and she guessed it would be a hot one today. She wondered if her skin burned easily. She didn't want to make the long trek into town on foot. But she had reached her limit with trusting this guy. Handsome did not win over crazy. Usually.

Maybe?

Blade leaned across the seat and called, "Tangle Lake is in the other direction!"

Zenia steeled herself against turning and looking back the way she'd walked. "I knew that," she said.

He tilted his head, as if to ask, "Really?"

"Fine." She marched toward the truck. "You win."

He popped the door lock open and she stepped up inside, setting her backpack on the floor. The tin circle poked out of the unzipped top.

"What's that?" he asked with an urgency that again alerted her that this guy wasn't all there in the head.

She tugged the pack onto her lap and pushed the circle inside, zipping it securely. "It's mine. Now, would you mind giving me a ride to the big cock? Or whatever it is you called it? And I recall you had mentioned something about helping a couple of nuns. You must have an appointment to get to, so the sooner you drive me into town, the faster we can both be done with each other."

"The big cock it is." Blade shifted into gear. He drove a few miles before turning the radio down to a whisper. "It's called The Red Rooster Inn."

"Whatever," she managed with as little interest as possible.

"I gave Beckett Severo a call while I was following you down the road. He's my sister's husband. Owns an auto-body shop. He has a sweet little Mini Cooper he can let me buy cheap. He's going to wash it and give the interior a good cleaning, then he'll call me when it's ready. Work for you?"

"What color is it?" she asked, only because she suddenly felt as if he was making all the decisions for her, and she needed to wrangle some control.

"Red?"

"Like a demon's eyes?"

"Yes, like a demon's eyes. Believe me, Zen. I'm not making this stuff up."

"Really? I want to believe you, but…" She sighed and tilted her head against the window. All out of argument. And so desperate for some small grace. "All right. Let me try out belief for a minute. You're a vampire? With fangs?"

"Got the fangs. I need warm blood to survive. Every few weeks. Though I prefer it more often."

He winked at her and it was all she could do not to drop her jaw in horror. He'd just confessed to drinking blood! And the truck was going the speed limit. If she opened the door and jumped now, could she get up and walk away as easily as she had after the bus incident?

But deep within, Zenia felt this man meant only good toward her. If he had a strange belief about his origins then she should allow him that. But that allowance should be countered with a healthy dose of caution on her part.

The giant red iron rooster swept by on her right as Blade pulled into the inn's parking lot. Zen wanted to dash out of the truck and run as far away as possible. She wasn't about to stay where he knew where to find her.

And yet. It was his kind eyes. And he had given her a huge roll of cash. And made arrangements for her to use a car. Balancing his crazy with his kindness was actually leveling out the scale.

So Zenia said something that surprised herself. "Come in with me."

"Why?"

"We need to talk."

He winced.

Yeah, so she'd just given him a standard girlfriend line. Poor guy. But she needed to get on the same page with him.

"I don't believe you're so lacking in curiosity that you can simply drive away, are you?"

He considered the subtle challenge. Twisting the key in the ignition, the truck settled to quiet.

After checking in, Zen filed down the narrow hallway with Blade in tow. Her room was small and fashioned with timber furnishings that sported green-and-red-plaid fabric on the chair and bedspread. Sure was a lot of plaid in this neck of the woods, she noted. She tossed the backpack on the bed, directed Blade to make them coffee and excused herself to the bathroom.

The blue-and-yellow dress was loud. She did need to pick up some new things. Something a little less crazy cat lady and a bit more sensual. Because she knew she was attractive, and Blade's admiring gaze hadn't gone unnoticed. Nor had his attractiveness gone unnoticed.

She wondered if he would flinch if she tried to touch his soft hair. She sensed that would be his first reaction. And then she wanted to test that theory because pushing him to his unknown boundaries felt important to her. To see if he could stand up to any challenge.

Because if pushed maybe he'd reveal his lies. That perhaps he clung to the fantasy of being a strange creature for reasons that helped him survive in this world. Or maybe it was simply that he watched too many movies. Believed women would go for the brooding vampire act. Ugh.

She tilted her head aside, her reflection tracing a finger down her neck. A vampire. Did he want to bite her? What would that feel like? *Orgasmic*, her knowledge provided on a whisper. And what was orgasmic? Had she ever had the experience of sex?

She didn't know. And that frustrated immensely.

She hadn't learned anything about herself out in the field yesterday. And maybe she had. Demons had been after her? Incredulous. She should have stopped to say goodbye to the old lady.

Why was he making up such an elaborate ruse? For what reason the lie? No, he was being truthful. And to test that theory she'd have to see proof.

"Fangs," she muttered.

And once he had to confess to a lack of such telling signs of vampirism, then she could move forward. Both of them could.

Nodding once, she turned off the bathroom light and found Blade waiting with two cups of coffee in hand.

"Dark?" she asked.

"As black as I could get it."

She glanced to the backpack. It was unopened. He hadn't snooped. Not that she had anything to hide. Just a bunch of stolen charity clothing and that weird tin circle. And her roll of cash. His cash. Yet she didn't feel as if she owed him for that generous gift. Was it because she couldn't recall if she was the sort of person who had guilt?

Sitting on the bed, she shuffled closer toward the head by the pillows when Blade sat not three feet from her. Inviting him in may have been a stupid idea. She'd hoped it a means to allow him to confess. Did the victim invite the serial killer in so easily?

"I need some proof," she said. "That you are what you say you are."

"Will that make you believe?"

"Of course." Or it would make him believe. One way or another, this was going to get settled.

"So you are not a woman of faith?"

"I don't know." She tapped her head. "Not all there, remember?"

"What kind of proof are you asking for?"

She set the coffee mug on the wood bedside table that looked as though it had been carved from an oak stump. "Whatever kind you're willing to offer."

She didn't want him to be crazy. She really did not.

Sliding closer on the bed, she raised her hand to touch his hair, then decided against it. "Fangs?"

"If that's what you need? I can do that."

Blade tilted his head back and closed his eyes. And when he rolled his head around, his nose drew along her cheek. Her skin tingled at the barely there touch. It seemed as if he was scenting her. And when the tip of his nose dusted her earlobe she felt her nipples tighten and couldn't decide whether to delight or be afraid of that feeling. Curling her fingers, she closed her eyes as a mix of anxiety and breathless anticipation stirred in her core.

A sharpness slid along her neck. Zen gasped in a breath. What the—? Blade's hand grabbed her by the chin, forcing her to look at him. His mouth was barely parted, yet bright white fangs jutted over his lower lip.

"Holy… How did you put those in so fast?"

"I didn't put them in. They are my teeth." A wide grin revealed his fangs rising to sit even with his upper teeth, and then again, they descended into the long, pointed, gleaming weapons. "You wanted proof."

"But… That means…" He was telling the truth? That was incredible. Impossible. Freaky. Real? "Oh, mercy."

Zen raced for the bathroom and closed the door behind her.

After a few seconds a rap sounded on the wood door. "Zen?"

"I'm good!" she called. "Just need a few minutes to process."

Chapter 6

Zenia leaned forward onto the vanity, peering at her eyes reflected in the mirror. What she saw there was not fear but uncertainty.

"He's a vampire. Those fangs were real."

She hissed out a breath and her shoulders sank. The man was really a vampire. Because his teeth had not been fake. No cheesy white plastic dentures. He'd lowered and raised them as she had watched.

So here she stood. Processing. And to do so, had locked herself in the bathroom to put herself away from the creature on the other side of the flimsy wood door. Who could probably knock it down if he wanted to and suck out all her blood before she could manage to scream for help.

She shook her head. "Don't let your imagination make this into something weird. Weird? Ha! The man is a vampire. Which means the mythology is real. And what makes me think all I know is real anyway?"

Of course, if vampires were real that also opened the door to other creepy critters being as real. Werewolves, ghosts and demons?

"He killed demons. There were real demons in that pink house. He was telling me the truth. And they'd mentioned me? What is going on?"

She'd fallen into some kind of creature feature. And while she should do the smart thing and run like hell, she couldn't resist a peek down the dark stairway.

"He's been nice to me so far," she reasoned with her reflection. "I can trust him." A nod confirmed her decision.

And so she turned the knob and walked out into the room. Blade leaned against the wall, arms crossed over his chest. Head bowed, his hair was tinted blue, no denying that. Was that indicative of his vampire nature?

Wow. Just wow.

"Are you going to bite me?" she asked calmly.

He smirked and shook his head. "No."

"Why don't you want to bite me?"

Now he laughed. "In the course of two questions you went from curiosity to fang junkie."

"Fang junkie?"

"Women and men who seek the vampire's bite. It gives them an orgasmic high. Sort of a thank-you for giving blood."

Zen blew out a breath. Shook her head. She'd asked for proof. And he'd given it to her in spades. The guy was a vampire. And the more she considered it, his fangs were actually kind of cool.

She walked up to him. "Let me see them again."

With a shrug, he opened his mouth to reveal the fangs. She touched the tip of a fang and he flinched away.

"What's wrong?"

"Women don't generally touch," he said defensively.

"I'm sorry. They are interesting to me. Don't you ever poke yourself in the lip?"

He smirked, again revealing the gorgeous fangs. "I've been living with them awhile."

"Since birth?"

"No, since my teen years. We vamps don't come into the blood hunger until puberty. A vampire baby is just wrong."

"I imagine so." Frowning, Zen ran the idea of a fanged baby drinking blood from its mother's nipple through her thoughts. Yeah, that was wrong in too many ways to consider. "Wow. So you are really a vampire."

"And you are having a tough time with this."

"No. Not anymore. I did some processing in the bathroom. Had a pep talk with my crazy ole self. So the myths are real? And you don't seem a danger to me."

"I have no reason to harm you, Zen. Believe me."

"I am inclined to trust you. You've shown me nothing but kindness thus far. Will you tell me about being a vampire? That'll help me to further process. You said you drink blood every few weeks? Is it a sexual thing?"

"You just ask whatever is on your mind, don't you?"

"Are you offended by my questions? You should be pleased I'm not screaming and whittling a stake."

"I am. Although the adrenaline that comes up when a person screams does season the blood nicely." He paused. Gauging her reaction? Likely.

Zen didn't feel disgust. She'd accepted that vampires existed. Now she needed to learn how and why.

"And so you know," he added, "it would take a damn long time to whittle a stake. Use an ax to hone a point on a thick wood dowel. It will go faster."

"Did you just tell me how to kill you?"

"I did. Feel better?"

"It's not as though I need to feel better about your condition—"

"It's not a condition. It is what I am."

"Okay. I understand. Blood is your means to survival?"

"Yes. I like drinking blood and it is a sensual experience if I'm having sex with the person when I bite them. But I can take someone in a dark club or back alley without it turning me on. My bite leaves the victim in a state of bliss. As I've said, a reward for giving blood."

"Do you ever, uh—" Zen ran her fingers along the plaid bedspread "—kill?"

His fangs retracted, and she missed them immediately. "When drinking blood? No."

That he'd categorized that question bothered her. "So you have killed at other times? Of course, the demons yesterday." She had no choice now but to believe they had been real.

He suddenly took her by the wrist and lifted her arm to hold her elbow toward the sunlight beaming through the window. "Those markings are faint but remarkable. Do you know what they mean?"

The man had deftly avoided the question about killing. She'd give him that. He had killed. Many times. She simply knew it. Perhaps he'd been protecting another damsel in distress from demons?

"I'm guessing it was something I drew on my skin before the accident," she offered. "Should fade away with a few more showers."

"Has it faded since you've noticed it?"

"No. I guess not."

"It doesn't look like ink or even one of those white tattoos that are so popular nowadays."

"Demonic?" she tossed out teasingly. She regretted it immediately. Demons were serious and real. What kind of nightmare had she fallen into?

"I don't know what it is," Blade said. "One of my brothers is full faery. He has pale violet markings on his skin. But the patterns don't look similar. Aren't you curious?"

"I am, but it's not as if I have any idea where to begin learning about such a thing. A faery brother? That's fascinating. How does that work exactly?"

"It's a long story. My family is a mix of races."

Nodding, she rubbed the inside of her elbow to distract herself from the need to delve into his family history. He'd been kind in answering her questions so far. She didn't want to press her luck. "How do I learn more about these markings?"

"There's a witch in Minneapolis. She might have a clue."

"Witches. Of course." And so many other species she would likely learn about the longer she hung around Blade. The idea of gaining such knowledge compelled her. If she couldn't learn about herself then she may as well gather info about the secret world that existed around her. "You know all the exciting people, eh?"

"Do you want me to take you to her?"

"I sense you are more eager to learn about these markings than I am. Digging up proof I'm not an evil demon?"

"I hate demons," Blade stated plainly. He paced to the window. His frame stiffened, shoulders tilting back and fingers curling into loose fists. Zen could palpably feel his cool anger. He was a man who didn't like to speak about himself, but he didn't have to. His emotions showed in his tightly strung physicality.

"Would you hate me if I were demon?" she asked.

He turned a glance over his shoulder. "I don't know what to think of you."

"Well, I think very highly of you, just so you know."

"Despite my being vampire?"

"Your race or species, or whatever you call it, matters little. It's you, the man, whom I make my judgment on."

"Not a lot of people in this world who can be so open-minded."

Zen smirked. "And look at me, not so much open-minded as absent of some of my mind."

His smile was an unexpected surprise. "You'll remember who you are."

"I hope so." She sat on the bed. "And then I wonder if it really matters. I don't know, I guess if I do have a family or job I would like to learn about that. Do you think vampires can get amnesia?"

He lifted a brow.

"They can?"

"There was a vampire who lived in the area, decades ago, who lost his memory. He got it back. We're very similar to humans, Zen."

"Except that part about needing human blood to survive."

"There is that."

"Would you, uh…bite me if I asked?"

"No."

"Why not? You said it wouldn't kill me. What if I wanted to experience the pleasure you said the bite gives a victim?"

"You're moving too fast, Zen. We haven't even gone on a date."

"Oh. Right. Sorry. But if we can't be friends, I don't hold out much hope for a date."

"Dates are…"

"Not your thing. I get it. Tall, dark, brooding guy has

a lot of issues and I should just shut up and be thankful he wants to help me. Hmm, but what if having a friend was part of the help I needed?"

"I don't know what you are."

She shrugged. "Does it matter?"

"It does. Instincts tell me you're not human. And there are certain species within this realm that I can't drink from."

"Really?"

He nodded. "Faery ichor is addictive to a vampire. And demon blood is just— It won't kill me, but I... Well, it's not important. Angel blood will kill me, though."

"I'm pretty sure I'm not an angel. I haven't any wings."

"I don't know much about angels. Those markings on your arm make me wonder if you're faery. You'd be able to bring your wings out if you were aware of them."

Wings? Bonus!

Zen closed her eyes and focused on the space between her shoulder blades and up and down her spine. She imagined wings popping out. Hey, if the man was a vampire, anything was possible.

"What are you doing?" he asked.

She opened one eye. "Trying to bring out my wings. I don't feel anything. Not even a flutter. Nope. I don't think so. Though it would be cool if I had faery dust. I like sparkly things."

His smile was always such a welcome change from stoicism that this time she stood and walked right up to him, lured by the seductive promise of his lips. She slid her hands up the front of his shirt and touched the tips of his long hair. It was soft, as she'd suspected. And then she tilted up on to her tiptoes and kissed him.

Chapter 7

Zen's mouth landed on Blade's with graceful precision. He grabbed her arms to push her away. Not expecting a kiss, he'd been blindsided. And when he wanted to shove her off and march out of the room, he suddenly relaxed his grip on her arms and leaned into the kiss.

And then he leaned in a little more.

He pulled her closer, sliding a hand up her back to keep her there. Her mouth fit his like no other woman's had. She felt…not so much right, but rather as if she'd found something and did not want to again lose it. A missing piece to her puzzle? Despite being unable to remember things about herself, she'd certainly not lost the skill of delivering a kiss.

He moaned deep in his throat and then opened her mouth with his and slid his tongue inside her heated kiss. She tasted like coffee. She felt impossibly exquisite. She smelled like honey and her body was warm and supple against his. A sweet thing.

And that was the kicker. Her scent did not allude to her identity. What *was* she? And worse, could whatever she was be bad for him?

Forcing himself to pull away from the kiss, he held her at a distance even as she leaned forward, attempting to ply him with another kiss. "What was that for?" he asked on a raspy tone.

"I had the compulsion to kiss you. You taste great. And your fangs didn't get in the way. Cool," she said with more enthusiasm than she probably should have. "Did I do it right? I mean, I'm not sure if I've kissed a man before."

"It was nice. Er, I mean… Yeah, it was okay."

"Okay? Hmm, that implies I need more practice."

The second kiss was firmer, more demanding, and was filled with an eagerness that rippled through Blade's system and hardened his cock. And then it jabbed at his vampiric need for a deeper, more intimate, connection. His fangs wanted down, and he fought against it.

He'd meant it when he'd said he would not bite her. Not when he didn't know what the hell she was.

Practice? This chick was an expert kisser.

"Zen, stop." He shrugged her off and backed toward the bed, but realized he was trapped unless he scrambled over the bed and out the door. "I can't do this. I—I don't do this."

"You don't do what? Kiss women? Are you gay? Stupid me. I don't have the gaydar that I know some do."

"I am not gay. Though, I wouldn't confine my sexual choices to women, either. I just don't do…this." *And leave it at that. Please.*

"Oh. You mean like the physical-contact thing? Or the emotion thing?"

"I think we've chatted enough for today."

"You mean kissed?"

He nodded. "Whatever you want to call it. Just drop it, will you?"

"If you insist. But you did share with me, so I guess that was my return share."

A kiss in exchange for a confession to vampirism. Worked for him. Until it did not. Blade did not want to get involved with a pretty woman in need of saving. He just. Did. Not. He either made love to them or rescued them. There was to be no in-between. Not anymore.

"Will you get me that car?" she asked sweetly. "The town is small but it's easier to get around in a vehicle."

He swung around the side of the bed, but the door was so far away, and did he really want to run out like a scared boy who'd just gotten his first kiss?

"Of course. And I want to take you to the witch. But I have to stop by the nuns' place today."

"Did you miss that appointment?"

"No, I told them I'd swing by when I was in town. Didn't specify a time."

"If I have a car I can run around on my own. I wouldn't need your help."

He wasn't sure if he should applaud that or lament not having a damsel to save. Because then his only other option would be to make love to her.

"I don't mind helping you, Zen. We'll get you figured out."

"You really think I could be something *not* human?"

"It's a possibility. It would help if I had some notion of what you are…"

Getting an idea, he bent and tugged out the knife from his boot. Turning to Zen, he held up the big bowie knife that had saved his ass on more than a few occasions. Her eyes widened. Her *gold* eyes.

Lowering the knife to his side, he leaned forward to peer at the irises. They changed color often.

"What? You looking for the best place to jab that big blade? I just start trusting you and then you go and freak me out of that trust, over and over—"

"They're gold now."

"My eyes? They were sort of a muddy green when I was in the bathroom processing things." She blinked. Rubbed an eyelid. "So what does that have to do with you bringing out the big bad weapon?"

"Nothing at all. And maybe everything." Jaw tensing, he weighed his options. The easiest choice was going to once again tug her out of trust and push her toward freak mode. "I want to make a small cut in your skin to see your blood." He grabbed her hand, holding her palm upward. "Will you let me?"

"Once again, you're making me think Brock was the better bet."

He frowned at her.

"Is this a vampire thing?"

"No. I have three brothers and one sister. One of my brothers is full-blood faery. He bleeds ichor. Ichor is clear and sparkles. Not red."

His blood was red, and yet—she didn't need to know that it had a tendency to sparkle, as well.

"So you think if you cut me…" She squeezed her fingers a couple times. A nervous reaction. Then she closed her eyes, squeezed them tightly and nodded. "Okay. I've processed. Go for it."

He wasn't going to argue and give her a chance to reconsider.

Blade dragged the tip of his blade in an inch-long cut down the center of her palm. She didn't make a peep. Points for bravery. Blue blood seeped out and dribbled toward his hand. He panicked and dropped her hand. And even as he backed away, the blood spilling from her palm changed color. Black droplets hit the worn beige carpeting.

Zen studied her hand and then the floor. "It changed color. And it's not red. Wow. I—don't think I'm human," she said with wonder. "How strange is that? I think I just passed you on the weirdness scale. But what bleeds blue?"

Heart falling in his chest, Blade stumbled backward, landing on the bed. "Angels."

The man sitting on the bed growled at her. And then he revealed a flash of fang. It was a combative display, and Zen didn't like it. Not coming from the man whom she trusted to help her learn about herself. And then she did not trust him.

And then she got over her freak-out to trust him again.

It was exhausting trusting this man.

But the display of fangs cautioned her that she knew little about him. And he could be very dangerous.

So back to not so much trust.

"Are you serious?" she asked with a gesture toward his fangs. "Don't go all warrior on me, Blade. Settle down. This is news to me. I'm an angel? I can't be." She thrust out her palm. It no longer bled, and had completely healed. "What the—? Do it again."

He held up his hands in protest, the knife in one of them and shook his head. "I'm not touching angel blood."

"I am not an angel. I mean…I don't feel angelic." She patted her chest, ran her hands over her hips. "What do angels feel like?"

"I don't know what you are, Zen. Angel is a guess."

"Right, but then my blood turned black. What does that mean?"

"Demons bleed black."

She gaped at him.

"That must have been your denizen back at the house."

"I am not part of a denizen."

"You have amnesia, so that argument is invalid."

Slamming her hands to her hips, Zen pinned the man with her best snappish look. Tossing the truth at her wasn't going to win him any points. All she wanted to do was move back to the window and resume their kiss. That perfect, delicious, erotic kiss. It had shimmered through her insides, warming in its wake, and had made her feel—things she wasn't sure she'd ever felt before.

But the evidence was not something she could ignore. Her blood wasn't red. That ruled out human. Right? For all the mythological knowledge she held in her brain, she could confirm that, yes, angels were the only creatures that bled blue. And quite a few things bled black, though the majority were demonic.

Maybe she was angel *and* demon? Was that possible? She didn't know. She'd only just begun to believe in creatures beyond humanity. She didn't feel particularly angelic. Where were her wings?

"This is," she started, "surprising. I need to process this." She inspected her palm. "Look."

Blade leaned over, without touching, though his hair did skim her wrist. "It's healed. You are not human by a long shot."

"We should talk to the witch."

"I'll give her a call."

"Blade." She grabbed his hand as he stood and fished out his cell phone. "Thank you."

He shrugged and pulled out of her grip.

"I know you think it's something you're doing, like helping the elderly. But you could have left me in that parking lot last night. And you could just walk away now. The door is right there. I won't protest if you leave. Too much. I mean, I *am* all alone. But you know, I've managed to survive this long. A week. I could probably manage awhile longer."

Now his body changed from the stiff defensive posture, his shoulders relaxing. He touched the ends of her hair. "You need my help. That's something I'm willing to give."

"Great. Let's seal that with a kiss." She tilted up on her toes, but he stopped her with a hand to her shoulder.

"The two of us kissing? I'm not cool with that."

"Why—"

His hand between them frustrated her. "No questions. Deal?"

If she didn't agree, he might take her invitation to walk out the door. But if she agreed, did that mean she'd never taste his kiss again? It seemed a ridiculous sacrifice in exchange for some information about herself. She had some ideas. Angel?

But not knowing would keep him from kissing her again for sure. So she'd choose the lesser of the two evils.

"Deal."

Blade hadn't forgotten about the nuns. He told Zen he'd give her a call when he was finished and they could go see the witch. She said she planned to do some shopping—which he didn't argue, as that dress was...

loud—so he said he'd look for her at the local strip mall later in the evening. He estimated a whole afternoon of work.

The nuns had been sitting out in the backyard sipping lemonade when he'd arrived. Thrilled at his arrival, they had helped him haul heavy stones around the fountain. A couple of workhorses. And their jokes had been surprisingly ribald. He'd ensured the water flowed and the fountain was secured to the concrete base with a couple heavy-duty bolts. When all was finished, he refused their offer to pay and promised he'd return with further landscaping assistance in a few days after the plants had arrived.

It was seven-thirty in the evening when he drove by the strip mall and spied Zen. Blade had told her he would park in the back lot. The lot butted up against an abandoned sewing-needle factory. The brick walls were crumbling, but he liked the decay. And the quiet.

Leaning against the pickup truck bed, he confirmed by phone call with Dez Merovich it was okay to stop by tonight. She was a nearly millennium-old witch who, a few years ago, had cured his brother Stryke of the silver poisoning he'd received after a hunter's arrow had cut him while in wolf shape. She also studied diabology. If anyone would have some answers for Zen, Blade suspected it could be Dez.

And while waiting, Beck called. The Mini Cooper was ready. He could take it off Beck's hands for three grand. A pittance if it would enable Zen to find her feet and survive on her own. The price tag wouldn't even dent his finances.

Was he going out of his way to help this chick to achieve his own redemption? The gods knew he was desperately in need of forgiveness. Or better yet, forgetting. He'd take Zen's amnesia from her if it were possible. A woman had died because of his indiscretions.

Could helping Zen find out who she was erase his sins?

All Blade wanted was to feel the weight of that horrible disaster lift from his shoulders. He'd wear the scars to remind him of it forever. The mental place he went to when Octavia's memory popped up threatened to bring him down so deep he'd never rise. It was why he kept to himself. Safer for him and those innocents with whom he came in contact.

Was Zenia an innocent? If she was an angel, he didn't know what to think. Same if she was demon. Either way, she was not a species he wanted to get involved with. He'd learned his lesson.

He had.

So when the taste of her kiss shimmered onto his tongue, he couldn't decide whether to savor it or grab the water bottle he kept in the truck cab and wash it away.

I am all alone. She'd said it with desperation, and he hadn't felt as if it had been a ploy.

He knew that desperate feeling. Sometimes being the loner wasn't what his soul desired. And that was why he couldn't walk away from Zen now.

A woman's scream alerted him. At the end of the alleyway he saw the silhouettes. Zen stood holding armloads of shopping bags. A tall, broad-shouldered man wielded a circular blade that he swung toward the hapless female.

Chapter 8

In a matter of two seconds Blade assessed and reacted. The attacker was big, but so was Blade. The enemy had a weapon, and Blade had the bowie knife. The alley was secluded. For the moment. He couldn't know how long before Zen's scream would bring curious onlookers. This matter needed to be dealt with. Fast.

So he shifted into his most powerful form.

With a warning growl, his wings emerged and his shirt tore across his biceps and abs. When in faery form his muscles tightened and grew more defined and powerful. Everything about his vampire was heightened, as well. His fangs slid down, pinprick sharp and longer than usual. Scents grew stronger and the air vibrated against his skin. He could navigate by sensation with his eyes closed and in the blackest cavern if need be.

He kept his eyes open and raced toward the intruder and Zen.

The attacker swung his weapon toward Blade, who caught the man by the forearm. The weapon clattered to the ground and Zen grabbed for it. At the sight of the circular weapon, Blade did not sink his fangs into the man's biceps. An angel halo? Which would make this guy an angel.

The last thing a vampire wanted to do was suck angel blood. That was the way to certain death.

The man swung Blade around and his spine hit the brick wall, wings folding about his shoulders in defense. The attacker's grasp was supernaturally strong, and he closed his fingers about Blade's throat. Blade slashed a wing forward, the edges of the black-and-silver appendage razor sharp and cutting through his opponent's cheek. Blue blood oozed from the cut.

Just as Blade felt a bone crack in his neck vertebra, the man—angel—suddenly gleamed bright white. His eyes glowed all colors. His mouth gaped. Then he dispersed in a cloud of crystal dust, dropping on the ground between Blade and Zen.

Zen held the circular weapon, dripping with blue angel blood. "Holy crap, that was awesome!"

Blade immediately shifted back to his vampire form, tucking his wings in and insinuating them into his system. His neck had cocked at an uncomfortable angle, and he jammed the heel of his palm against his vertebrae to shove them back into position. That smarted, and took his senses from him. Landing on his knees before the pile of crystal ash, he was aware of his torn jeans. Didn't matter. Zen was safe.

"That was interesting," Zen announced with more glee than a woman who had almost died at an angel's hands should have.

"You just killed an angel."

"I know! This thing rocks. I picked it up from the ground when he dropped it. It's just like mine."

"Yours?" He gasped and looked up at her. Did she beam unnaturally? Her smile was effusive. Not at all like someone who had just killed. And those marks inside her elbows seemed to glow. "What do you mean it's like yours?"

She flipped the halo over and over then made to put it over her head.

"No!" Blade blurted out and stood. He put up placating hands. "Don't do that."

She cringed and lowered the halo. "Uh, sorry?"

"If there is any chance you might be angel, if you put a halo in its rightful place—above your head—you will turn human."

"Oh. Okay. I think I need to process that."

"Yeah, you do that. Maybe I should hang on to that for you?"

She clasped it to her chest possessively. Okay, maybe not. He wasn't too keen on touching the blue blood tracing the circular metal anyway.

"So!" Her eyes wandered down his form and lingered at his crotch, where he felt a draft due to his ripped jeans. "You're going to need some new pants. The store just closed, but maybe there's a Target at the edge of town?"

"Zen!"

"Oh." She waved the angel halo before her. "I suppose you can have it. Mine is in my backpack. So this blood is blue." She inspected the bladed edge of the halo. "I didn't think it would be so easy to kill an angel. What's up with that?"

"It's the halo. It can be used as a weapon against the divine."

"I'd hardly call someone who had the intent of killing me divine."

"Neither would I."

She wiped the blood across her skirt, then thrust it toward him. "Here."

He accepted the cleaned halo, putting it around his wrist for the moment, and grabbed her shopping bags by the handles and strode toward the truck. "You get what you need?" Seriously? He'd just asked about her shopping trip instead of the obvious, like how was she able to kill a freaking angel?

"Yes!" She scrambled after him. "But, oh, there was this tiara. It was part of a display. It sparkled madly. They wouldn't sell it to me. It was just rhinestones, but it was so pretty—"

"Zen."

"What?"

"We need to get out of here before someone comes. But before we do…" He opened the truck door and dumped one of the shopping bags out, littering the floor with frilly clothing, and handed it to her. "Go scoop up the angel dust. We can give it to Dez in repayment for any info she might give us."

"Cool. I love the sparkly stuff." She gestured to his shoulder. "Nice wings, by the way."

"I am so out of my element with your easy acceptance of me," he admitted.

"Yeah?" Her eyes glided down to his crotch. "You're easy on the eyes, no matter what your form. I'll be right back."

"Hurry!"

He slid into the driver's seat and pulled a shirt from her bag over his lap. He hadn't a clean shirt to pull on to cover his back and prevent her from seeing the scars. Maybe she wouldn't notice.

Hell, she'd notice. The woman's eyes had practically licked every part of him just now.

Shaking his head and trying not to smile, Blade focused on the serious stuff. He'd shifted into faery shape in the middle of the city. Not something he'd ever done before. Too risky. Yet when weighing the risk against Zen's death, it hadn't required thought.

And yet, she had made the killing strike. The woman was utterly remarkable. And that was not a good thing. Because the more she fascinated him, the harder it would be to stand back and not get emotionally involved.

The passenger door opened and Zen stepped up into the truck. "Got it! And there was this." She held up a soft red feather as long as an ostrich plume but with tighter barbs.

"We'll show it to Dez. First I want to swing by my place and put some clothes on."

"Good plan. I don't really understand why your clothes are all ripped and…" Her eyes landed on his bare chest. "Missing."

Blade bowed his head to catch her gaze.

Zen shook her head as if to jar herself out of the stare. "Right. So vampires have wings?"

"Uh, not full-blood vamps."

"You're not full blood? What does that make you?"

No avoiding this conversation because the woman was persistent. He shifted into gear and headed north toward home. "I told you one of my brothers is faery."

"That you did. Can I assume one of your parents is faery?"

"My mother. And I got some of her sidhe mojo. Sidhe

is the universal term for faeries. I consider myself vamp, but I have the faery wings, so there you go."

"I'm surprised."

"Why?"

"That you can be more than one thing."

He found her gaze in the rearview mirror. "If you know so much about the world, you must be aware that the humans carry a mix of many heritages in their DNA. Look at you. Your skin color is light brown and your eyes are bright and your hair is almost red. Whatever you are, I'd guess you have a mixture of races in you."

"So? Oh."

"So that would imply I am allowed a mix of as many different breeds."

"Fair enough. And when you saw the big bad guy standing over me, you determined your faery had the best chance against whatever it was and you reacted. Good call."

"Lot of good it did. You were the one who killed the angel."

"I did, didn't I? Felt kind of empowering." She flexed her skinny biceps, and when she noted his frown, added, "You held him in place for me."

"I can live with that." And despite himself, he laughed at that one, and drove onward.

Yep, this woman was going to try his every staunch effort to never get involved again.

Chapter 9

Blade pulled on a change of clothing and tossed his torn jeans into a sack he kept to collect the damaged stuff. His mother was able to fix some, and with the unpatchable things, she made quilts. With five shape-shifting children, she had a lot of torn clothing to work with. Yes, his faery mother was into making quilts. For the grandchildren, she'd say with a wink.

Stryke was the only Saint-Pierre sibling who had a child on the way. His wife, Blyss, was due next month. Blade wasn't ready to be a father, nor was his brother Trouble. He wasn't sure about Kelyn's designs on family. The youngest was a hard one to figure.

Zen had changed in his bathroom and emerged in slim-fitted purple jeans and a blousy white top with multicolored embroidery around the neckline, which further attested to her bohemian nature. On her feet sparkled rhinestone-encrusted sandals. She spun before him and he nodded his approval, which made her beam.

And Blade found himself turning away to hide his own beaming smile. He could get over the fact that a woman had been the successor in that struggle in the alley. But he didn't want to dismiss the bright and sexy appeal of her. Ever. Because how often did a man get to appreciate the bright and sexy?

The twosome hopped in his truck and headed to Minneapolis. The sun yet lingered on the horizon and painted the sky orange and crimson. Rush-hour traffic had subsided. And the city lights had blinked on. Forty-five minutes later, he parked before the Washington Street high-rise nestled on the bank of the Mississippi River, and Dez buzzed them in to her penthouse loft.

Dez was married to the phoenix vampire Ivan Drake, who sat on The Council, which oversaw the paranormal nations. Blade recalled his grandfather Creed mentioning that Dez had been French royalty over nine hundred years ago, an illegitimate daughter of a Merovingian king.

Cool.

He enjoyed listening to his grandfather's tales of life in medieval times and walking through the centuries. To have lived in a simpler world appealed to Blade. Though, he knew no time was simpler, only that it had less technology. And he wasn't sure he could give up the coffeemaker for swords and bucket-topped boots.

The door opened and a cheerful greeting from a slender woman with chestnut hair and clad in a black T-shirt and a long floaty white skirt encouraged Blade to cross the threshold and shake the woman's hand.

"Thank you for seeing us, Dez," he said. He shivered then as a sort of electrical vibe ran down his spine. It was that witch radar he had. But it felt like something stronger.

"The wards," Dez offered in explanation. "I softened them for your entry. And who is this?"

Zen stepped forward and peered through the threshold.

"This is Zen. She's lost her memory and we're trying to remember her past. Uh, and figure out *what* she is. She's had demons and angels after her."

"And you have interesting blood. Or so Blade has told me," Dez said, gesturing Zen enter.

When she attempted to cross the threshold, Zen was repulsed across the hallway. She hit the wall so hard, the sheetrock cracked. Tiny dust particles settled onto her shoulders.

Blade rushed to her side but she shook it off. "I'm good. Whew! What was that?"

"I've warded against all species," Dez said. Arms crossed, the witch stepped out into the hallway and peered down into Zen's eyes. "I'm sorry, but I never take them down completely. It's not wise. I lowered the vampire and sidhe wards for Blade, but you are something else entirely, aren't you, my exotic one?"

"That's what we were hoping you could help us with," Blade said.

"Do you mind if I place my hands on your head?" Dez asked Zen.

"Go ahead. Work your witch magic."

The witch pressed her hands aside Zen's temples and placed her thumbs low, near the corners of her eyes. Closing her eyes, Dez bowed her head toward Zen's in a silent communion.

Blade stepped back and leaned against the open door frame. He wasn't sure how witches worked, and didn't have curiosity about it. That the wards had repelled Zen so violently, and yet she seemed to have brushed it off did make him wonder. Whatever she was, the woman was strong.

But not strong enough to have avoided getting amnesia from an apparent bump on the head. Interesting. If she were an angel, shouldn't she be able to endure a much greater blow? *Could* angels get amnesia? He knew nothing about them. With hope, Dez could fill him in on that, as well.

With a heavy exhale Dez stepped back from Zen and looked about as if she were emerging from a long sleep. Zen opened her eyes and Blade saw they were now pink. He'd never seen that color iris on anyone before.

"What?" Zen asked them both.

"Your eyes are pink," he offered. "What does that mean, Dez?"

The witch swept a palm up her arm as if cold. "I honestly don't know. I can't get a read on her. She's… not anything. Specifically."

Zen quirked a brow. "Well, I have to be something. Human?"

"Oh, no," Dez said quickly. "I can feel power rushing through you. It is immense. Supernatural. You can't feel it?"

Zen shrugged. "I did kill an angel an hour ago. That wasn't due to strength, but rather the halo I'd picked up from the ground."

Dez cast a wondering glance at Blade. He nodded. "We had an altercation before coming here. An angel tried to kill her."

Dez had no reply, but now she did shiver, rubbing a palm up one of her arms.

"I cut her palm and she healed instantly," Blade offered. "She also bleeds blue, but then it quickly changes to black."

"Yes, so you said. And an angel after you? Your arm," Dez noted. "Can I see?"

Zen held up her arm, the inside of her elbow exposed so Dez could study the markings. The witch looked them over carefully, her long fingers tracing the air above her arm, but did not touch Zen's skin.

"They look sidhe in nature," she said carefully.

Blade studied the markings over Dez's shoulder. "They don't look anything like Kelyn's markings."

"The breeds of sidhe are vast, Blade. Some have markings to denote tribes or birthright. Others are completely without such notable skin designs. If I knew any more about Faery and its occupants I'd be a far wiser woman. I regret that Faery is not one of my more studied banks of knowledge."

"If Zen has sidhe markings, then why are demons and angels after her?"

"You're sure it was an angel? It's not often they fall to this realm."

Blade unhooked the circular weapon from the back of his leather belt and handed it to Dez. She didn't take it, but nodded knowingly.

"Well, well," she said. "A halo. The angel had that on him?"

"Yes. It's the one Zen used to slay it. One slice took him out and reduced him to angel dust."

"Interesting. And remarkable. I need some tea. Yes, a lot of tea." Dez strode back inside the loft, and Blade followed.

Then he remembered and looked back at Zen, who stood just outside the threshold, clutching her backpack. He had the notion that she was like one of the oddball kids that never got invited to the cool kids' table.

"I can wait out here," Zen said. "I'm fine."

"Dez? Can you let down your wards so Zen can enter?"

"I haven't a clue what ward that would be. And I refuse to drop them all. Not wise in my profession. I'm sorry, Zen. I'll leave the door open."

"No problem." Zen squatted against the wall.

At that moment she looked…lost. Her pink eyes fluttered a glance across the threshold and she wrapped her arms about her chest.

Blade resisted reaching out to her. The urge to pull her against him and offer reassurance surfaced. Because it felt right. Connection tended to soften fears and worries. He knew that. He wasn't a hermit who denied himself touch or communication with others.

But it was easier to not offer that comfort, to keep up the shield around his heart. He wore the scars from caring too much about a woman—scars he'd deftly hidden from Zen when he'd taken her home to change. He wouldn't so easily embrace another helpless female again. But he would stand before her with weapons in hand and a fierce determination to protect. That part was easy.

"Won't be long," he muttered, and walked inside.

The south wall of the loft featured floor-to-ceiling windows and overlooked the Mississippi. Pale floorboards and white furnishings gave the area a clean feeling. Didn't look like a witch's home, but then, Blade decided pentagrams and hex bags were just movie lies. The real witches blended into society and took advantage of their surroundings to create the illusion of being merely human.

"Ivan is in Berlin," Dez said as she put a pot of water on the stove. "You'll have to say hello for me to your grandfather Creed next time you see him."

"I will." He sat before the kitchen table where he could keep Zen in sight through the open doorway. She gave him a little wave and he winked at her. To Dez he asked, "You think she's faery?"

"I suspect she isn't anything right now." Dez leaned a hip against the end of the white marble kitchen counter, positioning herself between Blade and the door. "I'm still considering the part where you encountered an angel with its halo. They don't normally have their halos when they come to this realm. When they fall from Above the halo falls away. The angel then seeks a muse—one specific female born for him—to mate with and ultimately give birth to Nephilim. If the angel ever does find its halo, it can be used to restore its earth-bound soul, and thus the angel becomes mortal. Perhaps it was another angel's halo?"

Blade shrugged. "Could be." He set the halo on the table. It was thin and clattered like cheap tin. At first glance, not a quality weapon, but to use it was another story. One slice down the angel's back had taken it out. He was going to hang on to this thing. "Zen has one, as well."

"What?" Dez turned to the doorway and Zen nodded in confirmation.

"It's in my backpack." She lifted the canvas pack from the floor. "Do you want me to show you?"

"No," Dez said hastily. "I don't like that power being in my home. The one Blade holds makes me nervous enough. It's only the angel dust that would truly interest me."

Zen pulled out a crunchy pink paper shopping bag from her pack and shoved it toward the threshold. Dez looked to Blade.

"The remains of the angel she slayed," he confirmed.

The witch took the bag and inspected the contents. "The feather, as well. It contains most powerful magic. I can use this."

"It's yours," Blade said. "For talking with us."

"Bless you."

The teapot whistled and Dez poured three cups. She stepped over the threshold and handed a cup to Zen, then returned to sit across from Blade. For a woman who had walked through nine centuries she looked no older than midthirties, and reminded Blade of a classic movie star with her perfect hair, smooth complexion and elegant moves.

He couldn't imagine living so long. If life intended to toss emotional challenges at him just for living he wasn't sure he wanted any more than the usual human's lifetime.

Then again, he never backed down from any challenge. Bring it all on. What didn't kill him only made him stronger.

"So when an angel falls," he said, "it immediately begins searching for its muse?"

"If it's the type of angel who has a muse," Dez explained. "But first and foremost the angel walks the world. It's a knowledge walk. They can walk the world in a day, crossing oceans and passing through cities at a speed that renders them imperceptible to all around. They glean facts and information about their surroundings. It's how they insinuate themselves into this realm."

Blade narrowed his gaze on Zen. "For a chick who lost her memory, she keeps saying she knows so much."

"I do," Zen provided. "I don't know why, but I do."

"If she was walking the world…" He considered the possibilities. "Maybe when she was passing through

Tangle Lake, the bus hit her and jarred her out of that knowledge walk."

Zen tilted her head in wonder.

It was just a guess, but it made sense. But that implied she truly was an angel. He wasn't buying that just yet. Because the part where her blue blood turned black remained suspicious.

"I suspect—" Dez sipped, lingering over the lavender steam that wafted from the delicate porcelain "—she's in the process of becoming. The halo…" Dez turned and studied Zen. "Did you bring the halo you claim as your own with you to this realm, Zen?"

"I don't know. When I came to after the bus hit me, it was in my hand. I've kept it with me. Figured whatever it was, I must have valued it to have held it through such an experience."

"So you could have either found it, or…come to this realm with it in your possession. Which doesn't make sense. It would have fallen away from you had you actually fallen."

"*If* she was an angel," Blade said.

"Exactly. Yet I get an odd sidhe vibe from her. You do know that betwixt Above and Beneath lies Faery?"

Blade pushed the tea away. The sweet smell wasn't for him and it actually made his eyelids heavy, as if he needed sleep. He'd heard about the location of Faery from his mother many times. It was imperceptible from the mortal realm and often overlapped less-populated areas of this realm. "So?"

"So." Dez set her teacup on the porcelain plate with a clink. "Besides the existence of a specific demon race who possess angelic origins, there is also a race of sidhe who originated as angels. They fall and get caught on this realm and become sidhe."

"If that were Zen's case, then why would angels *and* demons be after her?"

"That I don't know. I'm sorry I can't be of more help." Dez turned her shoulder so her back was to the doorway. She spoke quietly. "I know about your trouble with demons. If she happens to be demon, then…what?"

Blade had briefly considered the implications. If Zen was demon then his faery could be a danger to her. That was, if he bit her and his ichor-tainted saliva got into her bloodstream. So he wouldn't bite her. Because one way or another, that bite would kill one or the both of them.

He shook his head and huffed out an exhale. The witch's expectant gaze brought up his defenses as if an invisible shield. He was finished talking.

"If you wish to help her, perhaps she should know about you," Dez insisted. "All of you."

"I don't see how that will help matters."

"It's your choice." Dez raised her voice so Zen could hear. "Perhaps your best source of knowledge might be Michael Donovan. He's a halo hunter. Knows a lot about angels. And I'm sure he'd pay a fine price for that halo."

Blade gripped the weapon. "If angels are after Zen, the halo hunter will have to pry it out of my cold, dead hands."

The witch touched him lightly on the wrist. "Don't lose yourself in this one," she warned. "You already feel as though you've lost so much, but there is yet much of you that remains. It is the bold warrior within, Blade Saint-Pierre. Be bold, be bold, be not too bold."

He didn't know what the hell that meant, but he wasn't in the mood for exploring his unlost parts with Zen sitting so close.

"Thanks, Dez." He shook her hand, then grabbed the halo and headed toward the door. "How can I find this halo hunter?"

"I'll give him a call, see if he's in the States. He travels the world in search of halos. I'll let you know what I find out. As for you, Zen…" Dez approached the doorway. "Trust this man. But don't ask too much of him."

Blade straightened at that odd warning. "She can ask me anything. If I'm capable, I'll do it."

The look Dez gave him was more sad than warning. He shook it off and strode down the hallway, leaving Zen to follow after she'd thanked the witch.

Zen followed Blade down the six flights of stairs—he'd avoided the elevator—and out to his truck. He had left the witch's place in a hurry, and she suspected it was because the witch had asked him to tell her his truth. Much as they'd thought they'd been talking quietly, Zen had heard.

Did Blade have something against demons? Well, sure, he'd said as much. But it must be bad if it had shut him up so quickly. And if the witch had warned him that it was something he should reveal to her? Hmm…

She rubbed her inner elbow, wondering about the markings. Blade had fired up the engine and waited behind the wheel. Sidhe markings? *Could* she be faery?

Didn't feel right. Though what *right* should feel like was beyond her. The most right thing she'd experienced since losing her memory had been standing in Blade's arms, falling into his kiss. And he didn't want any more of that romantic nonsense.

Zen sighed. All she really needed was a friend, and she wasn't going to get that from Blade, either. He was a challenging bit of mystery and darkness. But he was her only hope. Because if she was involved in all this paranormal hoodoo, a vampire would probably be her best bet at keeping her in the loop.

And did she want to be in that loop? When she

thought about it she realized she did, and it didn't bother her as much as she thought it should. Consorting with vampires and witches? She, possibly an angel or even demon or faery? She could deal.

Really, she could. She just needed to process.

And she carried an angel's halo in her backpack. That was beyond cool. Unless it was hers. Because that would mean she was, or had been, an angel.

Why hadn't the halo fallen away from her when she'd fallen to earth, as Dez had suggested should have been the case? And had she really been on a walk around the world to gain knowledge?

"I do know stuff," she murmured. "Weird, odd stuff." All but the important stuff.

She didn't feel particularly angelic. The tug of wings between her shoulder blades was remarkably absent. And she'd already tried to pop out her faery wings. But what did an angel feel like? She had easily defeated the angel in the alley, but only because he'd been occupied with trying to choke the life out of Blade.

There were so many questions, and she was beginning to feel overwhelmed. The hot tub in her room at the inn sounded like a terrific escape from it all.

Once outside, the half-moon sat in the pale night sky, which was decorated with wisps of gray clouds. Opening the truck door, Zen climbed up and buckled in and Blade took off before she even got the door closed.

"You don't have to tell me what the witch asked you to reveal," she offered when they veered onto the freeway that would take them back to Tangle Lake.

"There's nothing to tell. You already know I don't like demons."

"All righty, then. For now, I'm going to stand on the side of not liking angels. One did try to kill you after

all. I didn't see the demons who were after me at the old
lady's house so I'll reserve judgment on that species."

"It's a free world. You can do what you want to, think
how you wish."

"I think I'm hungry. Would you mind pulling through
a fast-food drive-through on the way? I'll buy."

The expected smile did move his mouth the tiniest
bit. Because really? It was his cash.

Zen sat back, satisfied she may have softened his
hard exterior just for a moment.

They sat on the grass below the red rooster statue
before the inn. As vampire, Blade was not a voracious
eater, yet he'd downed two hamburgers in the time Zen
had finished a cheeseburger. The faery in him needed
sustenance. A hearty meal usually dampened his vampire's urges, as well. The vamp in him got nauseated to
consider drinking blood after a greasy meal.

The struggle within was always a kick. Blade had
mastered it. Mostly. But the times his faery ruled without discretion—well, as he'd told Zen, there was nothing to tell.

"Doesn't halo hunting sound like a fascinating job?"
Zen asked as she sipped from the milk carton and crumbled up her paper wrapper and napkin. "I wonder what
breed he is?"

"Halo hunters are usually human. I hope Dez can
contact the guy."

"You're really interested in helping me."

"I've said as much."

"And yet, you push me away at every opportunity
when we are just beginning to connect." She tapped the
toe of her sandal against his boot. "What does it take
to crack your armor, big guy?"

"I'm not wearing armor. And do we need a connection to find your memory?"

"I don't know. I feel as though if we're spending time together, conversation and general niceties toward one another would be, well, nice."

"We are conversing right now."

"Indeed we are. And yet I'm not allowed to befriend you. Or kiss you. So many rules for a man of so few words."

Blade grabbed the paper bag and crumbled it. "You were headed inside?"

"Right. I guess that's my cue to leave. Thanks again, Blade. For everything. But I can't promise I'm not going to try to crack that icy exterior of yours. I'm alone on a raft floating in the middle of a big ocean. I need contact. Connection. Someone to anchor me."

She leaned over and quickly kissed him on the cheek. "And touch. Good night."

She grabbed the paper bag and tossed it in the garbage can on her way toward the hotel lobby.

Blade touched his cheek where the brief warmth of her touch lingered. His fangs descended. Despite the hearty meal, his vampire insisted on blood. Something to quell the ache deep inside him.

And yet, the hunger he felt was a familiar one. One that called for demon blood. He'd tasted it once. Craved it again.

And Zen may very well have that wicked black treat gushing through her veins. Was that the only reason he was attracted to her? Hell, he was attracted to her, no denying it.

He just hoped it was for a better reason than to feed his craving.

Chapter 10

Blade handed the lumber deliveryman the signed bill of lading and waved him off as he drove down the long gravel road away from the designated compound grounds. His younger brother Stryke was building a compound for his newly formed pack. Blade was tossing around the idea of being his brother's scion, or second-in-command.

He'd not accepted the offer when Stryke had made it last winter. He'd simply said he'd think about it. Because for as much a loner he was—and he liked it—family was everything to him. And if he could stand by Stryke's side and help him to build a solid pack, then he was all for that.

But the pack building was going slowly. And that suited Blade fine. He still needed time. And things were working that way for him because Stryke wanted to select the pack members carefully. Yet also he wanted to expand beyond the family pack in which the brothers had grown up. He wanted to diversify, and if the prospective pack wolves were married to other breeds, they were more than welcome.

Hell, having a vampire as scion was radical.

Blade was behind Stryke's diversification goals 100 percent. Except when it came to demons. He would stand firm on his suggestion that no demons were allowed in the pack.

His brother strode across the cleared building site, rolled plans in hand, and slapped Blade across the back. "You're up bright and early, Dracula."

Stryke was the only one Blade would allow to remain standing after such a tease. It had started when they were teens and Stryke had seen the movie on a late-night creature feature. Only then had Stryke begun to understand that his brother was different from him. Now, if Trouble used the moniker Blade would deliver him a swift fist to the jaw. And Trouble would love it. And then they'd fight. And then Stryke would have to break it up. And Kelyn would stand off to the side snickering.

Brothers. Can't live with 'em, but sure as hell couldn't survive without 'em.

"Had some things to do," Blade said. "And it's going to rain today so I always get out early when I can avoid the sun. I signed for the lumber. When does the construction crew begin?"

"Next week. I wanted to get everything shipped to the site and ready to go. Let's go in and have some coffee."

"You don't do coffee."

"Yeah, but Blyss does. She likes it as dark as Beneath, just like you."

Blade strode beside his brother up to the cabin-like house where Stryke had settled in with his Parisian wife. Yep, Stryke had gone all the way to Europe to find his werewolf wife. Thing was, she hadn't wanted to be a werewolf, and had taken pills to suppress her wolf, until she'd met Stryke, and he'd brought out the wild in her.

A very pregnant, gorgeous woman with long black hair stood in the doorway wearing a terrycloth robe and pink slippers that sported tufts of pink fuzzy stuff on the toes. She was 100 percent feminine and always smelled like candy. Trouble, who picked up a lot of French words from Grandpa Creed, said she had je ne sais quoi.

"Blade!"

He kissed Blyss on both cheeks—the French way—and startled when her belly nudged his hip. "What was that?"

"I don't know." Blyss ran her palm over her belly. "I'm hoping it's a girl, but she kicks like a boy, *oui*?"

"Feels like there's a little bit of Trouble in there," Blade teased, with a wink to his brother.

"Blyss, give this guy some coffee before his jokes kill us all."

She poured a cup for Blade and herself, then kissed Stryke and excused herself with a wink over her shoulder at her husband.

"I haven't forgotten our date tonight, glamour girl," Stryke called after his wife. "A hot tub and massage." Stryke met Blade's wonky gaze. "What? Can't a man be in love?"

"My condolences," Blade offered.

"Love will find you again some day," Stryke said, "and when you least expect it."

"I didn't come here to discuss something as stupid as love. Have you any knowledge about angels?"

Stryke whistled and sat on the stool next to Blade. The two men wrapped fingers around their mugs— Stryke drank chai, as coffee gave him the jitters—and gazed out the picture window over the kitchen counter that revealed the razed building plot framed by mature oak trees.

"Angels," Stryke muttered. "What the hell have you gotten your hands into now, big bro?"

"I met a woman the other night."

"Really?" Stryke turned completely toward him.

Blade did not miss his brother's inquisitive raise of brow. "It's not what you think."

"What do you think I think?"

He wasn't going to say it. His brothers knew how he operated. He saw a pretty woman, he took her home and had sex with her—and usually a bite—then never saw her again. It was safest that way. For his damaged heart.

"She's in trouble, Stryke. Lost her memory. So she's in town to try to piece things together. In the past few days I've killed three demons and one angel, all of them in pursuit of her. And Dez doesn't know what she is."

Stryke set down his mug. "The witch doesn't know? That's strange."

"And she's got one of these." Blade laid the halo he'd decided to carry on him at all times on the counter.

"What is this?" Stryke picked it up to inspect. He ran his thumb along the edge and blood oozed from the fine slice in his skin. "Ouch! Doesn't look as sharp as it is."

"It's a halo. From the angel I killed. Or rather, Zen killed it while I distracted the bastard."

"I'm not following. I know you're into the calm, meditative stuff, but when did you start practicing Zen?"

"Zen is the chick's name. And I don't want her to be demon. Or for that matter, an angel."

There, he'd said it. And he knew exactly what Stryke was thinking. So let him assume the pretty chick with the copper hair and ever-changing irises meant something to him. She didn't. Hell, he hardly knew her. She couldn't mean a thing to him. Yet.

"Sorry, brother. I would have sent you to Dez for answers, but looks as though you've already tried that. Does Zen have wings? If she's got a halo that's a pretty big mark in the angel column. Don't angels have multicolored eyes?"

Blade knew that about angels. Only, he'd always thought that meant all colors at once. Not ever changing as Zen's eyes had displayed. "Shit. And her blood is blue, but then turns black."

"Some kind of angel-demon mix? Blade."

He shrugged off his brother's hand from his shoulder. Stryke was the one he and his other brothers always went to when they needed to talk because he listened and didn't judge and always seemed to offer some wise words. But he didn't want the emotional, reassuring touch today. It would mess with his determination to stand aside unaffected.

"Whatever she is," he muttered, "I won't let this one bring me down."

"It's always the ones you most want to avoid that you really need in your life, bro. Trust me on that one." He smirked and sipped his chai.

Stryke also had a weird way of extolling advice in cryptic form. Blade decided not to question. He could handle this one.

And he would.

* * *

The long floral skirt with pink flowers on a white background felt sexy and looked great paired with the white T-shirt. A few cheap rhinestone rings twinkled on her fingers and a necklace flashed more bling as the sunlight landed on the stones. Zen slipped on the rhinestone-bedazzled sandals and twirled before the bathroom mirror. Felt good to have some things that fit her and which hadn't come from a smelly donation box.

And she owned a comb now! So she pulled her thick copper hair up into a blowsy bun and stabbed a few hair sticks in it. It worked for her. Before dashing out, she leaned forward, peering into her eyes.

"Blue," she said and then wrinkled her nose. "They really do change colors. Beats contact lenses, I guess."

But what she knew about angels was that their eyes were like kaleidoscopes, all colors at once.

"I can't be," she said. "Don't feel as though I've ever had wings."

The witch had suggested she could be sidhe. Again, where were her wings?

Though the halo was an interesting clue. She stuffed it in her backpack and headed toward the lobby, intent on getting some breakfast at the Panera down the road. The afternoon goal was to find the library and look up the newspapers from a week ago, see if they had reported the accident.

"Ma'am!"

She turned before pushing the glass door open and spied the inn receptionist dangling a key chain. "This was left for you by a handsome man."

"Handsome man?" She took the key. The Mini Cooper logo was emblazoned on the black rubber fob.

"Guy had long bluish hair. He said you'd find the car in the parking lot. Is he your boyfriend?"

"Uh, no. Why do you ask?"

"Don't you want him to be? He's hot. All those muscles bulging under his shirt. He stood there like some kind of warrior."

Zen searched her knowledge for the slang explanation of hot as related to a man, and had to agree. "He is, but he doesn't believe in friends."

"*Uff-da*, you're going to have to change his mind about that one, sweetie. Have a nice day!"

"Thanks. You, too."

Outside, the sun warmed her cheeks and the back of her neck. A breeze tickled the skirt fabric between her calves as she aimed for the little red car. It was an older model and the paint was matte instead of glossy. A dent creased the back quarter panel, and the silver trim was pitted in a few places. Overall, it looked roadworthy.

And she wasn't going to look a gift cow, er—she couldn't recall the proper animal for that one, so she dismissed the thought.

Sliding in and discovering it was a stick shift, Zen wondered if she could manage it. The truck had been an automatic. Just shift into gear, press on the accelerator and go.

Pulling the halo out of her backpack and hanging it from the rearview mirror as a sort of good-luck charm, she shifted and put her foot on the gas. And the car sputtered to a clunking stop.

A rap on the driver's window alerted her to the man who stood outside. Zen rolled down her window without thinking. "I'm not sure how to drive this—"

He shoved a neon green flyer inside the car. "Party tonight! Only the coolest are invited."

She took the paper and glanced over it. "You don't even know me. How do you know I'm cool?"

Tall and blond, he looked Nordic, and Zen guessed him for a skier with his long lean lines and the athletic wear. Yet a beard didn't hide the tattoos climbing up his neck. "It's a guess," he said. "You like to dance?"

She considered the question. "I'm not sure."

"Come on, everyone likes to dance. We'll see you tonight, sure? It's just out of town. A map is on the back of the flyer. Come alone. There will be plenty of guys there to hook up with."

"I don't think I need to hook up."

"That's cool. Like I said, dance! It's going to be a blast."

"A blast sounds…like a blast."

"You betcha."

And he strode off across the lot, looking back a few times over his shoulder at the Mini Cooper.

Zen studied the flyer. The picture depicted a mansion more resembling a spooky Halloween haunt than a dance club. The guy hadn't known who she was. And he would have said something if he had, right?

"Come alone?" she muttered.

She wasn't sure if she should be creeped out by the invite or excited for the prospects. She couldn't remember when she'd last had a blast. Certainly it must be overdue.

Hookups? Obviously she would get nowhere with Blade romantically. But did she need romance right now?

"A little dancing never hurt anyone."

She set the flyer aside. She'd think about it.

Now to figure how to operate this vehicle.

* * *

No incident report was listed in the *Tangle Lake Tattler*, the local paper that was issued each Monday. The newspaper featured local news, which tended to be on the homey side. Mavis Butler had won best quilt design in the United States for the third year running. Red MacPherson was having a sale on taxidermy for the critters, including wolves.

Zen wondered what the local werewolves thought about that. And then she had to grin at her knowledge. How quickly she'd accepted that the realm of the paranormal existed.

She wondered if others were in the know. Probably not. If so, she would have never doubted Blade's confession in the first place.

She thanked the librarian for the use of the microfiche and headed back to the car, which she had finally figured how to operate after three dry starts in the inn parking lot.

Had the bus driver even been aware he or she had hit a person? Should she have stayed on the scene after being hit? Probably. But at the time she had felt like getting out of there, not causing a scene. Staying away from notice.

Weird to think that now. What instinctual part of her had reacted that way? Almost protectively of her origins. Whatever those origins were. An angel who had fallen to the mortal realm and wanted to keep her secret? Or a demon who perhaps couldn't shift to demonic form now because of the bump to her head.

Was her amnesia something that had resulted from her angelic fall?

Would certainly explain why angels are after me. But why demons?

While in the library she should have checked out the mythology section. Any details about the various species she could learn would be helpful. And yet, if she simply thought about it, mined the weirdly vast knowledge she seemed to possess, she knew a few things.

Angels did indeed fall, and most often it was to find their muse and procreate. Nephilim were the result. Nasty things, for sure.

Demons were a vast species, and while many occupied the mortal realm, many more lived in Daemonia. Zen wasn't sure what Daemonia was. Something similar to Hell or Beneath?

Faeries were few and far between on the mortal realm, most choosing to live in Faery. They were a hard bunch to figure, and she hadn't any more knowledge on them.

Witches were of all sorts and some were the Light and others the Dark. Warlocks were witches who had committed a grave transgression against their own.

"Wow," she muttered. "I really do have a lot of information in this noggin. I just need to think about something and it comes to me. Maybe a little mindless entertainment tonight will put my brain in a new place. I wonder if Blade would like to go along with me?"

At the very least, she could ask him about the club. Get his two cents on it. He didn't seem the club type. Definitely not the free-for-all dance type. He was more the blade-swinging warrior.

Which, she didn't mind at all.

Realizing she didn't have his phone number—and why should she, she didn't own a phone—Zen decided to drive over to Blade's place.

Chapter 11

"I don't do clubs."

Blade couldn't guess why Zen chuckled at his statement, but she did as she wandered over to the window and pressed a palm to it. The sun beaming across her hair lighted her as if…she was an angel.

He shook off the image of her floating in the air with a glowing halo suspended above her head. If she was angel then why had her blood turned from blue to black?

"But you've been there before?" she asked over a shoulder.

"I haven't heard of that club. Must be new. You think it's wise to go to a nightclub by yourself? Even if you didn't have demons and angels on your ass, a single woman alone in a bar…"

"You think I can't handle myself?"

"I'll go with you."

Her nod said so much more than just an acceptance

of his offer. Women and their secretive ways. He'd never been curious about them, until it was too late.

"What's the nod for?" he asked, strolling over to stand beside her. Outside, the rain was trying hard to become a downpour but the sun kept interrupting.

"I knew you'd go along with me."

Did she, now? "You know nothing about me, Zen."

"And as much as I'd like to change that, you do have your rules." She turned and tapped his chest. "No friends. Don't get too close. Don't touch. That kiss must have had you reeling."

"I kiss women all the time."

Her arched brow made another statement that he didn't want to be curious about—but was.

"Now what?" he asked.

"So you're a love-'em-and-leave-'em kind of guy? How's that working out for you, Stoic Warrior Dude?"

"Actually, quite well. And it's none of your business, is it?"

"Of course not." She flounced toward the couch. A bohemian goddess with added glints of sparkle today. "I think the club is going to be just what I need tonight."

"And what exactly do you need?"

Did he want to know? If she was looking to hook up that was her own business. Then again, he did want to know. Everything.

Zen plopped onto the big plaid couch, picked up the backpack and pulled her legs up to tuck her feet under her thighs. Tendrils of her hair spilled forward over the soft cleavage her low-cut T-shirt revealed. "Maybe I need connection."

So she did want to hook up.

Blade gripped his hands into fists. She looked so comfortable sorting through the backpack. As if she belonged there, on his couch. In his life. But that was wrong—hell. It was getting tiresome making up excuses to protect himself. He wasn't the guy who tossed out excuses as if they were ammo to blockade emotional shrapnel. If something bothered him he took a stand and showed it his teeth.

And right now Zen's earlier teasing bothered him. He should ask her to leave. Make it easy on them both. Because his life wasn't an easy fit for any woman.

"Let me show you something." She patted the couch beside her. Waited for him with those dazzling pale green eyes.

Why did her eyes have to constantly change color? It was a warning. He sensed it. And yet, the multicolored irises fascinated him. Did they change with her moods? Like those rings the giggling girls used to wear in high school? He'd have to take a survey of her eye color as compared to her mood.

Right now her green eyes indicated a—hmm—flirtatious mood. If he read her correctly.

He sat three feet away from Zen on the couch. "You know, the longer you stay the longer Oogie has to hide out in my bedroom."

"It's not my problem the cat doesn't like me. And he's a cat. Aren't they the supreme I-don't-give-a-shit of all creatures? He can deal."

Oogie probably could deal. From under the bed. Poor guy. Did the cat sense Zen's otherness? He had to. So why couldn't Blade get a fix on her nature?

Zen scooted closer and handed him a postcard.

"What's this?"

"I got it a couple days after the accident."

"Got it?" He studied the image of a painting in vibrant greens and blues.

"Stole it," she corrected. "I didn't have any money then and that picture spoke to me."

The computer-generated image depicted an angel with wings of binary code, white hair and kaleidoscope eyes. The attribution was to a New York artist who was now living in Italy.

"An angel," he said, and gave her back the card.

"Weird, huh?"

"Maybe. Maybe it means you used to be a klepto."

"Do kleptos take trucks?"

"Probably not. They're usually into the small stuff."

"Thought so." She slid her hand into his. "I want to try something with you."

He knew what was coming. But he didn't dash. A gorgeous woman sitting next to him, casting him the big green eyes and a curious smile? He could handle anything she wanted to *try*.

Leaning in, Zen's eyes took in his face, roving from his hair, to nose, down to his mouth. Her tongue dashed her upper lip. She smelled fresh, summery, like the grass on a rainy summer evening. But he couldn't get a read on her. "Does me being this close bother you?" she asked. Emerald eyes danced over his face, teasing him—no, defying him to meet her boldly sensual challenge.

He shook his head.

"But you'd rather I was sitting over there, two cushions away from you."

Enough. She thought to tease him? He'd show her the man he really was.

Blade threaded his fingers up through her silky copper hair and pulled her in for a kiss. Her body melded against his, and before he knew it, she had straddled him and was taking as much as giving. Now her scent drifted into his senses, summery sweet and addictive. His vampiric instincts matched pulse beats with the blood coursing beneath her skin. His fangs tingled, but he had this.

Too dangerous to bite.

Clasping her hip, he eased her down onto his lap so her breasts hugged his chest. He dipped his mouth to kiss her where the low-cut T-shirt revealed the beckoning crease between her generous breasts. Holding her, a woman intent on seducing him, stirred up desires that he wanted to satisfy. Often.

"Oh, I like it when you kiss me there," she said on a sultry sigh.

Her hair spilled over his face, a faery flutter. He kissed her breast through the T-shirt, and thumbed the nipple that had perked up beneath. "I like it, too. But this—"

"Don't say you don't want to do this. Just let me have this moment, Blade. You think I've done this before? I don't know if I have."

"You've kissed a man before. You're good at it."

"Yeah? Well, I don't remember, so help me to at least get back that memory. Or better yet. Make new ones."

She pushed him and he fell backward onto the plaid cushions, pulling her down along with him.

Kissing him deeply, Zen took control. She had kissed men. No virgin kissed like this, so aggressively. So curiously. And Blade was inclined to let her continue. To see how far she would take it. Because if she was unsure or inexperienced, sooner rather than later she'd come up short and have to stop. And then he'd have a new wonder about her beyond that of what species she could possibly be.

"Will you take off your shirt?" she asked, kissing down his chin and to his neck.

The vampire within him stirred as her firm kisses neared his carotid artery. The sensual touch was like an electric shock to his system, but in a good, erotic way.

He pulled off his T-shirt and tossed it behind the couch. Zen's hands played over his pecs and abs. The warmth of her was ridiculous, the firm, exploratory touches stirring up sensation, and he hissed with pleasure.

Her eyes sparkled like the rhinestones at her neck as she admired his torso. "You are ripped. But you don't lift weights, do you?"

"Not unless it's to toss them out of my way."

"It's a vampire thing, then? Or maybe faery? Do you ever have sex with women when you have shifted to faery like when you brought your wings out last night?"

He wasn't going to answer that. She was too curious, and moving too fast regarding those kinds of questions.

"Let's just kiss," he suggested and teased the ends of her hair between his fingers. "All of me, vampire and faery, likes it when you press your breasts against my chest and push your tongue into my mouth."

"Mmm…I can do that." She lay down on top of him, twining a leg between his, and then kissed him deeply, toying with his tongue, and licking his lips and teeth. "What does your vampire like?"

She wasn't going to give it up.

"Not important right now."

"Your faery?"

"Zen. Do you want to talk or make out?"

She paused, her hands holding her away from his chest, as she seemed to be considering the two options he'd given her. He threaded his fingers up into her hair and tugged gently. "Come here. Let's make Oogie jealous."

The cat had crept out from the bedroom and now, perched like a gargoyle on the kitchen counter, was watching. He hadn't hissed yet, so Blade was counting that as a favorable sign.

Zen's hands slid down his sides and her fingers tucked into his jeans. He followed her straying mouth, seeking the lush kiss, the wetness of her lips, the heat of her, but when she landed his neck with a teasing nip, he grabbed her by the neck. A little less than gently.

"Too much for you?" she challenged boldly.

The tease of her catching her lower lip with her teeth made his erection throb. The woman had no idea what she played with. And he wasn't about to let this liaison go bad. As in, turn bloody.

Reaching for the hem of her shirt, he tugged it up over her breasts and was nicely surprised she wore no bra underneath. He cupped her breasts and sat up, guiding her onto her back against the couch arm so he could kiss and suckle at her nipples.

She wrapped her legs about his torso. Squeezing a nipple with his fingers elicited a delicious moan from her. "You like that, too?"

"Oh, yes, please. This is better than sleeping in a truck. Better than wearing used clothes. Better than killing an angel."

The remark struck Blade, and he paused, lips about her nipple. Prepared to walk away, to put his brain back in the right place, and not indulge in his desires...

The tickle of her fingernail along his waistband, above where his cock strained against the tough denim, obliterated the need to retreat. He'd give her one more chance.

Feasting upon her skin, he savored and licked and suckled her nipples, her generously curved breasts and down her rib cage. And then back up to linger between the cozy snug of her breasts. Between them he pressed his cheek and closed his eyes. Nice here. Her body heat brewed her summery scent to a heady perfume that he wanted to soak in, get lost in.

When was the last time he'd simply held a woman and admired her softness and scent? *You remember.* But he was this close to forgetting. He needed the distraction of Zen. He needed this sensual venture.

Lost in her, he didn't realize when Zen had unbuttoned his jeans. Her finger brushed the head of his cock, eliciting a shock of desire that radiated through his system. His fangs reacted of their own volition, descending.

Blade pressed his mouth against her neck.

Chapter 12

Zen felt the sharp prick of Blade's fangs against her neck. She didn't flinch. So he'd changed his mind? *Yes*. The fangs nudging against her skin heightened the erotic appeal of his hands gliding over her breasts. She wanted to feel him sink deep into her. To know the rapture of a vampire's bite.

But when she slid her hand behind his head and pulled him closer, he suddenly jerked away. Standing above her, arms splaying and a wild look in his eyes, she watched as his fangs retracted, moving up to sit in line with his other teeth. His pecs flexed. And his opened jeans revealed a thatch of dark hair below the rows of tight abdomen muscles.

"A bite would feel so good," she pleaded. "I want to give it a try. Please?"

"Are you crazy?" He pulled his hair behind his head and then dropped it, fisting the air forcefully. "I can't believe I let this go so far."

"Blade, it's okay. I'm not afraid of your bite."

"Really? Well, that's great for you. Not so great for me. Do you remember what I told you happens when a vampire bites an angel? Shit." He picked up his shirt and then tossed hers onto her chest. "Put that on. Please."

"What happens— Ooh." She winced. "I'm sorry. I forgot. Angel blood makes vampires explode. That's what you said, right? But we don't actually know what I am."

"Exactly. And you were cool with me taking that chance? Nice."

He strode into the kitchen and opened the fridge. Tilting back a bottle of water, his anger vibes were tangible from the couch where Zen pulled on her shirt.

"Way to end a perfectly good make-out session, Zen," she muttered. But stupid of her to have expected the bite when it could have harmed him. Wrong decision. Made in the heat of the moment. Because she was all about new experiences. Especially the ones that made her feel good. She'd have to watch herself. "I should probably leave."

"Don't let the door hit you on the way out."

Zen cast Blade a pleading gaze as she passed him, but he didn't meet her eyes. What a cruel thing to say. Was he so mad that he couldn't understand she was new at this? That she had been following her instincts and emotions instead of logic?

Apparently. He didn't look at her, even though she waited before the stairs, just out of his eyesight.

"The invite to accompany me to the club is rescinded," she said. "If you don't like me, just say so. I can do the memory search myself. Thanks for all your help. I'll find some way to repay you and get the car back to you as soon as possible."

Grabbing her backpack, she marched down the stairs and realized, as she charged outside toward the Mini Cooper, that she had let anger get the better of her. She had no reason to not appreciate the man for all the wonderful things he had done for her. He'd given her a freakin' car.

And he had been right. She shouldn't have expected him to bite her. Not when neither of them knew what she was. He could have risked death if she really was an angel.

"I'm certainly no angel," she muttered as she slid into the car and fired up the ignition. "Angels aren't so cruel to kind souls."

Three hours later, after the sun had set and Zen had found the road leading to the club, she couldn't lament the car's sudden decision to sputter to a halt halfway there, stranding her in the middle of nowhere. The road was paralleled by tall birch trees and the night was dark thanks to the shimmer of moon she couldn't see beyond the tree line.

"Out of gas. Figures. Thanks, karma. I'll try harder next time. I won't be so selfish when it comes to making out with a man."

And she'd never again ask a vampire for a bite. At least, not until she knew what she was. Did she have deadly blue angel blood coursing through her veins? If so, seemed as if she should also have some kind of superpowers. What could angels do? She felt like a normal woman.

A normal woman who didn't know who she was.

A normal woman who just wanted some touch time with one very sexy man. A man who needed time to take things slowly. To gradually work up to closer. He was sexually skittish, which was an odd thing considering his incredible physicality and heart-racing allure.

"Guess I haven't a clue about men," she muttered.

Getting out of the tiny car and gazing up and down the dark road, she wondered which was a shorter walk: toward the club or back to town. Sitting on the hood of the car, she leaned back against the windshield and stared up at the row of stars framed by the treetops.

"Is there a reason I'm not supposed to know?" she asked the heavens. "Am I supposed to go on with life and take what comes to me? If so, I don't get the attacks. Do they want me dead or do they just want to mess with me? And what about the halo?"

She turned and spied the halo hanging on the rearview mirror. "Am I some kind of warrior? But for what reason? Shouldn't a warrior know what she's to fight? Or defend?"

The sudden spatter of raindrops on the hood and her head was not the answer she'd hoped for.

"Terrific. Guess karma wasn't quite finished with me, eh?"

Headlights appeared down the road and Zen hopped off the hood. Maybe she could hitch a ride to the club. Because tonight was for setting her worries aside. She didn't want to think about what she didn't know. And she figured a distraction from the things she did know about, like Blade and his amazing kisses, was necessary.

So when she recognized the big black truck as Blade's, Zen could but shake her head. "Oh, karma, you sneak."

The passenger window rolled down and a man she did not know popped his head out. He had thick short black hair, and a rugged facial structure. He winked at her. "Hey, sweetie, it's raining."

No kidding.

Zen gave him a curious lift of her brow. Hands on her hips, she peered past him to Blade who sat behind the steering wheel. "You don't have anything better to do than follow me around?"

The vampire shrugged. "What makes you think I was following you? My brother and I are headed to the club. You having problems with the Mini? Beck promised me the car was in fine condition."

"Oh, it is. Apparently the ability to remember to put gas in the tank was also wiped from my memory. Maybe I could hitch a ride with you to the club?"

"This the one you told me about?" the man in the passenger seat asked Blade.

Blade nodded.

The passenger door opened and the man hopped out. Clad in black leather pants and a leather vest, but no shirt underneath, he had a remarkable physique. "I'm Trouble," he offered and took her hand to help her up into the truck.

"I bet you are," Zen said as his dark eyes took her in. He hopped in beside her and closed the door. "Brothers?"

"I'm the eldest," Trouble offered as Blade silently drove onward. "Did you lock up your car?"

"Yes, and I have all my valuables here in my backpack. It's not really my car. Blade bought it."

"Yeah, I know he did. Beck told me," Trouble said to Blade, who apparently had not filled his brother in on his recent charity work. "I hear you're a fine bit of interesting," he said to her. "Lost your mind?"

"I have possession of my mind. It's just my memories that are playing hard to get at the moment."

"Sounds as though you like to play easy, actually."

"Trouble," Blade cautioned.

"Sorry, Zen. Just stupid guy talk. You know. Or do you know? Probably you don't. So you were planning to go clubbing all by your lonesome? Looking to hook up?"

"Why is everyone so concerned about me hooking up? I just wanted to dance and forget about things."

"Forget even more?"

"No, I—"

"Trouble, give it a rest," Blade insisted. "She's looking for a night out by herself. Leave it at that."

A bump in the road settled Zen's thigh against Blade's. He didn't move away and the connection felt like the most amazing kind of fire. *Burn me*, she wanted to plead of him. She sensed he had driven this way in search of her. And the fact he'd brought along his brother indicated that, if found, he didn't want to be alone with her.

"So are you a mix of breeds, as well?" she asked Trouble. "Like your brother?"

"Hell no. I am one hundred percent werewolf."

"And damned cocky about it, too," Blade muttered.

"So Blade says you could be an angel or maybe a demon," Trouble stated.

"Or who knows," Zen added. "Maybe even faery." Though, at the moment, she was doubtful for all of the above. She felt so normal. On the other hand, what was normal?

"Really? Our brother Kelyn is faery," Trouble offered. "Stryke is full wolf like me. And our sister, Daisy

Blu—ah, you don't need the family history. Blade tells me a bus hit you. And you walked away from it?"

"I guess so."

"That makes you one hell of a woman. Good catch, Blade. Whoa."

The truck's headlights beamed onto a grassy parking lot that was lined with a few dozen cars that were getting pummeled by the summer rain. But they wouldn't have noticed without the headlights. There was no outside lighting in the lot. And a huge mansion that looked like something out of a gothic horror show lurked on the horizon. In the darkness, Zen could only make out a scatter of people-shaped shadows walking toward it.

"This is a nightclub?" she asked. "I thought clubs were all flashy and uh…not haunted. Does it look haunted to you? It does to me."

"Ah, ghosts won't hurt you," Trouble joked and nudged her elbow with his. "I don't recall hearing about an old mansion out this way. You, Blade?"

"Nope." He rolled down the window but didn't open the door. "You smell anything off?"

The eldest brother opened his door and leaned out. Crickets chirped and the wind bristled through the leaves. Zen picked up the scent of dirt and the usual fresh ozone tang from the rain.

"Nothing," Trouble offered. "Kind of odd, but maybe it's supposed to have the creepy vibe. Like one of those goth clubs. You sure you want to go dancing that badly, Miss Zen of the Missing Memories?"

"Oh, come on, you guys, it's just atmosphere. I'm going up. You don't have to stay." She slid out on Trouble's side behind him and walked around on the squishy grass to the front of the truck. "Thanks for the ride, Blade. Sorry to bother you again."

He remained behind the driver's wheel, but nodded once.

Sensing he wasn't going to link arms with her and escort her inside, she turned and wandered through the parked cars until she landed on a cobbled sidewalk. Sort of Dorothy's brick road, but all in black. She didn't want to turn around to check if the brothers were watching her. She hoped they were. Because she suddenly felt very alone. And wet.

And maybe a little unsafe. But no fear.

"Not yet," she muttered as she gained a group of people who nodded and chattered.

The air was noticeably cooler, and she rubbed her hands up and down her arms as, at the back of the group, she followed them up a fieldstone stairway littered with red rose petals.

They were really working the goth atmosphere. But she did like the rose petals. As they neared the front of the mansion the doors swung inward. Myriad candelabras lit the interior and loud thumping music tunneled out. One of the women in the group giggled and grabbed another woman's hand. They skipped through the doors and starting dancing before they even hit the dance floor.

Zen wandered in slowly, shook off the wet from her arms and noticed the tall dark man who stood to her left, his arms crossed high over his chest. He nodded and bowed toward her, but didn't speak.

"Hey." She gave him a little wave. "Just here to dance. No hookups for this girl."

No response.

"Good to meet you, too."

The music had a lively beat. It coaxed her inward, and she didn't resist.

Time to get her wild on.

* * *

"She's got an exotic look to her," Trouble said as the brothers strode up the black-bricked walk. The rain had settled to a light sprinkle. "I can see why you like her."

"I don't like her. I'm just keeping an eye on her."

"Right. Because getting all up in that sexy hair and body would just be wrong. I know how you are about falling in love, bro. That's cool. But I also know you can get a woman in your bed if you want one."

"Maybe I don't want this one."

"Why? Because you don't know what she is? What if she's an angel? That'd be cool."

"Trouble, shut up. We're going to keep an eye on her, and then give her a ride home. That's it."

"Fine. But my eyes will be straying to all the ladies in the house."

"Go ahead and hook up. Zen doesn't need two baby-sitters."

"Then why'd you ask me along?"

"I have a funny feeling about this club."

Blade stopped before the stone stairway. The night hung heavy and wet, not a breeze in the air. The black mansion loomed amidst the gray shadowed surroundings. It was as if he'd walked onto a Tim Burton set. Head tilted, he sniffed the air. Trouble sniffed, as well. When the brothers met gazes, they shook their heads.

"Demons," Blade said.

"Shit."

Chapter 13

Blade charged up the stairs before the mansion. With every step he took the demon scent grew stronger. At his side, Trouble growled, and he sensed his brother's need to shift. Trouble was a smash-and-bang kind of guy. He reacted before looking. And that reaction was always accompanied by fists.

Blade preferred the stealthier approach. But he already sensed that what lay behind the tall black doors was not going to be the party either of them had expected.

"You said that some stranger invited her here?" Trouble asked.

"Yeah. Stopped her in the parking lot and told her about the club."

"Think the invite came from a demon?"

"I'm betting on it. Zen has no sense of the paranormal. She couldn't have known." He clamped a hand on his brother's shoulder. "We go in and look around. Don't start beating in skulls until we're sure there's clear danger. Got that?"

Trouble strode up to the door, clenching his fists at his sides.

"Trouble."

"Yeah, yeah." He bounced from foot to foot, a boxer move he employed whenever he was pumped for a fight. "Wait for danger. Do we need some kind of bat signal, too, boss?"

His brother's cocky attitude could never annoy him. Trouble was what he was. All wolf, and itching for a fight. Always.

Blade pushed the doors open and strode in, but was stopped by a wall of a man with arms crossed high over his chest. Leather and silver studs wrapped his biceps and his block of a body.

"No admittance," the wall said in a gravelly voice.

"We're looking for a friend," Trouble said. "She just walked in. Tall, copper hair, flowers on her skirt?"

The wall's eyes glowed red.

"She doesn't belong here," Blade tried. He sniffed, but the air was tainted with incense or some odd, sweet scent. "We'll just find her and leave. No trouble, eh?"

"She's exactly where she needs to be," the wall said.

"So you have seen her. And you're stopping us from going in to find her?"

The wall nodded.

"She's in danger," Blade said.

The wall shook its head. Neon club lights glinted in the curl of silver spikes that stuck out along his earlobes.

"Yeah, I think she is."

Swinging the angel halo before him, Blade caught the wall across the chest, cutting through leather, chains and skin and bone. The beast let out a yowl before disintegrating into obsidian ash indicative of the demonic nature.

"Wait for danger?" Trouble said. "Right. You just wanted to be the first one to draw demon blood. I'll give you that, bro. You're owed, that's for sure. *Now* can I bash in some heads?"

"Whatever gets your rocks off, Trouble. What's that?"

Blade pushed toward the edge of the dance floor, where, peopled with hundreds, the flashing glass floor opened in the center. A bright red oval or some kind of portal loomed amidst the dancers. They danced around it but not closer than twenty feet in all directions.

And standing before the weird portal was Zen, looking upon it as if it were a marvel. She reached out to touch...

"Zen, no!"

Blade charged through the crowd, but as he did, every head turned to growl and gnash at him. Human faces shifted to demon. Scales, horns and red eyes replaced the human glamour. Talons clawed at his arms and hair. Sulfur formed a sickening miasma in the air.

Slashing the halo took out two who stood between Blade and Zen. He leaped over the demon ash and managed to grab her before she could step into the glowing portal.

Stumbling against his body, she shook her head and blinked, as if coming out of a trance. "Blade? What are you— Watch out!"

Struck from behind, a demonic talon cut through his shirt and opened his skin in searing pain. Wincing, and swinging around, Blade cut the halo through two demon heads—both attached to the same body. A cloud of demon ash formed and he dodged to avoid inhaling the noxious dust.

Grabbing Zen, he shoved her through the crowd and she landed in Trouble's arms. "Get her out of here!"

Trouble took Zen by the arm.

Blade hadn't time to follow their retreat. A diminutive demon missing a lower jaw jumped onto his chest and when it snarled at him, hot spit spattered across his face. Elbowing the clinging miscreant, he couldn't quite get him off.

"If you're not going to kill me," he muttered to any who would listen, "then I suggest you run."

With that warning, Blade shifted to faery. The demon shrieked and sprang away from him. Faery ichor was poisonous to demons. Blade's bones stretched and muscles pulled to reshape into the powerful winged creature. Wings unfurling, he snapped a flying demon out from above and flung it toward the red glowing portal.

The music thumped hard, pounding in his eardrums. Demons screeched, fleeing the entity that could prove their death.

Trouble appeared before Blade. Black demon blood dripped from his cheek. "Good call, man. Bringing out the big guns. She's safe in the truck. No demons out in the parking lot. Weird. Anyway. Time to party!"

Trouble shifted into a big black werewolf. Two heads taller than his human form, he was half-furred with a head like a wolf and a long toothy maw.

The brothers stood at the center of the dance floor, werewolf shouldered next to vamp-faery, and welcomed the melee that aimed for them. Fangs descending, Blade opened his mouth. He had craved demon blood for months.

Time to party, indeed.

* * *

Zen did as Trouble demanded after he'd roughly shoved her into the pickup. *Sit. Do not come out. No matter what.*

Demons had been everywhere inside the club. But they'd initially all appeared human to her. No horns. No glowing red eyes. She was glad to be out of there, and hugged herself as she pulled her legs up and settled into the truck seat. Hitting the door lock provided added security. Felt like it anyway.

And yet, when she had spied the fiery red oval glowing in the middle of the dance floor she had been compelled to walk up to it. It had pulsed. Hummed, actually, a tune that had felt more to her like heartbeats than the raucous dance music that had boomed from the speakers. It had also felt warm, as if it was a sun. Or even a hug. She'd wanted to walk through to see what would happen. To answer the silvery whispers slithering through her veins that had beckoned her forth.

Now, removed from the craziness inside, her senses reset and she wondered: If she had walked through the red glow might she have never returned?

"Oh, no." The marks on the inside of her elbows had brightened to a creamy glow against her light brown skin. And she felt them pulse, and realized that must have been what she'd felt when inside. Was it a calling? From demons?

So what did that mean?

She rubbed her skin. The marks were definitely not something she had put there herself, nor were they going to fade. They glowed. Demonic? Surely there must be someone who could tell her about them. Wasn't there a friendly demon in the area?

Her arm felt warm, and that warmth moved through

her blood, softening her muscles and relaxing her tension. And Zen felt…wanted. Needed, actually.

"I should go back inside. They need me."

Just as she opened the truck door, a black wolf raced up to the door and yipped at her. She retreated, and then saw the winged man. His black-and-silver wings were immense, and tipped in deadly points. Demonic in appearance. Yet she knew better. He was vampire with faery blood coursing through his veins.

She glanced toward the mansion. It was dark, as it had been when they'd first arrived. None of the demons had followed their retreat outside.

The wolf propped his front legs on the truck frame and sniffed toward the backpack that was shoved behind the seat. Zen pulled it out and shuffled through it. Men's clothing inside.

"I get it. If you shift back to your human form, you'll be naked." She tossed the backpack out onto the ground.

Blade held vigil twenty feet away, observing the mansion, his wings erect and ready as if he expected the rage of demons within to come at them any moment.

Zen rubbed her arms and shivered. "Blade?"

"Turn away," he said, nodding toward his brother. "He'll shift with you watching, but I'd prefer you not."

She nodded, and shuffled back into the passenger seat, focusing on the mansion. "Right. I won't look." But knowing that the strapping man was shifting, totally naked, just outside the truck, made it very difficult not to twist her head and peek.

Of course, she had no interest in Trouble. It was Blade, who apparently had but to put away his wings to shift back to the regular form, who enticed her. But he no longer stood in view. Had he gone back into the mansion?

The driver's door opened and Blade slid in, sans wings. He wore jeans and no shirt, though he stuffed a wad of gray shirt between his thigh and the seat. Bringing out the wings must be hell on his wardrobe. She didn't even want to consider how many torn seams occurred when shifting to werewolf.

"You okay?" He didn't look at her, but fired up the engine. "Hurry, Trouble!"

The other brother popped in with a pair of jeans on and no shirt. "You are a size smaller than me, bro." He sat awkwardly on the seat, plucking unsuccessfully at the denim wrapping his thigh. "These suckers are tight."

"Be thankful I had an extra pair." He turned the truck around and spun out onto the dark gravel road. "That was a trap, I'm sure of it. Why the hell do demons want you?"

Zen realized he'd asked her that. The tension in the cab was tight, and she felt as if she dangled by her fingers from a tightrope between the two brothers.

"You didn't notice the demons?" Trouble asked as he eased a hand over his crotch.

"Not until you two arrived," she said. "Everyone looked human when I walked in. And I was distracted by the…"

"The portal?" Blade asked.

"You think that's what it was? Where do you think it leads to?"

"Hell if I know. You were going to step into it."

"I was," she said softly, then sank against the seat and pulled up her legs before her chest. She felt so small, being rescued from something that could have been disastrous to both men. They could have been hurt. And she may very well have entered a portal to a place even her curiosity couldn't have fathomed.

She'd sought a night of dancing and mindless fun. Instead, she'd gotten something far more dangerous.

"I'm sorry," she muttered. "I should have stayed at the inn. Or found a quiet place in town to distract me. Like more shopping."

"Not your fault," Blade said briskly. "The guy who told you about the club. He was in on it, I'm sure."

"He said I was cool and only the cool people were invited."

"Ha! Remember when you wanted to be cool in high school?" Trouble asked Blade.

"I was cool."

"No way, man. I was the cool one. The rest of you guys were pussies. But what was that portal thing?" Trouble asked. "And since when do demons gather in Tangle Lake?"

"Since never," Blade said on a hiss. "The last time was…" He shifted roughly, and the truck stirred them into a rumble down the road.

"The last time?" Zen asked.

"Never mind," Blade muttered.

They passed her parked car on the road and Trouble promised he'd drive out with their brother Kelyn and a gas can in the morning. Kelyn could drive the Mini back to the big red cock. He chuckled and rapped his knuckles on the door window.

Zen could but smirk. The brothers did like to work that joke.

"Thank you," she said to Trouble when Blade pulled up to his house and he hopped out.

"You just stay out of demon clubs," Trouble said. "And give my brother a break. He's skittish," he said. "About women and, uh, demons in general."

"Trouble!" Blade growled.

"See ya!" The elder brother winked at Zen and loped off.

Blade pulled away and drove back toward town. He drove past the inn, and Zen didn't bother to ask him why. She recognized the road he was taking. It led to the highway and eventually his place.

He must feel he had to protect her. And in truth, she felt in need of that protection. If he would allow her to stay with him tonight, she would be grateful. Because who knew if she might wake to find a pair of red eyes staring at her?

"Your cat will be pissed," she said after he'd parked and they strode up to the barn.

"He'll survive," Blade offered. "You can sleep in my bed. Oogie and I will take the couch."

"I don't want to put you out. Oh." Even in the darkness, she noticed the cut on his neck. It had scabbed and had probably bled quite a bit for the dried blood crusted on his skin. "Your faery is so valiant. And the wings."

"I'm all vampire even when my wings come out. The faery is sort of…seasoning."

"Okay." Was there something about his faery he didn't like to claim? She wouldn't press.

"I don't like to kill, Zen." And with that he strode inside, leaving the door open for her to enter if she wished.

He'd had to kill to protect her. That had been her fault. It cut into her heart to know she'd been the cause of his angst. Probably even pain. What man could kill so freely and not take some of the consequences of such a terrible act into his soul with every swing of blade or halo?

Squeezing her arm, she remembered the glowing design.

Zen rushed after Blade and only caught up to him at

the top of the stairs. "I think you should see this." She thrust out her arms, inner elbows facing upward. "I only noticed it after Trouble brought me out to the truck."

He hissed when he saw the still-glowing marks. "They're getting brighter, more defined."

She nodded. "Do you think they are demon marks?"

"Demonic marks are usually darker. And like I said, they don't look like my brother Kelyn's marks."

"What about you? As part faery, don't you have them?"

"No, just the wings and a touch of ichor in my blood. Do they hurt? Or feel different?"

"They feel kind of good, actually. Makes my blood warm and my whole body sort of relaxes. But as well…" She turned and looked down the stairs. The club was miles away. Yet she could feel the beckon. "I wonder about that portal. It couldn't have been so bad. I was compelled toward it. I feel as if I should have at least peeked through it. Maybe someone inside needed me."

"Needed you?" Blade tilted her chin up with an abrupt move. "That's demon magic luring you toward something you don't want to know about, Zen. Trust me. Nothing good comes from associating with demons."

"Because of the last time they were in Tangle Lake?"

"What? What do you mean?"

"You said something in the truck about the last time demons were in town. When I asked you about it, you dismissed it."

"There's nothing to say." He stroked a thumb over her arm and the marks actually stopped glowing. "You see that? What's that about?"

"I'm not sure. My skin is cooling fast, too. Huh. Your touch stopped the good feeling. What's this?" She lifted the hem of her T-shirt. Black blood spattered the white fabric.

Blade tilted his head and his hair fell over one eye. And then Zen noticed the fang peeking between his lips. "What's wrong?"

He stepped back, putting up his hands.

"Your vampire," she guessed, "likes demon blood?"

"I'm not talking about this anymore, Zen. You know where the bedroom is. You can use the shower. Pull a shirt out of my drawer to sleep in. I'm racked and need to get some sleep."

"You shower first, then, before I take over the bedroom."

"Fine." He strode past her, whisking up a breeze in his haste that chilled her to the core.

Zen pulled the wet hem away from her skin. He had been eying the blood fiercely. He was closed about so much. It was as if the man wanted to hide things, or even forget things, about himself.

"About demons," she whispered.

Whatever nightmare he fled, she had just led him back toward it.

While Zen was in the shower, Blade picked up the clothes from his bedroom floor and straightened up the room. In the kitchen he pulled out the full trash and he and Oogie went out into the night. He tossed the trash bag in the can outside the barn.

The night was dark for the clouds that shielded the moon. A scuffle in the grass that edged the Darkwood sent Oogie scrambling inside the barn. Smelled like a fox. Must have been chasing a mouse. That cat was skittish lately.

He turned to go back inside. But when his skin prickled from neck to wrist, he lifted his head and closed his eyes. Spreading his arms and opening his hands, he felt the presence on the air. Someone stood behind him. It was the absence of scent that informed him who that was. "Sim."

"You in now, Saint-Pierre?"

The creature who had asked him to help slay the demons in Tangle Lake. He wasn't sure what Sim was, but that didn't matter. Blade didn't have to think more than a few seconds to give an answer. "Yeah. I'm in."

"Excellent. I see you've already begun. Keep it up. I'll be watching."

"I don't understand. I don't know how you expect that I can take out all—"

Blade turned but no one stood behind him. The crickets chirped. And the red fox ran across the grass with a mouse hanging from its maw.

Zen showered, and after she'd dried off, found a long soft T-shirt in one of the dresser drawers. Swimming in the shirt, she tugged at the hem and climbed into Blade's bed. The well-worn black sheets were cozy. They smelled like him, which was an indefinable woodsy scent with a hard edge of steel. She wanted nothing more than to lay her head on his pillow and inhale his essence. To dream about what the man might be like if only his rules didn't exist to push her away.

After lying there an hour, she realized she couldn't sleep alone in this dark room with the crickets chirping outside the window he'd left cracked open. She was still unnerved from the club disaster. A trip to the bathroom to splash water on her face, and she returned to pace before the bed. She thought of Blade lying out on the couch with the ugly naked cat sleeping on his chest.

If she sneaked out there and curled up in the chair, would the cat hiss and throw a fuss? She didn't want to be alone. She needed to feel another beating heart in the same room with her. To somehow anesthetize the still pulsing vibrations in her skin that induced images of the weird portal in her thoughts.

And to know Blade was close should a pair of wicked red eyes peek through the window in search of her.

Navigating the darkness proved easy for the lack of furniture in the loft. Zen sneaked through the living room, homing in on the soft snores that came from the couch. Moonlight spilled through the cathedral windows and glistened in Blade's blue hair. A dark blue that was black, but not. Like the folds in azure velvet, she decided. Rich and luxurious. She longed to run her fingers through it and just…fall into him.

The cat crept along the front of the couch like a demon's golem. But it didn't hiss at her. Instead, when she approached, it skedaddled toward the kitchen.

The man didn't have a blanket. The evening was warm. A big fan at the top of the high, curved ceiling rotated slowly. Torso bared, spare moonlight etched his muscles.

Daringly, she lay on the edge of the couch in front of him, using his arm as a pillow. He'd didn't stir, and so she thought she was safe from discovery.

And then he did. His arm moved over her torso and his hand clasped across her stomach, pulling her up against his chest.

Smiling, Zen closed her eyes and drifted to sleep.

Chapter 14

Around two in the morning Blade stirred, his body tilting to turn over, but he sensed a warm presence lay close and under his arm. The wings between his shoulder blades tingled, seeking to unfurl, to feel her skin against the gossamer sheen of them. His entire body shivered, a sexual thrill that shimmied from ears to chest, to cock, to toes.

And then the vampire lifted its head. Her blood scent was exotic, yet dark and perhaps even dangerous. A marked change from when he'd originally scented her as merely human. To bite her would bring immense pleasure, perhaps even a moment of ecstasy. To taste an angel's blood...

Blade pushed down the desire. He wasn't stupid. No moment of pleasure was worth death.

Yawning, he curled his hand tighter, bringing Zen's back close against his bare chest. This felt right, and almost too good to be real. He didn't deserve to touch such innocence.

Yet was she innocent?

With that troubling thought stirring through his muggy brain, he drifted into reverie.

She slept like a log. Though Blade wasn't exactly sure how logs slept. It was a phrase his father had used often to describe his eldest brother Trouble's sleep habits when they had been kids.

Standing before the stove in comfy loose jeans that hung low on his hips, Blade stirred the scrambled eggs and turned the burner to simmer for the final finishing minutes. He wasn't much of an eater, but when he did consume food he stuck to plants and the occasional egg. Or, okay, burgers fed some weird craving for salt, or something like that.

Glancing to the couch he saw movement. Zen's arms stretched up and she twisted her spine to work out the kinks.

He'd been surprised to wake this morning and find her still snuggled up against him, and had to cautiously work himself out over the back of the couch without waking her. He'd quickly pulled on a shirt to hide his back, while she had continued to snore. So he had stared at her. The T-shirt she wore had ridden up high on her thighs but not high enough to satisfy his curiosity. And then he recalled the weird dream of wanting to have sex with her while his wings were out.

His vampire might be the more sexually voracious of his two halves, as well as wicked and demanding, but his faery was pure pleasure. When his wings were out while having sex every touch was magnified tenfold.

And if Zen were faery? The sex could be incredible. Or so he guessed. He'd never been with a faery.

He'd only the pleasure of having sex with his wings out with a woman once. And that had been a brief yet deliriously blissful joining. And to think of her now brought no pleasure whatsoever.

Fuck, he hated demons.

"Hungry?" he asked over a shoulder, and to redirect his darkening thoughts.

Zen sat up, shrugging her fingers through her fluff of copper hair. "Very. That smells great." She scampered across the room.

He dished up eggs and toast for her and then a small portion of fluffy eggs for himself and sat beside her at the kitchen counter. She tilted back a whole glass of orange juice before turning to him and smiling.

"I hope you don't mind me stealing the snuggle last night. Your room was so dark and lonely. Everything is black in there."

"We vampires appreciate the darkness."

"Yeah? But no coffin, eh?"

"A coffin? If you know so much about the world, how come you don't know that vamps and coffins are a fictional trope?"

"Really? Seems like it would be the perfect, snuggly, dark rest."

He hadn't thought much about it. And okay, so he had heard about some vamps who did sleep in coffins. He didn't have claustrophobia, but wedging his wide shoulders into a narrow box and pulling the lid down? Nope.

"I've been sleeping in total darkness since I was a kid. I've known nothing else."

"I wish I could know myself. And then." She set down her fork and turned to really look at him. This morning her eyes were blue. "Maybe it's not so important I remember? Maybe I'm meant to move forward with the knowledge I have."

"Sounds good. In theory. But there's that sticky situation with angels trying to kill you and demons trying to lure you into a vast glowing portal. What was with that?"

"I don't know. I do know I felt compelled to walk toward the glowy circle and the closer I got—let's just say, I'm glad you arrived when you did. You saved my ass once again."

She kissed him then. A sweet kiss to the corner of his mouth that wasn't seductive or teasing, but instead, a simple thank-you. Yet Blade was compelled, as if to a glowing portal, to pull her closer and kiss her deeper. The tingle between his shoulder blades alerted him as it had last night, but he ignored it. And no way would he let his fangs down.

"Mmm, you're a great bit of muscle and blue to wake up to in the morning," she said, and teased the ends of his hair that lay against his biceps. She turned and scooped in more eggs. "Did I dream that you pulled me closer last night?"

"Not sure. I think you were snoring so much there was no room for dreams," he said.

"What? I do not snore."

No, she didn't, but how else to dodge the "pulling her closer" question?

Ah, hell, what should he do about her? He wanted to deny the intimacy that seemed natural for the two of them to share, and at the same time he *had* just kissed her. And he'd liked it. And he wasn't going to regret it, either.

To kiss her or to push her away? Life would have

been a whole lot easier had he never seen those demons in the house across from Mr. Larson's lot.

"What's your plan for today?" he asked. "Luring more demons to you?"

"If I knew how and why that happened, I'd avoid it, believe me. I shouldn't have gone into the club alone. That was stupid. I was just…"

Feeling rejected by him after their weird embrace and then his pushing her away to prevent his vampire from biting her. So sometimes he wanted to kiss her and other times he didn't.

Pull it together, man!

"I'm complicated," he offered. "Sorry about last night. I should have been there to protect you, no matter what."

"Don't be sorry. You couldn't have known I'd need protection. And you know, I think I like complicated."

He smiled at that declaration. If the chick wanted complicated, he was the poster boy for that.

Zen crunched a piece of toast. "So let me get this straight, you can't bite me. That's cool. But when you're attracted to me it's your faery that reigns?"

"Not all the time. I can be normal. As normal as a guy like me is. I can kiss a woman, have sex with her, without wanting to bite her. It's when I'm in faery shape and am mating with a woman that my vampire wants to join in. Something about having my wings out heightens my vamp's craving for blood. That's never cool."

"Yet you were in plain old human shape when making out with me last night."

"I'm never plain or human." He chuckled, thinking that had sounded narcissistic. "If you have to label me as something, I'm vampire. And the vamp likes to make out with a pretty woman as much as any other man would."

"What about your faery?"

"Sex on steroids," he muttered, then grinned. He wasn't bragging, that was just how it worked. "So I'm a case. I did tell you to stay away from me."

"Everything I learn about you only makes me want to learn more. You're brave. Honorable. Handsome. Contradictory. We're alike in many ways. But while I strive to remember, I sense there is some part of you that wants to forget."

"Forget what?"

"You tell me. It's to do with demons—I know that much."

"Maybe you don't know that."

"I'm pretty sure I do. But if you're not cool with talking about it then I'll have to be cool with ignoring you're trying to hide it." She patted his arm. "So you wanted to know what I'm doing today? Nothing. At least not that I can think of."

"I was planning on stopping by my father's place this afternoon," Blade offered. "I want to show him the halo, see if he can modify it for me. He's a sword smith. Makes amazing swords and weapons."

"Can I come along?"

He nodded. "I'd like that."

Malakai Saint-Pierre wore his muscles like armor, and was gruffly handsome. Blade resembled him in pale skin tone, dark hair and height, but the father was a bit broader across the shoulders—if that was possible. Kai was a full werewolf, as Blade had explained to Zen on the drive over. Now she noticed him sniffing the air before her as Blade introduced them. Had to be a wolf thing.

He had a sure, almost painful grip, but when he saw her wince, he apologized and then slapped his son on the shoulder. "What do you have for me?"

"Something surprising."

"Come out into the work shed, you two. Let's have a look."

Zen clasped Blade's hand. She squeezed, more for her reassurance than his. Kai noted the clasp and grinned widely at his son.

"It's not fancy," Kai said to her as they strolled along the back of the house and into the shed. The rough-hewn log work shed was surprisingly bright thanks to exposure windows set into the vaulted ceiling. "But it's where I do all my work."

Scents of charcoal and burned steel mixed with the earth floor and an acidic chemical scent Zen couldn't place. She wandered up to the log wall where half a dozen swords hung from leather straps. The polished steel blades gleamed. Some featured elaborately etched blades; others offered a sleek swash of deadly beauty. She almost touched, but decided she shouldn't without first asking.

"You made all these?" she asked. "You possess amazing skill."

"My dad can make steel sing," Blade said proudly. "So here's what I've got."

Kai hissed at sight of the halo held in his son's hand. "Is that...?"

Blade nodded. "Slayed the bastard who owned it the other night. It was after Zen. Actually, she did the slaying."

"But you distracted the angel," Zen added with a wink to her man.

Kai delivered her a curious once-over. She shivered at the touch of his gaze. "Why are angels after you? My son told me you lost your memory. Are you an angel?"

"I don't know. I have a halo, too. Have had it with me since after the accident that boggled my memory. Does that make me an angel? Or maybe I found it somewhere and it's just a trinket?"

"Interesting. You talk to a witch?" Kai asked Blade.

"Dez hadn't any idea what she could be. Though she did think she was in the process of becoming."

"What does that mean?" the werewolf asked.

"Haven't a clue."

Both men glanced at Zen. She toyed with the rhinestones around her neck, suddenly aware of the overwhelming power a man's stare could deliver. Times two. It was…kind of nice. Made her stand a little straighter.

"Let's take a look." Kai held out his hand and Blade gave him the halo.

The imposing werewolf inspected the circular weapon, tapped it against the wood-and-steel-block table where he must fashion his weapons and put it around his wrist as if a bangle, then popped it off with a flick of his hand and caught it expertly. "Mind if I pound on this a bit?"

"Go for it," Blade said. "I was thinking you could modify it for me. Make it more blade like."

"Halos are the toughest substance to show up in the mortal realm. I doubt any tools I have will even dent it. But I'll give it a go. Maybe a little of your mother's faery dust worked in might soften it up? This could be sweet!"

"Thanks, Dad. Mom isn't home?"

"Nope, but she made some killer red-velvet cake this

morning. It's in the fridge. You two better go have some. Nice meeting you, Zen. And, Blade?"

"Yes?"

"Serve your woman some cake and then come back out, okay?"

The house was a gorgeous cabin-like structure. The open-floor design featured a vast living area and kitchen on the lower level. The second level consisted of an enclosed room with a king-size bed, and an open living area, one wall of which was entirely windows that stretched up to a peak at the pinnacle of the two-story ceiling. The view was lush and green, and a stream bubbled not far beyond the patio that hugged the house.

The cabin was a dream escape, Zen thought. Must have been an awesome place to grow up living in the middle of nature. Now, this was her kind of home.

Blade dished up some cake for her, but not himself— though he did lick the knife clean. "That will make you believe in heaven on earth. My mother makes the best sweet stuff. I almost miss moving away from home when I get a taste of her cookies and cakes."

"Better than blood?" she asked.

"Sometimes."

She sampled a forkful of the dense red cake capped with a cream-cheese frosting and decided not to talk because that would only hamper her from eating more, more and more.

"I'm heading out to see what Dad wants. Probably wants to give me his opinion on the new girl."

"Am I your girl?" she muttered through a mouthful of cake. "We're not even friends."

"That's right," he said, and left out the side door.

"Mmm…" Heaven, indeed.

But what would be more heavenly? To actually be

Blade's girl. And to convince the man that there were more interesting things to do than merely kissing her. She wouldn't ask for his bite again. But she really wanted to get back to where they had been the other night when they'd been making out on the couch, and he had licked her nipples. Just thinking about it made her toes curl.

Memory? Who cared about what she couldn't remember? She was making delicious new memories with a man who had begun to hold and kiss her in her dreams.

Now, how to convince him to take a chance on her in real life?

"She's trouble," Kai said. He gave the halo a good whack with his ball peen hammer. Not even a dent. "Angel? That's not good for your vamp, son. Your faery might like to dally with her, but if you whip out the fangs…" His father shook his head.

"I don't think she's angel. Or if she is, if she actually fell to earth, I don't believe she's angel anymore. Though her blood does initially bleed blue."

Kai hissed. "Keep your fangs away from that woman's neck."

"I will. But I sense other things about her. Or so Dez put the idea into my head."

"Like what?"

"Faery."

Kai set the hammer down and turned to his son, arms crossed and head tilted. "She got wings?"

"If she does, she doesn't remember how to bring them out. And she's got some interesting markings on her arms. Sort of like Kelyn's, but not. They glow."

Kai nodded. Thought about it. "So why are demons

after her? And what is with this new club at the edge of town? I've never heard of it. And I usually have a pretty good eye out for all paranormal activity in the area."

"Really, Dad? You're not even pack principal anymore. You've retired."

Kai puffed up his chest. "Are you saying I'm losing my edge?"

Blade shook his head. His dad would always have the edge, but he was more focused on making a good life with his wife right now than pack politics or even the paranormal goings-on in Tangle Lake.

"I didn't know about the club, either," Blade reassured Kai. "It's some creepy old mansion that looks as if it's been sitting on that property for centuries. Which makes no sense whatsoever because I'm sure all of us have been in the area where it sits, probably snowmobiling in the wintertime. And it had this portal in the middle of the dance floor that was sucking Zen toward it."

Kai blew out his breath. "Portals are not cool. If it's a demon hotspot it might suck her into Daemonia."

Blade hadn't considered Daemonia. Thinking about that place gave him a shiver. His parents had told him about it during their Teen Talk. It was the Place of All Demons. No place for any vampire, wolf or faery to go. They'd much prefer he smoke or start drinking than consider visiting Daemonia.

Kai asked, "You think this chick is worth the trouble?"

Blade ran a hand through his hair, but didn't meet his father's eyes.

"I get it. You're afraid if you let yourself care about her this will go down like the last one. What was her name?"

Blade bowed his head and turned a shoulder away from his father. "Octavia."

The last one. Why wouldn't his family stop mentioning her? There was no way he could ever forget until everyone else did.

"That wasn't your fault, Blade. You didn't know Octavia was a *mimicus* demon. And you sure as hell couldn't have known her denizen would let her die."

They could have saved her with intervention from a witch, even demonic magic. A simple spell. But Ryckt, the denizen leader, had allowed Octavia to fade—to death. Blade didn't want to stir into that muck again. He marched toward the door.

"I know you seek forgiveness, son," his father called. "You're the only one who can do that for yourself!"

Blade veered toward the stream that paralleled the back of the house. He stopped on a mossy stone that edged the crisp, gurgling water. Even the fresh, verdant scent couldn't lessen his anxiety. His shoulders felt as tight as his jaw. And his heart squeezed in his chest.

Had he known they would let her die he would have done something. What, he didn't know. He had been so out of it after the torture. But—hell. She didn't have to die!

When he heard Zen's soft voice, Blade cringed. She stood right behind him. Shit.

"I won't ask," she said softly. And she embraced him from behind and tilted her head against his back. "Let me in, Blade. I promise I won't look too deep. I just… I need someone to anchor me to this realm."

He clasped her hand against his chest. He could do that for her, the anchoring part. But the letting her in part was what made him clench his teeth.

"Whatever you've done that makes you feel as

though you are better off to push people away," she said, "doesn't matter to me. I'm starting fresh. You can start fresh with me. Deal?"

It would matter to her if she knew his dark truth. It mattered to every family member who still cringed whenever his past was mentioned. He had been responsible for a woman's death. Because of his bite.

"I'm lost," Zen whispered. "But standing close to you makes me feel found. Or at least, safe."

"I can't protect you forever, Zen. So long as I remain clueless about what you are and why so many are coming after you, I can't completely protect you."

"Maybe you should put the halo over my head? I know the mythology. If I am really an angel that'll give me my earthbound soul."

True. It would also make her human.

"And make you mortal. Do you want that? What if you fell to this realm for a reason? With a purpose? Let's keep looking. We'll figure you out."

He turned and she kissed him, and this time he didn't push her away. Because maybe he could protect her. And yes, it did something to his aching heart when he held her close. And he liked that feeling. It was a dangerous path to tread, but he'd never feared danger before.

Losing his heart to Zen could be the worst thing for him, but the best thing for his future.

Chapter 15

Blade dropped Zen off at The Red Rooster. He told her he had something to do with Stryke. He said he'd pick her up later if she wanted to get a bite to eat.

Of course she did. She was never not hungry. That red-velvet cake had only stoked her craving for more food.

Waving him off, she turned in time to see the Mini Cooper pull into the parking lot. Trouble hopped out and handed her the keys.

"Thanks." She tucked the keys into her skirt pocket. "Now how will you get back to your truck, which must be out on that country road?"

"Kelyn drove me out to your car. He'll swing by here in a few minutes and pick me up. Everything's cool. You and Blade getting along?"

"Yes."

"That's good. I thought for sure he'd never want to see you again after the demon affair at the club."

Zen slung the backpack over her shoulder and met Trouble's dark gaze, which was just as high up as Blade's was. "What is it with Blade and demons? Something really terrible must have happened because he always clams up when I ask him about it."

Trouble leaned forward, sticking his face right before hers. He smelled great, like pine trees and fresh-cut wood. "You really want to know?"

Zen nodded.

"Well—"

"Wait!" She put up her hands between them. "Forget it. If Blade wants me to know, he'll tell me. It wouldn't be right to go behind his back and ask about something if he wants to keep it private."

Trouble whistled. "I like you. Even if you do turn out to be demon, I'll have your back."

"I think I can handle myself."

"Really? 'Cause if we hadn't rescued you from the Demon Dance Hall you would be Hades knows where right now."

She rubbed her arm and shrugged. "Fair enough. Just tell me one thing about Blade."

Trouble shrugged his massive shoulders back and puffed up his chest, then shot out, "Maybe."

"Was it a woman? Someone who hurt him?"

She wanted to know, and then she didn't. She didn't have a right to know. Again, Blade would tell her if he wanted her to have that knowledge.

"No," she quickly said. "Forget it."

Trouble smirked. "Wasn't going to tell you anyway. But so you know, you are barking up the right tree. See you later, Zen." He strode off toward the big iron rooster and gave its tail a slap as he passed.

"A woman hurt him," she muttered. "So it's heartbreak that keeps him from being open with me. How to help him get beyond something so devastating?"

The man needed space. And a reasonable means to trust her, if he was going to fess up and tell her something so deeply personal. So she'd give him space. She could do that. If any nasty demons came after her she'd just whip out the halo and…

"Where is the halo?"

Unzipping the backpack she shuffled through it and found the halo nestled in a hoodie jacket. Taking it out, she decided she would have to keep it on her at all times. If it could take out an angel, it sure as heck could take out a demon.

"Watch out, bad guys." She swung the blade defensively in a close arc before her. "I am armed and ready."

The statement felt empowering. But really? She'd accidentally slain the angel, and that was only because it had been distracted by Blade. What if she was alone and trapped by an angel or demon?

Zen gulped down a meek squeak. She sure hoped Blade stuck to his promise to protect her.

"It's like a beacon," the demon said. He was visiting the mortal realm as first hand to his commander, who sat across the table from him. He set the coffee cup down and broke off a big bite of the sugared donut the café advertised as "heart attacks." "We can track her when she's got that halo in hand."

"But so can the angels," Kesabel said. He rapped pointed fingernails on his coffee cup and sneered at the coating of sugar that painted his cohort's lips white. "And we don't want them to get to her before we do."

"We were so close last night." The lackey demon sucked the sugar from his fingertips. "Until the vampire and the werewolf crashed the party."

"That idiot vampire thinks he's got to protect her."

"Someone needs to have words with him."

Kesabel nodded. "Done."

At the back of the garage where once a farmer had herded dairy cattle in and out to be milked twice daily, Blade leaned over the steel worktable his father had designed for him. He worked on cars as a hobby, but he wasn't a die-hard car fanatic who fixed them up and polished and shined and then parked them at shows for display. He liked a good, solid car and preferred not to buy new. Recycling was the way he'd been raised. He did the same with the weapons he stocked in the small arsenal here in the cool shadows of the garage. He rescued rusted blades from antiques shows and flea markets, took them home and polished and honed them. He liked blades, and it wasn't because of his name. When in combat, being up close and able to feel his opponent's breath on his face was the most challenging and satisfying way to win the fight.

He didn't own a gun. They were too loud, and really, it was too easy to kill with them. If a man were committed to defense, to protecting himself and others, he had better be willing to stand before that threat and give it good and fair fight. A bullet was too impersonal. A coward's weapon.

He drew his fingertips over the one blade he wouldn't leave home without. The bowie knife his father had forged for him when he was a teen. As well…he reached high for the salt dagger that hung above the assorted weaponry. It was fragile, but the hardened salt that had been compressed into the cheese-grater-like base of steel was an effective weapon against demons. Daisy Blu's husband, Beck, had given it to him; it was from his late father, Severo's, arsenal.

And now he'd added an angel halo to his necessity weapons. Or he would if his dad was able to modify it.

So he had told the mysterious Sim he was going to help him annihilate the demons in Tangle Lake. They had threatened Zen. And that was a good enough reason for him to go after the next demon he laid eyes on. And the next. And so on, until he was confident the threat had been eliminated.

He sniffed the bowie knife and then licked it. Traces of demon blood still clung to the polished steel. Fangs descending, he grinned wickedly. He was growing stronger with every demon he killed. It wasn't as though he needed more strength. Only, the gaining of said strength fed his faery's vicious desire for power. As well, strength bolstered his mission. He'd need muscles of steel if he were to fight more angels.

He wondered who Sim was and what his beef was with demons.

Didn't matter. There were no wrongs about this situation. Humans were protected from demons. He got to slay demons. And in the process Zen was also protected. Everybody won.

And because he was feeling so confident, Blade tugged out his cell phone and called Zen at the inn. "I'll pick you up in an hour," he said after suggesting dinner at a local restaurant, and clicked off.

Time to start treating that remarkable woman like the lady she was. And in keeping her close, he'd also be able to protect her.

Dinner at an Italian family-owned place called Man-setti's was followed by a movie. Which Zen had been very excited about. She'd never seen a movie before. Not that she recalled. Afterward, she strolled with Blade, hand in hand, out to his truck, which he'd parked around back in the theater lot far from other patrons.

"That was awesome," she said. "But I still don't think it's possible to shoot a man so many times and he'd continue to rise up, shake it off and go after the hero."

"That's why they call it a fantasy action/adventure flick. He did eventually die after they sliced off his head."

"Yeah, but his body still twitched." Zen thrust her arms out before her in a zombie imitation and twitched her limbs. "I will never die! Fear me!"

Blade's laughter was a startling surprise. She dropped her arms, and wrapped them around his neck. "Do that again."

"What?"

"Laugh."

He grinned and shook his head. "You're a strange one."

"If I told you I thought your laughter was sexy would you do it again?"

"I don't do sexy on command." He chuckled softly and playfully pushed her away. Zen beamed at him. "That wasn't on purpose!" he called as he strode to the truck.

"Doesn't matter." She skipped to meet him at the passenger door. "You've already gone and done it."

"And what have I done?"

He teased the ends of her hair. Such an absentminded move. His guard was down. She liked that. "You are seducing me with your charm."

"I...don't have a charming bone in my body."

"Oh, I think this one is." She ran a finger down his arm and stopped at the wrist, where he flexed his powerful fingers. "This one, too." She tapped his shoulder. "It's not your classic charm, to be sure."

"Like you would know, Amnesia Girl. Hop in." He held the truck door open and helped her up with a hand to her hip.

"Can I drive?"

"No one touches the steering wheel," he called as he swung around the hood, then opened his door and slid in, "or the radio. Driver rules."

"Sidekick shuts his cakehole?"

Blade tilted a curious gaze on her. "Where'd you hear that?"

"I don't know. Should I have heard it somewhere?"

"It's a quote from a popular TV show that features monster hunters."

"Huh. Must have picked it up when I walked the world."

Blade turned completely on the seat. His stare was so intense, she felt a shiver ripple through her system. "What?" she said in a panic.

"That's the first time you've ever said that. Actually acknowledged it. That you walked the world."

"So?"

"Angels walk the world after their fall to take in knowledge."

"I knew that. Because…huh." She sat back, considering the implications. "Because I walked the world. That's what I was doing before the bus hit me. I know it as truth."

"You getting back your memory?"

"I don't know. A little? But if I am an angel, that doesn't explain why my blood turns black."

Blade turned the key in the ignition, and, still looking at her, shifted into gear. "Explains why you have a halo."

He let his foot off the gas, and Zen screamed.

Chapter 16

Zen's scream startled him so thoroughly Blade slammed his foot on the brake.

Before the truck stood a man, who wasn't a human, but an angel. Blade knew that because the creature's wings stretched out twenty feet or more on either side of his shoulders. They weren't the standard feathered wings, either. These were fashioned from ice. And they weren't melting in the eighty-degree summer heat.

The angel heaved out a breath of frost that iced over the truck's windshield. Blade felt the chill enter his veins. He'd not felt so cold since the polar vortex had dropped temps below negative thirty degrees this past winter.

He heard Zen audibly shiver.

"Stay here," he said to her.

She slapped the halo into his hand. "You'll need this."

Right. His dad still had the one he'd claimed.

The angel slammed a fist onto the hood, denting the metal surface into the engine a good eight inches.

"Beating on inanimate objects isn't impressive," he muttered. "How about you try me?" To Zen he said, "Keep the engine running."

He kicked open the door and hopped out. He lunged for the angel, but got caught by an icy wing that thwapped him across the chest and flung him away from the truck. His spine landed against a street pole, the overhead light flickering from the impact.

The angel grasped the front of the truck and lifted. The front tires left the ground.

"Why are you after her?" Blade yelled as he pushed from the pole and charged the angel.

He jumped onto the hood, which didn't stop the angel from lifting it, and reached down to grip the bastard by its thick white hair. Ice flowed up Blade's fingers and hardened the veins in his wrist. "Why?"

The angel roared in a deafening blend of animal sounds and screams. Blade gritted his teeth as he struggled to maintain hold on the creature while his fingers felt as if they'd snap off from frostbite. Out of the corner of his eye he saw the clear ice wing sweep toward him. He slashed the angel's hand with the halo and on the follow-through managed to slice the wing in half. Ice shattered onto the pavement and the truck hood. The truck wheels dropped to the ground, toppling Blade off-balance.

To his advantage, the wings did not bleed.

Going with the momentum, Blade flipped over the top of the angel's head, slicing the halo over its shoulder and down the back as he did so. He landed the ground behind him and twisted to see the blue blood spill from the cavernous icy wound.

The undamaged wing collided with Blade's back. The force expelled the halo from his grip and pushed him forward to catch his palms against the angel's chest. The creature's skin was like dry ice. His flesh stuck to the thing. So he shifted. The subtle changes to his musculature and body were enough to free him from the icy opponent.

With wings out and in full faery form, Blade pranced around the angel, turning it away from the vehicle and Zen. "What do you want from her?"

Nothing but brain-shattering cacophony spilled from the creature's mouth. Either it hadn't mastered the human tongue or it was focused on annoying the hell out of Blade. The sound was louder than standing next to a stack of speakers at a heavy metal concert—turned up to eleven.

Holding his hands out in placation, Blade walked farther backward, luring the creature forward. Its wounded shoulder spilled copious blood that he kept an eye on. If it touched his skin he'd live, but the instant it permeated his bloodstream he was a goner.

Spying the halo on the tarmac, he swept down a hand and snagged it. A wing whooshed toward him, lifting his hair but not cutting him. Rolling up to stand, Blade eyed the truck. Zen sat inside. Safe.

"You're the second one," he said to the angel, guessing the thing understood him, no matter his language skills. "I will protect her with my life." He stretched his wings out behind him then arrowed backward, making him a narrow target. "Time for you to return to where you came from. But this time? I'm sending you to St. Peter's gate."

The angel lunged for him. An icy wing tip cut through Blade's jeans. Heat seared his skin. Slashing an arm down, he drew the halo upward, cutting the angel's leg and across his chest. The angel's body opened up, blood spilling and a bright light emitting. Blade dodged the gush of blue blood. A wicked growl preceded a brilliant flash. The angel dispersed in a scatter of crystal dust and settled like winter snow upon the ground.

"Yes!" carried out from inside the truck.

Blade shook the icicles off his wings and yowled. The angel's icy touch still hurt like a mother. He slapped a hand over his thigh. No blood. He was safe.

A police siren sounded and he guessed it was a few miles away.

The truck drove up beside him and Zen called out the driver's window, "Get in! The cops! Hurry!"

Trying to shift resulted in a vicious twinge to his system. The lingering shock of cold kept him from shifting. Folding his wings up behind him, Blade managed to fit himself inside the truck cab, but had to pull in the top of his right wing and bend it uncomfortably.

"We'll have to return for the angel dust later," Zen said.

"Don't need it. Only a witch would have use for it."

"Fine." Zen pulled the vehicle out of the parking lot. The truck sputtered and clunked and with a lurching heave forward—sped out into the darkness.

"That was close," she said. "That thing might have turned you to ice. And look at your wing! It's bleeding. I think. It's sparkly."

He hadn't been aware he'd taken damage. Blade pulled up the peak of his right wing and examined the cut, which healed even as he ran his fingers over it. Ichor-tainted blood spilled over the dark wing fabric and dropped onto his lap, staining the denim darkly.

Had any angel blood entered his bloodstream? He
didn't feel as if he would explode. Because that was
what would happen. One minute the vamp was smiling and going about his business. Angel blood gets into
his veins—bam!

Zen eyed him for so long the truck swerved toward
the ditch. It was only then he realized his pants had
split down the thigh and crotch during the shift. And
he wasn't wearing anything beneath the jeans.

"Eyes on the road," he directed her. "Don't take your
foot off the gas. The engine might be damaged. The
minute this truck stops, I think it'll be for good."

"Right." She turned sharply onto the gravel road that
led toward his home.

"I'd put my wings back but I need to stretch them
out to furl them back up. Gotta wait until we get home.
Sorry."

"For what? Saving my life? Again! Dude, you can put
those wings anywhere you like. And uh…those pants
are going to fall off when you stand up is my guess. I
can't wait."

"I just dodged death and you're excited to see me
drop trou?"

She shrugged, and while she kept her eyes on the
road, Blade took in her broad smile. He forgot about
the danger. That smile would undo him.

Hell, it already had.

Zen handled the truck well. And as Blade had suspected, when she stepped on the brake to park, the vehicle heaved to a clattering death.

"Sorry," she said.

"Not your fault. I think it had something to do with

the angel." He shivered. "And all that ice. I can still feel it on my skin. It's creepy."

"I'll run inside and get you a towel."

While Zen ran up to the house, Blade stepped out of the truck. Though it was a sultry evening, he shivered again. The angel's touch lingered on his skin, in his very veins. He clutched the jeans' waistband to his stomach, but it wasn't doing much good. The crotch was ripped open.

He smirked. Zen wasn't the sort he wanted to attract in this manner. Because those *sorts* were one-night stands. On the other hand, she'd let him know that she liked to tease him and push their intimate boundaries. And those boundaries of his were fast softening.

Striding up to the barn, he cupped a hand over his crotch when Zen reemerged with a towel. She tossed it at him and turned to face the door.

He wrapped it about his hips, dropping the tattered jeans, but suspected it wouldn't be long before his cock got the better of him and tented the towel. Zen led the way up the stairs, her hips shifting and hair spilling like a sexy veil across her shoulders. She did have some gorgeous curves, and those curves distracted. At the top of the stairs, she turned and caught him in a kiss before he could land on the top step.

"Thank you again. Ooh, you're shivering. You need to put some clothes on."

"Here I thought you wanted to see them fall off me."

"More than anything. But I don't want it to happen at the expense of your health."

"I'm not shivering because I'm cold." Clad in just the towel, Blade wandered into the kitchen, while keeping his back away from Zen's curious gaze, and ran himself a glass of water from the faucet. "The angel's touch iced under my skin." He drank the water then shivered boldly. "You want some?"

"I do want something." She fidgeted with the ends of her hair, then smiled as she tried to avoid looking at him. Classic subtle flirtation moves. Combined with, he suspected, a healthy dose of nerves. "So here we are."

"Yep." He felt a sneaky desire to toy with her discomfort, so he leaned against the counter, hand on his hip. "Here we are. I'd say that date was a disaster, wouldn't you?"

"Not the majority of it. It was just the last part that was harrowing. And that did end well. The villain died the first time. All in all, I had a good time. And you know, I've never seen a naked man before."

"That you know of."

"That I remember. So, uh…could I…" She eyed his towel.

"Seriously?"

She nodded eagerly. Clasped together her beringed fingers in expectation.

"I don't—" She reached for the towel and Blade grabbed it before she could tug it from his hips. "Whoa! Boundaries, Zen."

"Yes, but I'm curious. Your muscles are so—" she spread her hands before him, taking in his abs and pecs "—solid. You're just so strong. And perfect. And—it makes my heart flutter and other parts of me get really warm."

He arched a brow. Did she actually not recognize when she was turned on? This chick did not cease to surprise him.

"And what is eyeing my main stick going to do for you?" he asked.

"I want to see all of you."

"You've seen more of me than you should. Wings?"

"They are gorgeous. And besides, you saw me with my shirt off the other night."

"And you are ogling me with my shirt off right now."

Would she attempt to finagle him out of the towel? He wanted to see if she could.

"Looking at you makes me want to take my clothes off," she confessed. "And press my body against yours. And kiss you. And—oh! I know that I know about this stuff, but I don't think I've experienced it. Does that make sense?"

"Nothing about you makes sense, Zen. You're weird."

Her smile dropped.

"And I like that," he quickly added. "So you want to get your experience with me? Is that all I am?" He crossed his arms. "A means to add a notch to your bedpost?"

"I don't understand that. Do I even own a bedpost?"

"Then, you obviously don't know as much as you think you know."

"Apparently not. Okay, let me try a different tact."

He smirked. Never had a woman's attempt at seduction been so awkward. And yet it was a turn-on to watch her fumble and find her way to more confident ground. Kind of like a flower opening her petals to take in the sun. And where the hell had that notion come from? He did not relate women to flowers.

Did he?

"I…admire you," Zen said. "I mean, we've only just met. And it is apparent to both of us that whatever it is that I am is going to be dangerous to your health. And yet all you want to do is protect me. That's so noble. And sexy."

He brushed a swish of copper hair over her shoulder and stroked his palm up her neck to cup her jaw. "I like you, Zen."

"Even though I'm weird?"

"Especially because you're weird. And if we're going to do confessions, I admit that I struggle inside my head far more than any physical struggles I've had with angels or demons. I've got to stop that. Take life moment to moment. Like right now, I want to kiss you."

She beamed up at him, bouncing on her toes. "Then, let's kiss."

That was easy. He leaned down to kiss her and she sighed into his breaths. And Blade forgot to question the right or wrong of the situation and just let it happen. He wrapped a hand across her back and pulled her against his bare chest. She had kissed before, or maybe it was that they kissed so well together. This kiss felt easy. Sure. Not dangerous.

Her fingers played over his biceps, and the shivers he'd felt earlier vanquished in the warm wake of her touch. He could kiss her all evening and never come up for air.

"You're not resisting," she whispered against his mouth. "That feels good. You're pulling me close to you. You are so strong and hard when I touch you. Your skin is..."

"Pale next to yours," he said on a chuckle. "So pretty." He tapped the marks on the inside of her elbow. "Take your shirt off, Zen."

She pulled the shirt over her head so quickly he thought she might give herself whiplash. And there she stood, without a bra, her caramel breasts high and full and with darker nipples. Blade could taste them already. And he didn't think to question his tactics as he grew more aroused.

She pressed her hips closer, purring an approving noise into his mouth.

"Can angels have sex?" she asked.

"I don't know. But I thought we were going with you not being an angel. At least, not anymore. That becoming thing Dez mentioned?"

"Right. Then, maybe I should give the sex thing a try?"

Yeah. This was getting too deep too fast. Right? But he was encouraging her. And the feel of her hand running down his abs and so close…

He gripped her wrist. "I think with you, slow would be a good idea."

She pouted.

Damn it, why was he so conflicted about this?

Then she sniffed. "You smell so good. I think you're warming up. At least…" She glanced down to the towel. "Some part of you is."

She was not going to let up. Nor did he want her to. This thing with Zen was different than his usual encounters with women who were intent on one thing. Much as she was also that intent, he sensed a playfulness in her that he'd never had the opportunity to experience with other women.

"I want you, Zen," he honestly declared. "I just don't want you to feel—"

"Rushed? Oh, no, I don't feel that way at all. Blade, I want to have sex with you. I mean, like…a lot." She hugged him. "We're not moving too quickly. Oh." Her fingers stroked across his back curiously.

He knew what she was doing and cringed.

"What is that?" She peered up at him. "Feels like a scar. Lots of them. Can I look?"

That she had asked and hadn't brazenly ducked

under his arm to gawk meant the world to Blade. It was the part of him that reminded him he had wronged a woman. The part he wanted to forget. And yet, he couldn't move forward with Zen and continue to hide.

He nodded. "I don't want to talk about the reason for the scars tonight, but you can look."

She kissed him, bowed her forehead to his lips, then slipped around behind him and spread her hands across his back. At her soft, exploratory touch, Blade sucked in a hiss. Eighteen scars in all. A one-night stand had counted them for him one evening. She'd been too drunk to care what they had come from and had accepted his lie about a farming accident.

In truth, every one of them had come from a demon talon.

"This makes me sad," she said quietly. "Aren't vampires supposed to heal fast?"

"Demon talons have poison in them. Counteracts the healing process."

"Demons," she whispered. He'd not intended to tell her that. It was too easy to relax with Zen.

And then the gentlest kiss landed on one of those scars, and he shivered. His muscles tightened and his heart trembled. It wasn't from the lingering chill of an unholy angel, but rather the promise of something he feared more than the pain. Connection. Goddess, but it reduced him to something he wasn't familiar with.

Something that felt better than he could ever imagine.

"I will treat you with care," Zen said. "Because you deserve it."

A kiss to one of the scars branded him with innocent kindness. And then another, and then she moved around in front of him, took his hand and led him into the bedroom.

They fell onto the bed in a tumble of sighs and kisses, strokes and moans. Zen's skin, fire under his palms, coaxed him closer, deeper, toward something so innocent. Untouchable.

Yet he held her now, and wasn't about to let go.

Gliding his tongue along her arm, he aimed toward the cream-colored markings, slipping a wet trail over the arabesques, and then toward her shoulder. He kissed her there. And there. And at the base of her jaw, and then her open mouth. She gasped into him, exhaling sweet breath. Giving to him.

"Zen," he whispered. A prayer. A sonnet to her beauty. Simply a name. Not even her name. But it fit her. And him.

Her hand glided down his abs and landed over his crotch. She cooed and nudged up her hip. "That feels interesting."

He would give her interesting. He tugged the towel loose and she eagerly tore it away from his hips. Before he could resume kissing her, she'd grabbed hold of his cock.

"Wow, it's so hard and hot."

He growled and bowed his head to her breast. "That feels good when you give it a squeeze. Mmm, and that firm stroking. Oh, Zen…"

She took to the exploratory touching with a zest that didn't surprise Blade at all. She was a curious woman. And for that, he would not complain.

As she continued to squeeze and stretch and stroke him, he kissed her breasts and teased her nipples with his tongue. She hadn't developed a rhythm but she didn't need to. Her awkward play was actually making him harder and increasing his breaths. She squirmed and hummed a satisfied tone. A supple explorer lay beside him. It felt so different from any encounter with a woman he'd had previously. This felt real.

"I trust you, Blade."

Though he'd heard it before, that statement meant a lot to him coming from a woman who had no solid grasp on her life. She needed to trust someone. And she trusted him. So he would treat her as the precious entity she was.

Feathering his fingers down her breast and tweaking her nipple to the accompaniment of her grateful moan, he then glided his fingertips over her stomach and parted her legs. She was warm and wet. So ready for him. Her hands bracketed his head, luring him to her breasts. He kissed them both, suckling them while he fingered her teasingly.

"So many sensations," she said on a gasp.

"You overwhelmed?" he asked.

She shook her head. "My heart is racing. Every part of me tingles in the coolest way. Your kisses feel like the best thing ever. And what you're doing with your fingers... Don't stop, Blade. Please, don't stop."

"I won't. I want to be inside you, Zen. You ready for that?"

She gripped the head of his cock and guided him between her legs. "Yes."

He entered her slowly, steadily. The tight squeeze of her made it difficult not to come immediately, but he was determined to give her pleasure first before he came and then just wanted to roll over and fall asleep.

She murmured next to his ear that he was so remarkable. Fingers clutching at his shoulders and back, she tilted back her head as his thrusts grew faster, deeper.

She hadn't cried out, as if a virgin, but that meant little. All women were different. There was no real way to know if she had done this before.

Didn't matter. She was here in his arms, and he had been gifted her trust.

"Oh…" Zen gasped, her hands dropping away from him as her body shuddered. "That's…" The orgasm shivered her body minutely beneath him. A smile curled onto her lips.

And Blade felt as if an angel had just fallen into his life.

Chapter 17

Zen woke in the black bedroom, which was more a slate gray thanks to the morning light beaming through the window. The forest was close, and a mosaic of leaves shifted in the soft breeze. She pulled the sheet up to her neck and tucked her legs against the heat lying beside her. And then she realized she was lying next to Blade and stretched down her legs so she could snuggle along the length of him.

And some other length suddenly bobbed against her belly.

She murmured in satisfaction. "I like that guy."

"He likes you" came a voice from under the sheet. He tugged it down and leaned in to kiss her through the hair spilled over his face. She swept it away to reveal one gray eye. "Morning. Would you mind pulling the shade? Vamps aren't keen on bright light so early in the day."

"Of course." She slipped out of bed and pulled the shade, reducing the room to a subtle darkness save for a glimmer of light sneaking in on either side of the shade. "Better?"

"Much. Come back to me."

She slid into bed, and he pulled her up against his body, then moved on top of her, supporting himself with his elbows and a knee. Pressing kisses to her breasts, he lingered in tasting her, feeling her, holding his ear against her chest to listen to her heartbeats.

"Do I sound normal?" she asked.

"I hope not. There's something so wrong about normal. On the other hand, normal is in the eye of the beholder, yes?"

"Like being an amnesia chick?"

"Yep. For me being vampire with wings is normal. My brothers find being werewolf normal. So who is to say what your normal is?"

"I do know not remembering isn't normal."

"If you are or were an angel, maybe the not-remembering part is all part of the plan?"

She screwed up her lips in thought. "Vampires and werewolves sound a lot easier to me. If your father is werewolf, and I think you mentioned your mother is faery, how did you manage the vampire part?"

"My grandfather. He is married to a werewolf. They had twins, Kambriel and Malakai. Kam's a vamp. Dad's the wolf. Grandpa's bloodsucking genes just happened to show up in me."

"Do you regret not being werewolf like your siblings?"

"No. I've known nothing else. And I've never been made to feel I was different. Besides, Kelyn is full faery. If there's a weirdo in our family, it's my little brother."

He chuckled and nuzzled his face between her breasts for a kiss. "But you know I like weirdoes."

"You're a weirdo, too," Zen said. "You're quiet and dark. It's because of these, isn't it?" She ran her fingers over the scars on his back that wrapped around to his sides. "Tell me about them. Please?"

She felt his fingers glide between her legs. "Later," he murmured. "Right now I want to delve into you."

He moved down on the bed, kissing her stomach, her hip, her thighs, until he kissed her deeply between her moist folds.

Zen squirmed and reached down to thread her fingers through his silken hair. She wasn't quite sure what he was doing with his tongue, but she didn't require an explanation. It was marvelous.

Blade watched Zen wander to the window to pull up the shade. Those waves of copper hair glinted like metal when the sun embraced her silhouette, as if she was some kind of goddess.

Or an angel.

"She was a demon," he suddenly said.

Sitting up on the bed, he smoothed a hand over the wrinkled sheet draped across his lap. The sun wasn't too bright on this north side of the barn. His skin wouldn't burn unless he endured prolonged exposure to direct rays. And the faery part of him provided added protection that most vamps didn't have and without which would see them running for the shade long before he did.

Zen spun around. "She?"

"The woman from my past who is the reason why I like to keep my distance from other women. The reason for these scars on my back."

"Oh." She planted a kiss on his forehead. Stroking his hair over a shoulder, she smiled warmly upon him. "You've kind of shot that need for distance to hell with us, eh?"

He kissed the top of her breast. "It was worth the risk."

"Risk? Right. You thought I could be demon. Or worse, an angel."

"I still don't know what you are."

"But she was demon. This woman from your past? And…things did not go well with her, I take it?"

He shoved down the sheets and swung his legs over the side of the bed. Patting the bed, he waited for her to sit beside him. The heat of her body was as blessed as spring rain. Every part of him shivered and joined together to embrace the goodness he'd been gifted by Zen's presence.

And because of that, he owed her his truth. She deserved to know him. Good, bad and so terrible.

"Her name was Octavia. I met her in the springtime. Midnight, at a local drive-in movie theater that was still open. It shows classics once a month and the whole town attends. She was wearing a yellow dress and flashed me a fanged smile. I thought she was vampire. She even gave off the telltale shimmer that we vamps feel when we touch another of our kind."

"What's that feel like?" she asked, hugging against his side.

"It's sort of a tickle with an electric-shock kick. But not as strong as when you walk across a carpet and touch metal. It's a *knowing*, is the best way to put it."

She placed her hand on his thigh and, tilting her head aside his shoulder, silently entreated him to continue.

"We had an affair," he said. "Brief. Heated. I fell

fast for her. That happens with me. If I like a woman, there's usually no going back."

He peered into Zen's bright azure eyes and saw worlds beyond his comprehension. And he liked it there. Lost in her world. He didn't desire to go back now that he had ventured in.

Yeah, so he fell hard and fast. He was a wimp when it came to love.

"I had no idea she was toying with me. Gaining my trust. Grooming me for something unspeakable."

The spill of her hair over his skin lightened his darkening mood. Yet at the same time, it reminded him that he held a woman, and women tended to be tricky. But how to trick him when she didn't even know herself?

"I wanted to bond with her. Vampires do that by sharing the bite and blood. It's a way of taking a mate. For life."

He let that settle in. Because yes, he'd thought to love her that much. Had thought he could spend the rest of his life with her. Once, love had been a marvelous thing to him. Something to value, to desire.

"She was my first real love. Or so I thought. So I bit her. If she had been merely vampire she would have responded with a bite. We'd not bitten each other before. And in fact, when I'd brought it up she had always said she wanted to save it for the bonding. Which is why I knew she would accept my bite. Anyway…"

He pressed his hands to his knees and exhaled, taking a moment to fortify his courage. Did the scars burn? No, it was his imagination. But memory burned deep into his being.

"My faery wanted to get in on the action as well, so my wings unfurled. And in that moment, with my fangs embedded in her neck, she let out a blood-curdling howl and shifted into her demonic shape. That was the first time I suspected she was half demon. I didn't even consider she could be completely demon. I was stunned. Felt betrayed. But still, I wanted to love her, to believe she'd merely forgotten to tell me her truth.

"But then she started to spasm and react to the bite. Because while vampires can bite demons and come away with nothing more than a nasty mouthful of black blood, vampires who are also part faery really work a number on demons. Faery ichor can poison demons. And she got a good mouthful of my faery saliva. She screamed that she was *mimicus*, a breed of demon that is capable of mimicking other breeds.

"I freaked out. I didn't know what to do. So I took her home. Waiting for her was her entire denizen. They were oddly pleased to see me, and didn't give Octavia much attention. And…they were wearing protective armor. It didn't occur to me until later what it would protect them from. They moved in on me swiftly. While I was stricken by what I had done to her, I learned that she had been toying with me. A demon trying to lure a vampire into the denizen so they could have their way with me. But she had no idea what the rest of her denizen knew—that I was part faery.

"What happened next I could have never anticipated."

He spread his fingers over Zen's hand, clasping it tightly against his chest. Heartbeats raced and his skin was clammy. An inhale; gasped breath. Difficult not to fall back into that feeling of danger even though he knew it was long past.

"They tortured me. I don't know how long. Days? Weeks? Felt like forever. And that armor I'd wondered over? It protected the demons from my ichor-tainted blood. All the while, the leader kept bringing Octavia out to show me that she was slowly dying. That hurt me more than any talon to my heart could have. The denizen could have saved her. Could have used demonic magic to force the faery taint from her system, or even witch magic, but they didn't. They let her suffer. And I couldn't do anything to help her because at times I was stretched out on a rack being clawed and beaten and burned."

Zen shivered against him.

"At other times I was free to fend off the dozens of monsters who came at me tearing at my skin and muscles and digging their talons in deep."

She spread a hand over his back. "These are from that torture."

He nodded. "The scars mean nothing. What haunts me is that I couldn't help her. That she was a sacrifice merely for the denizen's twisted penchant for torturing others. No woman should be treated that way. Just left to die. And she wouldn't have died had I not bitten her. She received a small amount of faery taint, which was why it took her so long to die. It was my fault. And, Zen…" He breathed in deeply. "I loved her."

She hugged him so tightly he felt her heartbeats match the pace of his own. Rib to rib, skin to skin. Pulse to pulse. It was too wondrous. Did he deserve this woman?

"I'm sorry, Blade. You shouldn't have had to face that. But if she was lying to you…"

"Yes, she was tricking me, toying with me. It hurts my heart to admit that. But still, it was no reason to allow her to die."

"You're right. You are an honorable man. You wouldn't wish pain on anyone."

Yes, well. She did not know he wanted to slay all the demons now. And the more painful their demise the better.

She hugged him and just let him be still. The silence did not feel heavy or awkward. His breathing was calm yet his heartbeats ran. He'd just revealed a part of himself he had kept locked and sealed. That he had trusted her enough to reveal that was immense. She would honor his trust.

"What can I do?" she asked. "To make this easier for you to bear?"

"Just listening is good. I…don't normally do this. Spill my guts. But I thought you should know. She was demon, Zen. And with us being uncertain what, exactly, you are…"

"I understand. You don't want to make the leap to complete trust with me. You can't. I respect that."

"I trust you. I just don't know what you are. And… you should also know I made a deal with a stranger to kill the demons in the area."

"What?"

"He came to me in the Darkwood not long before I met you. Said the demons are rising, increasing their numbers. He asked me to annihilate them. At first I refused. But after slaying the demons who would have gone after you, I agreed to help. Innocent humans could be harmed. They all need to die, Zen."

She pulled away and turned to sit facing him. She ran a shaky hand over her hair. "I, uh, don't know what to say to that."

"I'm sorry."

And if she was a demon? His declaration that all demons needed to die went against his conviction to save the one demon who had tricked him into the torture into the first place.

If he had saved her, then how could he conceive of slaying so many others?

"I don't feel as if I am demon," Zen felt it necessary to state. "But then, I don't feel as if I am anything in particular." She spied the bowie knife lying on the floor beside Blade's combat boots and lunged to grab it. "Cut me," she said, handing him the blade. "I want to check again."

He took the knife and she held out her palm to him. "Don't worry. I'll heal."

Without a word, he drew the knife tip across her skin. Black blood bubbled up, then spilled in clear, glinting streams down the side of her hand before hitting the black bed sheet.

"No more blue," she said in awe.

"But still black," he offered.

"But then it turned clear. That's ichor, isn't it?"

He nodded. "It could be anything."

"Becoming." She whispered the word the witch had used. "What do you think I will become?"

He clasped her hand and kissed the back of it. "My ally," he said.

"Not in the fight against demons. I don't think... I don't want to be a part of that destruction. But I can stand by your side."

"How about you simply be my friend?"

"Really? You're willing to let me be a friend?"

"Actually, I think we've gone beyond that. What with the sex."

She glided a hand down his back. "You are an amazing lover, Blade. And to be honest, I think that was my first time."

He tilted a look at her. "Could have been. No regrets?"

"Never. I'd love to do it again. Anytime you're willing."

"Is that so?"

She nodded.

Blade twisted and pushed her back against the pillows. "How about a good-morning shag?"

"Does shag mean sex?"

"It does."

"I'm in."

Chapter 18

Zen got out of the shower first and called out that she was going to make breakfast for him today. Or maybe she'd said she was going to get the things ready for him to make breakfast. Blade wasn't sure she had the talent for cooking. Did she remember how? Had she ever cooked?

He turned off the shower. Probably better not to linger in case she did attempt to master the stove. Grabbing a towel, he patted his hair and stepped onto the tiled floor.

Immense relief had relaxed his very being after telling Zen his history with demons. With one demon in particular. He could never forgive himself for biting Octavia. He blamed his vampire for the bite and he blamed his faery for delivering the deadly poison. But really? He was responsible for himself, all of himself. That included vampire and faery. And if one got out of line, it was his responsibility to kick it back in line.

Thing was, the vampire was so strong. Yet it was his faery that craved the demon blood. He had to keep his winged desires in check. That was easy enough. He wasn't sure he'd ever fall so deeply again that he'd feel compelled to mate with a woman and bite her. And until Zen knew what she was he could have sex with her, befriend her—hell, he could even fall in love. But that didn't have to mean forever.

Fall in love? No. He'd meant it when he'd offered his brother condolences after he'd admitted to being in love with his wife. Love was...tough.

But since when had he resisted a challenge?

Smirking and shaking his head, he finished drying off. In the bedroom he slipped on jeans. Raking his fingers through his hair was sufficient. From the smell that wafted in from the kitchen something was up.

A cloud of smoke hung over the stove. Blade hustled by a fleeing Oogie and commandeered the spatula from Zen.

"Sorry," she said. "I didn't think eggs could burn."

"It's okay. I can rescue them. Why don't you get the juice and toast on the table?"

"How did you become such a master chef?" she asked as she plopped two pieces of bread into the toaster. She wore one of his longer T-shirts and nothing else. The neckline spilled over one shoulder, attracting his eye. And his kiss. She met his gaze after that kiss and he winked at her.

"Cooking breakfast hardly qualifies me as a master. My mom used to let us help her in the kitchen when we were little. We all picked up a talent. I think by the time we were in our teens Mom had trained us so well we could cook the entire day's meals and she didn't have to lift a finger."

"Smart mom. You said she is faery?"

"Yes, and so is my brother Kelyn."

"When you shifted last night behind the theater, besides the obvious wings, your body changed subtly."

"That was my faery shape. Same me, just…bulkier."

"That's interesting. I would expect a faery to be slender and, well, fae."

"They come in all shape and sizes. Just like humans."

She hugged him around the waist and kissed his biceps. He didn't mind the closeness. She liked closeness. He could live with that. And she smelled so good, despite the lingering burn scent. Freshly showered and like a spring blossom.

"Can you bring your wings out without shifting?" she asked.

"I can, but rarely do."

"Because it's a sex thing?"

He chuckled. "You really like sex, don't you?"

"I don't understand why anyone wouldn't like it. Anything wrong with wanting to learn all I can about it?" she asked playfully as her fingers slipped beneath his "Do you want to eat or have sex?"

Her bright eyes flashed up at him. "Do you really have to ask?"

He turned off the burner, setting the eggs, which were a lost cause, aside. He swung around, catching Zen at the waist and set her down on the counter beside the sink. She pulled off the T-shirt, rendering her naked, and he kissed her breasts.

"Mmm, that's one of my favorites," she said. "You can do that as much as you like." She wrapped her legs about his bare torso.

"Is it always this awesome when people have sex?" she asked, gliding her fingers down his wet hair. "Why aren't people constantly doing this? I mean, who has time to eat or sleep when you can kiss and touch and, oh…I like that."

He suckled her nipple and teased at the skin with the tip of his fang. It was a brief glide of tooth over flesh, nothing promising, because he couldn't promise the bite. Much as he desired it. Her blood had been black and ichor laced last night. But there was no guarantee some angel blood did not linger.

"I'll show you what I'd prefer over eggs for breakfast," he whispered in her ear, then glided down to part her legs and kiss her copper thatch.

Zen chirped a surprised sound, then settled into the feeling. She lay back across the counter and allowed him to put her legs over his shoulders. Eventually her head tilted into the sink, so he moved her down onto the floor.

Half an hour later, he picked her up from the floor and carried her into the bedroom so they could finally get dressed.

"Why don't I give you a ride into town," he suggested. "You can pick up your car and pay off the room bill."

"Why? Don't I need the room anymore?"

He shrugged. "If you want to, you can stay here for a while. I'll have a talk with Oogie. Let him know you're cool."

"I'd like that. I can do some more shopping while in town, as well. I really enjoy shopping."

"I'll drop you off, then we'll meet later at Panera for the breakfast we ignored earlier. Deal?"

"Deal."

After he'd dropped Zen off at the inn, Blade drove into the filling station and topped off the gas tank. Then he stopped in at the local hardware store. Stryke had emailed a list of tools for him to pick up. Though they had hired a construction firm to build the compound, Stryke was also working on a porch for the main house. Said Blyss liked to sit out there on a swinging bench in the summer. And he wanted a place for the baby to play without toddling too far into the yard.

Stryke would probably be an overprotective father. Blade thought it would be wiser to let the infant run. Unless Stryke carried some latent faery or vampire in him, his child would be born werewolf. Its instincts would be to run free.

But what did he know about child rearing?

Blade wondered if a half-breed man could ever have a child with a woman of unknown nature. Then he caught himself and shook his head at such erratic thoughts. Children were not for him. He could barely get the love thing right.

Hadn't he fallen in love too quickly with the demoness Octavia? He didn't want to analyze it. He'd spent far too much time lamenting that decision in the days and weeks following her death.

Right now, he felt as though life nudged him to move forward. To set his past aside, and—though it could never be forgotten—forge a new future. The feeling was light, and as soon as he recognized it, he again shook his head.

Not in the cards for this unforgivable bastard.

Especially an unforgivable bastard who was currently on a crusade to assassinate every living demon he laid eyes on—as well as the undead ones. Yeah, there were breeds that were classified as undead.

Strolling past a coffee shop, he paused. The rich scent of dark roast curled into his nostrils and drew him in. He ordered a venti black, no cream, and then headed around the corner, down the alleyway. He had parked three blocks down from the hardware store. The town was small, which meant little to no parking, and it was Blade's habit to choose an out-of-the-way spot. One never knew when a demon—or angel—might leap out from nowhere. Best to contain any encounters and keep them from public eyesight as much as possible.

Striding through a shadow cast by a church steeple— he wasn't baptized, so holy objects and images had no power over him—Blade was suddenly ripped from his strides. His back slammed against a brick wall. Coffee splattered the concrete.

He reacted by swinging a punch toward the blond man's narrow face, but his fist stopped an inch from nose. Impact did not happen, and yet his knuckles crunched as if he'd just punched a steel wall.

The man dropped him and stepped back. Splaying his fingers up near his face revealed the dark markings on his skin. "Runes to ward me against whatever the hell you are, *hic niger est*."

"Who are you?" Blade asked of the creature who'd said he had a dark heart.

"Ah? You don't care *what* I am?"

"You're demon." Blade spat at the ground near the man's booted feet. He was as tall as he but slim, and his short blond hair was slicked back tightly against his scalp, the severe coif revealing the nubs of horns above each ear. "You've got two seconds before I kill you."

"Give it a go. Unlike the other demons you've slain thus far, I have come to this realm protected."

Blade afforded a more studied look over the runes marked in crossed black lines all over the demon's fingers, hands and neck. Below his ears ran a trail of the marks, as well. The demon's eyes flickered red, then resumed a fathomless black iris.

The demon offered his hand to shake. "Kesabel, Lord of the Casipheans. And you are Blade Saint-Pierre."

"What do you want?" Blade asked, ignoring the offer to shake.

Again the demon gripped him by the throat and slammed him to the wall. Blade's feet momentarily left the ground. He aimed a fist for the demon's gut but his knuckles crunched against an invisible steel barrier.

"Quit killing us," the demon hissed. "We are not the bad guys."

"Yeah? Then, why are you trying to kill Zen?"

"Is that what she told you?"

"She didn't have to tell me anything. I saw the trio you sent after her."

"They were sent to persuade her toward the portal. For some reason she has been able to resist our efforts. A major fuckup in the plan, let me tell you."

"What plan? To murder an innocent woman?"

The demon dropped Blade's throat. "We're on her side." Spreading out his arms, he declared royally, "She is our queen."

Chapter 19

Blade considered asking the demon to repeat himself. But there was no need. His hearing was excellent.

Zen was their *queen*? Whose queen? If she was any kind of paranormal breed, she was an angel. Though, there was the case of her blue blood turning black. Which was no longer blue but now black and then clear.

"Yes, I can see your confusion," the demon Kesabel offered. He stabbed the air. "Allow me to explain how the fallen angel you've hooked up with was supposed to fall all the way to Daemonia, yet, for some reason, did not."

"You're lying."

The demon spread his arms out. "I have no reason to."

"It is the demonic nature to speak mistruths. Always. You are trying to get me on your side so you can get your hands on Zen."

"I do want to get my hands on her, but I need her alive. The Casiphean queen must be crowned, and that can only occur in Daemonia."

"Casiphean?" Blade had heard the breed name, but that was all. He'd spent more time lamenting his involvement with the *mimicus* to bother learning about any other in the vast profusion of demonic breeds.

Kesabel nodded. "You don't know much about demons, do you?"

"I know I don't like you."

"Yes, well, I am familiar with your troubles regarding a denizen of *mimicus*. Tough bit of luck, eh?"

The scars on Blade's back twinged. "You could say that."

"And now it seems you've a death wish for all our species."

"You could say that, too."

"Isn't really fair, is it? To make all suffer for the sins of so few?"

The demon had no right to place himself above others when it concerned sin. "I thought we were talking about Zen. She is a fallen angel. I'm sure of it. She has her halo."

"Yes, you've guessed correctly about her. Fallen from Above. Yet she was supposed to fall to Daemonia. Why she stopped here on the mortal realm is beyond me. It was destined that she would become our queen. She should have been on board with the plan before falling. All she had to do was—" the demon spread out his arms "—spread her wings and let gravity do the rest."

"She landed here in Tangle Lake," Blade said.

Maybe. If she'd walked the world, as he suspected, then she could have landed anywhere. Tangle Lake may have just been a spot on her route to consume knowledge.

He wasn't trying to fill in details for the demon. He was attempting to piece this together for himself. He didn't trust the demon Kesabel as far as he could spit, but he'd listen. Until the urge struck to slice him in two.

"If you're so keen on welcoming her into your folds as queen," Blade said, "then, why the death threats?"

"Oh, we haven't laid a hand on her. Think about it."

He wasn't going to—but, really? The demons in the house hadn't gone near Zen. Because he had stopped them before they could leave the house. The demons in the club hadn't touched her, either. They had tried to lure her into the portal, though. Beyond that, it had only been *angels* who had attempted to physically harm Zen.

"You were the one who thought it would be a good idea to slay my minions in the house by the field," Kesabel said. "And you and that damned werewolf brother of yours thought it would be fun to slay an entire club filled with my kind. You get some kind of sexual thrill from that, buddy? Taking the lives of innocents?"

Demons were never innocent. But Blade wouldn't give the man the challenge of a protest.

"Right. You're not going to speak when you know I'm in the right," Kesabel said. "You, vampire, like the taste of demon blood. That is known."

Blade flinched at that statement. So his faery half craved demon blood. But it was known? Of course, Sim had said as much to him, as well. What was it with all the riffraff knowing so much about him and what it was that got him off?

"The only time I'm aware that Zenia has ever been in danger is when those damned angels landed," Kesabel provided. "They want to take her out before we can lure her to Daemonia. Or so it appears. Those holier-than-thou assholes are possessive. Even though she's no longer of their lofty caliber, they'd rather kill her than see we Casipheans gain our queen."

"*Lure* her to Daemonia?"

"Yes. You see, it's not as if we can tie her up and take her there. She has to sit on the throne voluntarily. Thus, the portal in the club. It's a straight shot to Daemonia from there. If you'll just allow her to return to the night-club, that'll take care of matters nicely."

That was going to happen never. Unless Zen wanted to be queen. The woman did have amnesia.

"What if she doesn't want to be your queen?"

"Oh, she does. That's the very reason she fell."

"But she doesn't remember that."

"She—what?"

"So you don't know everything." Blade crossed his arms and spread his feet for a commanding stance. "Zen has amnesia. She doesn't know who or what she was or where she came from. You might believe she's your queen, but she doesn't know that."

"Well, that's a bit of tough balls." The demon's temples flared and the tips of the horn nubs briefly glowed red. "I sense we won't have any luck luring her to the throne until she gets her memory back."

"Why would you crown an angel your queen anyway?"

"She is no longer angel. The moment she landed on earth her angelic nature vaporized, so to speak. Though I've never heard of an angel losing their memory from landing in the mortal realm. Most arrive without memory of their angelic rank, but they walk the world to gain knowledge so they can insinuate into this realm."

"She was hit by a bus."

"Is that so?" Kesabel noticeably shuddered. "So she's in memory limbo."

"So is Zen demon?" Blade had to ask.

"She'll not become completely demon until she takes the throne."

Blade hissed. Hell, she was demon. Or would be soon enough.

And he had sworn to slay any demon that crossed his path. This was not good. Worse than not good. It sucked fifty ways to Beneath. But just because the demon talked a feasible story didn't mean he was speaking the truth.

"But until that occurs," Kesabel continued, "she is a sort of nothing, if you will. Much closer to faery, actually, than angel or demon. That's what happens when an angel doesn't quite make it to demon. They become sidhe. Curse those bastard angels! There is a time frame we are working with. Not sure how long it'll require for her faery to completely settle in. I'm pleased you let me in on the amnesia issue, despite the new challenge this presents."

Shit. No points for helping the enemy.

"So," Kesabel said, "I'll be needing you to, A, stop slaying my Casiphean denizen. Our race is dying out. It's why we need the queen in the first place, to repopulate our numbers. And, B, take the girl out for a night of dancing at the club and then ditch her and leave her to bigger and better things."

Repopulate their numbers? Blade didn't want to consider how that one would go down. No matter what Zen remembered, or wanted to do, he could not allow her to be used in such a manner.

Fingers curling into fists at his sides, Blade said, "How about C? None of the above."

The demon thrust Blade against the wall with but a flick of his wrist. "Don't make me call in the big guns, vampire."

Blade smirked. He liked a challenge. "The bigger the better. Now fuck off. And stay away from Zen. If I see one of you sulfurheads near her, I will slay you."

The demon exhaled heavily and shook his head. "You don't want this war, Saint-Pierre. And yet, it seems you invite trouble around every corner. Perhaps it is your nature. You cannot exist without strife?"

He'd love to live a peaceful life without war. Or demons.

"Bring it," Blade muttered. He wandered off, leaving the demon lurking in the shadows.

"Help!"

Zen looked up from the coffee she was stirring. Outside the café window a woman whose arms were loaded with two toddlers was trying to catch the handle of a stroller, in which lay a baby, as it rolled toward the street. A big black car veered near the curb.

Dashing out from the table and through the café doors, Zen yelled at the driver, but knew that he wouldn't hear her through the car's rolled-up windows. She dodged the mother who was crying and— why didn't she set the kids down?

Without thinking Zen lunged toward the stroller. Its front wheels rolled off the curb. The stroller tilted forward. The sun glinted on the car's chrome bumper, but a foot away from the infant carrier.

She felt the warm body under her palm and curled her fingers about an arm or leg, grasping more baby with her other hand, and snatched it just as the bumper hit the stroller and sent it soaring through the air.

The mother screamed.

Zen tilted her body backward, landing on the concrete sidewalk, the infant clutched against her chest. She fell to her back and pulled up her legs from the street.

"She's got the baby!" someone said.

Above her, two faces appeared. Zen handed up the infant and it was delivered to the distraught mother. Heartbeats thundered. Adrenaline raced. And in the moment the sun flickered in her eyes, Zen's memory burst with a familiar reckoning.

You came here with a purpose. You are from Above.

And she knew what she was.

A hand lifted her by the arm and asked if she was all right. Zen nodded. "Yes, okay." She walked away, even as someone followed her, asking her to stay because she was a hero.

"Anyone would have done it," she muttered and quickened her steps away from the growing crowd around the mother and her children.

"I…" She pressed fingers to her temples. "I remember."

Chapter 20

Blade grabbed the newly purchased tools out of the truck bed and carried them up to Stryke's work shed. His brother wasn't around, which was a good thing. Blade's mind was anywhere but in the moment. It was still back in the alleyway, shoved up against the wall by that arrogant demon.

Kesabel? Did he know someone, anyone, who had knowledge of demons and who might tell him something about the pale intruder? Maybe Dez, who studied diabology, could help him?

None of that mattered right now. Zen was destined to become a demon queen? That was twenty ways wrong. She'd fallen from Above with the intention of being crowned queen.

So why was he trying to stop that from happening?

Because until now he hadn't known it was supposed to go down that way. And now that he did, what would he do? Would it be fair to Zen to force her to become something she had no knowledge of agreeing to? Maybe being crowned the Casiphean queen would bring back her memory?

Only one thing mattered. Zen was destined to become demon. And that trumped all.

He'd opened his home and his life to a woman who was demon. Or who was supposed to become demon. But according to Kesabel, if she remained in this realm for much longer she could instead become faery.

He set the skill saw on a workbench and decided against leaving Stryke a note. His brother would figure things out when he saw the tools. Hopping back into the rusty old white Ford he'd driven because his usual ride did indeed need a new radiator, Blade shifted into gear, but didn't take his foot off the brake pedal. "Ah, hell, I forgot."

He was supposed to meet Zen at Panera. And… He glanced at the dashboard clock. He was an hour late.

He tugged out his cell phone, then remembered she didn't have a phone. Nor did she know her real name. Neither did she know her wicked destiny.

Gripping the steering wheel he squeezed.

Could he tell her? Had he a right to tell her? What if he kept this information to himself? He could continue to slay any demon that went near Zen and take out the occasional angel, as well. She'd never have to know.

As long as she never got back her memory.

"Stupid," he muttered, and shifted into gear, letting the truck roll down the gravel road. The two of them had started something. A relationship of sorts. Maybe? He'd been firm about not being friends with her. Look what had come of that.

It was a relationship. And that bond demanded truth and trust. "I have to tell her."

And then it would be up to Zen to decide which direction her future would move—toward continuing the relationship with him, or toward Daemonia.

Blade knew what he wanted her to decide. He didn't want to hope, either, but somewhere along the line he'd fallen for the woman. Fangs, wings and heart.

Pulling into the garage beneath the loft, Blade was relieved to see Zen's Mini parked outside. Of course, he had invited her to stay with him. She had nowhere else to go.

He'd invited a demon queen to stay with him. What. The. Hell?

And she would probably be angry. He had stood her up for lunch.

So the best way to do this, he decided as he strode up the stairs, was to blurt out everything he had to say right away. Distract her from his mistake of being late. Make it all about her. Because it was.

This situation had become all about her in all the wrong ways.

He couldn't think about it that way. She deserved compassion and understanding. And probably a place to sit and a shoulder to cry on after he revealed her truth. He could do that. He wanted to do that. Because Zen meant something to him. And yet the thought to push her away was strong.

He smelled something savory as he topped the stairs and Oogie scampered up to curl about his ankle. She was cooking again? This could not end well.

Bending to give the attention-starved feline a scratch at the base of his spine, Blade scooped up the purring cat and wandered toward the kitchen. Zen pulled a couple bowls out of the microwave oven. Oogie didn't even flinch when he entered the kitchen. Had the two come to some kind of understanding?

She spied him. "Oh, hi! I'm so sorry, but I missed our date."

"Uh, you did?"

Oogie squirmed in his grasp so he let the now-nervous cat drop to the floor to race out of the room. Did the cat know what she really was? Oogie liked demons less than Blade did. Hell, Oogie had known all along. What an idiot he had been not to pay more attention to his pet's discomfort around her.

"So we missed our date. But you brought home supper?" he asked.

"As an apology. I was so busy shopping—I really like shopping. And I got this!" She shifted her hip forward to display the rhinestone-encrusted belt wrapped around her pink sundress. The woman did love to sparkle. "Anyway, the time slipped away from me. It's baked potato soup with bacon and cheese. Doesn't that sound delicious? And I didn't cook it. It's from the restaurant, so it's safe. Oh! Guess what?"

"I, uh…"

She wasn't angry. She was just her usual, gorgeous, bright self. Completely unaware. And always trying to please him, of all things.

"Zen, we need to talk. I learned something today—"

"So did I." She set the bowls on the counter and took his hand. "I rescued a baby."

"You—what?" This conversation was all over the place. Blade needed to give her the truth about herself. Before he chickened out and decided to keep it to himself. "Listen, Zen, there's something you should know."

"Exactly." She beamed up at him, her eyes as bright as rhinestones. "I *do* know. Blade, after I rescued the baby, I experienced this weird zinging jolt to my head. And then…"

"And then?"

"I remembered." She grabbed his hands and bounced with giddy glee. "I know who I am."

Chapter 21

Her eyes were emerald, Blade realized. Not kaleido-scope, as would be an angel's eyes. Nor were they red, as would be a demon's eyes. Not even violet, indica-tive of the sidhe. And she stood...straighter. With more poise than he had noted up to this point. She exuded well-being and a certain strength. Confidence. Not to mention the effusive joy that spilled from her like sun-shine.

She had come into herself. Because she had remem-bered. And Blade found himself walking up to her to be close, a part of her excitement, and yet, at the same time, his heart cringed and dropped.

She knew.

Would she walk away from him now? Go on to be-come a demon queen? The thought was revolting to him. But was it more because of the idea of losing someone who was a species he hated or whom he was starting to care about?

She took his hands and was literally bouncing on her toes. "I fell," she said. "And I am meant to be the Casiphean queen."

Yep, she knew it all. Damn. He'd lost this one. But had she ever been his? Did it matter to him?

Yes. Damn it, yes. She'd touched his scars. She'd kissed them. Had accepted him.

"So you know that you were once an angel?" he asked.

She nodded. "I fell with a purpose. Or so I assume. I know who I was and that I fell to become a queen, but there's some fuzzy stuff in there, too. It'll probably come back to me slowly. Or who knows? Maybe it'll pop back into my head if I have another harrowing moment like the one with the baby."

"The baby?"

"I saved a baby from being hit by a car. I think, in that moment, with my heart pumping and my body out of sorts, is when it all returned. Anyway, I know there is a denizen of demons awaiting their queen."

"And…you're eager to join them?"

"Well." She squeezed his hand and settled her enthusiasm. "I know how you feel about demons. I'm so sorry to give you this news."

"No, that's okay." It was far from okay, but he wasn't going to spoil her good mood. He had no right. "My only goal was to help you get your memory back. Now you have it. What happens next…" No, he couldn't tell her what he wanted to happen next. "You gotta do what you gotta do."

"And so do you. Which is slaying demons. Does that mean you're going to slay me now?"

"Don't be ridiculous." He crossed his arms over his

chest. Yeah, put up a shield. Easier that way. "You still bleeding ichor as well as the black stuff?"

"Not sure. Do you want to check again?"

"No, that's uh…"

Words felt wrong. He could never harm her. But could she really walk away from him and put on a demon crown like a pretty accessory? Never looking back at what could have been?

What could have been with him. Ah, hell, he'd gone and started caring for this woman. Just like before.

And just like before, she was demon.

But at least this time he had advance warning of her nature. Not that it would do his hurting heart any good. The damage had been done.

She'd touched him.

"Blade." She stroked his hair and caressed his cheek. He almost pulled away, but then he realized if he did, he might be pulling away from the last touch she would ever give him. "What we've started? I like it. The sex. The sharing and companionship. The trust."

Trust was everything. And now he could not trust her.

Or could he?

"But I've always had it in the back of my mind that you would never commit to me," she continued. "Because you couldn't be sure what I was."

"And now I know."

"And it's not your favorite species in the world. Well. I'm not demon yet. Right now I'm sort of in the middle. Becoming, like the witch said. I could become faery if I stayed here on the mortal realm."

"But you won't do that because you have a goal. A destiny."

"Yes. Destiny." She sighed. Her giddy smile did

not escape his notice. But she saw him looking at her and pulled on a straight face. "You're upset. Do you… Blade, do you care about me?"

If he lied he'd lose her. If he told the truth, his heart would break. He didn't like either option.

She bracketed his head, slipping her fingers through his hair, and kissed him. Urgently. Deeply. Forever. And it felt as though he was falling alongside an angel swiftly plummeting from Above. Her wings enveloped him and he felt safe—yet leery. He didn't want either of them to land. Could he stop this fall and keep her in a free fall forever?

He wrapped his hands around her back and pulled her in. What luck that the second time he should find someone to care about she turned out to be another demon. Did the gods have something against him? Was he never meant to be happy?

Don't think about it. Take this kiss. Remember it. Never forget the intensity of it. The soft regard of it. The knowing that it was more right than any kiss he'd ever had before.

Take the fall.

Because Zen made him realize that it didn't matter what you were but who you were. What went on in your thoughts, and how you responded to the actions of others. To arrogantly assume that all demons should die simply because one group of them had hurt him? How dare he? He wasn't making the world a better place. He was harming it. Demon by demon.

Blade stood back, still holding Zen's head between his hands. He pressed his forehead to hers. He wanted to ask her, to beg her to stay. To be his. To be the demon he could welcome without judgment.

To be his woman.

But something kept that want from leaping free.

She pulled his hands from her head, and as she lowered them, he reluctantly dropped their connection. "I'm heading to the club tonight," she said. "You know, the place with the portal."

Whoa. She was moving fast. And with a determination that felt similar to when he'd been going after demons.

"There's just one thing," she said, and she turned to pick up the halo from the couch. "I'm not sure why I held on to this. Like I said, some things are fuzzy. But it'll be a nice souvenir, I guess. I'll see if I can take it with me."

So it was as easy as that for her? Memory returned. Back to her mission. Leave the vampire standing in the lurch.

Of course it had to be that easy.

"What's wrong, Blade?"

"I, uh…" Sighing out his apprehension, Blade pulled back his shoulders and blurted out what had to be said, "I talked to Kesabel earlier today."

"Kesabel?"

"You don't know that name?" Shouldn't she know the leader of the demon denizen she was to eventually help repopulate? Although, he wasn't sure if Kesabel was the leader. He had named himself lord of the Casipheans. Whatever that meant. "He's demon. The Casiphean agent come to this realm to ensure you complete your journey to Daemonia."

"Oh. So you knew? Why didn't you say anything?"

"I was going to, but you and your happy bouncing feet beat me to it."

She nodded. Bounced once more. "It's pretty cool, isn't it?"

No. Not cool at all.

"You betcha. Cool. Are you sure about this, Zen? I mean, you don't even know these demons. And to become their queen… That's a big commitment."

"Oh, listen to you, the master of avoiding commitment."

That snarky response slapped Blade across the face as if her hand had done it. He touched his cheek, because the feeling was that palpable. "I suppose you did want this. It's why you fell."

She nodded. "I can't say why I want this, but if I made the fall it must have been for good reason. So you want some soup?"

Soup? What the— On to a new tangent when he was still drowning in the reality of her truth? Blade shoved his hands into his jeans' pockets. "I'm not hungry. But thanks for thinking of me."

"Then, I should probably get going. Things to do before I leave. I was going to donate the car to a homeless shelter. Would that be okay?"

She had really thought this through. "Great idea." He forced on a smile.

"Then, I'll be seeing you!"

She grabbed the backpack by the fridge and headed toward the stairs. Blade couldn't bring himself to call out to her, to ask her to reconsider. To stay. To stop the fall to Daemonia.

She had a mission. He had no right to stop her.

And he had made the fall—only to crash, wings splayed and heart completely shattered.

Zen drove mindlessly toward town. The birch trees lining the gravel road shushed by like slats on a fence and revealed open field at the stop where she turned left and drove toward Tangle Lake.

She'd had to leave Blade's place quickly. And without lingering in that incredible kiss. A kiss that had felt like falling. A good kind of falling. But to stay and draw out her exit would have killed her.

Why had she had to remember that she was waited for by an entire demon race? That they needed her to take her place as their queen? To marry and repopulate a dying breed. She'd not told Blade that part. He wouldn't have taken it lightly.

"I'm a queen?" she muttered. And then with the pride it instilled within her, she announced, "I'm a queen. That's cool. Right? Queens get crowns. I could so rock a crown."

Her fingers curved tightly about the steering wheel as anxiety reared up. "Why?" she asked. She didn't want to lead a denizen of demons. Or an entire race. She didn't need the crown. She just wanted to stand in Blade's arms and know he loved her.

But she'd had to leave. Because he'd never said he loved her.

The man—vampire, faery—had just been helping her to get her memory back. A man who had been hurt in the past because he had loved a demoness. There was no way she could expect him to accept her truth now.

She had lost him.

As much as she'd wanted to stay, leaving had been her only option.

She touched her mouth, trying to remember the irrepressible heat of his kiss. Too quickly it faded. She couldn't remember his mouth against hers. She needed that feeling back!

Slowing at a stop sign at the entry to town, she

shifted into Park and bowed her head against the steering wheel.

"I don't want to do this."

But she had been destined to this. By falling she had taken on the task, had agreed to this monumental undertaking. She mustn't disappoint the Casipheans. For if she did, might she risk their anger and a rage of demons storming this mortal realm?

If Blade thought he could take out the few demons that tread this earth now, he'd never be able to handle an entire rage. She had to do this. To save Blade.

Chapter 22

A shout from outside the barn alerted Blade. He rested his elbows on the battered hood of the truck. There was no saving this heap. The angel had obliterated the radiator and the surrounding engine and he bet Beck would tell him he needed to install a whole new engine. He had a few vehicles to choose from to drive, so he'd junk this one. The rusted white Ford had started to leak oil when he'd returned home earlier so he'd drive the Mustang for a while.

The shout came again and he recognized it as his father's voice.

"In here!" Blade called. He flexed his fingers in and out of fists. He wasn't in the mood to talk to anyone.

Zen had run away from him. She hadn't been able to get away from him fast enough. Away, and then on to Daemonia. Where she would be crowned a queen. That had to count for something.

And really, he knew not all demons were evil. He just didn't like them as a species. And he had every right to that opinion.

But he needed to talk to Sim. This was no longer his war. Blade couldn't, in good conscience, slay the next demon he saw. Not if it was Zen.

"What the hell happened to the truck?" Kai asked as he strolled into the evening shadows of the garage. His father wore a T-shirt, suede jeans and was barefoot. The lack of footwear was a wolf thing that Blade had picked up as a child.

"Had a disagreement with an angel." He wiped the grease from his hands on a cloth, then tossed it aside to the open toolbox. "What's up, Dad?"

"I do believe I've outdone myself."

Kai pulled a sword from behind his back and handed it, hilt up, to Blade. "All it took was some of your mother's faery dust, and I was able to manipulate the metal. Still don't know what kind of metal it is, but it's strong and true. This blade needs but to whisper across flesh to draw a deep cut."

The sword blade was about a foot and a half long, and it was wide, honed to cut along each edge. It gleamed and seemed to sing as Blade turned it side to side to look it over. The hilt was simple, wrapped in black leather and impressed with the Saint-Pierre monogram. Yet where the blade joined the hilt words had been impressed in a language Blade did not understand.

"Sidhe writing?"

"It means *warrior*," Kai offered. "Your mother thought it appropriate for you. Can't say that I ever wish for you to be in a situation where you'd need such a weapon, but if so, then you will be well armed. You like it?"

"It's amazing, Dad." He swung the sword, testing the weight. It was light, and yet as he curved through the thrust, the weapon carried a definite direction, a focus. Wielding this he could take out a line of demons with but a sweep of his hand. Or one pissed-off angel. "Thank you."

"My pleasure. It'll probably kill angels. Uh, you don't think there are any more angels walking around Tangle Lake, do you?"

"Not sure." Because if they were determined to stop Zen from making it to Daemonia, now would be the time to kick it into high gear and invade. Did Kesabel know about the angels who were after his queen? "Zen got her memory back."

"Yeah? So what's up with her?"

"She's a fallen angel who was supposed to fall all the way to Daemonia to become the Casiphean queen."

Kai was rarely speechless, but that announcement hit its mark. His dad leaned a palm on the truck bed and raked fingers through his shoulder-length hair.

"She remembered falling, and that she has a mission," Blade explained. "She was hit by the bus, so some memories are a little fuzzy."

"Yikes. So why didn't she fall all the way to Daemonia? Why stop on this realm? I can't imagine the bus stopped such a momentous fall."

"That's the question. And—" Blade swung the sword before him in an exact cut through the air "—she's still got her halo."

"I thought the halo fell away from the angel during the fall?" Kai said.

"Exactly. So she must have been holding it."

And then it hit him like a demon fist colliding with

his heart. Blade's jaw dropped open. Nothing felt more true to him. Nothing.

"Because she didn't want to go all the way to Daemonia," he muttered.

"What?" Kai asked.

"Dad, I think having the halo in hand kept her here on this realm. Has to be," he said, working the options through. "She didn't want to become their queen."

"But why not?"

He met his dad's wondering gaze. "I have no idea. But I don't have time to wonder. I've got to save Zen before she makes a huge mistake. Will you lock up for me?"

Blade grabbed the keys for the 1964 Mustang he'd fixed last year but which was still waiting for a coat of paint. He slid in behind the steering wheel.

"Need me to come along?" Kai called as Blade backed out of the garage.

He could use backup. But he wasn't about to put his father in danger. His mother would never forgive him. "I've got this, Dad! If you see Trouble, tell him I went back to the club."

Because if Trouble showed, then he'd have all the help he needed.

"I'll give him a call!" Kai said, waving him off. "Is she worth it?"

Blade backed the Mustang down the gravel driveway. Worth it? Hell yes.

Zen entered the mansion with a confidence that virtually floated her across the marble floor. The dancing crowd silenced at the sight of her. They were people. And demons. Or maybe demons that wore a human disguise. All eyes were red. And it didn't disturb her.

Because they were *her* people.

Or that was what she told herself. She didn't really have a people at the moment. She wasn't fully demon. Nor was she fully angel. She could become…

Could she toss the crown aside and become something else?

She paused at the edge of the dance floor that now flickered to darkness as the music was pulled to a halt. A few dancers looked around like "what happened?" until they noticed her standing there in a simple yellow dress that fluttered to below her knees. Were they all stuck in this nightclub endlessly dancing in wait to lure her toward the portal?

The thought creeped her out. Why not just walk up and ask, "Will you join us? Be our queen?"

The demons on the dance floor separated to form an open aisle for her that led up to the pulsating red oval of—now she was close enough to see it—fire. A fire that blazed yet didn't seem to give off heat.

The doorway to her destiny. The beginning of her life as a queen who would repopulate the Casiphean denizens and bring—well, she was fuzzy on the details.

Just like she was still unclear on how she'd landed in Tangle Lake. Angels never failed in their course. So why had she?

The clank of the halo, secured at the thin rhinestone chain she'd belted around her waist, alerted her. She shouldn't have brought it along. The Casipheans would view it as something that belonged to their enemy.

Really? If she had originated as the enemy, why now did she intend to walk through the portal to become their queen? Another question that didn't make sense. But she was missing all the information that would put the pieces together and show her the complete picture.

Zen didn't want to turn and look over her shoulder for him.

But she did.

Why she thought Blade would be standing there in the center of the aisle, arms held out to receive her was a question she could not answer. And shouldn't answer. She had a duty. All those standing in silence around her waited for her to accept that calling.

She turned toward the portal, trying to avoid eye contact, but it was impossible not to. Red eyes looked hopeful. Even pleading. Some thrust back their shoulders in defiance, while the ones standing next to them clasped their hands, settling their ire.

Zen set her gaze straight ahead for the portal even as a vile shriek echoed up from the ranks at the back of the nightclub. Demons all around her mobilized. Feet scuffled and the ripple of wings unfurled. While a few remained at her side, bowing, encouraging her to walk forward into the flames, she was aware of so many others who shifted into their demonic forms and soared away.

As if in defense.

Swinging the halo blade obliterated the vanguard of demons charging Blade. Black blood spattered his face and shoulders. He licked it off his lips. The faery in him grinned. *Oh, yeah, that hit the spot.* His fangs descended, eager for a longer, deeper drink.

He didn't hesitate on the upswing, returning the blade across the throats and chests of the next assault. From behind, he was attacked. Claws cut through his shirt and skin. Teeth gnawed at his boot. He kicked aimlessly, and managed to unloose the ravenous threat.

Ahead, the flaming portal glowed. And silhouetted

before it stood Zen, looking small and alone, lost in a greater plan that he feared might swallow her up. She couldn't step through that portal until she knew what he had guessed. He had to at least try to make her hear him.

Taking a fist to his jaw, he growled at the perpetrator. He grabbed him by the shoulder and sank his fangs into the sinuous black-fleshed neck. Lusciously bitter demon blood oozed over his palate. It tasted so good. Because of the ichor running through his system, and in his saliva, the demon yowled from the burning bite and scrambled off, clutching its neck. It wouldn't survive long.

"Zen!" His shout was lost in the melee of crazed demons who wanted to ensure their queen made it to the throne. "Zen!"

She was so close. Blade took a knee-bending hit to the back of his legs. Felt as if he'd been plowed into by a truck. He wobbled, grasping at the closest thing—a demon's bald and slimy head—to break his fall. An inhale filled his lungs with sulfur. His faery pleaded for release. And just as he began to unfurl his wings, the next injury he took was a deep cut to his chest that spilled out his blood, dazzled with ichor. The attacker retreated from the sting of the ichor. It could eat away a demon's skin in seconds.

Now thoroughly angered, Blade unfurled his wings. The serrated edges cut through demon throats and appendages and sent some fleeing, while others dived for him, only to be slashed away by a precise sweep of wing.

Ahead, a wall of demons began to form, literally, demons climbing atop one another's shoulders and linking arms before the dance floor to block him from getting near Zen.

Blade charged the wall. Wings lifting him into a soar, he glided to the top of the demonic wall and slashed the halo sword. He managed to bring down three from the top row, which then toppled them all.

And behind them Zen turned to see Blade land on the dance floor twenty feet away from where she stood. He spread his wings wide to prevent the demons from getting near her, but felt the enemy beat against his wings repeatedly. He couldn't hold them off much longer.

"You held the halo tight so you wouldn't land in Daemonia!" he yelled. "You don't want this, Zen. Don't go!"

She unlatched the halo secured at her hip and looked at it. A crew of demons that flanked her gestured for her to walk toward the portal. Of course, they couldn't touch her, or even push her through. As Kesabel had explained, she had to enter Daemonia of her free will.

"Think about it!" he called. A demon landed on his shoulders and fangs sank into his skull above the ear. Blade reached up and ripped the intruder away, flinging it toward an oncoming pack of its brethren. "Come with me!"

"I…" She clutched the halo with both hands. "I don't know!"

Blade rushed for her, grabbing her by the shoulders. He coiled his wings around them to give them a momentary shield. Her heartbeats were palpable against his palms. Frightened blue irises sought his eyes. Secluding her within his wings, he spoke from his heart. "Zen, you have a choice to step through that portal and become queen. Or…"

"Or?" Her fingers clutched his shirt. Desperation glowed in her eyes.

His heart prodded him toward truth. Surrender. Want. "You choose me."

The brightness he so admired returned to her eyes. Zen exhaled a heavy gasp. "I wasn't aware you were an option."

"I am."

The demons shrieked an awful chorus of mayhem. As soon as Zen's hand landed in Blade's, he knew what she'd decided.

"I choose you," she said.

"Let's get out of here." He pulled her across the dance floor littered with slippery demon blood and some of his own, for sure.

Once outside, they were followed by the denizen but not attacked. They couldn't risk harming their queen. The sky blackened, the moon blinking out as the rage pursued from the sky. Blade pushed Zen in through the driver's side of the Mustang and slid in after her. He risked the rage following him home, but what was worse was the strange cloud looming out from the top of the spooky mansion-cum-nightclub.

"What is that?" he muttered as he backed up, plowing over a couple demons in the process. "Zen, are you okay?"

She studied the halo in her hand. Nodding, she didn't reply.

The cloud moved toward them. He slammed on the gas pedal and barreled down the country road. "Zen?"

She remained silent, turning the halo over in her grasp. Stunned? Under some kind of demonic power?

"Zen!" He shook her by the shoulder and she startled out of it.

"I'm good," she said. "Just need to process."

He smiled at that. She was always good and in need of processing. God, he loved her. He actually loved her.

"I think they're pulling back," he said, observing

the sky in the rearview mirror. "What the hell? It's as though they don't want to get too close to you unless it's before that fiery portal."

A mile away from the nightmare he realized the rage had given up on tracking him. But the thick black cloud, as big as a football field, loomed directly overhead. It wasn't composed of demons, and didn't look like bats or even insects. It was a mist, cloud-like.

Some kind of demonic tracking system? Whatever it was, it wouldn't be able to fly over his property, for he'd warded the skies above for many miles.

All that mattered was that Zen sat next to him. She had chosen him. But what was she thinking now? She hadn't stopped turning the halo over and over. It was as if she were enraptured by it. A remnant of her fall. A reminder of her destiny. Was she reconsidering?

She could be.

A trickle of anxiety tightened his grip on the steering wheel and he couldn't force himself to look at the beautiful woman beside him. How long did he have before she left him again in pursuit of a crown? Had he done the right thing?

Hell. This love stuff was a lot harder than it had been before. He'd made the wrong move.

Blade parked the Mustang inside the garage, got out, slammed the door and strode up to the barn. He took the stairs two at a time, disappearing from Zen's view before she got the car door open and slid out onto the dirt garage floor. Angry? He seemed so. A man who had just battled dozens of demons to rescue her had a right to anger.

But had it been a rescue?

She turned the halo over, remembering what he'd

shouted to her. She'd held tight to this when falling so she wouldn't land in Daemonia? But why? Why fall with the intent of meeting her destiny as the Casiphean queen, and then—not?

It was late. It was dark down in the garage, and Zen was oddly hungry. She needed to think about this. But at the same time, she'd just walked away from destiny and toward something entirely unplanned.

"Blade."

She glanced up toward the ceiling, where his footsteps were imperceptible. He had offered himself to her as an option. And she had taken that option. So what was up with his sudden need for distance now?

She ran up the stairs to the loft. He stood before the cathedral windows looking out at the waxing moon. The black cloud hovered over the dark forest, but it didn't encroach on his property.

Zen approached slowly. "Thank you," she said, slipping the halo around her wrist to let it dangle. "I think."

The weapon around her wrist felt as if it belonged to her. It did belong to her. But she knew well that when an angel fell from Above the halo fell away. Those angels destined to seek their muse did so, never caring to find the lost halo. Others, well, who knew?

She knew that the halo contained the angel's earthbound soul. To place it atop their head in its original position would restore that soul and make them completely mortal. Human.

It had not fallen away from her. Because…

"I *did* hold on to the halo as I fell," she said with surprise. She wrinkled a brow. She knew that as fact, and yet— "But I'm not sure why. When I figure that out, I'll know whether or not I should return to the portal or run like hell. Blade?"

She touched his shoulder and he flinched. Demon blood spattered his neck. His bare back boasted bloody smears. Yet Zen could see the fresh wounds had healed. Most of them.

He'd taken more scars to save her. He was reliving the one nightmare he'd fiercely tried to never live again. Because of her.

"You have every right to be angry with me," she said quietly. "But I never asked you to rescue me."

He twisted his head around and the darkness in his eyes sucked away her breath.

"Wh-what's wrong? Did I do something to make you so angry?"

He exhaled, his shoulders falling. The sword he held firmly, he tilted out to the side. Streaked with black demon blood, it glinted in the moonlight. He was a warrior to the bone.

"You just left," he said. "Walked away without a goodbye or even bothering to ask if I wanted you to leave."

Because she'd had a destiny to meet. And yet she'd had to force herself to leave him.

Zen bowed her head, glancing over the floorboards. "I didn't think you cared."

He noticeably stiffened. The sword fell to his side.

"You've made it very clear you are not interested in a relationship," she continued, daring to meet his eyes. "You never said you love me."

"I offered myself as a choice!"

"And I took that option! Yet why do I feel it was just a ruse to get me away from the portal?"

"A ruse?"

He turned. Sliding a forefinger down the blade he held, he wiped the black blood from it. He lifted his bloodied fingers to his mouth, and just when Zen thought he'd lick it, he flicked his fingers aside and tossed the halo blade to the floor, as well.

Her heart fluttered, but she wasn't sure if she felt anticipatory or fearful. His eyes were so dark. Had his wings been out surely she would have screamed.

And then he did the most remarkable thing.

Blade dropped to his knees before her. Eyes brightening and fixed to hers, he said, "I love you, Zen. I should have told you. But I didn't want to stand in the way of your destiny."

She brushed his hair over his ear, which glowed bright blue under the moonlight. "Truly?"

He nodded. "I mean it. I love you. You've made my life…lighter. You make me want to leave my past where it is."

"But that means you've fallen in love with a demon queen. That goes against all that you've tried to protect yourself from. And what of your deal with Sim to slay all the demons?"

"It's done. I won't harm another soul unless it first intends you harm."

Still on his knees, he clasped his arms about her hips and pressed his face against her belly. And he didn't say anything, because he didn't need to. Zen ran her fingers through his hair and bowed over him. At this moment he was most vulnerable, and she wanted him to know that he was safe with her. Because she knew who she was. Strong, capable, determined. An angel on a quest to become.

Could she love him when there was something that felt so much greater standing between them? She wanted to. But she didn't want to let him down, if she ultimately descended to Daemonia to take the crown.

But she couldn't tell him that. Not now when it was apparent this man needed her.

And she needed him.

Kneeling before him, she kissed Blade. "I think I've fallen far enough."

He nodded. "Stay here with me. You didn't intend to fall all the way to Daemonia. There's a reason behind your hanging on to the halo. We'll find out what that reason was. I'll help you."

"I'd like that. But what I'd like even more is a kiss." She kissed him. "And a hug." She fell into his hug and he stood, lifting her in his arms. "Take me to bed, Blade."

Chapter 23

"If you can hear me, Sim—and I'm sure you can—we need to talk."

Blade stepped onto the grass behind the barn and scanned the darkness. Zen was inside, sleeping peacefully in his bed after they'd made love. She was his.

For now. And...he would have to be cool with that.

Above, the black cloud had left the sky. Or maybe it was hovering over the Darkwood, out of his vision and looming at the edge of his property, which only cut into a small portion of the forest. He stepped across the grounds, shifting as he did so. He'd left his shirt off and worn a loose pair of jeans in anticipation of the shift. His wings cut the air and soared him up over the Darkwood treetops. No black cloud up here.

Arrowing toward the freshwater stream that cut through the north side of the woods, he this time sent out a mental call to Sim.

He landed at the edge of the stream, his bare feet sinking into the cool water. Bending, he plucked up a small stone and skipped it across the shallow water. A rabbit tucked in the undergrowth scampered out and away, its white tail bobbing.

A scatter of crickets suddenly stopped chirping. Even the breeze stilled. Something had arrived. It wasn't wolf, demon or even of this realm.

Why hadn't he picked up on that before?

Blade stretched out his wings and turned to face the approaching entity. Halo blade held at the ready, he waited for whatever stalked through the trees. He used the darkness as camouflage, but was aware the moonlight on his wings or hair would give him away in a flash. So be it. Whatever approached must do so knowing exactly what waited for it.

A blue glow preceded the stranger's sure strides.

"Angel," Blade murmured. He swung the blade in a defiant slash before him. "Come at me, other one!"

The angel stepped into view, and Blade saw the blue glow was actually its wings. The shape of feathers was crafted as if with finely wrought blue LEDs, like one of those fast-action photos a person takes while drawing with light. Yet the wings moved as if fashioned from feathers, while Blade knew they were not. Wearing some kind of draped loincloth over its muscled hips, the angel resembled something a medieval artist might have painted.

Perhaps it *was* biblical.

And when its face pierced a ray of moonlight and the odd gill-like scars were revealed, Blade hissed out an oath. "You?"

Sim bowed his head and stretched out his arms as

if to accept the accusation, but with a prideful smirk. "You called me?"

The bastard was an angel. Why hadn't he assumed that from the start? Who—or rather, what—would want to extinguish demons? And ultimately Zen.

"Stay away from her!" Blade warned. "She is no longer one of you."

"Until she ceases to breathe this mortal air, the being you call Zen will be a problem." The angel's wing slashed forward. "Just as you have become a problem, vampire. I sense you've given up the quest to slay demons?"

"I won't be a party to the senseless destruction. And now that I know Zen might become demon—"

"She was destined to become demon! And yet she changed that destiny." Sim dashed his wingtip before Blade, the hiss of it as tangible as a steel sword.

Blade jerked his head backward, avoiding the cut of the deadly wing. He swung up the blade, parting the retreating feathers in the odd blue appendage, but not cutting.

The angel hissed. "Where did you get that weapon? It feels angelic."

"Fashioned this from a halo. A halo I got from one of you guys. Picked it out of his crystal ash."

"You must stop killing our kind!"

"Yeah? Why is it both the demons and the angels think asking me to stop killing them is going to work?"

"You are bloodthirsty, half-breed."

Blade straightened his shoulders and his wings spread wide. Not quite as wide as the angel's, but he could do battle with what he had. "Says the guy who wanted me to take out an entire denizen. Hell, a rage of Casipheans. Why couldn't you do it yourself? Aren't angels all-powerful?"

"This mortal realm weakens us."

Blade quirked a brow. The two angels he'd battled had been strong. Yet they hadn't wielded any supernatural powers beyond strength.

"And our numbers are few," Sim continued. "But I was foolish to ask you, demon slayer, to help me. I had no idea you would get entangled with Synestriel, Keeper of the Second Light."

"Is that Zen's angel name?"

Sim nodded. "She is from my ranks. I, Simaseel, Master of the Ninth Void, sent her on the Fall."

With a sweep of its wings, the angel soared high, and just when he tilted down to dive toward Blade, Blade took to the air to meet his challenger. He dragged the halo blade along the supportive high bone of one of Sim's wings. The angel shrieked in a myriad of voices, and dodged midair. Blue blood dripped over the glowing wing.

"She is a traitor!" the angel insisted.

Suspended in the air, Blade maintained his position with slow sweeps of his gossamer black wings. He kept the angel's bleeding wing in focus while he twirled the hilt of the sword and caught it, blade down.

"How is Zen a traitor?" he asked.

The angel's multicolored eyes seemed to spin as if a child's toy, hypnotizing Blade with their radiance. When they'd spoken previously they had been white. A glamour? Most likely. He shook his head and returned his focus to the deadly wings.

"The plan was made before Synestriel fell. We have been watching the Casipheans for eons. It is their time for elimination."

"So you angels take it upon yourself to eliminate entire races whenever the mood strikes you?"

"It is ordained."

"Don't give me that bible crap."

"We do not subscribe to the humans' book of biblical stories. We live on truths and follow the destiny of the universe."

"Big talk. Small act. So you wanted to destroy the demons without lifting a finger? Fine. You talked an idiot into helping you. I'm over that now. What does Zen have to do with any of this? Why did she fall?"

"Synestriel agreed to fall to Daemonia to insinuate herself into the Casiphean order. Once crowned their queen she would have utmost control and access to the denizens. She could open Daemonia to our numbers. We would slaughter them before they might growl and hiss and strike back at us."

Blade swallowed. Zen had agreed to participate in genocide? Not all the demons in the world, but an entire breed of them in Daemonia. But that was when she'd been angel. Now that she had landed the mortal realm she had changed. Right?

"This is not your fight," Sim said. Its wings hadn't even to move and the angel maintained its position before Blade above the treetops. "Stand down."

"She doesn't want that anymore."

"This, I have come to know. Why do you think I recruited you to extinguish the demons running rampant on mortal grounds? You are my backup plan. And because of her absence of memory Synestriel has become a liability. She must be destroyed."

Wrong answer. Blade would protect Zen with every ounce of muster he had. Good, bad or otherwise.

It was worth a try. Because, really? He could handle

one angel, but if a cavalcade of them came at him, then he was as good as toast. "You know, Zen still doesn't have her memory completely restored. But I don't understand your need to exterminate the demons. Seems to me if you sit back and let the Casipheans lure her into Daemonia, then your work is done. Once she's there, she'll become demon, yes?"

The angel nodded.

"She'll have all that remarkable power to open Daemonia to the angels."

Sim's eyes glowed as blue as his wings. "You suggest we do nothing? Hmm…" The angel folded back its wings and descended to the forest floor.

Blade followed, but kept his wings spread as a sign of aggression. He wasn't letting down his guard around an angel. Even if the blade was capable of killing the creature, the bastard could still do Blade some major harm before dying.

"If she's not got all her memory back," Sim said, "there is no guarantee she will know the plan when she arrives in Daemonia. And she's been on this realm too long. The longer she remains harnessed to human flesh the less capability she has of assuming the demonic form."

"She went to the nightclub last night with the intent of entering the portal to Daemonia. I'd say that's pretty damned determined, wouldn't you?"

"But you stopped her! And I am quite sure you will continue to impede her quest."

"Seems as if your problem is with me, not Zen."

The angel tilted his head sharply. A glint of blue flashed in his kaleidoscope eyes. His sneer could have cut diamonds. "So I'll take you out—"

Blade dodged the sweep of wing that would have

sliced his head from his neck had he not moved. Lunging upward, he caught Sim against the chest with a shoulder and pushed him to ground. The angel's wings spread across the mossy rocks and earth. Blade's wings curved forward, pinning the angel's wings down with the sharp tips.

"I'm glad to be your problem," Blade said, wrapping his fingers about Sim's throat. "You want that?"

With his other hand he wielded the halo blade, drawing the tip along the man's outstretched arm, but not hard enough to cut through flesh and release blood. He didn't need to give the angel another weapon against him.

"I will consider your suggestion." And with that, the angel kicked Blade off him and swept away, soaring out of sight over the treetops.

Blade dropped his wings and let out a breath. "That was easier than expected."

But how soon before the angel realized that even if they did leave Zen alone, she wasn't going near the demon portal?

Not if Blade had any say about it.

Zen munched a crisp green apple she'd found in the fridge. She hadn't been able to sleep after noticing Blade had slipped out of bed to go outside. So food it was. She wondered if, as a vampire, he was repulsed when he ate for his faery. Gotta be weird.

But he liked weird. And so did she.

Wandering barefoot in front of the cathedral windows, wearing but the long T-shirt that belonged to her lover, she reveled in the moment. The act of being in his home, eating a sweet, juicy apple. For all other moments would be different, some urgent, some not so urgent. Some gorgeous, some weird. Some would challenge her and…

And it was the challenge she wanted to avoid now. Breathing in, she inhaled the air that designed this mortal realm. And knew that she was no longer one from Above. That realm was no longer her place.

And yet the place she had been destined for, Daemonia, teased in incomprehensible ways. So when it did not—as now—she could enjoy the moment.

When the door opened, she listened as Blade ascended the stairs. He wandered into the kitchen and poured a glass of water, drank it down, exhaled, then padded across the hardwood floor toward her.

From behind, he embraced her, wrapping his hands across her stomach and leaning down to kiss her at the base of her neck. His hair tickled her skin. He smelled like a wild, dark forest. She smiled and offered the half-eaten apple.

"Hungry?"

"Only for you," he said. "I want to hold you now. Forever."

"That's sounds like a choice I'd like to accept."

Zen turned and touched the scar that curled around from the back of his torso, and she bent to kiss the raised flesh. It was a new scar. Because of her.

That was over. She wouldn't again purposely do something that would cause him danger.

"Bring out your wings, lover. I want to have sex with you in faery shape."

"I'm never completely one or the other. If you want the faery, you also get the vampire."

"Would that be so terrible? My blood is no longer blue."

His eyes took her in from head to shoulders and

then paused there at her throat. Fangs descended over his lower lip. Zen inhaled a shiver at the incredible sight. The thought of him sinking those into her skin appealed. He would never harm her. And if the bite was a sensual experience, the urge to have him do so would consume her.

"I crave demon blood," he said. It seemed like a confession to her. "It's the faery in me that has the craving, and it makes my vamp go after it like a hound. I don't want to crave yours."

"But if it's mixed with ichor?" She knew that faery ichor was like a drug to vampires. "Can you, a vampire, drink ichor?"

He nodded. "I'm half faery, so ichor is not addictive to me."

"So maybe the demon blood is safe, too? If you crave it?"

"It is safe to me. But, Zen, I don't want something simply because I crave it. It tastes awful. But I feel… stronger after I've drunk it."

"I see. It is a habit, then."

"The only habit I will admit to is wanting to hold you. To kiss you." He leaned forward and kissed her. "To touch your skin." His strokes under her jaw and down her neck caused a shiver of goose bumps to ripple her flesh, as well as tighten her nipples in anticipation.

"Wings," she said softly. "Please? And fangs. Promise I won't ask for the bite."

Her lover's wings unfurled behind him in a glorious spill of crisp autumn scents and winter ice, capped with the luscious hint of spring. Moonlight spilling through the windows shimmered on them. His wings were black and blue and silver, formed in a demonic shape, like something depicted in Doré's etchings of *Dante's Inferno*, and serrated around the edges in gothic peaks and curls. Black filaments dusted the tips and a faint blue arabesque designed curls in the shimmery silver.

Zen reached over his shoulder to touch one, but Blade put up a finger to stop her. "Be careful. You touch my wings, you'd better mean business."

"I'm all about the business, lover."

"Yeah, but the kind of business I'm talking about is an erotic touch."

"I know what happens when a person touches a faery's wings." Because know-so-much chick was in her zone. "I'm in."

Dipping under his arm, Zen stepped around behind him and between his wings. She spread her palms over the soft, yet tellingly strong appendages. They fluttered under her touch. Blade hissed in a gasp, indicating his arousal.

"Hold me," she said.

He wrapped his wings about her, caressing her torso firmly. She raised her arms over her head and tilted her head back against his neck. The sensations of warmth and erotic massage across her skin were irresistible. One of his wing tips pushed up under her shirt and coaxed the garment off over her head. The man was talented with those things.

A wing swept over her breast, her nipple growing instantly rigid. Soft as feathers but warm, so warm, his wings permeated her skin with a kind of anticipatory joy.

"Blade, that's amazing."

The wings swept away and he turned to kiss her, wrapping his wings forward to again embrace and pull her forward. And he lifted her, cradled by his wings, and held her to him as he dipped his head to lick her breasts.

She gripped the hard, bony upper portions of his

wings and felt the gush of life within them. Much like a firm erection in her grasp, the wing was supple yet solid. He growled against her breast, a hungry, wanting plead for more.

She stepped back and lazily took him in. Regal, exquisite, a gorgeous creature of wing and…yes, the fangs were down. Muscles flexed and drew her eye to the skin that felt so soft under her fingertips, yet was hard as stone. And when he grinned, it was the most wickedly appealing invitation she'd ever received.

"Come at me, woman."

Zen actually jumped into his arms, her legs wrapping about his hips. "Show me some of that wing action," she whispered at his ear, then bit the lobe and tugged.

The soft wings, which were not made of feathers but rather a suede-like material, caressed Zen's back, and with Blade's nod, she leaned back into the cradle of them and spread her hands over the strong but soft appendages. Holding her with but his wings allowed Blade to kiss her breasts and glide his hand down to her mons, where he dipped one finger over her clit and slowly massaged the swelling, wet bud.

She clutched at Blade's wings, gripping the edges to anchor herself to the exquisite feeling. He moaned deeply against her chest and lashed his tongue over her nipple. "Touch them. Stroke them," he said.

So she matched the rhythm of his finger between her legs and stroked the fabric of his wings. She could feel the hot blood rushing through them. Blood and ichor? Or was it all ichor since this was the faery part of him?

Who cared? Zen squirmed and shifted her hips, accepting his ministrations and wanting him to go faster, deeper… And then the rush of sensation frenzied through her system.

Chapter 24

So there was a new plan. Zen would lie low, keeping herself off the radars of both the angels and demons. And Blade would stand his ground of no longer killing demons for the sake of killing them.

Right now, in Blade's mind, the angels were the bad guys. Zen was still holding out judgment on the demons, and that was her right. Perhaps the middle ground was the best place to stand, but defense was so ingrained in Blade that this step to setting down arms was big enough.

It was well past noon. They'd lingered in bed making love again with the rising sun, though the shades were pulled. He couldn't get enough of Zen's body, and she seemed to want all of him. Constantly. He was cool with that.

Sharing himself was…easy with Zen. This relationship was not the same as that with Octavia. He wouldn't allow it to be. He'd walked into this one with eyes wide-open, and now that he had the facts—as dire as they were—he would continue to protect and love her. Because he had fallen. And unlike Zen's fall, his had been accidental, and yet, he was pleased about the step into this new, yet strangely familiar territory.

But he had a few errands to run today, and rather than answer his brother's curious questions about why he had forgotten, Blade kissed Zen on the forehead and promised to return in an hour or so with some lunch for her.

He stopped by Stryke's place. The construction crew had arrived and had begun to dig the basement, but they needed a permit to pour concrete footings.

On his way in to town he got a phone call from Michael Donovan, the halo hunter Dez had said she'd track down for him. He was in town for the day, passing through, visiting old friends, and he wanted to talk.

After stopping at the city hall for the permit, Blade drove to the city park. He wandered past the football field where a couple guys were tossing the ball and toward the docks that overlooked the lake. The straightest lake in the state, his sister, Daisy Blu, often said of Tangle Lake. It disturbed her that the town's namesake wasn't tangled. Blade could but snicker over her frustration.

He parked himself under an awning set into a rectangular concrete base where a picnic table had once sat. Work-release crews from an area prison were repairing and repainting the tables this weekend in preparation for the big city shindig that celebrated the summer.

Pulling a pair of sunglasses out of his pocket, he slid them on. The sun's rays didn't touch his skin here, and he could walk in daylight, no problem. But vampires did burn faster than most, and he avoided direct sunlight for more than a few minutes whenever possible.

Tonguing the tips of his fangs, he realized he'd not bitten Zen when they'd been making love. And his wings had been out. She had intimated she'd like a bite, and he'd thought it might be okay. No more blue blood? She should be safe for him.

Maybe.

He still wasn't willing to risk it if even the tiniest bit of angel remained in her. Would she ever be completely angel-free? He hoped so. Because the bite would allow him into a part of her more valuable to a vampire than anything else. Her very soul. They could bond.

He wasn't ready to bond with her. He wouldn't jump so quickly as he had with Octavia. A slow, trusting relationship felt right to him. And he wanted that from Zen.

He wanted a lot from her. And that realization made him sit up straight. He really had fallen in love with her. Idiot. Love was for fools. And never ended well.

"Saint-Pierre?"

Turning, Blade nodded acknowledgment to a man with short dark hair who wore aviator shades. Khaki cargo pants and a crisp white shirt rolled up to the elbows gave him a big-city casual look. He shook his hand and determined he was merely human.

"Michael Donovan," he said. "The witch said you've come upon a couple halos lately?"

Blade drew up the halo sword and held it, tip up, before Donovan. "You talking about this?"

The halo hunter preened over the weapon, even snapped his finger against the blade, then said, "Wow. That used to be a halo. How did you manage to rework it? An angel halo is formed from the most indestructible metal known to man. And angels, for that matter."

"My dad is a sword smith. Add a touch of my mother's faery dust, and voilà."

Michael whistled in appreciation. "May I?"

Blade clasped the hilt tighter. "You going to give me some answers?"

"I'll do my best. I know a lot about angels, but not everything. I've been hunting halos for over a decade. Ran into an angel or two in the process. And just so you know, you can trust me. My girlfriend's a vampire. So I know about all the species."

Blade eyed the man discerningly. He wasn't about to trust him, but should the human attempt anything funny he'd not get farther than two steps before Blade made him understand it wasn't wise to mess with him.

He handed the sword over, hilt pointing toward the halo hunter. Donovan took it and, with an awe-filled sigh, studied the blade, running a finger carefully along the metal, and then balancing the precise weight.

"How many halos do you have?" Blade asked.

"Eighteen. Found them all over the world. When the angel falls the halo falls away."

"Right. Unless the angel holds tight to the halo when falling."

"Why would they do that?" he asked, handing over the sword. "Doesn't make sense. The very purpose of the fall is to maintain their angelic nature so they can stalk the mortal realm. Of course, the halo could serve as a handy weapon, but it could also be put over the angel's head, rendering it merely human as the earthbound soul is returned to the body."

"An angel might hold on to the halo because they didn't want to fall for the original reason intended."

Donovan wobbled his head in an uncertain nod. "Maybe."

"There's another halo in town, unchanged and in original form. It's in the hands of the angel who fell with it."

"No way. Where is it? I've got to get my hands—" Donovan dropped his shoulders and relaxed his enthusiasm. "Well, you know. I'd like to take a look at it."

"You're not going anywhere near that halo. The owner is partial to it."

"Is this the angel who could be a demon that Dez told me about?"

Blade nodded. "Tell me about angels who fall to become demon."

"Hmm…I do fancy myself a bit of an angelologist as I learn more about them." Michael crossed his arms and considered the question. "There is a race of demons who were once angel. The Casipheans."

"Yes, that's the breed I'm dealing with."

"Okay. The Casipheans fell eons ago and landed directly in Daemonia. They are the only race of demons who possess divinity."

"Divinity?"

"An angelic birthright. And believe me, if I were an angel from Above I'd want to take out the Casipheans because it's not right, you know, a demon walking around with divinity. Divinity is only for the chosen. Or so the angels believe. Yet they are the ones who taint it most."

"Do the Casipheans know this?"

Michael shrugged. "My demonic knowledge isn't top-notch. I only knew that tidbit because I've had a conversation with an angel slayer. The Sinistari are angels who are specifically chosen to slay those angels who hunt their muses. They fall to Beneath, become the Sinistari demon and sit in wait until they are called to slay a Fallen."

"This angel lore is complicated."

"That it is. But just imagine, whether or not the Casipheans know, their divine vibrations are constantly infusing the entirety of Daemonia. It's gotta be interesting in the Place of All Demons. Ha! I bet it drives those bastard angels mad."

Blade quirked a brow. "You don't like angels much?"

"I believe they are far more evil than some demons. Bunch of self-righteous assholes. I am a big fan of the Sinistari."

The angel slayers. Interesting. There was so much Blade did not know about other species and breeds. And there were days he wished to remain oblivious.

But not today. He needed all the information he could get to protect Zen.

"So have you spoken to these angels who seem to be giving you trouble?" Donovan asked.

"One of them recruited me to slay any demon I laid eyes on. I initially refused, but then—I hate demons."

"Everyone has a right to their opinions."

"Simaseel is the angel heading the demon-slaying mission. The angels are trying to infiltrate the Casipheans and annihilate them."

"Makes sense."

It shouldn't, but it did if the angels were jealous that breed of demons possessed divinity. And it was wrong in ways Blade could not begin to understand.

"So how do we stop a cavalcade of angels?" he asked.

"Why? Have you switched sides? Are you fighting for the Casipheans now?"

"No." Stand for the demons? Never. "I just…" He

exhaled and shoved the sword back in the sheath he wore at his hip. "I need to know everything to help her."

"Who her? The angel demon?"

"Zen. Or Synestriel, as Simaseel called her."

"The Keeper of the Second Light," Michael said with a knowing nod. "She created all light that beams from manmade sources."

"Really?"

"Yep. Anything that gives off a glint, sparkle or glow, but which is not naturally generated."

"Like...rhinestones?"

Donovan shrugged. "Yes, I suppose."

"Makes weird sense." And he did like weird. "Zen's blood is no longer blue, so I believe whatever angel she had in her has faded."

"But she was angel for a while?"

Blade nodded. "Simaseel sent her to fall and become the Casiphean queen."

"That's where the infiltration plays in." Donovan leaned against the wood post. "Clever."

"But she—Zen—has amnesia, and is only just beginning to remember her mission. Right now, she's swaying regarding her alliances. I want to push her over to the right side."

"And which side is that?"

"Mine."

"Ah, love."

"I didn't say anything about love, man."

"Yeah, but that's generally the catalyst that makes a man do crazy things. Like stand up for an amnesiac Fallen One when the angels will surely rip him to shreds. And speaking of crazy, you, uh, won't mention my name to any of the involved parties, will you?"

"No reason to."

"Whew. I've been living a relatively quiet life lately. Not sure I'm up for angel battles. I don't mind taking out the occasional vamp, if need be, though."

"What does your girlfriend say about that?"

"Vinny is cool with me doing what is necessary for the two of us to survive. She's been through a lot. I'd protect her with my life."

Blade could relate.

"You sure I can't take a look at the halo your Zen has?"

"Positive."

"Had to try. There is one other thing."

"What's that?"

"I suspect the divinity that's been festering in Daemonia can be used as a weapon against the angels. You know once an angel touches mortal ground it loses power?"

"Sim had mentioned something similar. They still seem damn strong to me. I've fought a couple in the past few days."

"Their strength is depleted, which gives you an idea of just how strong they could be in Above. But what I'm talking about is their ability to move objects with but a gesture, the mind control and general badassness. Angel feet touch mortal ground? So long badassery," Donovan added. "And the Casipheans are überstrong as well— at least with all that divinity coursing within them."

"I don't think they are aware of that hidden talent. How do they use it?"

Michael shrugged. "You got me. But it's something, right?"

"Could be." Rain started to sprinkle the grass, and Blade held out a palm to catch the droplets. "Thanks, man. I appreciate you taking the time to talk to me."

"No problem. I won't be leaving town until noon to-morrow. So, you know, if you think you might want to do a little more show-and-tell…"

"Give it up, man."

"All right, all right. I'll leave you to your apocalyptic troubles."

"I do have one other thing." Blade pulled out the postcard he'd nicked from Zen's stuff before leaving and handed it to Michael. "You know anything about that?"

"Wow." Michael merely glanced at it, then handed it back to Blade. "Where'd you get that?"

"You know the painting?"

"Of course. It was done by Eden Campbell. She used to be a muse, until a Sinistari demon rescued her from the angel who wanted to impregnate her with a Nephilim baby. Name was Zaqiel. He was an asshole. Eden has been painting angels all her life, without knowing that she was connected to them. That's how it works for a muse. One day it's life as usual. The next, they're being chased by a horny angel. Where did you get that postcard?"

"Zen had this on her. She said it spoke to her, even not knowing what she was."

"Interesting. But you already know how she's connected in this big circle that ever fascinates."

"That I do. Thanks again." Blade strode off, leaving the halo hunter by lake's edge tossing stones into the water.

Chapter 25

While she was drying off from the shower in the bath-room, Zen heard the door shut and Blade's footsteps rushing up the stairs. It was late in the day, but the sweltering heat had compelled her to hop in for a quick and cool rinse.

"In here!" she called, letting the towel drop to the floor as she walked out into the bedroom.

"Wow." He walked in and strolled his gaze up and down her naked skin. "That's a nice way to greet a guy." He thumbed a gesture over his shoulder. "I picked up a salad and sandwich for you. Left it in the fridge."

"Thanks. I am hungry. But it can wait."

She climbed onto the bed and patted the sheet be-side her. He sat and she kissed him and pulled off his T-shirt. It wasn't necessary to ask him to take off his jeans; he'd already quickly shoved them down. After-noon sex was awesome, but with the rain pinging the window—and the man always had the windows open a crack—a humid breeze floated over the bed. She nestled into the black sheets and stroked her fingers along his leg, delighting in the soft dark hairs. No blue here.

He kissed her head and drew her hand up to kiss each finger. Down her wrist, and up to her elbow, he paused. "These markings are brighter."

"Yes, I noticed that. What do you think?"

"Faery?" he offered with a shrug.

"You know as much as I do." She walked her fingers over his abs and tapped one of his steely pecs. "How did the chat with the halo hunter go?" she asked.

"Interesting. He really wants to get his hands on your halo."

"Did you tell him it was mine?"

"I did."

"I own very few things. I value what I have. I would never give the halo up, even if…"

He sat up against the headboard and ran his fingers through her hair, brushing it from her face. "Keep the halo on you at all times, Zen. Promise me."

"I will. The Casipheans will have to accept it is mine. Does that mean you're worried someone is going to attack me again?"

"The Casipheans still have a chance of luring you to their side."

"I won't go."

"But you just said—"

Zen sighed heavily. "I know. I'm not sure what is right anymore." She stretched out her arm and stroked the marks, which had brightened to white from the original cream. "Why did I fall to become their queen?"

"I can answer that. I spoke to Sim last night before

returning and making love to you all night long. That bastard is an angel."

"He is?"

Blade nodded. "Simaseel, Master of—uh, I don't recall. Doesn't matter. You ready for this?"

"It's not good, is it?"

He shrugged. "We all react and move through life according to how we've been raised. Or in your case, created."

Yes, because angels were not born and nurtured from an infant, they were created. Come into being fully mature and ready to do…whatever it was they had been assigned—or perhaps even destined—to do.

"Simaseel knew why I fell, didn't he?"

"Do you remember that name?" he asked. "Simaseel?"

"No. Should I?"

"He said you were in his ranks in the Ninth Void. That he sent you to fall. Called you Synestriel, Keeper of the Second Light."

"Really?" Her posture straightened and she lifted her chin. "That sounds so regal."

"I think it's a reason why you are into the sparkly stuff." He tapped the many rings that glinted on her fingers, then took her hand and kissed the knuckles. "Zen, you were destined to become the Casiphean queen. But it's not for the reason you believe. According to Sim, once inserted within the demonic ranks, you were then to open the gates to Daemonia, allowing the angels to invade and kill off the entire Casiphean race."

Her mouth dropped open. For a moment she was aware that she could not sense her heartbeats. Empty inside, she grasped at her chest. "But that's genocide."

Blade nodded.

"I don't want…"

Was that what she really wanted? Before she'd lost her memory, had her goal been to infiltrate the demons so her former race of angels could destroy them all?

It was hideous to consider. Unthinkable.

Blade clasped her hand. "Zen. Think about it. When you fell you held tight to your halo. You knew, either right before making the fall, or moments after beginning that long descent, that you didn't want to go through with it. Holding on to your halo prevented you from entering Daemonia. It is what stopped you here on the mortal realm. Don't you see? You couldn't go through with it."

Shoulders dropping, she breathed out slowly as she drew a knee up to her chest and propped her chin on it. Her heartbeats resumed a more regular pace. His version sounded good. Not so violent. And much less evil.

Had she been an evil angel? What made her think she could ever move beyond that?

Her lover moved up onto his knees and bent over her, stroking her hair and tilting up her chin to meet his searching gaze. "Zen, you're not that angel anymore."

"Sure, but what am I? What must I become?"

"Whatever you become, you're not going to join the demons. That's not you, either."

"How do you know?" came out in a panicked question. "Maybe…maybe the Casipheans *need* a queen to lead them? To protect them from the imminent angel invasion?"

"They've their own means of defense against the angels. Trust me on that one."

"But—"

"Zen." He kissed her softly. All she wanted was his kisses. The world faded away when their mouths connected. And that was a world she wanted to live in. "The invasion won't happen as long as you keep out of Daemonia. If you want to protect the Casipheans, stay here in the mortal realm." He looked aside and said softly, "With me."

He wanted her to stay? Zen had never felt so needed, so special. So…real. And that she belonged someplace. Could she stay with this beautiful man who embraced her despite his own dark troubles? Of course she could. But would her origins ever remain a brutal reminder to his awful torture by demons?

"I love you, Blade. I mean, I think I do. I'm not sure what love is, but if it's something that makes a person feel certain of their position in the world—right here with you—then that's the definition I'm using."

He stroked her cheek and brushed his mouth over her lips. Oh, that world that only they two could create. She was in for the long haul.

"You are love, Zen. You've been nothing but open and wondering and positive since landing in this realm. You were meant to be here. I think you wanted to be here. Maybe as an angel, agreeing to the plot to eradicate the Casipheans was your means to escape?"

"Could have been. That's the part I'm still blurry on. Oh, but, Blade, how can you allow me into your heart knowing that I had planned to be part of such an annihilation?"

"Because we all do what we must. I agreed to much the same when Sim asked. When we learn more, we do better. I'm no angel, Zen."

"Well, no, you're faery and vampire. Which is exactly how I prefer you."

"Weirdo." He kissed her softly, his nose nuzzling

hers. "I won't force you to stay. I just want to keep you here awhile longer, until we figure things out."

"Sounds like a plan. So I don't have to worry about angels anymore?"

"I wouldn't go as far as to get comfy. I'd keep one eye out to the sky. I did give Sim something to think about regarding backing off from you. But when he figures out that was a crock I'm not sure what to expect. What we need to do is give the angels good reason to retreat, and the demons, as well."

"Which is?"

"Haven't a clue. You hungry?"

"I could eat anything you put in front of me."

He smirked and his eyes flitted down to his cock, which was erect.

"Is that so?" Zen tapped the head of the hopeful appendage.

"It has to stop with me," Zen said later as she finished the salad Blade had picked up. They'd had a quickie and then just knowing food waited for her in the fridge, she had dragged herself away from her naked lover for sustenance. "I've been muddling on things, and I recall the moment I agreed to Simaseel to fall and insinuate myself into the Casipheans."

"You do?"

She nodded, and placed her palms together before her, closing her eyes reverently. She nodded again, decided, and opened her eyes, spreading out her palms. "It was a lie, as you suspected. I wanted to be the change. To stand on the side of life."

"But the Casipheans are not without sin."

"Who am I to judge?"

"Well, you do come from divine beginnings. If anyone is allowed to judge—"

"That's not me," she said. And she felt it in every atom of her being. This was what she had fallen for. To save lives. And to stop an annihilation. "I will stand for the Casipheans. Simaseel must be stopped."

She laid a hand over his. She had no right to ask, but she wanted to. Because with him she felt whole, strong and capable. "Join me."

"You're asking me to protect the demons."

"Yes, the very species who tortured you and left you for dead."

"I…don't know if I can do that," he answered. "I can step back. Do them no harm. But protect them?"

"It's a lot to ask. You're right. Let's leave things where they are right now. Me and you. Together. We're together, yes?"

He kissed her and nodded. "For as long as you'll have me."

She would have him forever, if that was possible. Though she was still torn between two worlds. She must help the demons, but would that wrench her lover from her arms?

And he couldn't commit completely to standing at her side in the defense of the Casipheans. Zen couldn't help but feel her heart fall a little to know she may have to stand alone and risk losing the best thing that ever happened to her.

Chapter 26

With Zen in the house flicking through the TV stations in fascination, Blade stalked out behind the barn and beyond the shed.

From the loft window, he had spied something moving in this direction. It wasn't an animal, because they were more stealthy, and anything from the Darkwood was usually cautious of the wards he'd put up surrounding his property.

Had Simaseel returned?

Now, as he tracked the edge of his property, the Darkwood grew up to his left, a black wall of gnarly barked trees with leaves that appeared drained of life even in the middle of summer. The wildlife within the forest moved about without fear. He liked to think that someday he would be as fearless. Because, really, he did fear some things.

Like losing the best thing that had happened to him lately.

She'd asked him to stand in defense of the demons. He couldn't do that. He wasn't that forgiving. But should he be?

The snap of a twig lifted his head. He stopped, turned toward the forest and looked over the row of red eyes that had likely tracked him since he'd left the barn.

He knew this denizen. All too well.

"Ryckt," he said coldly.

"Foul One," the leader of the *mimicus* denizen addressed him.

The demon stood before his ranks. His body was as black as night, his clothing blending in with the foliage—if he wore any—for he was in demon form. Horns curled over and behind his ears, and his elongated face dipped his chin low to a narrow chest. Blade knew well that their limbs appeared emaciated, their black flesh clinging to bone, but they were deceptively strong. And they could take on any form, and go undetected by those of the species they mimicked.

"We are watching you," Ryckt stated.

"Is that so? Never would have guessed," Blade said lightly. Though it took all his bravery to do so. The scars on his body pulled tightly.

This was the denizen who had tortured him while Octavia had slowly died. These were the demons that would play with a man's very soul just to see it quiver. And they would stalk a vampire-faery half-breed because their leader had the twisted desire to see how much torture it could withstand. And to test their armor against the ichor.

"Step forward if you wish to talk," Blade said.

"I know your wards are fierce. I am perfectly capable of conversing with you from where I stand."

Not fierce enough if they had allowed the denizen so close to his home.

"What do you want?" He had the bowie knife stuffed in his waistband, but wished he held the halo blade.

He prayed that Zen stayed inside the barn and did not come out looking for him.

The demon leader shifted from one foot to the other. "You are giving Kesabel a difficult time."

"So he sent you to look after me?"

"Indeed."

"Since when do the royal denizens of Daemonia associate with the lowlife *mimicus* demons who haunt the mortal realm?"

"The Casiphean numbers in this realm dwindle."

Blade smirked. He'd had something to do with that. Though he'd decided he wasn't going to slay another demon, he'd take out this entire denizen right now if they attempted to cross his wards. Because he had a reason to kill them. Slowly.

"She's never going to join their ranks," he said. "Tell Kesabel to give up. The angels are determined to infiltrate their denizen—through Zen—and destroy them all."

"So say you?"

Blade sensed the demon's genuine concern. "So I say. I spoke to Simaseel yesterday. He revealed his plan to me. Best thing for the Casipheans to do? Retreat."

"Our kind never retreat."

"Then, your denizen will be obliterated alongside the Casipheans. Idiot demons."

And Blade turned and walked off, forcing himself not to look over his shoulder.

"The moment she leaves your property she is ours!" Ryckt called.

"You can't force her to enter the portal!" Blade yelled.

"She will do just that if the stakes are high enough."

Blade fisted a rude gesture at the denizen and strode back toward the barn.

"Who was that?" Zen asked as Blade topped the stairs in the loft. "I glanced out the bathroom window and saw you talking to someone at the edge of the woods. A brother?"

"The *mimicus* denizen."

"Demons?" Her jaw dropped open. That was the denizen who had tortured Blade. "I don't understand. I thought you had wards?"

"I do. Guess I need to have them renewed. Kesabel sicced Ryckt and his denizen on me since I won't hand you over to him."

"But even if you did 'hand me over'—" she made air quotes for those words "—it wouldn't matter. I'm supposed to go willingly into Daemonia."

"They know that. They just want to piss me off."

"Oh." She rubbed a palm down her arm and gave him a sidelong glance. He seemed just a bit too casual about this announcement. "Have they?"

"Yep." He smacked a fist into his palm. "I told them the angels have it out for them, and that they should head for the hills, but I don't think the warning was taken for what it was. I need to talk to Kesabel again. If you are intent on protecting the Casipheans, then we need to get them on our side."

"We don't have a side, Blade. We, or rather I—since you haven't agreed to defend the demons—am the center, trying to keep the peace."

He pushed his fingers through his hair and tilted

back his head. Zen could sense his anger and the uneasy acceptance of her goal to make peace between the angels and demons. Of course he couldn't stand by her side, defending the very creatures he hated most. And now the denizen who had tortured him and left permanent scars in his flesh was watching him?

"I want to stand on your side, Zen, but…" He sighed heavily.

"Your heart is true. But you mustn't sacrifice your principles to please me."

"Sounds like the best reason to sacrifice." His smile was genuine. "For you."

If he was serious, she could so get behind his help.

"You don't need to do this." She wrapped her arms around his waist from behind. "I am capable."

"I believe you are capable. And I'm not particularly keen about protecting demons. But I want to stand at your side. If you'll have me." He pulled her around to stand before him. "You're becoming more faery every day. The moment you are fully faery you are no good to either the angels or the demons."

"So we just wait it out?"

"No. I don't like hiding, doing nothing."

"You would not." She tilted up on her toes to kiss him. "But can we wait through the night?"

"Of course. The denizen can't cross my wards. You're safe here."

"And so are you."

"Is that so?" He kissed her. "I do feel safe in your arms. That, no matter what the world tosses my way, I can overcome. Because if you're standing there waiting for me when the dust clears, then everything is right."

"I'll be there. I promise."

"What about being queen? Can you give that up?"

"Oh, hell, yes. Though I will miss the crown."

"You think there's a crown?"

"There had better be. One can hardly be queen without some sparkly headgear."

He kissed her head. "When this is over I'll give you the prettiest, sparkliest crown I can find."

"Promise?"

"You have my word."

They had sex in the shower, and afterward, Zen curled up on the couch with Blade to watch a late-night showing of *Dracula*. She laughed at all the right places. He loved her for that. He was distracted from the black-and-white flick by the flash of headlights on the ceiling.

Now what?

"Who's that?"

"Stay here." Grabbing the halo blade from the kitchen counter, he headed down the stairs and outside.

Trouble hopped out of his truck and strode up to the open garage entrance where Blade stood staring skyward. The massive black cloud had returned. "What the hell is that? Can you ever not attract danger, little brother?"

"I can use your help again," Blade said. "That cloud comes from the nightclub. Must be some form of demonic spy cloud. And you see those red eyes at the edge of the Darkwood?"

Trouble cast his gaze along the forest edge, and he suddenly jumped. "What the hell?"

"The *mimicus* denizen," Blade confirmed. "They're keeping an eye on me."

"That's the ones who fucked you up?"

"Yep."

Trouble punched a fist into his palm. "How do they play into all this?"

"Kesabel hired them."

"Kesabel?"

"The Casiphean leader who wants to make Zen their queen."

Trouble whistled. "This is way beyond my story line, bro. You're going to have to catch me up. I just stopped by for some gas. Was headed to the casino in the next town and realized I needed a fill."

"You can fill up and then come inside for coffee. If I'm right, we're going to have an all-nighter."

"So you're a demon?"

Zen sat up from the couch, where she'd almost dozed during a commercial, and eyed the cocky werewolf who approached. "Trouble, hi. Uh, not demon. Yet."

"That's what Blade tells me. We're heading to the nightclub to take a look around. Guess my casino plans are spoiled…" He plopped onto the couch beside her. "*Dracula*! I love this one. Did my brother tell you we used to tease him about being Dracula when we were kids?"

"And how many times did I let you get away with that?" Blade called as he topped the stairs.

"Once." Trouble winked at Zen. "He beat the shit out of me and I gave it up. No one ever gets my jokes."

Zen pushed the blanket off and sat up straight, stretching out her arms. "If you guys are going to the nightclub, I'm coming along."

"No," Blade called as he disappeared into the bedroom. He reappeared with the bowie knife and stuffed it down the side of his combat boot. The halo sword he shoved in the sheath strapped at his hip. "You're safe if you stay in the barn. I've wards that will keep everything out."

"Those same wards that you said needed refreshing? I don't want to stay alone. Not with demons lurking in the woods. Besides, I could be of help. I do have the halo."

"No," Blade said at the same time that Trouble said, "She could be helpful. If the demons want her, she could play bait."

Blade gaped at his brother.

Zen shrugged and nodded eagerly. "I can do bait. I think."

Trouble winked at Blade. He had to admit he'd rather keep Zen in eyesight even if it meant added danger.

"Fine," he conceded.

Zen slipped on her shoes and bounced.

"But no bait. You do as I say, and keep out of sight when possible. Promise?"

"Whatever you say, boss."

Chapter 27

Trouble drove because he owned the big, bad Dodge half-ton diesel. The abomination was painted olive-green camouflage. Trouble thought the paint job ironic. His brothers snickered about it behind his back. He navigated the truck down the country road toward the club.

Zen sat next to Blade, arm wrapped around his and head tilted onto his shoulder. She was warm and smelled like sex and apples.

He kissed the crown of her head. "You got your halo along?"

"In my backpack. You told me never to go anywhere without it."

"In case of emergency…" He wondered if it was wise to suggest such a thing? There could be no other option if things got hairy. "Put the halo above your head."

He felt her peer up at him but he kept his eyes on the dark country road, peeled for red eyes or moving objects not in human form.

"What if it's too late?" she said in the tiniest voice.

He caught Trouble's glance that seemed to echo, *yeah, what if*? What if the angel within her was gone and wouldn't react to the halo and accept her earth-bound soul?

"I'll have your back," he said. "Promise."

She snuggled even closer to him and he wished they were not driving toward danger, but instead away from it all. Could he steal a moment out of time to simply enjoy being with Zen? They'd shared a few moments of bliss, but that had been between running from demons and angels. Could life ever be normal?

Did he want normal?

"Yes," he murmured. With all his heart and soul he wanted the freedom to exist without having to look over his shoulder all the time.

"Your brother Stryke lives a good life?" she asked.

"Uh…yes?"

"Do you want that?"

"Perfection? No." Had she been privy to his thoughts? Or was it they shared a connection that they mustn't ignore? "I want peace," he said. "Quiet."

"Seems as if you have quiet out on your little plot of land far from the city and your family members."

True. And he had been generally demon-free until Zen had entered his life.

"I've brought you something more," she said. "The question is, will it be too much for you? Will you want to return to the peace you had when this is all over? Demons forced back to Daemonia and angels extinguished?"

"All I want is you, Zen."

"You have me. Now let's see what you do to keep me."

He looked down at her and she beamed up a smile

curved beneath violet eyes. Violet? Was she so close to faery, then?

Trouble's grin was so loud that Blade could but smile in response. So he'd gone sappy. If Trouble said something he'd give him the fistfight he deserved. Only problem was, his brother would enjoy that too much.

"Kelyn's behind us," Trouble announced.

He slowed the vehicle to a stop. Blade rolled down the window. Kelyn, his faery brother, called out to be heard over the idling diesel engine, "Need some help?"

"You bet. Follow us to the nightclub."

"You going to kick more demon ass?" Kelyn yelled.

"With hope, no."

But Blade knew that hope had long been siphoned from his soul.

After the brothers got out, Zen moved over to the driver's seat. They stalked up to the stone staircase before the mansion. There stood a man, or probably the demon Kesabel, waiting for him. Zen hadn't seen Kesabel so she could only guess.

She rolled down the window and the blond brother, Kelyn, was standing by the door. He said, "No matter what happens you stay in the truck. Blade's orders. And roll up the window."

She nodded, but didn't feel like a weakling damsel who needed to be protected by the boys. She was smart enough to know to stay out of the fray, if that should occur. But that didn't mean she wasn't going to jump in should things require another hand. Though she saw no other demons in the darkness surrounding the mansion. And surely their red eyes would reveal them.

She tried to hear what Blade was saying to Kesabel, but the obnoxious rumble of the truck engine made it impossible. Trouble had asked her to keep it idling for a fast getaway, if need be. So she strained to hear through the closed window.

"You brought an army?" Kesabel asked as Blade stopped at the bottom step. The demon, clad in maroon leather armor Blade was all too familiar with, stood two steps up.

"If you consider three men an army," Blade said, "then my numbers won't even blink should you call on yours."

Kesabel chuckled. "You know my fellow Casipheans are few in this realm."

"Right. You had to call out the *mimicus* denizen to help you. I see they lent you some armor. They don't scare me, Kesabel. You're going to have to try harder."

"I'm not attempting to scare. I'm going for the win." He made a show of glancing over Blade's shoulder toward the truck. "I see you brought our queen. If you would be so kind as to escort her into the club, we can get started."

"Started?" Kelyn, who flanked Blade's side, glanced to him.

Blade shook his head at the idiot demon's audacity. "She has no desire to become your queen. Listen, Kesabel, and I say this with sincerity and the genuine desire not to slaughter more of your ranks."

The demon crossed his arms. The small portion of his neck that was exposed revealed many of the dark runes, no doubt, wards against vampires.

"I spoke with Simaseel," Blade said.

"The very angel who sicced you on us. You finally figured that one out?"

Yeah, so he'd been slow on that one.

"The angels sent Zen to infiltrate your denizen. If you invite her through the portal and make her your queen? She'll open Daemonia to Sim's ranks and they will eradicate you."

"Impossible. Angels cannot access Daemonia."

"Yeah? All right, then. Let's give it a go." Blade made a show of turning toward the trucks. He didn't give a signal to his brothers to follow because Kesabel cleared his throat.

As expected.

"Truly?" the demon asked.

Blade nodded. "Sim wants to take you guys out. I assume because you possess divinity."

"A faery tale. Fat lot of good divinity does us in Daemonia."

"You don't actually know how to utilize it, do you? You know, you can fight the angels with divinity."

"Lies told to you by the angel to lure us closer to the brink."

"Actually, it was told to me by a halo hunter. What did he call himself? An angelologist."

"A made-up word for a boastful human who thinks he knows things."

"All righty. If you want to ignore the truth."

"Divinity is but a remnant. Trust me, vampire. Are you or are you not going to allow Synestriel to approach the portal?"

"That's a big not."

Kesabel scratched his head near the horn. "Then, we'll have to give her reason to want to make such a sacrifice." The demon glanced at Trouble, who flanked Blade five feet to the right, and then to Kelyn, who stood to his left.

"There's nothing you can do that will make her come to you."

"How about this?"

Blade saw the demon swing forward his arm, but as he deflected it expertly with a forearm, the demon's other arm shot up with an undercut. He felt the wooden stake enter his chest, plunge between rib bones and tear through heart muscle.

Gripping the wood dowel stuck in his chest, Blade dropped to his knees. Behind him Trouble and Kelyn swore. And Zen's scream was the sound that kept him in this world, alive, but struggling for consciousness.

Chapter 28

Zen ran toward her lover, on his knees before the demon. The brothers hadn't had a chance to stop the inevitable staking. Even Blade hadn't seen it coming in time to retreat. Damned demon!

A skitter in the air averted her gaze upward as she ran. A black cloud swirled toward earth.

"Demons!" Trouble yelled. The eldest brother shifted to werewolf shape in a matter of seconds. His clothing tore and fell away from the incredible growing musculature, and his wolf head and maw tilted back to howl.

From out of the mansion poured the denizen in demon form, talons scything the air and wicked menace clouding the night atmosphere.

Kelyn grasped Zen's arm before she could get to Blade. "You're not safe! Get back in the truck."

"No! He's been staked."

And yet, when most vampires would disintegrate and

sift to ash on the ground, Blade had not. He knelt there, gripping the thick wooden dowel as Kesabel looked over him.

"It's what the demons want," Kelyn said. "To get you out in the open."

Zen met her lover's fierce gaze. He yelled something at her, but she couldn't hear for the noise from above. It wasn't the usual demonic din that accompanied their ranks, but instead was populated with animal sounds of all species. They weren't demons…

"Angels," Kesabel hissed. And to the heavens he shouted, "Thou shall not pass!"

The spoken angel ward was not effective when issued by a demon. Dozens of angels aimed for the ground where the vampire knelt, flanked by a werewolf and a faery.

Zen wielded her halo. She managed to make it to Blade's side. He stood, still clasping the stake.

"Get in the truck," he demanded.

"Nope. Got a battle going on right now. And you look as though you need some help."

"I'm fine."

She studied the stake in his chest. "That's your definition of fine?"

"If I don't yank it out…" He winced. "I'm good."

"Just need to process, eh?"

He nodded and managed a smile.

"Blade!" Kelyn stopped before Blade and Zen, back to them. He wielded a bow and arrow aimed toward the descending angels. "You good?"

Blade nodded to his brother. "Let's do this!"

The werewolf took a hit to the chest from two demons working in tandem. But even as the wolf's back landed on the ground, his arms arced forward, catching his attackers by the necks and crushing their heads together. He flung them aside and leaped into the fray.

Bow and arrows in hand, Kelyn utilized his wings effectively as weapons as he flew over demon heads and clashed with angels. Before placing the arrow to the bow, he sliced through his skin with the arrow tip. Ichor glittered on the sharp point. Sure poison that dropped the demons to the ground and momentarily stunned the angels.

Blade held strong, even though the stake in his heart pulsed and burned like a mother. But he knew to keep it in. Removing it would allow his heart to deflate and burst—sure death. He swung at Kesabel, then realized who it was and pulled the swing just before the halo blade slashed the demon.

Kesabel paused, hands up in surrender. "Take your shot, demon slayer."

"You are not my enemy. Use your divinity," Blade growled. "It's the only way to defeat these bastards!"

"But I don't— I've…staked you. And still you insist…" Kesabel studied his palms. "Really?"

All around the two men the battle raged, angels taking out demons and vice versa. The werewolf and faery had joined forces and stood back-to-back, with Zen at their sides. She wielded her halo expertly, having learned that throwing it toward an opponent would slice through skin and bone, and then the halo would return to her grip. Like a boomerang with unholy intent.

While Kesabel considered the power within him, Blade struck the angel who loomed overhead. The opponent grasped him by the wrist and took flight. Midair, Blade unfurled his wings, but one appendage was struck by a passing angel, and that upset the sword from his grasp. The halo blade fell to earth. Trouble looked up just in time to catch the sword and wield it, leaping over falling demons to go for the angel who shrieked in defiance.

Using his wings as weapons, Blade sliced at the angel but only succeeded in cutting arms and legs. He couldn't get to any part that would cause death. And really, the only effective weapon for killing these bedamned things was the halo blade or Zen's intact halo.

Fangs descending in anger, he resisted the urge to bite, for that would bring his death. And yet, death sat lodged in his heart. The organ pulsed and pushed blood around the wood column, yet had not given up on him. On life.

On Zen. He had to survive for Zen.

Sure that his brothers would have Zen's back while he was air-bound, Blade twisted in the air, bringing the angel around with him, so he was under him. He slashed his wing across the angel's, and his opponent retaliated with a howl. It was then Blade realized he fought Simaseel. The bastard who had tricked him into taking demon lives. Easy enough to do when he'd been so down on himself over the torture.

No longer. He would rise above his torment. He'd begun by helping out in the community. And he would continue by opening his heart even more. He could live life without always looking over his shoulder.

With a swift angle of wing, Sim turned them both in the air and forced Blade to ground. His spine and hips landed on the fieldstone staircase before the mansion. Blade felt his bones break, his jaw crack and his brain shudder inside his skull.

Sim clutched the stake, intent on yanking it out. "Time to die, vampire."

"You first!" A sweep of the halo blade sliced the stake off right at Blade's chest. It cut his skin, it was so close. But it also shaved off the stake and released Sim's grip on it. The angel hissed, clutching his hand. Blue blood seeped from a slice on his fingers.

Kesabel landed over Blade and offered him a hand, tugging him up to stand. When the angel lunged for them both, Kesabel shoved the sword hilt into Blade's grip. "This belongs to you."

Blade reacted and stabbed, piercing the angel through his glass heart. "Meet you in Beneath, asshole." Sim yowled the horrifying din of the angels. A blue glow crept out at the sword wound. The tinkling sound of glass shattering preceded Sim's abrupt silence. The angel dusted to crystal ash and dropped in a mound at Blade's feet.

"Good riddance," Kesabel said. "Duplicitous asshole."

"Zen was his cohort," Blade said.

"Indeed. Yet I scent a soul in her. She is not the queen for us. I took that from one of your brothers," Kesabel offered, gesturing to the halo sword. "The werewolf was faring well enough with claws and fangs."

Blade slapped a hand over his chest. The wooden stake sat flush with his rib cage and little blood seeped out around it. "You saved my life. What was that for?" he asked the demon.

"I figured out how this divinity thing works. And you know, it does repel the angels. Pisses them off, too, which is the sweet part. Thanks." He clamped a hand on Blade's shoulder. "We may not have a queen, but the Casipheans will survive now that we know how to protect ourselves from our greatest foe."

"So you're going to leave Zen alone?"

Kesabel nodded. "She's more faery now than anything. I'm not convinced she'd even become demon if she did willingly descend to Daemonia. And if it was all a plot to kill us, well, then…"

"Forgive me for the ranks of Casipheans I've killed," Blade said. "I was doing what I thought right. But now I know it wasn't."

"I believe forgiveness is a human weakness," Kesabel offered. "Survival is a valuable trait to possess, especially for a vampire. No forgiveness is necessary. We will find a fitting queen. Some day. I offer you my friendship and a lifelong alliance, if you will accept."

"I do."

"You are a warrior, Blade Saint-Pierre."

Blade slapped his palm into Kesabel's and they shook. And as an angel with fiery wings soared in toward Kesabel's back, Blade leaped over the demon's head and tangled with the predator. A slice of the halo blade took off the angel's head. Blade shoved him away quickly to avoid the blue blood that spewed out.

And as he spun in the air, taking in the grounds below, he saw the angels retreating with the Casipheans tight on their wake. Kesabel commanded his few but powerful forces. Below on the ground stood Kelyn, gossamer violet wings spread wide and bow aimed toward the sky. And with her shoulders pressed against Kelyn's shoulders, Zen held guard at his back. No enemies dared approach the twosome.

Trouble loped across the battlegrounds, sniffing at the fallen dead and dashing his claws through the heaps of angel and demon dust. He did not see the emaciated demon stalking close behind him.

"Ryckt." Blade soared downward toward his nemesis, catching the demon through the shoulder with his pointed wingtip and lifting him from the ground seconds before he would have landed on Trouble.

The demon struggled but remained pierced through, even as he turned to face Blade. Suspended in the air high above the waning battle below, Blade looked into his enemy's red eyes for the first time as an aggressor.

And yet, he could not force himself to end the bastard's life, for his heart had altered.

"She didn't need to die," he said. "Octavia. You used her to lure me to your denizen."

"That I did." Ryckt lashed out his long black tongue and managed to flick it across the wingtip that pierced his shoulder. "You going to crush me now, vampire? This armor is strong and sure."

"Yeah? But it's got a weak point. I'm going to do for you what I should have done long ago."

With a bend of wing, Blade forced the demon toward him and sank his fangs into the thick vein that pulsed on its neck. There was just enough room above the armor to get a good hold. He drank deeply of the horrible blood. His faery writhed with pleasure. But he would take no joy in this win. Spitting upon the wound, he then rubbed it into the open flesh, ensuring his ichortainted saliva seeped in.

"No!" Ryckt squirmed and Blade released him, allowing the demon to fall. He didn't make it to the ground in one piece. The burst of demon ash showered the other piles of ash below.

So his heart hadn't altered completely. That had been a debt he needed to pay. Now he could move on.

Casting his gaze over the ground below, Blade focused on one figure in particular. Zen looked up and her eyes met his. He slapped a palm over his heart and winced. He'd forgotten about the stake.

* * *

Zen watched as the man who would slay angels for her descended from the sky. His tattered black wings allowed the moonlight to seep through in the holes torn here and there. He looked a dark angel, but he was the furthest thing from a creature from Above.

And she was glad for that.

"All's well," Kelyn announced. He'd stood beside her most of the time Blade had not been able to, taking out the enemy with bow and arrow. The faery was swift, to the degree that she hadn't seen him move most of the time.

Kelyn clasped her hand and the faint violet symbol on his wrist glowed. And in turn, Zen noticed the white marks on her inner elbows glowed.

"Does that mean…?" she said.

"I think you're sidhe," Kelyn said. "Only time will tell." He brushed her cheek and showed her the black smeared on his finger.

"That's not my blood," she said.

"Good. You had me worried. There's Blade."

The vampire landed on the ground behind them. His wings swept the air, stirring up a pile of crystal angel dust in a flurry.

Zen ran to her lover as he stumbled toward her. Hand clasped over his chest, only then did she remember he'd taken a stake to his heart. How could he be alive? Vampires died when staked through the heart. Had she only moments before he might suddenly be reduced to dust?

"No, please no."

Just as her arms touched his, he fell to his knees before her. Head wobbling, he managed a weak smile up at her. "Love you," he muttered. Then he dropped to his side.

"Blade!"

The werewolf shifted down to his four-legged wolf shape and loped over to his vampire brother's side. He sniffed at the wood stuck in his chest and growled lowly. Kelyn joined Zen and touched Blade's throat over the carotid artery. "He's alive."

"He's got a stake in his chest." Zen stated the obvious. "We have to get it out!"

"No." Kelyn stayed her with a hand to hers. "That's the worst thing you can do. Pulling the stake out will cause the heart to explode. Right now, it's the only thing holding him together, so to speak. Have to leave it in and allow it to push out naturally as he heals."

"That's crazy. He's going to die!"

The wolf barked, echoing his brother's insistence.

"Really?" She touched Blade's cheek. "He's cold."

"He's going to need blood, and lots of it. I'll put him in the truck. Trouble, you drive into town and find blood donors. Zen, you go along with Trouble and he'll—" The brothers exchanged looks. Trouble nodded agreement to some silent command Kelyn had given him. Then the faery said, "I'll take him home. And hold vigil."

Chapter 29

Blade existed in a bleary state of exhaustion and orgasmic high. He was aware of his brothers' presence. They wandered near the couch where he lay, talking about everyday things such as women and who was going to help Stryke with the construction work. Every so often he would smell a human woman's perfume, and she would coo over him. One of his brothers would explain to the nameless woman how he was sick, and as a dying man he wanted one last kiss from a beautiful woman.

He knew what they were doing. It was a sneaky method he'd never engage to get blood. But he needed the blood and was too weak to protest the trickery, so he didn't argue. After about the fifth or sixth woman, he licked the wound on her neck and used his vampiric persuasion to make her believe she'd had a blind date with a man she had liked but wasn't interested in seeing again, as he'd done with those previously. Kelyn drove her back to town.

Trouble was off in the kitchen making something that smelled awful. Meat. Blade did hate the smell of cooked meat.

"Where's Zen?"

"You up and at 'em, bro?" Trouble's head appeared from over the back of the couch. He was chewing on something Blade didn't want to know about. "Hungry?"

"Not for that crap."

"How you feeling?"

"Alive." He patted his chest. Had the stake moved out of his body about a quarter of an inch? He was sure when Kesabel had sliced it off it had been shaved even with his chest, so much so he'd been skinned. The skin had healed. "How many days has it been?"

"Three. You're holding on, though. Getting stronger with every neck you tap. Kelyn was right. We just keep feeding you blood and your body will heal. Soon enough it'll push that stake right out."

Blade shuffled up to a half sitting position. A dizzy wave washed through his skull. "Where is she?"

Trouble's jaw pulsed. "Uh, I told Zen to leave you be."

"She left?"

Trouble shrugged. "It's best for the both of you, bro. Sure you don't want something? I made deer sausage and kraut."

Blade had to forcibly keep from gagging. "I need Zen. She wouldn't have left town."

"She didn't leave town. Hey! Sit down. You have to rest."

Blade stood, wobbled and caught a hand on the back of the couch. This infirmity was for the birds. He needed to move, to finish what he'd started. "I need to find Zen."

"Dude." Trouble pulled off a pink ruffled apron—where he'd found that, Blade had no idea—and tossed it aside. "Fine. But tell me one thing. Do you love that chick? The one who doesn't know what she is? The one who brought a war between the angels and the demons to your doorstep?"

"Hell yes."

Trouble's smile preceded his feisty punch of fists before him. "Yes! Then let's go find her."

"Just me."

"I don't think so, man. You're wobbly at best. You're going to need more blood. I can hook you up with this chick—"

Blade clutched Trouble's shirt and jerked him to a stunning silence. "Just. Me," he muttered. "You get that nasty smell of meat out of my house before I return."

"Dude, you are no fun when you're dying."

"I'm not dying," he muttered as he wandered down the hallway to clean up.

Zen had denied the Casiphean crown in favor of choosing him. It was the right choice. The only choice. But Blade did not forget the promise he'd made Zen. After showering, he dressed and headed in to Tangle Lake, to Zen's favorite clothing store. It took some fast-talking and a little flirting, but he accomplished his mission.

Now with a black velvet bag in hand, he plodded through the forest, thick with undergrowth and few worn paths. The paths had been tromped down by his father and siblings when they went out for a run in wolf shape.

After Trouble had come clean about Zen's where-abouts he'd revealed he had suggested Zen go to his parents to stay while Blade recovered. And Kelyn had taken her there.

Blade couldn't believe she'd agreed to it. And then he knew Trouble could be persuasive, if not intimidating. But the last thing he needed right now was distance from the one vital being who gave him life. He was suffering. The stake would take another week or two to completely push out, and that meant lots of blood to invoke the healing process.

It hurt like hell, but he was thankful that Simaseel hadn't ripped it out of his chest. The demon Kesabel had saved him. Guess not all demons were worthy of death. For without the demon's quick action he wouldn't be wandering through the woods, stumbling here and there because he wasn't at full strength, in search of a woman.

Not just any woman. The one woman who made him believe he could do better.

The gurgle of the falls signaled he was near his destination. Behind the falls was a cove of rocks where he and his brothers often rested after swimming up the stream. The water was always cool but refreshing. He was compelled to strip and plunge in, but that could wait. He had to find Zen.

A scurry of rabbits bounced to his right. Overhead, a dazzle of dragonflies, their iridescent wings catching the sun through the tree canopy, bobbled in the air, flying the same direction he was headed. The hiss of a snake clued him in on one slithering beneath the fallen leaves and grasses. And a doe leaped into view before him, glanced his way, then dashed onward, but not as if she needed to flee.

They were—all of them—headed somewhere. Together.

And then Blade felt it, the distinctive vibrations that

scurried over his skin and hummed in his veins. His faery alighted within and his furled wings shivered. For moments he forgot the pain of the stake in his heart. A gorgeous perfume lured him forward, near the stream's edge, where, lying on a wet stone, he spied the halo.

She stood there, arms spread out and head tilted back. Facing him, he saw her eyes were closed as she communed with nature. Calling out to all the creatures that arrived the same time as he did. The doe walked up to Zen and sniffed at her fingers. She opened her eyes, and without startling the deer, smiled and whispered something he couldn't hear.

Clad in a floaty white dress that was so sheer he could see her dark nipples, with a start, she noticed him. The doe didn't dash away; instead, it stepped to the stream's edge for a drink.

"Blade."

Dropping the velvet sack near the halo, he approached cautiously, so as not to frighten any of the animals that surrounded Zen as if she was a Disney princess and they were waiting for her to break into song. But once close enough, he rushed into her arms and pulled her in for a hug.

"I needed you," he whispered aside her ear. "Had to find you."

"You've found me."

"What are you doing out here?"

"Your brothers told me to stay away while you healed."

"So you did?" He pulled back and studied her eyes. They were violet, like Kelyn's eyes. And the markings on her arms were bright white. He traced the curving lines inside her elbow. She was faery. "I would have you stay with me. Always."

"I didn't want to interfere in the healing process. And Trouble said there would be women. Lots of them."

Good ole Trouble. Never as much help as he thought he was.

"There weren't that many," he offered. "And I only drank their blood. Needed it to heal."

"And it worked?"

He tugged up his shirt and she pushed it higher to reveal the end of the severed stake sticking out of his chest. "Still more to go."

"You should be home. Resting. Drinking blood."

"Zen, seeing you makes me stronger. Don't ask me to leave." He twined his fingers in hers. "Please, let me stay and look at you."

"Look at me?"

"You are gorgeous. You've become, haven't you?"

She nodded. "Yes. Full faery now. You like?"

"I like you no matter what."

"I'm still waiting for a kiss. It has been days. I should think—"

He kissed her. Soundly. Firmly. Deeply. He kissed her so she would know that she was his and he hers. He kissed her to let her feel his pulse and know he was alive. He kissed her to taste her sweetness and know her strength. For she was strong and powerful.

And she was his.

"That's better. I won't ask you to leave. Ever," she said. "In fact, I want to show you something. But only if you promise to sit down on that rock there by the bunny. You are more pale than usual and you're swaying."

"Fair enough." When he landed on the rock, Blade realized he needed the rest more than he could have imagined because his head swam, as did his brain. Yeah, more blood was a necessity. He should have found a donor before searching for Zen. "What do you want to show me?"

"I've been spending my days out here in the forest just sort of…becoming."

He lifted a brow. "And?"

"This is what I've become."

Bowing her head, the breeze listed through her copper hair. The rabbit sitting next to Blade sat up on its hind legs, as did the pair of squirrels on the other side of him. A red fox poked its nose through a frond of greenery and sniffed the air. A lush scent of flowers filled the atmosphere, accompanied by the ozone aroma of rain. It was a heady scent that seeped into Blade's being. Zen's innate perfume. He placed a hand over his heart. The wound had stopped aching.

With a sweep, her wings unfurled behind her. They were quartered as if a dragonfly's wings, and though clear they shimmered a coppery sheen to match her hair. They fluttered and then snapped out behind her and began to flap, lifting Zen from the ground.

Legs bending, then straightening as if a ballerina doing a plié, she giggled and clasped her hands to her mouth as she looked down at him. "Aren't they cool?"

He stood, following her as she floated up about ten feet from the ground. "You are the most gorgeous woman I've laid eyes on, Zen. And you sparkle."

"I know! Faery dust. That's the coolest part!"

"Can I join you?"

"Please!"

He tugged off his shirt and his wings snapped out. That startled the animals, but only for a few moments, and they sneaked back to witness as he soared up to hug Zen.

"I'm completely faery now," she said. "Your mother

said so. My eyes have been this color for days. What do you think?"

"I think I'm in love."

He pulled her into his embrace, and his tattered wings curled around hers, twining within one another as they hovered above the forest floor. The dragonflies circled them, and birds fluttered close by.

"You feel that?" he asked.

"Oh, yeah. When our wings touch that's ten kinds of all right. We could have sex like this, floating in the air, clinging to one another with our wings."

"I think we should."

She placed her hand over the stake. "But first you have to heal." She circled the wood, and in her wake a glittering of faery dust coated his skin. "You can bite me, yes? My ichor won't harm your vampire?"

"It won't, thanks to the ichor that runs through my veins."

"Then, bite me, lover. Take my blood for your strength. And to make me yours."

He didn't vacillate with the consequences, because damn the consequences. He'd waited too long for this.

Blade sank his teeth into Zen's neck, drawing out the sweet, warm ichor and drinking from her deeply. No blood tainted her ichor, neither the dark taste of demon blood nor the deadly blue angel stuff. She moaned and her body hugged to his, her breasts conforming against his chest. Their wings flapped slowly, turning them minutely. Zen's faery dust spilled onto the water below, sparkling in the sun.

And as he drew her life into his body, he felt the immense power infuse him. His muscles spasmed and Zen grasped on to his arms, but he kept his lips against her neck, drinking of her. Marrying himself to her in the unspoken act of shared life.

She was *his* queen.

And the ache in his chest burned suddenly. He grunted. Zen sighed up from the exquisite pleasure of his bite and met his gaze. "What is it?"

"I think your ichor is healing me." He looked down.

She gasped as they watched the stake ease its way out of his chest. The skin around it tightened as the stake narrowed to the point, and when it was out it fell to the water below. Blade's skin knit and healed completely. He felt his bones repair and the muscles about his heart sew into strong fabric.

She kissed the bare spot where once the deadly stake had been. "Did I do that?"

He smirked and wiped a smear of ichor from his lip. "You sure did. That's some powerful ichor in your veins. Born of the angels and forged by the demons. You, Zen, are exquisite."

"You're pretty awesome yourself. Can you love a faery?"

"I already do. Can you love a vampire faery?"

"Best gift I've ever received."

"That reminds me...I brought a gift for you."

"Really? You mean I get something more than your love?"

"It's on the ground by your halo." He clasped her across the back and they descended to the soft, moss-frosted earth. Handing her the velvet bag, he waited for her reaction.

"Oh, my mercy!" She pulled out the crown, which was the cheap display-model tiara from the clothing store she had tried to buy with little luck. Sun glinted in the rhinestones. It was gaudy, but suited for her.

"Would you trade a halo for that?" he asked.

She toed the halo toward his foot, ignoring it for the prize in her hands. "You have to ask? You can give it to the halo hunter. Just let me try on this gorgeous crown."

"You are my queen," he said as he placed it on her head and kissed her.

"Take me home with you," she said. "And never let me go."

"I promise to hold you always."

* * * * *

THE WORLD IS BETTER WITH

Romance

Harlequin has everything from contemporary, passionate and heartwarming to suspenseful and inspirational stories.

Whatever your mood, we have a romance just for you!

Connect with us to find your next great read, special offers and more.

f /HarlequinBooks

🐦 @HarlequinBooks

www.HarlequinBlog.com

www.Harlequin.com/Newsletters

HARLEQUIN®

A *Romance* FOR EVERY MOOD™

www.Harlequin.com

Love the Harlequin book you just read?

Your opinion matters.

Review this book on your favorite book site, review site, blog or your own social media properties and share your opinion with other readers!

Be sure to connect with us at:
Harlequin.com/Newsletters
Facebook.com/HarlequinBooks
Twitter.com/HarlequinBooks

HARLEQUIN®

A *Romance* FOR EVERY MOOD™

Stay up-to-date on all your
romance-reading news with the
Harlequin Shopping Guide,
featuring bestselling authors, exciting new
miniseries, books to watch and more!

The newest issue will be delivered right to you
with our compliments! There are 4 each year.

Signing up is easy.

EMAIL

ShoppingGuide@Harlequin.ca

WRITE TO US

HARLEQUIN BOOKS
Attention: Customer Service Department
P.O. Box 9057, Buffalo, NY 14269-9057

OR PHONE

1-800-873-8635 in the United States
1-888-343-9777 in Canada

Please allow 4-6 weeks for delivery of the first issue by mail.